# Man the Guns, my mate

## my mate

a Night Stalkers romance story

by

M. L. Buchman

Buchman Bookworks

# Other works by M.L. Buchman

## The Night Stalkers
*The Night Is Mine*
*I Own the Dawn*
*Daniel's Christmas*
*Wait Until Dark*
*Frank's Independence Day*
*Peter's Christmas*
*Take Over at Midnight*
*Light Up the Night*

## Firehawks
*Pure Heat*
*Wildfire at Dawn*
*Full Blaze*

## Angelo's Hearth
*Where Dreams are Born*
*Where Dreams Reside*
*Maria's Christmas Table*
*Where Dreams Unfold*
*Where Dreams Are Written*

## Dieties Anonymous
*Cookbook from Hell: Reheated*
*Saviors 101*

## Dead Chef Thrillers
*Swap Out!*

*One Chef!*

**SF/F Titles**
*Nara*
*Monk's Maze*

# 1

**Roy Wilkinson won the** lottery.

Finally!

For a decade he'd entered the drawing to board the USS *Constitution* for her yearly "Turnaround Cruise"—the one time each year that the majestic sailing ship left dock and crisscrossed Boston Harbor. At the midpoint, she'd fire off a cannonade in salute to old Fort Independence that had guarded the harbor during the Revolution and the War of 1812. At the end, she'd be docked facing the opposite direction—

turned around—so that the sides of the old wooden ship would weather evenly.

Ten long years he'd had to eat his growing disappointment at not making it through the drawing for a ride on "Old Ironsides," the greatest of the U.S. Navy's sailing ships. He'd always brought along some of his marine engineering students to watch the event from a tour boat—the tall majestic three-master, gliding out under tow across a Boston that had looked so different when she'd leapt to her city's defense in the War of 1812. She lost none of her nobility for moving through a harbor transformed by buildings of glass and steel rather than brick and stone.

The *Constitution* was scheduled into dry dock for the next couple of years and he'd been dreading that deeply if he missed the lottery this year. But he hadn't.

Roy had certainly walked her decks enough times, but that was far different from riding aboard as she crossed the harbor, even if it was only under tow.

She'd only raised her sails twice in the last century.

But now he had his "Golden Ticket," his E-coupon, his season pass—actually, his friendly little email with a code. He was allowed one guest.

A colleague? Most of them already thought him a little off center, he really didn't need to prove that hypothesis for them.

His sister? She was in Seattle married to a Microsoft engineer.

No, he'd go himself and simply enjoy his three-hour tour. Maybe they'd get marooned on some desert island…in Boston Harbor. He really had to get a life one of these days. Soon! Maybe he'd meet somebody there. A pretty, intelligent woman who lived in the Back Bay or Beacon Hill, was interested in old sailing ships, and ran a small but highly successful catering business.

Or maybe he'd win a free trip to the moon. The latter was far more likely.

There were certainly strings he could have pulled to get on the Turnaround Cruise sooner, but it didn't feel right. While he wasn't in the Navy, but rather was a professor of naval architecture, he worked with the Navy. That connection had left him with a feeling of duty to follow the honorable path to finding his own way aboard. Taking advantage of his friendships in the Navy or his MIT professorship had simply not been an ethical course.

But ten years had been a long time to wait.

That the email of his success arrived on the same day his taxes were due only made it all the sweeter. This year, some small portion of his taxes would be taking him on a cruise around Boston Harbor aboard the country's oldest Naval vessel; only the third ever commissioned—this one by old George Washington himself.

With a heavy black marker he'd blocked out the week before July 4th on his wall calendar in addition to his electronic one to make sure he didn't double-schedule himself, plus a day after to relish the experience. He had summer school classes to teach in the mornings, but had posted a notice weeks in advance on his door: "No office hours June 30-July 5 for *Constitutio*nal."

Anyone who'd commented on his odd use of italics would launch him into a long-winded history of the origin of the word *constitution* dating back to the Latin *constitutio* "act of settling and order" (which itself went back to *constituere* "to cause to stand") and the "al" being a Johnny-come-lately addition in the 1670s.

Torturing students and colleagues was just one of the many fine perks of a tenured MIT professorship.

Roy mapped out his plan of attack. While still in college—rather than teaching it—he'd purchased and read most of the books on the design of the *Constitution* and her famous career. But to truly appreciate every aspect of his cruise along with a hundred and fifty other lucky lottery winners, he now prepared to immerse himself each day after teaching.

He would start with a brief tour of the ship. Then he'd plunge into the museum for two days and gather everything he could there. Afterwards, he'd spend July second and third aboard the ship, going over her carefully, from Humphrey's forward-thinking design choices starting at the keel to her most recent restorations of the original curvature to the Spar Deck to aid in rainwater shedding.

He knew it was being ridiculously anal, but he'd gone to the local craft and farmer's market and found a hand-sewn tooled-leather journal to record his impressions and sketches. He already owned a perfectly serviceable fountain pen, so he avoided being utterly irredeemable.

After his morning's lecture on Naval Ship Conversion Design and hydrodynamic implications of hull extensions—something for which the modern Navy had been showing a recent penchant—he set out to stroll the two miles from campus to the Charlestown Naval Shipyard on the walking path along the Charles River Basin.

Late June at the Boston waterfront was a delightful temperature and he walked along with some anticipation of his first glimpse of the towering 220-foot tall mainmast. The modern world of a hustling, blaring Boston seemed to fade away the closer he came to the ship.

## 2

**Commander Deborah Reynolds stepped** out of her four-hundredth meeting about the upcoming Turnaround Cruise, at least it felt that way. She'd been aboard less than a week, so it was probably only the two hundredth.

And then, impossibly, as if stepping through a time machine, she climbed the stern gangway onto the wooden deck of the greatest sailing ship of the U.S. Navy. It took her breath away every time and she hoped it would never stop doing so.

The three-masted frigate towered above the urban port. Hundreds of lines, over thirty-five miles of rope, held and serviced those towering sticks. She tried to imagine the wonder of the multiple booms filled with canvas, but could never quite do it. Despite the lack, the old ship rested here and still she filled tourists' hearts with wonder.

Even though her two-year stint in command of the USS *Constitution* wouldn't technically begin for four weeks, the ship already felt as if it was hers, as if they'd only been waiting for each other.

She'd been released early from her command of a Perry-class long-hull frigate because they'd decommissioned the USS *Reuben James* right out from under her. Despite it being a part of the planned retirement of the entire class, it had been a hard duty nonetheless. They had a final deployment down the western side of the Pacific—Japan to the Philippines—and then her ship was retired after thirty-one years.

She'd ignore any ominous implications of her own age matching her ship's.

She'd had no real hope of gaining a tour of command aboard the Constitution, but she'd certainly been trying for it. The first woman and the first of African descent to command the old sailing vessel. The former was a matter of some pride, the latter no longer seemed to matter in the modern Navy. About damned time, even if the news was making a deal out of it. She'd wanted to be known for her ability to sail, but while she'd won a lot of races, she hadn't been Olympic level good. Being known for her ability to command was as much a surprise to herself as to the review boards that kept promoting her—she'd found a deep joy in leading a smooth-running ship and hoped to go on doing so for a long time to come.

Her two ships, technically both classed as frigates, had a few similarities and a lot of differences. Her new command was a hundred feet shorter and a hundred and fifty taller, though nearly identical in side-to-side beam and draft depth.

Instead of two hundred crew on the *James,* she now commanded seventy—though *Constitution* had carried five hundred in her heyday. They paused from their tasks or chatting with tourists to salute her as she strolled across the quarterdeck to catch her breath. Her boots softly thumping her progress on wood rather than ringing on steel as she was used to.

The *Constitution* had been designed almost two hundred years earlier than the *Reuben James.* Wood rather than steel. She had a top speed of twelve knots, versus thirty. Forty-four twenty-four pound cannons compared with enough heavy firepower, missile power, and torpedo power to put anything other than a destroyer to shame. And her rope rigging would kill any helicopter that even thought about coming close. The *Constitution* lacked the pair of Seahawk helicopters that could kick some serious anti-submarine butt when needed.

But there was one overwhelming factor in the old ship's favor. Instead of forty-one thousand shaft horsepower of roaring twin diesel engines, she ran on chunks of canvas the size of a basketball court...each. That was certainly enough to humble a girl about her new command.

Actually, this command was humbling her in a wide variety of ways; she would soon be in charge of the most visited ship of the Navy. *Intrepid, Midway, Missouri,* and *Arizona* were all decommissioned.

*Constitution* was still a commissioned ship of the Navy since 1797. The next oldest ship was the *Pueblo* commissioned in 1967 and she was still in the hands of North Korea.

Deborah could feel the weight of her new command threatening to choke her as surely as the high collar of her 1812-era uniform.

"Walk the ship." That's what the former *Reuben James* commander had said to her as he'd handed over his ship to her care.

"When in doubt, walk the ship and listen. She'll talk to you."

It was surprising how often it worked.

So, she left the wide, flat quarterdeck, and walked slowly forward.

By the great twin, spoked wheels of the helm, she received a casual salute from a tourist. He really snapped to when he realized she wasn't just an actor inside the period uniform, which was surprisingly gratifying. He turned out to be a Navy SEAL Lieutenant. She chatted with him and his red-headed helicopter pilot girlfriend for a few moments and left feeling somewhat better and more cheerful about her new role working out. She also appreciated that bit of respect due her rank, which she'd worked damned hard to attain.

It had surprised her how often over the last week she'd received salutes from Navy personnel, and occasionally other forces' soldiers who were touring the ship.

A naval commander was still a naval commander.

And a ship was still a ship.

If she could handle a Perry-class frigate, she could handle a sailing frigate as well.

# 3

**Roy watched the commander** work her
way along the deck. He'd been up at the
bow sketching the long lines of the ship as
seen from the foremast hand's perspective.
Joshua Humphreys had designed the
*Constitution* to be longer and leaner than any
other fighting ship of her size. It made her
fast and it made her strong, especially
backed up by a two-foot thick oak hull.
That was how she'd earned the nickname
"Old Ironsides"—the British eighteen-
pound cannon balls had bounced off her

thick, well-braced sides in the first battle in the War of 1812.

The woman walking toward him had those aspects in common with the ship: long, lean, and looking impossibly strong. Her period costume only enhanced the impression. Mid-calf black leather "Hessian" boots with scalloped tops, white slacks, dark blue woolen jacket with tails, brass buttons, and a high collar making her neck appear impossibly long. A tall bicorn —a hat pointed to the front and back and folded upward into a peak on the sides— sat neatly atop her short dark hair.

The twin gold tassels on her shoulders lent her a feminine air for they bounced and fluttered as she walked.

They also marked her as the ship's commander.

"If I were in the service, I'd offer you a salute, Commander. You look incredible."

"Thank you," her tone was pleasant but she looked at him askance with those dark eyes.

Roy reviewed his words and grimaced, "Okay, that didn't come out right. I meant the uniform. The attention to detail is amazing. You look exactly as if you walked out of the history books."

"Other than being black and female."

"Well, yes, other than that."

She almost began to move off, then paused with a half smile to herself.

"So, my uniform looks incredible."

"Yes, sir." He'd almost said "Yes, ma'am." While that might have been more proper in today's Navy, neither she nor this ship belonged in the present.

"You didn't mean me."

"No, sir."

She stood there waiting, then raised her eyebrows slightly.

Oh god. Now he'd said that she wasn't pretty, where in truth she was stunning. Her skin looked smooth and creamy, strong eyebrows, full lips, and…he absolutely needed a brain transplant. The only question was how fast could he get one. A monkey's brain would be more adept than his. Perhaps even a gerbil's.

"Okay," he resisted the urge to beat himself over the head with his notebook; the ink on his sketch was still wet and would probably smear across his forehead. "A gorgeous woman in a stunning uniform is clearly beyond my capacity to process rationally. My apologies, Commander."

# 4

***Deborah let the laugh*** out. The man looked so pitiful that she couldn't help herself.

He flushed and looked down at his notebook, which was pretty damn cute in such a handsome man.

His wavy hair was nearly the same shade as her new command's polished oaken brightwork. His dark eyes a surprising contrast. There was a neatness about him that she rather liked; as if he were ship-shape and Bristol fashion. She must be adapting to the *Constitution* to use such an arcane metaphor.

She looked down at his notebook.

"That's a fine rendering." He didn't look like an artist with his jeans, Rockports, and a neat button-down. And then she saw that it was less of an artist's view than… "An engineer?"

He looked back up at her in surprise. "You got me in one. Actually an engineering professor."

"With a taste for old ships," she could see the detailed notes down the page opposite the drawings noting rail heights, cannon distributions, rope sizes—properly noted by circumference rather than diameter. The workmanship was as neat as the man, a reflection of each other that she would wager carried through to his very core.

"I teach naval architecture at the Pratt School of Naval Architecture and Marine Engineering at MIT."

"That explains it."

He looked at her quizzically, but she liked keeping him off balance a bit.

"Well, I hope you enjoy your day aboard."

"Days," he inspected his drawing at an angle in the bright afternoon sun before closing it carefully. "I'm afraid you are going to become rather sick of me before the next seven days are over." His smile was bright, but she could see more behind it. Something that she couldn't identify, but was intriguing.

"Seven days?" She moved to an at-ease stance. Was he a secret government inspector? If so, he was lousy at the secret part.

"I won the lottery."

"Congratulations. But I still can't let you buy the USS *Constitution* with your winnings."

"No, no."

She'd known exactly what he meant, but he actually took her line straight.

"The 'Turnaround Cruise' lottery. Took me ten years to win. So, I want to familiarize myself as thoroughly as possible with the ship before the event."

Deborah looked to see if he was joking. Then she looked away and looked back. But he wasn't.

What was being the torture of her first week appeared to be the highlight of this man's decade.

"You love this ship that much?"

"I'm kind of a nerd that way. Did I mention: engineer?" He flipped open his notebook to reveal a drawing of the running rigging, specifically tracing how the Fore Royal Topgallant Studding sail's outriggers were extended and retracted, starting from the deck and detailing every run and turning block to a hundred and fifty feet above the deck. Down the side were force estimate calculations to extend and retract the outriggers. It was the most complex piece of line on the entire ship.

"Perhaps I should let you command the ship as you know so much about her."

"I know how she was designed and built, I don't know how to sail her."

"Can't sail her?" Why was she teasing the man? It was not a proper military demeanor to portray to a tourist.

"I don't know how to sail."

"You're a marine engineer, designing ships for the Navy, you love the *Constitution,* and you don't know how to sail?"

"Well, I train students to do the designs, though I have certainly consulted for the Navy on several occasions. I'm a specialist in long-hull conversions, like the Perry-class frigates, though that wasn't one of mine. My mentor did that one. That design was done the same year I was born."

"My, but it's a small world."

"What?"

"As former commander of the USS *Reuben James* Perry-class long-hull, I am going to take you out tomorrow and teach you how to sail." Now why had she gone and said that? She'd been looking forward to a quiet day off, sailing out in Boston

Harbor by herself. She had a sweet little Dragon class boat rented for the day.

"I was going to spend tomorrow in the museum…" he looked doubtful. Then he smiled up at her with such a genuine grin and she was glad she'd asked. "I'd love to."

They made arrangements to meet the next morning at nine at the marina just a few hundred meters to the west. He would bring lunch.

Deborah left him and continued her walking tour of the ship. She was down through the gun deck and halfway along the berth deck before she realized that they were each short a crucial piece of information.

She returned to the spar deck, but her guest was nowhere to be seen.

It might have helped if they knew each others' names.

# 5

***Roy hadn't been thinking*** at all. It was pure chance that the next day was a Wednesday and he'd had no classes under the summer schedule.

Sailing?

Correction: Sailing with a beautiful Naval commander?

Him?

Of all people!

He logged onto the Internet the instant he reached his apartment and ran a search. Commander Jeffries was still listed as the man in charge of the Constitution. His replacement wasn't announced anywhere that he could find, a ceremony typically held in late July.

The *Rueben James.*

She said she had commanded the Rueben James, which had been retired and decommissioned. The only article he could find on the event had her photograph in front of her ship, but not her name. She looked even more daunting in her dress whites than her 1812 dress blues.

Then he'd started worrying about what he should wear? Normal attire and a windbreaker. Did he need his own lifejacket? He hoped not because he had no idea where to find a marine supply store in downtown Boston. Lunch. Did she have any food allergies? What kind of things were good for eating on a boat? Should he buy two thermoses? What kind of…

Nine a.m. finally arrived and found him standing at the head of Pier 4, just outside the locked gate and staring down at the small sail and power boats that filled the two hundred slips there. They were mostly small ones. Under ten meters. Or were small boats defined in Standard Units the way the *Constitution* was, "thirty-two-point-eight feet or less?" Or—

He almost cried aloud in relief from his own thoughts when someone touched him on the arm.

The woman standing beside him was very different from the one who'd greeted him aboard ship yesterday. So different, he almost didn't recognize her. She wore slacks, sneakers, and a blouse that showed her curves were curvier than her heavy Melton dress jacket had implied. Her dark hair was a shiny practical bob that just reached her jaw line. Jarringly modern wrap-around sunglasses hid those dark eyes. She too carried a windbreaker, but no lifejacket.

At least he'd gotten that part of it right.

He held up a small cooler. "I wasn't sure what you ate, so I went to Michael's Deli. I got corned beef, pastrami, and turkey sandwiches (I can eat the leftover one for dinner or tomorrow or something), root beer and cream soda and a cola (I may have gone a little overboard), pickles…" and he was babbling, "…and potato and macaroni salad as well as coleslaw. I would have gotten knishes, but they should really be hot. And—"

"I'm Deborah Reynolds," she cut him off, thank god, with a smile as well. "And I love deli food."

"Whew!" Again her smile said he was missing something.

Oh. Right.

"Roy Wilkinson. Pleased to meet you." It seemed ridiculous to be shaking hands with the woman he'd already agreed to spend the morning with in a small sailboat, but he wasn't complaining about how it felt. He'd worked with enough Naval personnel to expect the surprising strength in the woman's hand, but he wasn't ready for the warmth of the clasp as if an observable heat was instantly conducted along his nervous system.

She led him to a small, narrow boat.

"It has lines like a meter-boat," the classic long, lean look of the big racing yachts that used to rule the America's Cup before all of the catamarans took over.

"It does," Deborah acknowledged. "Full-keel on a twenty-nine foot hull. It's a Dragon design."

"Johan Anker's work." He wondered if she was ever Deb or Debby. If she was, he decided that he didn't like them as well. This was a woman who commanded the use of her full name.

"How is it that you know so much about boats and have never sailed?" Clearly an expert, she began preparations so quickly that he didn't know how to help and didn't like feeling useless. He needed to learn this.

"I've worked on the Independence Class littoral combat ship designs, but I've never sailed one of those either."

"That's not sailing."

"But—" she was a commander who had sailed… served… Roy decided *he* was best served by keeping his mouth shut and helped her ready the boat as well as he could.

# 6

*There was a fresh* breeze across the harbor, so Deborah raised sail and cut the engine before they were even fully out of the marina.

The boat heeled, dug in, and took off flying.

"Oh my god!" Roy's shout was one of pure exhilaration.

He was an interesting puzzle that Deborah felt herself reacting to, and she couldn't figure out why. His innate eagerness was a plus, but that only carried a man so

far. He was like a young boy trying to
gather in the world about him as fast as he
could. The sails, the rushing water, the
fresh wind all engaged an instinctual joy.

But he was also an MIT professor of
some note. She'd asked around; there were
only so many professors of naval conversion
hydrodynamics on the planet, making him
easy to find. His reputation was sterling, his
classes very popular despite being noted for
their difficulty.

And the way he'd looked at her with
those frank, assessing eyes. Either he was a
macho jerk who didn't care if it was rude to
inspect her head to toe, or he was simply
interested in what she looked like and
wasn't aware of how it seemed. A bet on
the latter was one she knew she would win.

As they tacked back and forth past the
busy wharves of Boston's Inner Harbor, he
took to the basics of sailing with surprising
speed. Of course he'd know the principles,
but that was a long way from a small sailboat
heeled over twenty degrees and scudding

fast before a sharp breeze. Not once did he pull the tiller the wrong way—he pulled left to turn the bow right from the very first time. The tricks of sail trim, coming about, and even jibing rapidly fell to his sharp mind and comfortable agility.

There was a neatness about him that she enjoyed watching. Every motion was thought out, but not in some drill instructor mandated precise motion. Roy Wilkinson moved like an efficiency expert, pre-judging each motion.

For a long time they sailed in silence, communicating with nothing more than a "Ready about" and a "Helm's a-lee." They crossed beneath the roaring jets climbing out of Logan Airport and soaring aloft over the water.

"That's where we'll be taking the *Constitution* in five days," she pointed to Fort Independence as they rounded Castle Island. The old pentagonal stone fort still an imposing presence atop the grassy-sloped island.

"Firing a twenty-one gun salute before being towed back. It's so sad that she can't be sailed." He did look deeply disappointed. Then his face cleared a moment later. "At least I'll get to be aboard her while she's underway."

"Do you always look at the positive side of things?" Deborah desperately wanted to sail her as well.

"Well, other than the low point after my failing to win the 'Turnaround Cruise' for the ninth year in a row, I do. I've never been a big fan of the darker side."

They swooped past the outer islands and into the heavier chop and stronger winds of Massachusetts Bay proper. It was still only a medium air to a boat as finely designed as the Dragon, but it made her move along smartly with the occasional light spray splashing up, filling the air with sparkling drops and the taste of salt.

Rather than being a seasicker, something she'd been watching for, he served lunch once he had the feel for the demands of the stronger breeze.

"How did you learn to sail?" It was Roy's first question not to do with the boat. Nothing about a woman serving in the Navy.

Neither did he start off speaking about himself and what he did.

It was about her and it was personal.

She was trying to think of the last time that had happened...and couldn't.

"My dad," she managed between bites of an amazing pastrami on rye with a rich mustard that slapped her right between the sinuses. "He raced for most of a decade before settling down. Even did a year on an America's Cup boat as a grinder—working a winch. A massive blow-up photo of the team and the Cup still hangs above our fireplace down in Maryland. He and Mom have a sail loft and still make some of the finest racing sails you can buy. I practically grew up on the water. How did you *not* learn to sail?"

And the afternoon passed more easily than any in a long time. He didn't put any moves on her, was the perfect student, and an ideal companion.

They sailed far longer than she'd planned. They split the third sandwich and the extra salad for their dinner as they worked their way back through the harbor under the light of the setting sun. They had her tied off and wrapped back into her berth at that perfect moment when the sky's golds and reds still ruled the evening, before the city lights took over.

"I'm finding myself very reluctant to go ashore." Roy was eying the dock a mere step away.

Deborah found her emotions were much the same, as if somehow the ease and connection they'd felt upon the water would evaporate should they touch dry land.

"Well, one of us must be brave." He stepped boldly forth onto the wooden dock as if it were a noble sacrifice and then held out a hand to assist her with the decorum of a perfect gentleman.

Despite the day spent together on a small boat, they hadn't touched a single time since their initial handshake. It wasn't as if they'd been avoiding each other, they simply hadn't touched.

Now she took his hand and squeezed it tightly in appreciation as she took the simple step.

She didn't want to release his grasp, but she would have if he hadn't at that moment brushed his thumb across the back of her hand.

As a female Naval commander, she kept men at a careful distance.

As a woman, she tugged ever so slightly on his hand. He turned easily and she took the half step into his arms and kissed him. His hesitation was brief, very brief, as if it was the most natural thing on the planet for them to kiss.

It was not like a first kiss. Testing, brief, or unsure. Nor was it just some flash of fire. It was as if they'd been lovers a long time. She slid a hand up into his hair and relished the softness. His hand around her waist snugged them together as if they'd always fit together perfectly.

When the kiss ended, they still held hands. No words were needed.

He escorted her to her car. They shared a last goodnight kiss and a smile, he closed her door for her and she drove out of there before she dragged him into the car with her and ravaged him.

She'd just been too long at sea. That's all.

# 7

**Roy stood dazed in** the parking lot after Deborah drove off and wondered what the hell had just happened. Veronica at the senior prom, Bethany from the History department, Caroline the assistant dean at Harvard, and others had all been good lovers. He was still friends with many of them, sometimes meeting for lunch. Veronica still sent him humorous Christmas cards about her twin boys. None were...

He couldn't label Deborah's kiss. He could only label what it wasn't. It wasn't casual or hasty or unwelcome—more than one coed had taken an unsuccessful run at him.

It was…familiar. As if through those various lovers of the last decade of his life, he'd been waiting for this one and had known it. Or at least his body had.

He didn't have her phone number, nor she his. But there was no question that they'd meet again.

# 8

***Roy spent most of*** the next day in the museum, attempting to cover all of the information in a single day that he had planned to cover in two. Only as the evening settled over the Boston piers did he approach the ship.

Deborah, once more attired in her formal historic wear, stood on the quarter-deck as if she'd never commanded anywhere else. She looked inviolable, impossibly powerful behind that dark blue Melton cloth and gold adornments.

"How was your day?"

Her smile was radiant at his simple question. He tried to puzzle it out but didn't have a chance.

"Gods, you really are that decent. Ask me out to dinner and I'll tell you."

He took her to a small pub near his place where they each had Irish stew and a pint of Guinness and shared their day. Halfway through the meal, their ankles brushed and neither pulled away.

That they wound up in his apartment was as natural as their first kiss. In his living room, she spent some time browsing his collection of naval history and naval architecture, took her time to inspect and appreciate as if she were perusing a library.

In his bedroom, he discovered that anything natural about Commander Deborah Reynolds had remained on the other side of the door. Only super-natural had crossed the threshold. All of the seriousness that wrapped about her in her formal attire, the watchful steadiness when she sailed, and the charming dinner companion were discarded the moment the bedroom door closed. She left all that aside and Roy now stood by the most striking and feminine woman he'd ever met.

On request, he rustled up a couple of dinner-table tapers and lit those, by the light of which she looked even more remarkable. They took turns undressing each other by that soft light, discovering the wonders of shape and texture. More than once they both burst into spontaneous laughter at how impossibly good it felt. He'd never wrestled with a lover before. Many more times than once they overbalanced and landed on the carpet in a snarl of sheets and pillows only to continue their bout there.

When finally spent beyond any possible recovery, they didn't sleep. Instead, they curled up beneath the covers, legs and arms tangled, forehead to forehead and simply talked. He learned that she'd joined the Navy because of her father's passion for the sea and her mother's training that she could do anything she wanted. She exuded a simple confidence in who she was and discarded any possibility of limitations on the future.

He told her of his mother who designed airplanes for Boeing and his father who taught history at the University of Washington.

"I decided on Naval architecture because I was fascinated by the complex math and the real world application of it. It's not some obscure calculation that doesn't attach to anything; it affects performance, fuel consumption, and dozens of other aspects of a design's success or failure."

They made love in the sunrise light glowing through his apartment window as if greeting each other, and showered together to prepare for their days.

"I'm planning to explore your ship for the next few days."

"As thoroughly as you've been exploring me?" Deborah offered with a happy sigh.

That he could make a woman like her sigh happily was a pretty shocking concept. "Well, perhaps not that thoroughly, but I'll try."

"I have a lot of meetings. It's amazing how much there is to know about a command that only moves once per year."

"I'll see you aboard once I finish teaching my morning classes."

They had showered, but still not slept when they parted at his front door and turned in opposite directions. He turned to watch her fine figure stride away. He now knew and could appreciate every curve of it, but in motion it took on new shapes and temporary configurations worthy of note.

Her flash of a smile, and then she was gone around the corner at the end of the block.

He looked down at his feet, he was still rooted two steps from his apartment's front door.

# 9

**Their next day's encounters** were only in passing. Deborah afforded him a bare nod and a quick smile as she went by. Commander Jeffries—also an avid sailor—was briefing her through the boat practically plank by plank which fit her way of thinking perfectly.

Seeing Roy didn't distract her, rather it steadied her. No pout at how little attention she paid him, simply a goofy happy look when he spotted her going one way while he was going the other.

That night he was waiting at the foot of the gangway. As they returned to his apartment, he picked up a pizza—that he'd clearly called ahead for not wanting to waste any time waiting. A wise man.

A while later they ate lukewarm pizza sitting naked on his bed.

"This is seriously decadent. I'm not really a decadent kind of girl. I think that you're a corrupting influence, Professor."

"No sir, Commander. It's not my doing. It might be your body and my body's interactions. Their mutual desire for significant exothermic activities appears to be insatiable. Speaking from a strictly personal perspective, I'm all in favor of their predilections."

"Really, Professor?"

"Really, Commander."

Deborah felt some feral lioness side of herself, one that she was only starting to discover, clamber to the surface. Halfway through a piece of Canadian bacon and pineapple, she jumped him.

# 10

***Deborah had some thinking*** to do the next morning, so she walked the ship. Tourists wanted their photograph with her in her historical uniform, which she was glad to oblige even if they thought she was merely a hired actor.

Normally she'd correct them and most were thrilled to discover she was a real commander and this was a commissioned ship of the U.S. Navy. But today she let herself drift along with their expectations and assumptions and allowed the rest of her mind to ponder the man even now leaning back against the stern rail and studying the mizzen mast rigging with a small pair of binoculars.

If it had only been "significant exo-thermic reactions," he really *was* cute, or even just serious sex, he really was that handsome, revving their motors into high gear for a while, she'd have been okay with it.

But it wasn't.

Deborah had been serious about only one man. But Henry Jones, on the very night she'd expected a proposal, had informed her that he wasn't the sort to wait at home for her while she went to sea. That had been the single hardest decision of her life, choosing the military career. Henry had found himself a comfortable wife who aspired to children and a husband who came home every night. He owned a small chain of fast-food franchises and his wife did the bookkeeping.

So not her.

Which meant Professor Roy Wilkinson was no more so.

But Deborah knew the feeling; deep down in her bones she knew the difference between a man she was enjoying time with and one that she was serious about. In an impossibly short time, the good professor was making definite progress toward serious.

Had it been only the sex, she could enjoy herself while it lasted, though it had set a new high-water mark since…ever. Had it been only his unthinking kindness or his consistent optimism or his—

Deborah heaved a sigh. He had definitely gotten under her skin. Way down deep below the surface.

She wandered the gun, berthing, and even the lowest orlap deck before allowing her circling patrol to return to his locale, even if it did so with the unerring intention of a compass needle aimed at true north. She eased to a station, standing close beside him, where she could see Roy's notes and sketches in his book.

"Hello, sir. I'm glad to see you are enjoying our ship."

"Thank you, Commander. She's a beautiful craft." His smile fully acknowledged his double meaning.

She too was smiling at the compliment, couldn't help herself. Roy made it so easy to be happy around him.

"Are there any parts of the ship you'd like to see that you haven't yet?" She really hadn't intended quite such a double entendre. Yet his eyes didn't even flicker to her chest, though she knew he took an insatiable joy in her breasts; a focus of intent that had always bothered her in other lovers, but she found herself quite enjoying from Roy.

"Well, there is one place I'd like to go," he drawled his voice just enough to show that he had not missed the double meaning. Then he looked aloft at the Main Top Platform.

"If you think you're going to get any up there, you're dreaming, Roy."

He looked at her in startled surprise.

"Uh, I hadn't really thought of that. But I must say, you do have a way of planting an image in a man's mind. An image that could be permanent."

The way he said the last of it, Deborah was left to wonder at his meaning. They'd had a few good days. There was no way that—

No. She simply wasn't going to go there.

But after the ship closed for the evening, she did lead him up to the Main Top Platform, sixty feet above the deck, and they sat for a long time observing the city at night. The lights were bright in every direction, even the narrow passage to the sea sparkled with small craft, channel markers, and tattered reflections of moonlight.

"Two dozen Marines used to crowd here," Roy circled his hand to indicate their perch on the small platform. "During battle, they'd be shooting down at the enemy with their single-shot muzzle-loading rifles. Jostling elbows with the topmen who were frantically resplicing lines cut by enemy fire. The mayhem must have been unbelievable."

"What are you doing to me, Professor?"

"Whatever it is, Commander," he didn't turn to face her but instead continued staring out across the harbor, "we're doing it to each other."

"Well, at least I'm not going mad alone."

"Do you think it would make any difference if we slept apart tonight or the rest of this week or even…" he trailed off.

"No." It wouldn't.

"That was my thought too." Then he did turn to face her and she could just see his dark eyes studying her face. "I feel as if every step I take beside you, I become a better man. Even if I were to simply walk away now, not even come on tomorrow's Turnaround Cruise, I would still be a better man for having known you. How is that even possible?"

"Well," she thought of the secret she'd kept from him these last forty-eight hours that had so consumed her every waking minute. "I have no idea how it's possible, but you'd better come tomorrow. I've been working on a surprise for you."

"Wouldn't miss another day with you for the world."

And she knew that no matter how important tomorrow's trip had become to him after a decade of trying, she was now more important than that. She'd never been that important to any man.

She certainly liked the way it felt.

# 11

**They had spent the** night together, sleeping. And when his alarm woke him two hours early, Deborah was already gone. A note on her pillow admonished him against being late, because, she reminded him, there was a surprise waiting.

He skipped breakfast and was at the dock within thirty minutes, which left him milling at the dockside with the other overeager winners and their guests. He tried to estimate average age of interest in the cruise, but it was too varied. Gender spread was pre-biased toward couples by the one guest rule, and the percentages of lesbian and gay couples didn't offer him a statistically clear bias either. He found that encouraging; everyone loved the USS *Constitution*. A symbol that had transcended age or gender.

When at last they were allowed to board, he felt like a sheep in a herd climbing the gangway. A very happy sheep. They were greeted at the top of the gangway by a phalanx of the ship's officers in full uniform. His hand was shaken by Commander Jeffries, Lieutenant Walters, and Commander Deborah Reynolds.

Even touching her took his breath away. He made sure he didn't linger overlong, but the impersonality of their brief contact was not impersonal at all. Somehow they were past all that and simply both content to be together on the *Constitution* on a fine July 4th morning.

When all were aboard, the voyage began. The Navy crew of seventy made a fine show of pulling in lines, accepting the tugboat's lines, and generally tending the ship. They tied the tug alongside near the stern where it would lend its power to the old sailing ship, but it was the helmsmen of the *Constitution* at her tall spoked, double wheel that guided their course.

There were informal lectures, and museum personnel, and spectacle. There was so much to watch, but Roy found much of his attention was on the quarter-deck. Even though not yet in command, he could see how perfectly it fit Deborah Reynolds, every bit of it. In her stance, her calm demeanor, and her air of authority, this is where she belonged.

Not merely in command of an old sailing ship, but it was almost as if he could visualize the four-dimensional timeline of her standing at each of her career's commands: the *Reuben James* and a succession of smaller ships behind her, the *Constitution* in the present, and perhaps one of the new LCS ships or a destroyer in her future and more beyond that.

He'd known he was a goner on this woman. Somehow he'd known it from their first meeting, but seeing her in such impossible magnificence he knew that there would never be another woman to match her. Not for him. Not ever.

That it had been under a week was as meaningless as how quickly he fell in love with ship design. He simply knew. He wanted to push aside the crowds on deck and rush up onto the quarterdeck to tell her, but he resisted, there would be plenty of time for that later.

Instead, he enjoyed the journey over the same water they had sailed together only five days ago. Part of him wished even now for their small boat and the world's winds rather than the crowds and the low rumble of the tug. All the years he'd spent imagining this moment aboard *Constitution,* he never would have thought a part of him could desire to be elsewhere.

They pulled abreast of Castle Island and the crowds were herded off the foredeck. Knowing what was coming, Roy had positioned himself to be right at the safety line that now stretched across the deck.

With a precision clearly born of long drill, the lieutenant exhorted his crew to the loading of the great black cannon. Deborah had remained astern on the quarterdeck, but he had an ideal view as they used block and tackle to back the cannon away from the gunports, ram loads of gunpowder and paper wadding down their maws—but sadly no cannonballs—and haul them back into place.

Directly opposite Fort Independence, Commander Jeffries called from the quarterdeck, "Salute, Fire!"

Down the line twenty-one cannons were sparked, firing off with a succession of roaring booms that had everyone covering their ears. Clouds of acrid smoke filled the air and still the cannons roared, jumped back against their rope stops, and ejected their wad and gunpowder plume. He was positioned at the rail and could actually see the tongue of flame that shot from the mouth of each gun on his side. Then the fort answered in turn.

It was a glorious statement of raw power and a tiny but terrible window into what her true battles must have been like. When the display was done and the breeze had cleared away the last of the gun smoke, the day seemed to shine brighter.

"We have a special treat for you today," Commander Jeffries called over the crowd. "A bit of a surprise. To carry it out, I would like to present my replacement who will be taking my place in three weeks when I depart for my next command. The first woman to command the USS *Constitution*, Commander Deborah Reynolds."

There was an enthusiastic round of applause as she stepped forward and Roy's palms hurt before the crowd quieted once more. He felt blinded by her magnificence and humbled that she shared it with him as she stepped to the fore.

The crowd finally quieted.

Deborah rested a hand on her sword hilt—an addition for the day that he hadn't noticed. Was that the surprise she'd mentioned for him? Even without close inspection he knew that by regulation it had to be a U.S. Navy Pattern 1813 Eagle hilt sword. It would be a beautiful piece and he couldn't wait to study it more closely.

"Since 1881," her voice carried easily over the waiting crowd, "the USS *Constitution* has sailed only twice under her own power. In 1997 on the two-hundredth anniversary of her commissioning and again in 2012 on the two-hundredth anniversary of her defeat of the HMS *Guerriere* during the War of 1812. Today we are simply going to sail the old lady because we can. Topmen aloft!" she roared out the last, startling the crowd, and able-bodied seamen in period dress began swarming up the ratlines.

While most of the crowd had moved forward to inspect the now quiescent cannons, Roy had worked his way aft through the crowd as Deborah was introduced and began speaking. By the time he arrived near the helmsman, the massive sheets of canvas descended with a snap of heavy cloth. He watched in wonder as the six sails of Constitution's "battle configuration" were released and trimmed. All she had of her full set of forty-two sails, but still an amazing amount of cloth.

Deborah ordered the tug's lines released and the old ship moved ahead under her own power. At first it was imperceptible, but she was soon moving neatly across Boston's outer harbor. The wind was perfect, so she could steer a clear line out past Deer Island and onto Massachusetts Bay.

Small boats zoomed about her, television helicopters circled nearby.

But he only had eyes for one person.

Deborah had spotted him in the crowd. She made it look like a casual one-finger salute; touching her index finger to her temple then sweeping it forward to point at him.

But the message was unmistakable.

"For you."

He had never received a more wonderful gift.

Except one: the woman who gave it to him.

# 12

**"Two years, Roy." Deborah** was seething with frustration. Roy was doing one of his dense-professor things. "It's a two-year assignment here. That's all. Then I'll be shipping out again."

"I know that."

"I take command of the *Constitution* in," she checked her watch, "twenty minutes." She so didn't have time for this. How had it all gotten so serious anyway? Of course he had come to the ceremony. They'd been inseparable for a month and it wouldn't feel right if he wasn't here when she took command. But to propose to her now? On the ship's quarterdeck? The man was totally nuts.

Roy stood before her just as calmly as could be, making her feel even more that she'd been sleeping with a lunatic.

"We've known each other for barely three weeks, you *can't* propose to me."

"Four weeks today, and you're too late, I already have."

"But—"

He raised his hand to stop her next broadside shot. Just as well. They were all bouncing harmlessly off his thick skull.

"Do you love me? Because that is the one thing I know with absolute certainty. I love you, Commander Deborah Reynolds."

"Of course I do." So much that it scared her. For four weeks they'd been living a romantic idyll that went so much deeper than mere fling or affair. It went all the way off the continental shelf and right out into the depths of the ocean blue.

"So, we'll have two great years together."

"Then what?" She didn't want just—

Again, he cut her off.

"Then, if you don't move on to your next command, I'll be pissed as hell at you, because the Navy is what you are passionate about. This career is where you need to go." Roy never swore, not even a little.

She opened her mouth and closed it again. Could feel the tears rising and knew if she tried to speak they'd come.

" 'But what about us'?" he said the words for her.

She nodded mute agreement with the question. Didn't dare do more.

"I'm not talking two years; I'm talking two lifetimes. Yours and mine. I'll be here teaching. Whenever you have leave, you come home. If you are assigned to Washington, D.C., I'll come there and do consulting work. Whenever *you* decide you're done, and not a moment before, then you come home to stay. Because your home is with me, Commander Reynolds. And don't even think of denying it, because you know better."

She did. She barely managed to suppress the next "But" before Roy continued.

"There are plenty of wives who've awaited their commander husbands. For you I'd gladly wait for each moment we can have together."

The man simply took her breath away. Leave it to the Professor to have considered all the angles.

"As simple as that?"

"Well, not quite."

She glanced at her watch, ten minutes until the ceremony. The newsies and the tourists were already gathering on the deck.

"Okay, what else does the Professor have up his sleeve?"

"You will be in Boston for two years."

"You know that. Get on with it, man, I'm running out of time."

"Getting on with it. Yes. Precisely," he hit her with one of those happy smiles that she'd so come to love. "I was thinking two years might be plenty of time to start a family. I can raise our child while you sail forth and keep us safe."

A child? She'd always wanted children but could never see how it was possible along with her career. But with this man…

"You think you've got it all figured out, Professor?"

"I certainly hope so, Commander."

The other officers and seamen were beginning to gather on the deck. It was not an appropriate place for a public display of affection. Leave it to Roy to have the craziest sense of mistiming.

But if he was insane enough to ask, maybe she was insane enough to answer, because the answer in her heart was as clear as water and as sure as the Great Deep.

She held out her hand and shook his when he took it.

"In that case, Professor, it will be a pleasure."

"The pleasure will be all mine, Commander."

Then she moved forward to take command of the USS *Constitution,* the oldest ship of the U.S. Navy, while wearing the biggest smile in the U.S. Navy.

# Author's Note

***In the brief span*** between the composition and publication of this story, they chose to sail the USS *Constitution* for the third time in over a century. She was headed into a three-year service in dry dock and so, much as described in this story, they sailed her *simply because they could.*

# About the Author

***M. L. Buchman has*** over 30 novels in print. His military romantic suspense books have been named Barnes & Noble and NPR "Top 5 of the year" and Booklist "Top 10 of the Year." In addition to romance, he also writes thrillers, fantasy, and science fiction. In among his career as a corporate project manager he has: rebuilt and single-handed a fifty-foot sailboat, both flown and jumped out of airplanes, designed and built two houses, and bicycled solo around the world. He is now making his living as a full-time writer on the Oregon Coast with his beloved wife. He is constantly amazed at what you can do with a degree in Geophysics. You may keep up with his writing by subscribing to his newsletter at *www.mlbuchman.com.*

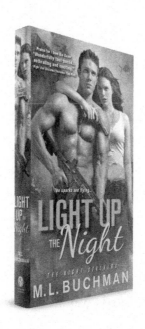

# Light Up the Night
## -a Night Stalkers romance-

***Second Lieutenant Trisha O'Malley*** waited
ten kilometers off the north coast of
Somalia for the mission "Go!" moment.
She held her AH-6M Little Bird attack
helicopter at wave height, exactly at wave

height. The long metal skids were practically being licked clean by the rolling crests heading ashore from the Gulf of Aden.

Through the large openings to either side of the tiny cockpit where the doors would be hung, the smell of the hot night ocean wafted thick with salt and bitter from the dust blown off the achingly dry land. Nobody flew a Little Bird with the doors on. She didn't know why they even ordered them. The only time they were used was to protect the birds when they were parked in harsh enviornments; a piece of plastic could do that. When they flew, the doors were off. Having them off also added freedom of movement to the tiny cockpit and, far more importantly, the visibility was much better.

Not that visibility was such a big deal at the moment. Outside the forward glass-and-polycarbonate windscreen, which reached from below her foot pedals to almost above her head, was nothing but impenetrable darkness. That was one of many things Trisha liked about the Little Birds. The console swept up between the pilots' seats but was confined to a narrow column on the front windscreen that stopped below eye level.

Flying an AH-6M was as close to flying with nothing between you and the sky as existed. No door beside you and bullet-resistant protection from below your feet to farther back than you could tilt your head while wearing a helmet. Everything a girl needed for a good time.

The console itself was dominated by a pair of LCD multifunction screens that could be switched at the tap of a button from engine performance to weather radar to digital terrain map. It made her feel like those science fiction movie heroes in superpowered suits, as if rather than flying a chopper, she herself was wearing a weaponized suit that happened to be in the shape of a helicopter.

Though there really was nothing to see at the moment. Even through her night-vision gear that projected infrared images from the cameras mounted on the outside of the chopper onto the inside of her helmet's visor, there was nothing to see ahead. Except more waves.

To her right hovered the DAP Hawk *Vengeance* with Chief Warrant 3 Lola Maloney commanding, and beyond that Dusty James's transport Black Hawk, the *Vicious*. To Trisha's left, if Chief Warrant 2 Roland Emerson weren't sitting shoulder to shoulder with her in his copilot seat, she'd be able to see the two other Little Birds of her flight formation, *Mad Max* and *Merchant of Death*—*Max* and *Merchant* for short.

When she'd named her bird May, everyone thought it was some stupid woman joke. But any fool who teased her about it being the *Merry Month of*…or *Mayfly* soon learned that it was short for *Mayhem*. She never had to explain it twice.

There was no "Go!" command and no need for risking that extra bit of encrypted communication. The mission "Go" had been given fifteen minutes earlier when they'd spun up their rotors and departed the USS *Peleliu* amphibious assault ship floating forty miles out in the Arabian Sea.

Now fifteen seconds to start of mission, she wound up on the throttle in her left hand. At five seconds to "Go!" both the bird and Trisha's body were humming with the need to get moving.

The clock on her dash hit 03:00—and she was gone. The *May* didn't fly, she leapt. Not like a racehorse, like a greyhound. With the collective full up and the cyclic forward, Trisha was tilted nose down five feet above the waves and a hundred meters in the lead of any other bird in the flight, right where she liked to be. They closed formation quickly, but she liked setting a higher standard even on this, her first operational flight. It had been two long years of training and she was way past ready.

Even with the low-noise blades and engine baffles, the roar inside the craft was loud enough that you wouldn't want to try a conversation without your headset. You could do it, but your voice would get tired really fast. Despite the full-enclosure helmet, she could feel the familiar beat of the machine and whine of the high-speed turbine engine against her body.

Everything in tune and running true. Sounded like an idea for a song, not that she could write music.

Three a.m. should be the sleepiest moment on the Somali coast. Intelligence said the guard change was at oh-four-hundred. Everyone else should be asleep.

Everyone except the Night Stalkers of the U.S. Army's 160th Special Operations Aviation Regiment (airborne). SOAR(a) ruled the night, the most elite Special Forces helicopter team on the planet.

Tonight they'd be ruling the northern coastal town of Bosaso, Somalia, on the Horn of Africa. Or at least one corner of it. They wouldn't be engaging within the third largest city in the country, because the pirates had made the mistake of using a compound outside of town. The local authorities were clamping down hard on piracy and, even if just for public image's sake alone, they wouldn't have been as tolerant of the pirates if they were right in town.

She'd expected to feel some serious nerves. It was her first mission-qualified flight for the Night Stalkers. She'd spent five years with the 101st Airborne flying Cobra attack and Little Birds. She had planned that the day she hit the five-year minimum-experience requirement, she'd walk across Fort Campbell and knock on the 160th's locked gate for an application. Instead, an invitation to apply had been waiting for her that very morning.

Trisha smiled even at the memory of that. Her old friend Major Beale had kept track of her despite roaring up the officer ranks. Trisha hadn't West Pointed in, though she could have. Instead she'd made her parents crazy by taking the NYU education

that she'd paid for herself, then enlisting
and bucking her way up from private.
Though stepping back to the basics of
Office Candidate School after she'd been a
non-commissioned officer for several years
had been tough. She didn't want any
advantages;she'd long since understood the
value of learning the hard way. She'd no
more climb up the broad ladder of her
father's political heft than she would
clamber up the lace-draped tiers of her
mother's social one.

Two more years had passed since she'd
been accepted to SOAR. She was used to
leading entire flights and planning operations for the Screaming Eagles. Not so with
the Night Stalkers. They'd spent two years
showing her just how little she knew. She
was glad to simply be allowed to fly with
them.

"One click," Roland said over the headset. She and Roland were the same rank,
though he'd been in a year longer than she
had. He was there in case she fucked up.

No! Trisha admonished herself. He was there as her copilot. If he were there to cover for her, she'd be in the left seat and he'd be in the right-hand pilot position. All they both cared about was doing this mission and doing it right.

One kilometer out.

Fifteen seconds to shore.

Right on cue, the breakwater came into view. A massive pile of car-sized concrete blocks protected the small harbor from storms coming in off the Arabian Sea.

But it wasn't ready for the storm that the Night Stalkers could unleash.

\*\*\*

Navy SEAL Lieutenant William Bruce squatted in the dust, wearing the standard clothes of a mercenary soldier looking for a quick buck by joining the Somali pirates. Bill wore camo pants, a dark tank-tee, and a black sweatband. He carried a very battered but immensely serviceable M-16 which marked him even more clearly as a merc for bringing his own weapon with him.

Most pirates wielded out-of-date Russian crap, some of it from all the way back to WWII, that was as likely to explode in their hands as to actually fire. He had a Russian TT-30 semi-auto pistol in the back of his waistband, a reliable enough weapon though he preferred a Sig Sauer, spare magazines in his thigh pouches, and a rusting but very sharp hunting knife strapped to his thigh.

He fit right in.

Bill checked his watch. Oh-three-hundred sharp.

The choppers should be here in three minutes, if they were to be trusted.

There was a laugh.

A decade in the Navy, the last five years as a SEAL, and he still didn't trust the Night Stalkers. He really should try to get over it, but he didn't see that happening anytime soon. They were dead reliable, anywhere on the planet, any time. But this was Somalia, and though it wasn't their fault, he couldn't help himself. He would never trust them on Somali soil.

Well, the time was now or never, and he'd have to bank on them actually showing up and doing it right. He slid up behind Abshir, the night guard assigned to the hostages taken in their latest successful piracy, and dropped him with a hard chop to the neck. He could have come from the front, Abshir knew him, but Bill didn't want to risk his undercover role being identified. Nor was Bill willing to kill the man in cold blood simply to protect his identity.

The local warlord, Mahan, would probably have the man shot for failing his guard duty, but that would be his choice. It wouldn't be any great loss to the world. Abshir was a nasty piece of work with a deep strain of cruelty that even the most hardened pirates rarely possessed.

Bill slipped into the low building holding most of the prisoners, dragging Abshir with

him. Let Mahan think that the prisoners
had overpowered the guard.

All of the male hostages were asleep.
No one on watch. No one waiting for the
least opportunity to escape. It just showed
how easily civilians became dispirited, and
this was only the second week of their
captivity.

He began waking them quietly. At first
they'd thought he was attacking them, and
he lost almost thirty seconds convincing
them they were about to be rescued. The
boat's owner, Wilkin something Junior, was
the slowest of the bunch. Senator's son. No
one ever said he was a bright bulb, just rich
and related to the right man to require an
immediate rescue. Who would name their
kid Wilkin anyway? And Junior was just salt
in the wound, like the father hadn't learned
from being stuck with it himself.

Eleven, six passengers and five crew,
taken off the hundred-and-fifty-foot
pleasure yacht *Gracie* in the Arabian Sea.
The same number of SEALs that fit in a

twenty-two-foot rubber boat along with all of their gear.

What the idiot yachties were doing out there alone in the constricted throat of the Gulf of Aden, he didn't want to know. Anyone transiting the Suez with even half a clue on board would wait for a military escort convoy before braving the waters between Somalia and Yemen. The Somali coast was one of the four most dangerous stretches of water on the planet, and they'd gone sightseeing. Probably on their way to explore the Straits of Malacca off Indonesia next. There they wouldn't be hostages, they'd just be robbed or dead if they resisted at all.

He knew the civilians would take another minute to get their acts together, so he told them to stay silent and be ready. They hadn't even asked about the women of their crew yet, a crime that made him think the men were the ones he shouldn't bother rescuing.

Bill slid out the door and moved in the darkest shadows of the moonless night, tight against the adobe walls on the right side of the street. At the last doorway before the cross street, he turned in. The three women yachties had been separated from the others and were tied to beds. So no guard. They were battered and bruised, but he was pretty sure that they'd only been mishandled, not raped. It had taken some risk, but he'd convinced Mahan that unless he wanted serious retribution after they were ransomed off, he'd better not let his men make a holiday of the ladies.

They were gagged, so he didn't bother to wake them gently. They wouldn't be making any noise. He just slashed their bonds and had them stumbling ahead of him before they were fully conscious.

*Available at fine retailers*
*everywhere*

*More information at:*
*www.mlbuchman.com*

CPSIA information can be obtained
at www.ICGtesting.com
Printed in the USA
BVOW03s1935220617
487624BV00001B/6/P

HIGHBALLER

# HIGHBALLER

True Tales from a Treeplanting Life

||||||||||||||||||||||||||||||||||||||||||||||||||||||||||||||||||||||||||||||||||||||||||||||||||||

# GREG NOLAN

HARBOUR
PUBLISHING

HARBOUR PUBLISHING CO. LTD.
P.O. Box 219, Madeira Park, BC, VON 2HO
www.harbourpublishing.com

ALL PHOTOS courtesy of the author
EDITED BY Caroline Skelton & Derek Fairbridge
COVER DESIGN BY Setareh Ashrafologhalai
TEXT DESIGN BY Shed Simas / Onça Design
PRINTED AND BOUND in Canada
PRINTED ON 100% recycled stock

Harbour Publishing acknowledges the support of the Canada Council for the Arts, which last year invested $153 million to bring the arts to Canadians throughout the country.

*Nous remercions le Conseil des arts du Canada de son soutien. L'an dernier, le Conseil a investi 153 millions de dollars pour mettre de l'art dans la vie des Canadiennes et des Canadiens de tout le pays.*

We also gratefully acknowledge financial support from the Government of Canada and from the Province of British Columbia through the BC Arts Council and the Book Publishing Tax Credit.

LIBRARY AND ARCHIVES CANADA CATALOGUING IN PUBLICATION
Title: Highballer : true tales from a treeplanting life / Greg Nolan.
Names: Nolan, Greg, author.
Identifiers: Canadiana (print) 20190090448 | Canadiana (ebook) 20190090537 |
    ISBN 9781550178685 (softcover) | ISBN 9781550178692 (HTML)
Subjects: LCSH: Nolan, Greg. | LCSH: Tree planters (Persons)—Canada—Biography. |
    LCSH: Tree planting—Canada.
Classification: LCC SD129.N65 A3 2019 | DDC 634.9092—dc23

This book is dedicated to all of the young men and women who braved their first few weeks on the slopes, who despite the unrelenting fatigue, the pain, the bruised body and mind, summoned the resolve to carry on, and thrive.

# CONTENTS

||||||||||||||||||||||||||||||||||||||||

# THE ROOKIE

||||||||||||||||||||||||||||||||||||||||||||||||||||||

IT'S MID-APRIL. YOU'RE IN A TENT PERCHED ON THE TOP OF A HILL overlooking camp. You're reluctant to leave the warmth of your sleeping bag, especially this early in the season when everything is coated in a thick layer of frost. Even the inside of your tent and the exterior of your sleeping bag are colonized by a thin layer of ice crystals.

Courage attained, you shed the insulation of your down-filled cocoon, pulling cold, damp work clothes over your goosebump-raised skin. You crawl on your hands and knees to the front of your tent and unzip the nylon flap that functions as a door—no matter how you approach this simple task, it's a zipper that always seems to stick.

You're on full display, at least that's how it seems as you stumble outside and confront the elements. Slowly pulling yourself upright, your joints and vertebrae creak and snap, a reminder that you may not be as invulnerable as you once thought. Shivering, you face the frigid landscape, and the first rays of light emerging from the distant eastern horizon hold your attention, but only for a second or two, even though you've tuned your senses to be on alert for these moments of extraordinary beauty—a mere snapshot will have to suffice.

You tentatively make your way toward camp, periodically stretching your stiff quadriceps and hamstrings as you advance. The frigid

1

ground crunches under the weight of your boots, and as you draw closer to the Quonset hut, reggae music suffuses the air, as does the bustle of an anxious crew milling about inside. Pulling the canvas flap open to the dining tent, you're immediately hit by a blast of warm air from a cedar fire burning inside the airtight wood stove. All around, a swirling mass of hippy treeplanters, vying for position at the lunch table and breakfast counter, are fixated on securing their nutritional needs for the day. It's an important task. Merging into the chaos, you fill your mug with hot coffee and brown-bag whatever is leftover from the feeding frenzy. You then plop yourself down on one of the empty chairs in front of the wood stove. As you try to choke down a few morsels of breakfast—you're not used to eating this early in the morning—you lean back in your chair and reflect on the day ahead. You have a few minutes to think.

You think about your reputation as a "highballer," how you'll soon be forced to throw your body in motion, expending more physical energy in a single eight-hour day than most people will in an entire week. The thought is intimidating, but you pretend to be at peace with it. You think about the drive to work, the ruts in the road and the lousy suspension on the truck you'll be forced to ride in. You think about the vapid conversation you'll have to endure in the cab of the truck along the way (you remind yourself to change the batteries in your Walkman, just in case). You think about arriving at your cutblock and being unceremoniously dumped at the bottom of your area, back into the cold morning air. You think about pulling back the tarp covering your tree cache and shattering that thin layer of ice that will have formed on the tops of the seedling boxes overnight. You think about the bitterly cold bundles of trees that lie underneath—you can already feel the icy bite on the tips of your fingers. You think about stuffing your treeplanting bags full of seedlings, stuffing them to the point of bursting. You think about your shoulders and hips straining under the weight of your bags as you pivot to face the mountain that rises before you—it's some five hundred metres, a single line of 150 trees to the top. You think about those first few shaky steps on broken terrain, poking through the debris on the surface of the ground with your shovel, attempting to home in on good soil. You think about that first tree—it's a grunt, but it's finally in the ground. You think about how you'll be required to repeat the same task, again and again, at least two thousand more times before your day is done. You think about the madness behind such an endeavour.

Several blasts from a truck horn snap you back into the moment, back into the here and now. You think about how you have less than five minutes remaining to enjoy the rest of your coffee in the warmth of the wood stove. It's nearly 7:00 a.m. The trucks leave at 7:00 sharp. As you step outside, back into the icy early morning air, and begin organizing your gear, the smell of truck exhaust tags your senses. It's time. It's time to hit the slopes.

THIS SCENE, WITH VARIATIONS ACCORDING TO SEASON AND LOCALE, was my daily reality for twenty-seven years, between the ages of nineteen and forty-five, beginning in 1983, when I was a hardcore British Columbian treeplanter. It was an exciting, exhilarating period of my life and I embraced the subculture enthusiastically, becoming a top producer, known in the trade as a highballer.[1] Looking back now, from sedentary middle age, I remember my early days of treeplanting as a kind of charmed existence, bound up in the glories of my youth, whereas in reality the times of triumph and joy were more than balanced by times of trial and even terror. But it was seldom dull, especially at first when I had the normal youthful doubts about being able to cut it on my first real job. I remember that first day so well.

Barrett Jardine was my sister Lina's partner. He was a treeplanting contractor. He was the man behind CRC Ltd. I would soon come to appreciate that Barrett's company was at the very top of the heap in the

---

1. "Highballers" are the highest-producing treeplanters on a crew and are generally held in the highest regard.

silviculture arena. It was *the* company to work for if you were an experienced treeplanter in BC. It had a waiting list with hundreds of names, and the reason for this enviable distinction: working for Barrett was not only lucrative, it was a total fucking blast.

Barrett picked his crews carefully, with an eye for physical prowess, character and, perhaps unintentionally, beauty—at least so it seemed to my adolescent eyes on first viewing the women I was to share camp with. Barrett recruited what struck me at the time as a very satisfactory balance between men and women. I wasn't expecting this. Barrett also chose his projects carefully, preferring remote contracts—those well off the beaten path—over those within hailing distance of paved roads and fast-food drive-thrus.

These remote and geographically isolated projects fetched significantly higher premiums due to their technical nature and complex logistics. Very few contractors possessed the skill set to pull them off. Of course the geographic isolation presented a host of other challenges, some of which made life difficult for a treeplanter, some of which added an element of risk, all of which generated heightened levels of adventure.

It had taken some serious arm-twisting on my sister's part to convince Barrett to take me on as a rookie treeplanter. He resisted at first. We had never met. I'm sure he imagined the worst, thinking I was some hapless city punk completely lacking in wilderness skills—some insufferable putz who would become an instant liability to him and to his finely tuned crew. But my sister knew how to apply pressure. Barrett finally relented. My name was added to the crew list, reluctantly.

Barrett didn't know, but he could have picked a worse candidate for the small rookie training crew he was assembling. I was athletic. I loved the outdoors. I craved adventure. I also hated school, even though I was surrounded by academically oriented siblings. I wanted nothing to do with post-secondary education—something every treeplanting contractor likes to hear. I was a nineteen-year-old boy, the youngest in a litter of five, who was determined to follow a decidedly different path

CHAPTER ONE

from that of his studious older siblings. I suppose it was partially out of spite that I arrived at this decision.

I trained hard for several months prior to meeting Barrett. I ran daily. I hiked. I lifted weights and I cross-country skied. I had also meticulously assembled my gear for this three-month wilderness gig, scouring every outdoor store, army surplus and second-hand shop for gear, clothing and equipment. Our basement took on the appearance of a marshalling station for a major expedition. My mom, impressed with her baby boy's zeal, actually ran guided tours through the basement whenever she had friends over. Every time I added to my stockpile, I ran a formal inventory check, complete with clipboard, felt marker and highlighter. I guess I was a little gung-ho.

In hindsight I suppose Barrett's first impression of me wasn't exactly confidence inspiring. Not owning a vehicle, and having a mother who had a difficult time letting go, I agreed to let her drive me the seven hundred and fifty kilometres to our designated meeting place at a small café near Purden Lake, BC. I was on pins and needles for the entire journey.

It was my mom who broke the ice on that first day.

She was a character. The only girl among five siblings, she'd led a life of slave labour on the family farm from the moment she was able to walk. Thrown out of the house in her mid-teens, she would later discover that her four younger brothers, the boys she helped raise, had colluded to cut her out of the family fortune (this is how it was explained to me). This not only deprived her of a better life, it shredded her sense of self-worth. She wore this humility, anger and sadness around her like a veil. Barely a day went by when she didn't reflect on this act of betrayal in some way. Human nature being the mystery it is, this brittle side of her personality was reserved mainly for the benefit of family. To the outside world she could seem as intimidating as a momma bear.

We had to push our way into the café that morning. It was standing room only. Neither of us had ever met Barrett, so my mom, summoning her momma bear persona, called out in a shrill demand, "Where can I find Barrett?!" After the laughter subsided, a reluctant voice called out from behind us, "Uh—that'll be me." One of the people we had unceremoniously brushed past at the entrance to the café was our guy.

Barrett was a good-looking man of average height and lean frame. He had an air of cool about him. He even dressed cool, wearing a grey down vest over a faded jean jacket, black denim pants and a pair of tired leather hiking boots. He greeted us with a warmth and affection that was so charming I sensed my mother getting weak in the knees. She responded by turning flirtatious, a side of her I wasn't even remotely familiar with and, given that I was already self-conscious enough in front of these new peers and this new boss, it made me cringe. I think I still bear psychological scars from that little display.

Barrett handled it graciously and I immediately liked him. Getting him to like me would be no easy task, as it turned out.

Having lived a relatively sheltered existence under my mother's wing in the big city didn't exactly help prepare me for what transpired next. Feigning courage as I bid my teary-eyed mother farewell, I found myself surrounded by forty complete strangers; a group that looked more like a band of gypsies than a bush crew. There was no time for introductions. We loaded ourselves into a number of idling bush trucks and made tracks, travelling a half-dozen kilometres back down the highway before turning onto a rough and rutted logging road.

There's a certain comfort and familiarity in driving on pavement—all of that is lost the second you hit gravel. From that point on we travelled deeper and deeper into the wilderness. I didn't fully realize it then, but nothing in my life would ever be the same again.

Within minutes our long convoy of vehicles kicked up an unbroken column of thick, choking dust. I couldn't see the vehicles out in front or the topography on either side of the road. I had nothing, no sense of the surrounding landscape to help divert my attention away from the feeling that I was being abducted, that I was being taken to a place where escape would be impossible. I imagined that this was how young men must've felt after being drafted and abruptly hauled off to war.

Finally we arrived. Our caravan pulled into a large landing—an area that had once been used as a staging area or log-sort by a previous logging operation. It was a level, one-acre teardrop-shaped clearing with a gently flowing creek running along the bottom perimeter—a creek that emptied into a series of ponds and marshes several hundred feet below.

Just beyond the landing and across the creek, looming over us like a thunderhead, was a rolling expanse of barren landscape stripped of every conceivable living thing for as far as the eye could see. This was where we were to set up camp. This was where we were to plant our trees. This was where it all began.

Barrett's camp, as I would later discover, was about as well equipped and elaborate as they came back in those days. It took a good number of vehicles and trailers to haul in the entire setup. A half-dozen trucks and trailers bore the weight of metal frames, lumber, appliances, generators, pumps, sheets of canvas, tarps, tools, fuel and, of course, mountains of food. The most prominent feature of Barrett's camp: a medium-sized travel trailer that had been gutted and converted into a kitchen-on-wheels. Inside were a large freezer, two commercial-sized refrigerators and a pair of gas-powered stoves. And judging by the assortment of meat, dried beans, grains, fresh fruit and vegetables that were on board, our meals were going to be anything but your standard meat and potatoes fare.

I had my first real look at the crew as the trucks were being unloaded. It was a spirited bunch. It was fairly young too, except for the managerial types who appeared to be in their mid- to late thirties. The men, who outnumbered the women by only a handful, appeared to be in excellent physical condition—lean and mean. A good number of them had long hair, some had ponytails, some wore headbands; nearly all of them sported beards or moustaches. I couldn't help noticing that several carried acoustic guitars, and perhaps twice as many had bongo drums poking out of their gear.

The women on Barrett's crew all looked magnificent to me. They seemed extraordinary in every respect: attractive, athletic and high-spirited. They were also generous in making eye contact with the new kid. But beneath the long flowing hair, the provocative assortment of tight-fitting jeans, rock-star tees and tie-dyed tunics, these women all had a certain ruggedness about them. I had no doubt that they could teach me a thing or two about thriving in a remote wilderness setting. I believe I fell in love several times over within the first few minutes of landing at our campsite. Suddenly, the idea of having been abducted by a band of gypsies didn't seem all that dire after all.

I sensed everyone was sizing me up as well. Apparently, nearly everyone knew who I was. My sister, Lina, who had served as camp cook for this same crew on a recent contract, was admired by all. She was a splendid cook. To this day, I don't believe I have met her equal. In bush camps few people are held in higher regard than a good cook, and of course she was also the boss's partner. I suppose this minor degree of celebrity by association gave me a bit of a confidence boost as I attempted to assert myself and find my place.

People knew who I was for one other reason. I was an obsessive guitarist at the time, and a few months earlier I'd sent Lina a thirty-minute cassette tape of my playing. She shared it with several members of the crew, who were apparently impressed. While helping unload gear from the trucks, I overheard a stray comment that I was some sort of a guitar prodigy. I didn't know it then, but getting together for evening jams was a favourite pastime for this crew and people had rather large expectations for some new sounds, especially when they spotted the acoustic guitar case poking out of my gear. I hoped I could live up to my advance billing.

After helping Denny, our cook, unload his supplies, I lent a hand with some of the bulkier camp components. The dining tent—a semi-circular, metal-framed Quonset hut, six metres high by nine metres wide by fifteen metres long—was the main structure. It required a dozen people to assemble. Once erect, it would comfortably accommodate up to sixty people. The front of this massive tent was lined with a series of wooden counters where Denny would lay out lunch items each morning. The back of the tent was open ended, allowing the kitchen trailer to be pulled snugly into place. There it functioned as both a wall and a food distribution centre, operating like a food truck. It had a large window and service counter that opened up inside the Quonset hut. People would line up and fill their plates from an array of food items laid out buffet style. In front of the kitchen trailer, elevated thirty centimetres above the ground, was an expansive wooden platform that served two purposes: it gave some of the smaller people in camp enough of a lift to access the buffet counter, and once dinner was over, it served as a stage for music and entertainment.

Another crew was outside assembling our shower stalls, nailing together two-by-four frames, stretching out tarps and tacking them down tight to create walls. Rolls of thick white hose were extended down to the creek where water was sucked up by a powerful pump and fed into a propane water heater. This supplied hot water to the kitchen, as well as to a half-dozen shower heads.

Lastly there was a group of people busy with shovels excavating a number of deep pits on the periphery of our little village. These pits were to be used as shitters. It was an unenviable task, but one given an appropriate amount of care and attention.

It took about five hours to construct our little village. No detail was overlooked or ignored. It was around that time, after the main camp had been meticulously pieced together, that I began to think about setting up my own campsite. There was a slight chill in the air and the sun was beginning its hastened retreat below the horizon.

I noticed that there were several preferences in site selection. Some people pitched their tents in the heart of the camp, within metres of the Quonset hut. I later discovered that this was for security reasons: we were in bear country after all. Others who were less concerned about bear danger paced off a good one hundred metres or so from the perimeter of our village, preferring to carve out a little piece of real estate near the creek, or up on a hill with a view of the surrounding landscape. The last group put a good distance between themselves and downtown CRC Ltd., up to five hundred metres or more, preferring total isolation when they bedded down at night. I picked the top of a hill that looked down over everything, some two hundred metres away.

As I was pitching my tent, I spotted Barrett on the road below and decided to have another go at establishing some rapport. I hadn't had a chance at the café earlier in the day. My mother succeeded in monopolizing his attention. Barrett didn't leap at the chance to make nice. Instead, he rebuffed my comradely approach and rather coldly handed over a brand-new set of multicoloured treeplanting bags and shovel.

"This is it, kid. This is where my responsibility ends," he said. I suddenly felt very alone in a very big and intimidating new world. I guess it was written all over my face.

"If you're starting to get butterflies, the highway is in that direction," he said, waving his arm in the general direction of Highway 16, our only escape route to civilization and home, which was much farther away than anyone could reasonably walk. I was taken aback by that brief, dismissive exchange and walked away with my tail between my legs. Family connections meant shit to Barrett. There would be no special treatment. I had no friend or ally in him.

The next day the breakfast horn sounded at 6:00 a.m. It was still dark. The early morning air was bracing. The sleeping bag I chose for the occasion wasn't anywhere near compatible with the chill we experienced that first night. Midway through the night I was forced to pile every stitch of clothing I owned on top of myself for additional insulation.

As I stood out in front of my tent, teeth chattering, looking down over the thin wisps of light emanating from the Quonset hut in the distance, I could hear what sounded like reggae music.

Making my way off the hill toward camp, I observed a blanket of icy fog that had settled over the surrounding landscape—it had a palpable density to it. Judging by the ruckus coming from inside the Quonset hut, I was the last person to arrive for breakfast that morning. The music I'd heard earlier was indeed reggae, and it was coming from inside the kitchen.

The atmosphere inside the Quonset hut was frenzied, filled with tension and nervous energy as people vied for position at the lunch and breakfast counters. The beautiful women I had observed only twelve hours earlier were barely recognizable in their ponytails, thick sweaters and down jackets. The bags under people's eyes spoke volumes. This was a time of transition. Swapping out the warmth and comfort of one's four-poster in the city for a thin foamy and sleeping bag was not an easy trade.

I was not a morning person. I preferred to begin my day in an environment completely free of chaos and stress. I wrestled with the idea that this discordant early morning routine would greet each and every one of my days for the next three months. Home had never felt so far away.

By 6:50 a.m. the mosh pit in the Quonset hut was reduced to a dull roar. By 7:00 a.m. the crew had assembled outside for a meeting with Barrett and his foreman. People were outfitted with backpacks, rain gear, work boots, water bottles, shovels and treeplanting bags.[2] After the meeting, people broke into three smaller crews and walked off in the direction of the large clearcut that loomed ominously over our tiny village. I, along with five other stragglers, watched as the procession of planters crossed a small bridge over the creek before disappearing into

---

2. Treeplanting bags are used to carry seedlings. They consist of a series of large pouches crafted out of heavy canvas or nylon. The pouches are attached and arranged along a thick belt with connecting shoulder straps. Two pouches ride along each hip, and a third pouch rides along one's butt. The three pouches, if fully loaded, can carry many hundreds of seedlings at a time.

the fog-shrouded landscape. Those of us who remained formed the "rookie" crew. And we were about to be served a very large dose of reality.

The rookie crew was equally split between genders—three guys, three gals. The women were the obvious standouts. They were all university students, athletic, high energy, attractive. I had an immediate connection with a tall, lean redhead named Debbie. She was a vision of loveliness. Her eyes were what drew me in: large, expressive, hazel. Her face was dotted with deep brown freckles, which I immediately found myself fixating on. Her copper hair, which tumbled along her shoulders when she walked, rounded out the vision. She also possessed a sharp wit, but you had to listen for it as she liked to speak in soft tones, especially when sarcasm was her objective. We were instant friends even though she was three years my senior. I was in love.

After a one-hour blackboard-assisted lecture on general safety and treeplanting basics, we were told what was expected of us: plant a minimum of one thousand high-quality seedlings per day by day fifteen, or go home. One thousand trees per day—judging by the stunned looks on peoples faces, I suspected there were those who doubted their ability to even count that high.

If achieving this seemingly unrealistic production goal wasn't enough pressure, we were informed that we would be strictly supervised, that every one of our planted trees would be examined "under a microscope." This was to ensure that the roots were planted properly, that they were in a specific soil, at a specific depth and that the rest of the tree was perpendicular to the ground. We were also expected to plant our seedlings at a specific distance apart from one another, ideally on a 3.2-metre grid pattern across our entire area. This criterion seemed doable *if* we were planting trees on a golf course putting green, with no obstacles to manoeuvre around. Of course there were no putting greens to be had within hundreds of kilometres of our camp, nor was there anything even remotely resembling one.

The terrain we were dealt on our first day consisted of a series of rolling hills rising high above the road on which were assembled. We stood, gazing up at the clearcut landscape with slack jaws. At the crest of each hill were layers of exposed bedrock forming sharp stratified ridges, some of which appeared to be completely devoid of soil, their bleached and weathered edges resembling whitecaps on a choppy sea. There were large boulders randomly distributed across the entire setting. Stumps and discarded "junk trees" littered the landscape like lifeless limbs and torsos on a medieval battlefield—the aftermath of the harvesting process. There were large concentrations of slash everywhere, and apparently these areas needed to be probed thoroughly for any hint of soil.[3] There was also water, both stagnant and flowing. Large volumes of it coursed through the numerous gullies and ravines that were chiselled into the landscape, fed by a source much higher in elevation, gravity mobilizing it downward. Much of the coursing water, after being channelled under our feet through a series of culverts buried beneath the road on which we stood, continued its rapid descent, disappearing into terrain below. Some of the water eventually collected in pools along flat benches near the bottom of the clearcut. We would soon discover that the fringes of these pools were swamp-like, with soft muck, even quicksand, lining their outer edges. And it was on this terrain that we were expected to plant our seedlings on a 3.2-metre grid to exacting standards. I swallowed hard several times and considered the futility of such a task.

Our taskmaster was an extremely arrogant and peevish character named Jeremy. He insisted on giving us his entire resumé—every annoying detail of it. He was a mountain climbing expert, a survival expert, a search-and-rescue expert, a martial arts expert, a treeplanting expert and, judging by his behaviour around Debbie, a smooth-operating female-treeplanter expert. I hated him.

Jeremy was a good instructor, though. He wasted no time arranging us in a line and setting us in motion. He demonstrated in minute detail the mechanics of putting one's shovel blade in the ground, opening a

---

3. "Slash" refers to piles, large and small, of wood debris and waste.

hole, sliding a seedling's roots in, closing the hole and pacing off the proper distance to the next spot. It wasn't easy. There were areas where the soil was simply too shallow, where the level of slash was too deep, where large obstacles and water courses impeded forward progress—where planting trees on a 3.2-metre grid was a physical impossibility.

Rattled by the lofty expectations thrust upon us, we worked non-stop that first day. I struggled to maintain my balance on the broken, uneven terrain. I attempted to use my athletic prowress to produce a fluid motion, but I couldn't develop a rhythm. It was like learning to walk for the very first time. My final tally at the end of day one: ninety-five trees! And I was by far the highest producer on our rookie crew.

We ended our first day as treeplanters feeling completely overwhelmed. One thousand trees by day fifteen, or else! They had to be out of their fucking minds. No one could conceive of attaining such an absurd goal in such a short period of time. This dominated our conversation on our hike back to camp. That is, until we approached the bridge near the edge of camp where our loud, boisterous discussion trailed off into stunned silence. Crossing the bridge, we were greeted by a half-dozen women from the regular crew who were bathing in the creek below. They were completely naked. I couldn't believe my eyes. I remember questioning my senses, wondering if what I was witnessing was real. It was real. And it was by far the most captivating display of the female form I had ever encountered in my nineteen years. Six voluptuous lily-white bodies, all in proximity and without even a hint of self-consciousness, using the cool clear creek water to wash away dirt and sweat from their exhausted, ethereal frames. They paused briefly, just long enough to toss us a friendly wave as we filed past—muffled giggles could be detected once we were clear. The images I took in during those precious few moments had a profound impact. They were indelibly imprinted in the pleasure centres of my brain. If I had felt even the slightest hesitation or doubt in my commitment to tough it out prior to this glorious and sublime event, those feelings were immediately cast aside.

Debbie and I ate dinner together that evening. We tried our best to console one another after a gruelling day on the slopes, a day that seemed to produce more questions than answers.[4] We both responded politely, albeit reluctantly, to the inevitable queries from some of the more experienced planters on the crew. Questions like: "Tough day on the slopes?" and "Did you pound in a grand today?" and the most annoying one of all, "How goes the war?" After enduring the same line of questions from over a dozen people, I broke away from Deb and sidled up to a small group of veterans who had assembled around the wood stove. The sun was low on the horizon and the temperature was dropping by the minute. Over the crackling of a cedar fire, peering through clouds of cannabis and tobacco smoke, I listened in on their conversations, hoping to glean any insight that might offer an edge. It wasn't long before they shifted their focus toward me and I became the centre of attention. The advice and counsel came rapid-fire and from every direction. Even those who weren't part of the conversation, who overheard bits and pieces as they were passing by, chimed in with nuggets of wisdom, all for my benefit.

The general consensus among this group of highly skilled individuals: don't stop moving—never pause—learn to conserve movement—eliminate any unnecessary motions—always scan the area ahead—learn to take mental snapshots of the ground immediately in front of you—plot your next three or four moves in your mind—*never* stop moving. Incredibly, this made sense to me, and with all of this fresh intel swimming around in my head, and after bidding Debbie a warm good night, I strolled off into the cold night air, in the general direction of my tent (I remembered to pack a flashlight with me from that evening on).

---

4. The terms "slopes," "clearcut," "cutblock," "block," "ground," "planting area," "area," "piece," "unit" and "land" are synonymous. They all refer to an area that has been harvested or cleared of trees—an area slated to be planted with seedlings in order to grow a new forest.

There's a strange phenomenon that plagues nearly every rookie treeplanter at night during their first few shifts. Their dreams are monopolized by planting scenarios, and in particular, grid patterns. Whether the setting of your dream is a shopping mall, your mom's kitchen or the surface of the moon, there's a powerful compulsion to establish a 3.2-metre grid pattern. Everywhere! I cannot tell you the number of times I woke up in a cold sweat, frustrated because I was unsuccessful in pacing off an acceptable grid pattern over my dreamscape.

The second night in my tent followed a similar pattern to the first. It became bitterly cold in the wee hours of the morning. Not only was I forced to pile every stitch of clothing I owned on top of my sleeping bag for additional insulation, I actually wore several pairs of underwear on my head in order to trap body heat. I remember waking up, wondering if I'd ever be able to restore my dignity.

I was determined to approach day two on the slopes with a new strategy and mindset. I was determined to stay in motion no matter what the circumstance. This is easier said than done, especially when one's terrain is riddled with obstacles that hinder forward progress and limit one's view of what's ahead. But the strategy began to pay off. By midday, I astounded Jeremy with a total of 120 trees. By day's end I managed to pound in 275 trees. Having shared some of my recently attained insights with Debbie, she too was able to plant over two hundred seedlings that day. The rest of our rookie crew were struggling to crack the one hundred level, and on the hike back to camp at day's end, I revealed my secret. Sadly the bathing beauties we'd encountered near the entrance to camp on the previous day were not in evidence. Apparently they had discovered the showers.

The strut in my step, having bettered my previous day's score by 200 per cent, was lost soon after returning to camp. The average number of trees planted across all three (experienced) crews that day was thirteen hundred trees, with some of the faster planters pounding in an astonishing sixteen hundred (I was told that those numbers were expected to rise as the people began hitting their stride). Still, my score was a vast improvement over the previous day, and for the first time since arriving in camp, Barrett acknowledged my presence with a mock tip of the hat.

After dinner that night, Debbie and I took a seat next to the wood stove. There, I found myself studying the behaviours of the crew as they mixed and mingled, paying special attention to the women I'd admired at the edge of the creek one day earlier. It appeared to be a very vibrant, animated and sexually charged atmosphere. It reminded me of some of the parties I attended back in high school. There seemed to be an inordinate amount of flirting and petting going on, and I couldn't decide if it was merely an extremely friendly group of people or the prologue to an orgy. Debbie sensed the heightened state of arousal too, and found it as intriguing as I.

Understanding that Deb had a few years on me, I decided to probe her for details regarding her private life anyway. She explained that she had a boyfriend back in Vancouver and that it was fairly serious. She also said that he planned to drive up to meet her in Prince George during the break between contracts. I wasn't surprised. I couldn't imagine such an incredible woman being single.

By day three, with the moral support and wise counsel of several veteran highballers, I was halfway to my target of one thousand trees per day. By the end of day four I managed to plant four full runs of two hundred trees per run—a grand total of eight hundred trees.[5] It was at that point that I came to the realization that planting large numbers of trees was as much a mental process, if not more so, as it was a physical one. There appeared to be a mysterious underlying dynamic at play, one that could be tapped and exploited with the right amount of focus, forward motion and conservation of movement. I also came to realize that things could become very interesting from a monetary perspective.

---

5. A "run" refers to the task of filling up one's treeplanting bags with a specific number of seedlings and planting said seedlings until one's treeplanting bags are empty.

The crew's average at that point was fourteen hundred trees per day. If I succeeded in achieving that level, at 11¢ per tree, I would gross $154 (the equivalent of $350 in 2019 terms). Righteous bucks!

Day five was a day of rest. Barrett had established a schedule of "four and ones"—four days on, one day off. I used the opportunity to sleep in until 6:30 a.m., do my laundry in the creek and take my first shower in nearly a week. Stripped naked, it appeared as if I were wearing a dark brown belt and suspenders—it was the exact outline of the mud-caked support straps on my treeplanting bags. It wouldn't wash off. The dirt and grime appeared to permeate my skin cells right down to the DNA. I then understood why some of the more fastidious planters on the crew showered daily and had long-handled brushes sticking out of their shower bags.

There was something very odd about the shower setup itself: there were no dividers, no stalls—only a single large enclosure with six shower heads spaced a metre apart. Oh, how the mind wanders when you're all of nineteen years of age, in a remote wilderness setting, surrounded by women who appeared to be more comfortable with their clothes off than on. But I was determined to stay focused. At the beginning of the contract, Barrett seemed convinced that I was some kind of a flake. He even had the temerity to show me in the direction of the highway. Despite the adversity, the punishing pace on the slopes, the dirt, the extremely cold nights and the humiliation of waking up with underwear on my head, I was determined to carve out a niche on this crew.

# CHAPTER TWO

# THE STALKER

||||||||||||||||||||||||||||||||||||||||||||||||||||||||||

THE MASSIVE CLEARCUT THAT LOOMED OVER OUR CAMP WAS COMpletely planted within five days. Our plantation of conifers stretched out across the landscape for nearly as far as the eye could see. I was told that it took four hundred thousand seedlings to cover the entire area. Our new ground—the next clearcut on our list—was several dozen kilometres away, and getting there required a fleet of trucks. As we got ready to depart, a half-dozen four-by-fours idled in the cold, early morning April air, and billows of steam and exhaust hung over our staging area in front of the Quonset hut.

As we suspected, our rookie crew was a farm team of sorts. We were about to be split up and divided among the three existing crews. Barrett's foremen were about to duke it out over who would get whom. The previous evening I caught Kelly, Barrett's highest-producing foreman, sneaking a peek at our individual tree scores[1] in Jeremy's ledger and entering figures into a little notebook that he liked to carry around

---

1. "Tree scores" or "tree totals" are the number of seedlings an individual manages to plant during the course of their day. These numbers are diligently collected and recorded at the end of each day for accounting and payroll purposes.

in his tit pocket. When he noticed that I had noticed him, he gave me a wink, as if to say, *Your ass is mine, pal.*

The road that led to our new ground wound through a maze of interconnected clearcuts, several dense patches of mature forest and a canyon that Nature had crudely chiselled into her landscape.

After forty-five minutes of hard driving, we crested a ridge and began descending into a wide sweeping valley, the back end of which had been mowed down into a bowl-shaped clearcut. Our destination was obvious. The road leading in was lined with tree caches, their bright white reflective tarps lending the appearance of snowbanks from a distance.[2] As we entered the block, the idle banter in our truck subsided as we eyed the harvested landscape on both sides of the road, sizing up the sloping terrain, homing in on the areas that appeared most desirable.

I was on a roll. I was determined to crack a grand—one thousand planted trees—by the end of that day. By 2:30 that afternoon, I was fifty trees away from that important milestone, and while loading up for my final run of the day, Barrett pulled up alongside me riding a big beautiful trike.[3] He was looking for a progress report.

Barrett had all of a sudden taken a keen interest in my progress. When I informed him that I was on the verge of cracking a grand, and then some, his face lit up like he had just flopped a full house.

A nineteen-year-old rookie who outgrows his training crew and manages to crack a grand in only a few short days is considered an extremely valuable asset to a treeplanting contractor. When I

---

2. A "cache," "tree cache" or "road cache" refers to a stockpile of seedlings that is strategically positioned along a roadside for treeplanters to draw from as they work their land. Each cache of trees is covered with a bright white Silvicool tarp—a tarp made with a special reflective material that keeps the fragile young seedlings cool and moist, even when exposed to direct sunlight.

3. A "trike" is a three-wheeled all-terrain vehicle (ATV). By the late 1980s it was taken off the market due to its instability on rough, steep terrain.

informed Barrett that a tally of thirteen hundred trees was a distinct possibility if I was given an extra hour or two at the end of the day, he asked if I knew how to operate the trike. Excited, I answered back, "Of course I can ride that thing." I lied.

I had been riding dirt bikes since I was twelve years old but I had no idea if that skill set would transfer over to the strange-looking three-wheeler. Barrett then made me an offer I simply could not refuse: I could stay on the block as late as I wanted as long as I was willing to ride the trike back to camp—if I was certain that I knew my way back home. I promised him that I had paid close attention to all of the major intersections on the road leading in, that finding my way back to camp would be a piece of cake. I wonder if I actually believed that at the time.

That day ended at 4:30 p.m. for everyone—almost everyone. Debbie paid me a little visit at my cache before packing up her gear and jumping in the truck. She was still panting, having just finished her last run of the day. Her shirt was soaked with perspiration, and there was a fair volume of mud smeared across her forehead, presumably from repeatedly wiping away the sweat from her brow with her dirty work glove. She was also incredulous that I was bagging-up at the end of the day, thinking I had lost track of time.[4] "You do realize it's quitting time, don't you?" she scolded, wiping her brow with her soiled glove, confirming my theory of moments earlier. When I told her my plan to stay late and ride the trike back home, she objected. She listed a number of reasons why it was an extremely bad idea, chief among them the number of bears that had been spotted around camp in recent days. Bears had just emerged from hibernation, she said, and were desperate in their pursuit of a meal—any meal. I dismissed her concerns and told her not to worry. I explained that there was a backup plan: Barrett would come looking for me in the event I wasn't back by a certain hour. I also boasted of my expertise in operating

---

4. "Bag-up" or "bagging-up" refers to the process of loading one's treeplanting bags full of seedlings in preparation for a run.

three-wheeled ATVs. These were barefaced lies, but they helped put her mind at ease.

It's quite an experience looking out over a large clearcut, spotting dozens of people spread out over a hundred acres of rolling terrain one minute, then being the only person left standing in the middle of all of that wilderness the next. I watched in awe as the taillights from the last truck disappeared below the road, leaving only a thin column of dust in its wake.

No more voices calling out in the distance. No more whistles, no more shouting, no more singing or spontaneous bursts of laughter. No more dogs barking or truck engines straining. Silence. The only interruption: the pounding inside my chest and the occasional ruffle from a stray breeze. Scanning the wide-open landscape heightened the senses. The air became heavier, the temperature cooler. It felt as if the sun had suddenly drawn blinds down on itself—light seemed denser. I don't believe I had ever felt so isolated, so exposed, so alone.

With my head down and 250 seedlings weighing heavy on my hips, I continued to work my land. By 5:30 the forest that bordered the top of the cutblock had cast a dark shadow over the upper third of my area. It was getting late in the day. I was beginning to feel more anxious. There were times when I thought I detected movement along the treeline, or within the shadow it cast below—a shadow that continued to creep down the slope toward me as the sun continued its inexorable retreat.

The setting was ripe for the overactive imagination. My nerves were on a hair-trigger. Though it was necessary to maintain a hurried pace, I paused periodically to scan the terrain above me, surveying the landscape for anything out of the ordinary, anything that might present a threat. I was a little more than halfway through my final run by 6:00 p.m. I calculated that I could bag-out by 7:00 p.m., but I needed to stay focused.

I bagged-out at 7:00 p.m. on the dot. Excited, I raced back to my cache and packed up my gear, preparing for the long trike ride back to camp. There was roughly one hour of sunlight remaining in my day. Barrett had estimated that the ride home would take ninety minutes.

The trike was a fairly simple ATV. It had no clutch and only four gears. It was a pull-start machine, though, and I knew from experience they could be moody. I took a couple of pulls on the starter cord, played with the choke, took another half-dozen pulls. Nothing. I stopped and examined it from top to bottom to make sure that I hadn't missed a step. The key was turned to the ON position, it had plenty of fuel, the fuel line was open. I took a few more pulls. Nothing. A dozen more pulls yielded the same damn result. After fifteen minutes of increasingly frantic pulling, I succeeded only in tearing the callouses off the palm of my hand. I was exhausted. My hand was bloody. After catching my breath, I took another half-dozen desperate pulls. Nothing. It was nearly 7:30 and I was losing daylight. Fast. With my heart pounding, I weighed my options. It didn't take long to conclude that my only real play was to begin hiking the thirty-five kilometres back to camp.

I couldn't spend the night on the block. Temperatures were still dipping well below zero in the wee hours after nightfall. My one hope was that, at some point, someone in camp would discover that I hadn't made it back and would send a truck out after me. Then, I was struck at once by several realizations:

One: I had been keeping a fairly low profile in camp in the evenings by heading to bed early. My absence in this case wouldn't have been deemed out of the ordinary.

Two: I had instructed Barrett not to fuss. I hated people fussing over me. Rejecting his offer to set aside my supper, I had told him that I'd simply raid the kitchen for leftovers once I arrived back in camp. That was a monumental error on my part. Someone at some point would have noticed an untouched plate of food. It would have set off alarm bells.

Three: I had convinced Debbie not to fuss on my account as well, knowing that she had worked her ass off that day and was thoroughly exhausted. I'd insisted that she not wait up for me.

Four: The camp took on a carnival-like atmosphere at night. I knew that my presence wouldn't be missed.

Taking inventory, I discovered one severely bruised Granny Smith apple at the bottom of my pack that had been taking abuse since day one. I also had a one-litre bottle of water—meager provisions, but better than nothing. For protection, I had my long-handled staff shovel with a heavy steel blade at the end. I also had a six-inch lock-blade knife. In the event of a hostile grizzly encounter, I figured I could escape the situation by using the knife to slit my wrists. Shaken but not deterred, I began my long trek home.

Separating reality from the forces one perceives to be threatening is no easy task, especially when one is physically and mentally exhausted. I was also famished, not to mention scared shitless. The reality: I had planted trees for over eleven hours, I was in the heart of bear country, I was defenceless, I had less than thirty minutes of daylight left and I faced a challenging five- to six-hour hike back to camp. The forces that I perceived to be threatening: whatever hungry or territorial carnivore that was already aware of my predicament, and whatever menacing element loomed, concealed in the shadows around the next bend in the road.

The road leading out of the cutblock rose to the top of a ridge before dropping back down into a long continuous series of older clearcuts. My view from the crest of the ridge was expansive, and it appeared that my road cut right through the centre of these clearcut areas. That was a good thing. My greatest fear in hiking through the darkness was following a road through a dense stand of mature timber, one where every vestige of available light would be blocked out by the canopy above. I worried that my visibility would be reduced to nothing. I worried about what might be lurking inside, concealed in the shadows. I remembered travelling through at least two such areas on the way in earlier that morning. It was only a matter of time before I'd be forced to confront them.

I was no more than thirty minutes into my long trek home when I came to a junction in the road that I didn't recognize. As I examined my two options carefully, I noticed a moist set of tire tracks leading away from a large puddle that spanned the width of the road on the left fork. I knew that my crew had left them. I was fortunate in having just enough residual light to spot them against the dry, hard-packed gravel. I could easily have missed them. A sense of uncertainty, one that had already taken hold, deepened. This was likely only the first of many such junctions. I thought the path home would be obvious. I thought wrong.

One hour into my trek, I came to a stretch of road that I did recognize, even though the sun had completely set. The road entered a narrow canyon with jagged walls that rose up steeply on both sides. I could hear the sound of fast-running water to my left, but it was difficult to pinpoint its location. Judging by the hollow roar, it was likely following a flume that had been cut deep into the rock along the far edge of the canyon. Though my visibility was limited, I scanned the canyon walls thoroughly as I walked. I was looking for movement…anything that might signal danger.

The steep topography of the canyon produced crazy echoes. The sound of my hiking boots scuffing against the gravel road bounced along the sharp, rugged terrain like an Indian rubber ball. If there was ever a time when I needed to walk softly, this was it.

Midway through the canyon, the sound of surging water began to intensify as the road tapered toward its source. Then the road swung hard to the left and I suddenly found myself crossing a bridge elevated high above the maelstrom. I felt my legs tremble as I crossed over. It was an old bridge. Large gaps between the deck planks exposed its support beams underneath. Beyond the beams, unimaginable darkness and deafening turbulence. The relief I experienced in stepping back onto hard-packed gravel at the other side was monumental.

At 9:30, the canyon was behind me. I was relieved to be out in the open again, but I was experiencing tremendous strain, particularly in my thighs, which were beginning to cramp. At that point, I estimated I had at least three hours of hard hiking ahead of me. One blessing I was afforded that night: a full moon and a clear sky. I didn't mind the dramatic drop in temperature that accompanied the clear moonlit air. I was generating more than enough internal heat from my brisk pace and elevated stress level.

Though my eyes were adjusting to the dark and the moonlight was illuminating certain features in the landscape, I was struggling to make sense of objects on the road ahead, particularly those off in the distance.

My mind was constantly playing tricks on me as I surveyed the surrounding terrain. On at least a dozen occasions I thought I detected a dark shape in motion along the edge of a treeline, or at the top of a rock bluff. Though they were all false alarms, I had the uneasy feeling that I was being watched.

I came upon two additional junctions over the next forty-five minutes. At the first, I was reasonably certain that the trucks had turned right, and so I followed. I wasn't nearly as confident at the second junction. It was a Y in the road and both forks appeared to be equally well travelled. Guessing, I chose the path to the right. After only a few minutes, I had a nagging suspicion that I had made the wrong choice. After fifteen minutes, I knew I had taken the wrong fork. By then, the moon was much higher on the horizon and I could clearly see that the road led to the top of a distant ridge. There was no such ridge on the drive in earlier that day—that much I was certain of. I glanced at my watch. It was 10:30 p.m.

The logical move was to simply turn around, hike back to the last junction and take the left fork. Continuing to press ahead, following the road to the top of the ridge, also had its merits. There, a view might open up, exposing the valley on the other side. I suspected that our camp was tucked away in there, somewhere deep in the valley on the other side of the ridge. I chose to push forward and attempt to gain the height of land.

It was an exhausting climb, but it was worth the effort. A filtered view of the valley below began to open up through a thin line of conifers that were sporadically spaced along the top of the ridge. It was breezy. The atmosphere was unsettling, eerie. I felt the tiny hairs on the back of my neck stand on end as I approached the edge of the precipice. Walking along the rim, carefully negotiating each step forward, I managed to find a ledge that offered an unobstructed 180-degree view of the valley below.

Though shrouded in darkness, shadows, thin layers of cloud and patches of fog, the moonlight infiltrated the landscape below, revealing a vague outline of its rolling contours. As I began scanning the area, I was suddenly struck by an odd vibration. It was only for the briefest of moments, but it sounded like distant drumming. I heard it again seconds later, but a gust of wind immediately displaced it. As I scoured the landscape for the source of the sound, something caught my eye to my extreme left. Nestled between a large black void and a series of small hills, perhaps ten kilometres away, was a faint undulating glow. It was my camp. It had to be my camp. There was no other explanation for the mysterious source of light. My mind raced as I attempted to carve out a mental map that would lead me there. I knew that I needed to hike back to the last junction and take the left fork. From that point on, I resolved to stay left whenever in doubt.

Checking my watch as I descended the steep road back toward the last junction, I was shocked when the digits lit up and I saw 11:30 p.m. I was at least ten kilometres from camp. I still had a long, difficult hike ahead of me. I had already worked through two major leg cramps and felt a third one coming on. I was also feeling a hunger unlike anything I had ever experienced. I knew the emptiness was exacerbating the cramping in my muscles, not to mention my ability to think straight. I then remembered the apple in my backpack and quickly devoured it, tossing the core behind my shoulder. Then, just as I was approaching the junction, I detected the sound of tumbling rocks approximately fifty metres behind me. Though it wasn't necessarily an unusual sound—the cutbanks on both sides of the road were steep and in a constant state of erosion—I suspected the disturbance was created by something other than mere gravity. I scolded myself for having discarded my apple core so carelessly.

Debbie's anxiety over the number of bear sightings reported in and around camp suddenly began to weigh heavily on my mind. As I pressed on, limping, attempting to stave off a third muscle cramp, I continued to sense movement on the road behind me. It was difficult to separate the sound of my own footsteps, heavy and irregular, from the other vibrations around me. Heightening my anxiety, the moonlit landscape I had been trekking through all evening appeared to end abruptly farther up the road at a solid black wall. It was inevitable. I was approaching a dense stand of timber, the canopy of which would block out the moonlight I was relying upon to navigate.

As I approached the edge of the forest, it was like peering into a lightless tunnel. The path behind me was bathed in moonlight, the path ahead plunged into a pitch-black void. Pausing to take one last look behind me, I entered the forest and immediately hastened my pace. My visibility was nearly nil. I was able to make out only the basic contours of the road ahead. After one or two minutes of being enveloped in near total darkness, I launched into a spontaneous jog. Panic began to set in. The tension ratcheted higher when I heard a knock deep within the forest to my left. My jog turned into a full-out sprint when I thought I heard another knock directly behind me. I lost track of both time and space. I remember the sensations all too well though: dread, terror, a grave reckoning that I was drawing my last few gulps of air. I was in both fight and flight mode, ready to stop, turn and savagely swing my shovel at whatever was behind me.

The threat that seemed so real, so immediate, failed to materialize in physical form. Eventually, after rounding a sharp bend in the road, I spotted a breach in the blackness several hundred metres ahead. I was coming back into the light.

I reached the edge of the timber. The stretch of road that broke through on the other side was drenched in moonlight. The transition between light and dark—the margin separating the two deeply conflicting elements—was astonishing. It was a glorious moment. My panic-stricken charge quickly deteriorated into a series of limps and staggers as my exhaustion triggered yet another severe leg cramp. This last stitch did some damage to the muscle in my right thigh. The pain was excruciating.

As I attempted to settle into a steady, consistent stride, I continued to hear sounds emanating from the dark corridor behind me. This time they were clear—heavy scrapes in the gravel. I was being followed.

Pressing ahead, looking over my shoulder every few seconds, I fixated on the road leading out of the dark wall of trees behind me. After advancing another two hundred metres or so, something caught my eye—a shape began to emerge slowly from the edge of the corridor. At first, I thought it was my imagination—a large rock, a stump perhaps. Then my worst fear materialized as the dark shape began to shift and take form, slowly pulling away and separating from the black wall.

I began shouting obscenities at the top of my lungs, hoping it would back off and blend back into the dark depths from which it emerged. My protests didn't seem to faze it, though. It advanced, slowly but steadily closing the gap between us. It was a bear—a large bear. An apex predator. Its unwavering swagger suggested that it was fully aware of its position at the very top of the food chain.

After another fifteen minutes of staggering and lurching forward, of constantly looking over my shoulder and attempting to maintain a safe distance between me and my stalker, I saw that the road ahead was in the direct path of yet another dark forest corridor. I began scouring the road berm for a long heavy stick. I was looking for another weapon to augment the shovel I was gripping tightly with my bloody right hand. I also began loading my pockets with sharp flat stones. I had a good throwing arm.

It's unsettling how different the woods appear at night. Any semblance of familiarity is lost or concealed in the absence of light. Individual trees that appear grand and majestic during daylight hours suddenly become menacing, threatening. I was experiencing a whole new set of negative emotions at this point. I had no idea that fear had so many layers, that it could probe so deep into one's psyche.

It was now 1:00 a.m. as I approached the edge of the forest. Entering this corridor was like walking through a portal. I was immediately enveloped in darkness. Again. The road, barely visible, twisted and wound for several hundred metres before crossing over a fast-running creek. The surge of rushing water made it impossible to discern any other sound in either direction. I began to panic. Again. Despite my crippled gate, I managed to press ahead in a bizarre combination of skips and hobbles. Finally, I could see moonlight peer through the blackness a few hundred metres ahead. I emerged from the densely wooded corridor, once again stunned by the dramatic contrast. It was another moment of monumental relief—another glorious moment.

As I continued to press forward, I fixated on the forest edge that was now a good two hundred metres behind me. I detected no activity, no shape or form materializing from the edge of the dark corridor. Sensing that the bear had lost interest, I gave up attempting to run and limped forward. I had no idea how far I was from camp, but I hoped and prayed it was within shouting distance.

It was 2:00 a.m. when I arrived at yet another junction, one where both forks in the road cut through a sparse stand of timber. I was on my last legs.

Pausing at the junction, sensing that I was close to camp but unsure if it was left or right, I took a cursory glance behind me as I pondered my two options. Something was wrong. A black shape occupied the left side of the road approximately 150 metres behind me—it shouldn't have been there. I could have sworn it wasn't there the last time I scanned the terrain. I studied it for the better part of thirty seconds, and just as I was about to dismiss it as a log or a stump, I detected subtle movement. Then, suddenly, it began slowly advancing toward me.

I hollered at the creature. I screamed until my voice cracked. I whacked the ground with my shovel blade, creating as much noise as I could muster. When it appeared to hesitate, I turned around to further examine the junction in the road. Just then, I spotted a narrow beam of light coming from a dense patch of conifers roughly two hundred metres along the road to the left. It vanished. Then it appeared again, darting across the woods before abruptly trailing off.

Excited, I ignored my limp and advanced as fast as I could in the direction of the light. Then I saw it. A tent! It was a treeplanter's tent. It belonged to one of those veteran planters on my crew who preferred privacy to convenience, carving out a nook a healthy distance away from the main camp. Pushing forward, while looking over my shoulder for evidence of my stalker, I stumbled and tripped on the road directly in front of the tent, making a horrible racket, provoking a very irritated, "What the fuck!" from within. I didn't bother answering back. What would I say?

I wasn't worried about my stalker from that moment on. The main Quonset hut was dead ahead.

Throwing my gear to the ground with a thud, I barged into the Quonset hut and made a beeline for the kitchen. Not bothering to grab a plate or utensils, I plucked a quarter chicken from a large baking tray in the fridge and tore into it, consuming bones, cartilage and all. Another deep tray had what appeared to be perfectly cut squares of lasagna—I fished one out with my free hand and inhaled it within seconds. Feeling only slightly satiated, I plated two additional quarter chickens, two slabs of lasagna and made my way to a table near the wood stove—it was still throwing off heat from a cedar fire that had burned hours earlier. I took my time with this plate of food, glancing at my watch every now and then, replaying the events of my evening over and over in my mind.

It was nearly 3:00 a.m. when I blew the candle out in my tent. I was asleep before my head settled into my pillow.

When I woke up it was 6:45 a.m. and Debbie was frantically unzipping the door to my tent. "What's the matter with you?" she said. "It's quarter to seven. The trucks leave in fifteen minutes." After I gave her a quick summary of what I had endured only hours earlier, she raced back to the Quonset hut, packed a lunch and tossed a heap of scrambled eggs into a plastic bag for me. When I arrived at the staging area where the entire crew was assembled, only a handful of people were aware of my little adventure. Of those, several erupted into spontaneous applause; others simply pointed in my direction and laughed. I spotted Barrett on the sidelines shaking his head. He wasn't sure what to think.

I later learned that the drumming I heard from the top of the ridge, immediately prior to spotting the distant glow from our camp, was a drum circle that had apparently built up to a climax at around that time—an obnoxious climax no doubt, but one that couldn't have been better timed. I developed a much greater tolerance for bongos after that episode.

And without the freaked-out treeplanter who probed the woods with his flashlight, unable to make heads or tails out of the horrible racket taking place a short distance his tent—I'm not sure I would have found my way home.

My final tally from the day before: 1,450 trees. My stalker, an enormous male black bear, was spotted along the road outside camp later that day. Denny apparently dealt with it, firing off several warning rounds with his shotgun. That bear was never seen again.

I was a minor celebrity that morning after my story circulated among the three crews. But by mid-morning, by the end of my second run, it became just another day on the slopes.

CHAPTER THREE

# THE HIGHBALLER

||||||||||||||||||||||||||||||||||||||||||||||||||||||||||||||||||||||||||||

BY WEEK FOUR OUR FIRST CONTRACT OF THE SEASON WAS WINDING down. Those of us who began the season as hapless rookies had become, by some minor miracle, *treeplanters*.

We were a proud lot, though we were all still adjusting to life in a remote camp. Toward the end of the last shift of the contract I began experiencing severe stomach cramps. Actually, a number of people in camp suffered from a similar malady. Playing amateur sleuth, following the downward track of the intake hose from the water pump, I found a possible cause for the intestinal distress: we appeared to be sucking water straight from the creek. Back then, it was often argued that if your creek water was running cold and fast, it was safe to drink directly from the source. I don't recall if Barrett had installed a filter farther up the water line, but most treeplanting camps operated without any sort of water filtration system back then. Parasite and protozoa exposure was typical.

At the time, there didn't seem to be any real urgency to enforce a list of camp standards. There was no government oversight—not that I can recall anyway—no outside controls of any kind. It was like the Wild West in many ways. I suppose the stomach bugs we endured were

33

a small price to pay for the freedoms we enjoyed. Bureaucrats have a way of ruining a good party.

As it turned out, Kelly, the foreman with the highest-producing crew in Barrett's arsenal, drafted both Debbie and me. My average daily production was slightly above the crew average at sixteen hundred trees. At 11¢ per tree, that worked out to $176 per day. In 1983 dollars, that had the same buying power as about $400 in 2019. For a nineteen-year-old kid fresh out of high school, that was a king's ransom.

For the final three days of the contract, Debbie and I were instructed to plant together, side by side. I believe Kelly, who was paid a commission based on our daily tree totals, hoped to motivate Debbie to up her game. For me, this was a very agreeable arrangement.

Like me, Debbie was extremely competitive. She strived to match me step for step, tree for tree. She also liked to clown around, injecting her uniquely twisted brand of comedy into our day in order to break up the routine. Sometimes, at the end of a particularly difficult run, she'd stop, turn and belt out a few lines of an Ethel Merman tune at the top of her lungs. I lost it every single time. It was right around that point in our friendship that I realized that I needed to be with this woman. I loved everything about her: the shimmer in her deep green eyes (I could swim in those eyes), her lithe frame, her nonchalance about having mud on her face, the sweet aroma of her jasmine oil, her flawless Ethel Merman impersonation. I wanted to spend the rest of my life with this woman, even though I knew I was nowhere near her equal—intellectually or emotionally.

The atmosphere around camp on the final night of the Purden Lake contract was jubilant. We were a tight crew. We were happy with the money we were making and our energy was good. We were also on the cusp of a two-day break. There was going to be a party in camp that night, the only question being: What form would it take?

It was from this buoyant reservoir of high spirits that the idea of a talent show surfaced. It seemed that everyone had something (or someone) that they wanted to interpret in their own way, in their own special humiliating way. The idea snowballed in a matter of minutes. Chairs were all turned toward the stage and people began huddling together in small troupes, hatching basic storylines for their moment in the spotlight.

Performances ranged from impromptu skits to poetry readings; from duelling bongos to John Wayne impersonations. Some of it was top-shelf entertainment. A couple of smartasses even decided to re-enact my long trek home from the cutblock that one night. Toward the end, as the creative juices began to ebb, people began pointing in my direction. It seemed to be a given that I'd break out my acoustic guitar for the final act of the evening. Truth was, I hadn't touched my guitar in over a month. It was lying on the floor of my tent, in its case, covered in candle wax, work socks and underwear nightcaps. When I announced that I had no intention of playing—due to a swollen injured index fin-ger—people unleashed a chorus of boos and hisses. Luckily, I was saved by a bright set of headlights spotted off in the distance, making their way toward camp. It was the head forester from the logging company. In the back of his truck were two large metal tubs filled with crushed ice and beer. It was his way of thanking us for planting healthy seedlings all across his division. Within minutes, there was an orgy of drinking, smoking, music and dancing inside the Quonset hut and out.

Copious amounts of cannabis were being consumed that night, and everyone seemed to be partaking except for a small group of new arrivals who were keeping to themselves. Among this group was a med-ical student named Dr. Josh. Josh was an interesting study. The man oozed charisma. He towered over us all at six foot seven and had a booming voice to match his imposing frame. He spoke his mind, and he liked to stir the pot. As a large hippy circle materialized outside— it rotated participants in such a way that everyone could pause and greet the person next to them, saying the first thing that came to mind before shifting to the person next in line—Josh and I watched wide-eyed from the sidelines. When the leader of the swirling mass of love and patchouli graciously encouraged Josh and me to join in, Josh, without skipping a beat, bellowed out, "We're good eyeballing it from here for now." I was pretty open-minded back then. I was curious. It appeared to be a little too delightful for Josh, though. He nudged my shoulder and proposed, a little louder than necessary, "Let's go shotgun some beer, young fella."

It was a great night. I was really beginning to feel as if I had found my place on Barrett's crew. The night would have been even greater had Debbie not made a point of reminding me that she was meeting her boyfriend in town the very next day while we were on our break. She retired early that night in order to be fully rested. I was a little hurt when she abandoned me, but there were plenty of distractions to be had that night.

The next morning, as the sun emerged from the cold eastern horizon, there was no time for hangovers or leisurely sleep-ins. The breakfast horn sounded at 7:00 a.m. and within one hour, the camp was completely dismantled, the Quonset hut lying flat on the ground like a giant deflated hot-air balloon. Gear was packed into large wooden crates, and a long line of trucks were idling, waiting, ready to receive their loads. What was once a thriving community, a myriad of multi-coloured tents spread out across four acres of wilderness, was now a string of tightly packed bundles assembled neatly on the side of the road, ready to be tossed aboard any vehicle with extra room. I remember being struck by the contradictions in this crew, from a gyrating mass of free-hippy-love-shit to a tight unit working with military discipline in the space of only a few hours.

As I helped load the trucks, Barrett approached me and asked if I wouldn't mind taking care of one of his four-by-fours over the course of our break. That's when I knew I was officially in. Barrett took great care in assigning responsibility for his vehicles. I was a bit blown away by the offer, which I eagerly accepted, and suddenly I found myself with a great set of wheels to boot around in during my two days of R and R.

\*

WHEN A TREEPLANTING CREW ARRIVES IN A COMMUNITY, IT'S AKIN to a circus rolling into town. We attract attention. We stand out with our parade of bush vehicles, our trailers loaded down with ATVs and gear, our wild hair and free-hippy-love-shit attire. Our hacky sack circles and impromptu jam sessions.

The Nechako Inn in Prince George was where every treeplanting company in the region settled themselves when they had time off between contracts. If you can imagine an uproarious wall-to-wall house party, one that spills out onto the front lawn and into the street, that's what the Nechako Inn was back in the day. It wasn't unusual to have a group of complete strangers—planters from other companies—barge into your room in the middle of the night looking for a lost friend, a beer or a couch to crash on. Most of the rooms, which reeked of weed and tobacco smoke, were pockmarked with dozens of cigarette burns about the carpets and drapes. The mattresses on the beds were all well broken in—from what, I dared not imagine—and the fabric on the couches and chairs was tattered and threadbare. But strangely enough, there was an easy, comfortable feel to the place. We were at ground level. We were also all living on borrowed time with the next project looming over us like a menacing storm front on the horizon.

Prince George was a thriving resource town back then. There were a number of mills in the region that supported a significant percentage of the population, and they paid very decent wages. Judging by the quality of many of the stores, restaurants and watering holes in town, those wages were generously plowed back into the local economy. There was a small price to pay for all of this prosperity, though: the pulp and paper mills belched out so much sulphur in their emissions, it was nearly impossible to escape the stench of rotting eggs. The locals proudly referred to this as the "smell of money." After a few hours in town, the olfactory senses somehow seemed to adapt.

While walking the streets of Prince George during my first real day off in four weeks, I marvelled at the number of treeplanters that had descended on the poor town. We were everywhere. We stood out, easily identified by our filthy work clothes and long hair; our backpacks and hacky sacks. It was a total invasion—I'm sure that was how the locals viewed it. We jaywalked along every street, forcing traffic to a standstill. We travelled in mobs. We monopolized public places. Worst of all, we formed drum circles in the middle of busy sidewalks, often near the entrances to health-food stores and all-you-can-eat buffet restaurants. It was a spectacle. If it wasn't for the fact that we were all flush with cash, we likely would've been rounded up, issued one-way bus tickets and stuffed on the next coach headed back east.

Our second contract of the season was along Williston Lake. I had never even heard of Williston Lake, a 250-kilometre-long monstrosity created by the W.A.C. Bennett Dam. There were no roads leading into this project, so Barrett had arranged for two water taxis and a barge to transport our trucks, camp and crew to a point along the lake where a series of logging roads had been pushed in, approximately halfway up the extremely remote eastern shore.

After one night at the Nechako Inn, a night that resulted in precious little rest or relaxation, I drove to the town of Mackenzie, where our trucks were to be loaded onto a barge later that evening. After dropping off Barrett's truck at the loading dock, I hooked up with the crew at a small motel at the edge of town where we all settled in for the night. It was a peaceful and uneventful night—until about two in the morning. That's when James, the hardest core of all hardcore tree-planters, spotted a peeping Tom outside of Debbie's bedroom window. A frantic chase over concrete, one that echoed across the motel compound and through our open windows, was followed by a cacophony of angry shouts and piercing screams. Too exhausted to investigate, and not entirely convinced that the commotion didn't emanate deep from within my own dream world, I kept my head on the pillow. As the story was brought to light early the next morning, it appeared that James had caught the pervert peeping into Debbie's bedroom window, chased him down and then proceeded to open up a can of whoop-ass. Barrett would later be heard to say, "You just had to know James was involved…"

The next morning, as we waited in the motel parking lot for a fleet of vans to transport us to our water taxis, I spotted Debbie moping around outside her motel room. I approached her cautiously and asked how she was coping after the peeping Tom incident. She blew it off, saying that she wasn't even aware of the commotion, having slept right through it. She wasn't functioning all that well. Her boyfriend had bailed on their planned two-day retreat, coming up with some lame excuse as to why he couldn't make the trip up north from Vancouver. It was plain to me that she was hurting, but she wasn't willing to admit it. Desperate to see her glow restored, I asked her, "What would Ethel say?" Without skipping a beat, she launched into an unbelievable rendition of Ethel's "Everything's Coming Up Roses," complete with flailing arms, gyrating hips and stomping feet. I lost it. Fits of laughter swept across half of the crew—the other half stood stunned, unable to calculate what the fuck was going on.

After packing ourselves into two big shiny aluminum water taxis, we began our long journey up Williston Lake. Cruising along the eastern edge of the reservoir, we spotted tree stumps dotting the shoreline and, occasionally, the black weathered tops of mature trees jutting straight out of the water, only metres from our boat. Apparently, when the construction of the W.A.C. Bennett Dam was given the green light back in the 1960s, a decision was made to leave much of this great northern forest standing. Vast expanses of conifer and deciduous trees were simply left to drown. It was a political decision—politicians needing to get things done fast in order to get re-elected and all. Even at my young, naive age, Williston Lake stood out to me as a monumental environmental disaster. With all of this devastation as our backdrop, a sombre mood hung over our crew that morning. The dark grey skies that challenged us in the distance offered little solace.

Our destination that morning turned out to be a narrow stretch of hard-packed sand, and what appeared to be a concrete ramp protruding from the water's edge. This was the genesis of the road system that would lead us inland to our project area. Creating an insurmountable barrier just beyond the ramp, however, was a four-metre-high wall of beached logs, one that stretched hundreds of metres in both directions. Our trucks were nowhere in sight. Radioing the barge captain from the water taxi, we discovered that he had arrived earlier that morning, discovered the huge volume of wood onshore—a consequence of several violent spring storms—and was forced to head back down the lake in order to pick up a large backhoe. His plan was to use the backhoe to punch a hole through the wall of wood—one large enough for him to offload our vehicles and send us on our way. In the meantime, we were stuck without our trucks for at least three or four hours.

Visible through the trees on the other side of the giant pile of beached logs, about half a kilometre inland, were several long rows of red and white trailers. It was a logging camp. With nothing else to do, nowhere else to go and with the skies threatening to open up on us, we grabbed our packs, bid farewell to our boat captains, climbed the wall of wood and cautiously made our way toward the camp.

As we entered the compound it was immediately obvious that it was an inactive camp—a ghost camp. It was clear that it hadn't been occupied for a good many years—perhaps decades—judging by the condition of the mattresses and furniture in the trailers. But it was shelter nonetheless, and the weather was unsettled and threatening.

Having scoped out several of the least offensive rooms, we packed ourselves in and tried to relax while we waited for the barge to return. Curt, veteran treeplanter and designated camp musician, pulled out his guitar and began grinding out a few Neil Young tunes while we settled in.

Curt was a gentle, wise and thoughtful man. He always paused to consider what you were saying before responding. I really liked that about him. He also had one eye that slightly crossed over toward the other. He wasn't self-conscious about it, not in the least. I liked that about him too. His partner was a black lab named Jessy, who Curt liked to burden with a backpack, one designed to carry precisely one hundred seedlings. With his backpack loaded, Jessy would hang out in the shade until Curt needed trees. "I feed him chow, he feeds me seedlings—that's a fair division of labour," Curt liked to say. One day, halfway through the first contract, while on his way to deliver trees to Curt, Jessy picked up on the scent of something he couldn't resist and gave chase. When he finally returned, panting from exhaustion, his tree bags were empty, having been jostled free during the wild chase through the woods. Curt didn't like being reminded of that little episode.

In the first two weeks of the season, Curt had urged me to join him up on stage with my guitar in the evenings. I rejected his invitations, time and again. One night, after listening to the same old litany of tired excuses, he advised, "You need to find a balance here—you're missing out on some really cool shit, man."

I happened to be carrying my acoustic guitar with me on the water taxi that morning. It was too valuable to risk sending off on the barge unattended. Having several hours of downtime until the barge arrived, I decided to take it out and tune it up in front of Curt. His face lit up like a pinball machine.

Curt was prepared. Apparently, he'd had a good listen to the cassette tape I sent to my sister months earlier and knew that I wasn't much of a rhythm guitar player. He understood that I was more into improvising rather than providing a foundation for others to play off of. He understood that I was selfish, that I liked to show off. The guitar rhythm he laid down for me was inspiring. We were off. Within a matter of minutes, we had twenty-five people packed into our tiny room and at least a dozen more in the hallway trying to squeeze inside. I'll never forget Barrett pushing his maps aside, turning his clipboard upside down and using it as a drum (thank goodness everyone's bongo drums were safely stowed away on the barge miles offshore). We played for well over an hour, and it was an incredibly moving experience for both of us. In my six years of obsessing on the frets, three of which were spent experimenting with a number of different bands, rarely had I achieved that level of musicianship. We would have continued playing long into the mid-morning drizzle if it weren't for the mysterious truck that pulled into the camp compound and blasted its horn.

From an old beat-up pickup truck, an elderly First Nations gentleman emerged, leaving a wide-eyed young girl behind in the front seat. He was more than a little overwhelmed when all forty of us spilled out of the gutted trailer. After hearing our story and shaking a half-dozen outstretched hands, his relief was palpable. He immediately asked us if we had any food. When Barrett threw his hands up in the air and joked about sending a small crew out into the woods to forage for grubs, the old guy, without saying a word, jumped back into his truck and sped off.

The sun had just broken through the clouds when he returned thirty minutes later. Without ceremony, he and his granddaughter, Anna, pulled down the tailgate to his truck, spread out a woollen blanket and carefully began laying out an assortment of local delicacies. There were jars of fish, bright red fillets of smoked trout, an assortment of pickled vegetables and two tall stacks of fried bannock. The outpouring of gratitude from every one of us nearly brought the old man to tears. Young Anna took the opportunity to mingle with the ladies on the crew, and before long, they were pampering her with every indulgence one might expect from a five-star spa. She sat propped on Debbie's knee while several of the girls worked on styling her hair, dabbing her with various perfume oils and applying "stuff" to her tiny excited face. It was a beautiful scene.

It was late in the afternoon when Dr. Josh, while engaged in a spirited round of hacky sack with the crew's French Canadian "hacky contingent," hollered with an outstretched finger in an exaggerated French Canadian accent, "*Oua de la barge!*" (I don't think Josh was much of a francophone.) That put an abrupt end to the festivities.

Positioned at the front of the barge was a large backhoe, and within minutes, it was up on the beach busily tossing logs in all directions. Within fifteen minutes, there was a gap in the wall of wood large enough to allow our vehicles to pass through. And just like that, we were a mobile crew again.

Bidding our First Nations friends farewell triggered the waterworks. Poor little Anna didn't want the afternoon to end. Her grandfather did his best to comfort her as we pulled away, but she couldn't hold back the tears. I don't think there was a dry eye among the crew either. We later learned that Anna's family was employed by the logging company to provide "care and maintenance" for the camp. It must have been extremely lonely for them in such a remote setting.

After a forty-five-minute drive through a succession of clearcuts and patches of mature virgin timber, across fast-running creeks and a river, our convoy came to rest in the middle of a large clearcut at the edge of a riparian zone—a lush oasis of trees and running water that was left untouched by the logging company.[1] This wasn't just any large clearcut. This was truly epic in scale.

It was apparent that we were about to set up our camp along the edge of the largest cutblock on the contract. Every square inch of land around us, right up to our tent pegs, would soon bear our seedlings. The fact that we would be walking to work, rather than driving, for the first few shifts of the contract anyway, spelled opportunity. I was planting an average of sixteen hundred trees per day at that point. I calculated that by working an extra hour or two each day, I could potentially tack several hundred additional trees onto my daily average. That would put me in the running to become Barrett's top planter—his top highballer. It was a ridiculous goal, especially for a rookie working among some of the best planters in the sector, but it became my objective nonetheless. It wasn't just a greed thing, it was a satisfaction thing. I felt sufficiently motivated to make my mark.

It was getting late in the day and we needed to erect a fully functional camp by sunset. We all knew what to do and we threw ourselves at the task. Due to the extended time frame of the project—six

---

1. A riparian zone refers to an area where land meets a river or stream. The interface between land and water is often dynamic. These zones are defined and recognizable by the abundance of trees and lush vegetation that border them.

weeks—an effort was made to create a more comfortable and fulsome setting. After the Quonset hut and kitchen were squared away, a spacious shower complex with multiple wings was envisaged, as was a sauna. Both structures were masterfully constructed, limb by limb, plank by plank, under the bountiful shade of the conifers that lined the edge of our cold-running creek.

With only thirty minutes of light remaining in the day, I followed the perimeter of our riparian zone and discovered a lush opening in the trees, some 250 metres away from our little village. The spot had shade, it was private and it was far enough away from the sounds of the camp generator—a very important consideration (Denny started his day at 4:30 a.m. and his first order of business was cranking up the camp generator in order to light his way around the kitchen). The generator weighed well over a hundred pounds and it made a racket. If you were camped too close to the kitchen and were a light sleeper, as I was, you risked being robbed of precious sleep. Of course, there's always a risk in separating yourself from the herd. There was a robust bear population in the area, and having been stalked earlier in the season, I moderated an internal debate. Peace, quiet and solitude won out in the end.

Having pitched my tent and arranged my bedding, I stood back and witnessed the last vestiges of light retreating from the stealthy approach of night. The luxuriant canopy above my campsite filtered a setting sun that cast a smoldering orange glow across the late evening sky. I was spellbound. It was a superb moment, one of cogitation and inward reflection. Aside from a few distant female voices, the only sounds I could detect were from leaves fluttering in the caress of a soft breeze above, and the gentle lapping of water from the brook below. This would be my home for the next six weeks.

Supper was late that night and, as predicted, very simple. Setting up the kitchen, unpacking, arranging and storing the tons of food that accompanied us left limited time for Denny to fuss over an elaborate dinner. On the menu that night: spaghetti with meat sauce and salad. Even the simplest of meals taste absolutely amazing when you're camped out under a big beautiful northern British Columbia sky.

There were several new additions to the crew, and curiously, one of the new girls seemed to know Barrett rather well. They both appeared to be quite taken with one another. Barrett and my sister lived together, as far as I knew, but I wasn't privy to their exact arrangement as a couple (my sister and I rarely communicated—I hadn't actually seen her in over eight years at the time). As I watched Barrett and the new girl, Brandi, disappear into Barrett's trailer later that evening, I simply assumed that he and my sister had an open relationship. As I would soon discover, there were a few characters around camp who had wives and significant others back home, something you never would have guessed judging by the company they entertained in their tents at night. The whole situation was far too sophisticated for me. I was strictly a one-woman kind of guy.

As I entered the Quonset hut the next morning for breakfast, I spotted Debbie at a table near the wood stove. As usual, she had a seat reserved just for me. By that time, the majority of the crew suspected that we were a couple, though it wasn't even remotely true, even if we were openly affectionate toward one another.

Debbie confessed that she was still in a funk over her boyfriend, "Mr. No-Show," having broken his promise to meet her in town during the break between contracts. She said that she was considering giving him an ultimatum, or just ending it outright. In deference to her fragile emotional state, I feigned regret, but secretly, selfishly, I was excited at the prospect of seeing that relationship end. Then an extraordinary thing occurred: Barrett and Brandi sat down directly across from us.

Barrett and I had never broken bread together and suddenly here we were, on a double date. In hindsight, I think he needed to know that I was cool with his arrangement with Brandi. It would have been impossible to hide, after all. Determined to set his mind at ease and establish once and for all that I really didn't care—that his personal life was none of my damn business—I broke the awkward silence by floating the idea of working extra hours. To my relief Barrett embraced the idea. "Whatever turns your crank, kid," he said. Curiously, Brandi also expressed interest in working extra hours, if I didn't mind the company in the evenings. Debbie immediately registered her opposition to that idea by poking me under the table, then quickly changed the subject by asking Brandi what her major was at university.

Having the freedom to walk to work was a rare opportunity. On most days, I woke up at 4:00 a.m., packed an extra-large lunch, and began my lonely walk just as the sun began casting its first rays of light on my day. By the time the crew arrived on the block later that morning, I'd already have four hundred trees pounded into the ground and would be well into my second run of the day. When the planting day wound down at 4:30 p.m. and people began their long hike back to camp, I'd stick around for one more run.

I loved watching the long procession of treeplanters as they made their way home at the end of the day, walking along the path at the bottom of my piece, chatting away, oblivious to my toil on the slopes above. It was always a welcome event when someone suddenly spotted me from below and called out my name, tossing an enthusiastic wave, causing others to follow suit. As the procession faded from sight, their laughter and conversations trailing off in the distance, a strange and heavy silence would often settle in around me. It was then, in those first few moments after losing visual contact with my crew, that I always felt exposed and vulnerable.

As I had discovered earlier in the season, there's an indefinable atmosphere on the block when you're the only one left standing in the middle of all of that wilderness. I loved pausing in those moments and scanning the rolling landscape. Every movement and vibration was significant. Even the sight of a small bird taking flight took on greater meaning. If I was high enough on the mountain, I could sometimes spot our Quonset hut off in the distance. The images shimmered. They didn't seem real at times. It was like a mirage as rising hot air along the ground played havoc with the light. Sometimes, I could make out the larger, more colourful tents that were tucked in against the lush halo of our riparian zone. I wasn't able to spot movement, though, no matter how hard I focused. If the wind was just right, however, I could sometimes hear voices emanating from camp, often as if they were only metres away. This, I found most unsettling.

It wasn't long before my early morning and late afternoon escapades earned me the nickname "Non-Stop." My daily production soared to an average of 2,100 trees per day—$231 (equivalent to $525 today). There was a price to pay for this crazy pace, though. After arriving home late in the evening, I was too exhausted to appreciate the rich, festive atmosphere at camp. For some, the money and the positive camp energy were on equal terms. For others, their primary reason for hooking up with Barrett's company was to bask in an atmosphere and lifestyle that they could not find anywhere else, in any other profession, or at least with any other treeplanting company. I was aware that I was depriving myself of a good many positive social experiences, but it was a sacrifice I felt compelled to make.

Many people, after hearing Curt and me play together at the ghost camp earlier in the week, expected us both to grace the Quonset hut stage each night. I rarely had enough energy to shower in the evenings, let alone perform in front of an audience. This bummed out more than a few people.

I promised Curt that I'd jam with him on the eve of the first day off. And of course, being the perfectionist that I was, I worried all through the final day of the shift that my guitar playing would fall flat. But as usual, my nervous energy morphed into creativity, and after several shots of tequila from Debbie's private stock, Curt and I produced some exceptionally stirring rhythms and melodies.

It was a wonderful scene in camp that night. The front panel of the Quonset hut had been unzipped and pulled away, extending our view from the stage down to the sauna and creek where a dozen naked bodies excitedly rotated back and forth between the hot and the cold.

As the sun began to set, a large pile of wood was gathered and set ablaze. There was drinking, dancing, singing and laughter. Veteran planters on the crew couldn't recall ever seeing spirits so high. After fulfilling my musical obligation, Debbie and I raided the kitchen for lemons and salt, cuddled up in front of the fire, and went to work polishing off the remainder of her pure blue agave nectar.

The latter part of that evening took on a warm and fuzzy quality. We talked about everything, from past relationships to our favourite pizza toppings. As the night wore on and people began drifting off to their tents, I summoned the courage to tell her how I really felt about her, but she interrupted me in mid-sentence, saying, "I need more time to think. I still have feelings for…" I'd be lying if I said I wasn't hurt. She was thinking more about *him* than me, at that very moment. It was more than my little brain could process emotionally. I abruptly rose to my feet and walked away, leaving her to gather up her things and clean up the mess we'd made around the fire with our discarded lemon peels, empty cups and bottle.

I wasn't quite halfway to my tent when I suddenly realized what an idiot I was. I couldn't allow her to navigate through the dark alone. I ran back to the fire, grabbed the stick that held the most flame and ran after her. She laughed as I attempted to light the way back to her tent, saying softly, "I know you're one of the good ones, Non-Stop."

IT WAS THE FINAL WEEK OF MAY AND THE MIDDAY SUN WAS UNRELENT-ing. My water intake increased to over eight litres per day as sweat gushed from every pore in my body. It had become so hot, I was unable to maintain normal eating habits. I couldn't eat breakfast. Barrett, instinctively knowing how our appetites would change as daytime temperatures rose, shipped in two tons of Granny Smith apples from New Zealand. These apples were very high quality—individually wrapped in green tissue, thirst quenching, satisfying. My lunch breaks involved jamming a fist full of crackers into my mouth, chasing them down with several large gulps of tepid water, devouring an apple or two, core and all, and repeating the same drill over again. Lunch was usually over in less than five minutes.

The concept of staying in motion took on a new urgency at this time as well. In the early morning and evening hours, hordes of no-see-ums and mosquitoes swarmed us relentlessly. As the morning chill lifted and the temperature began to rise, clouds of blackflies descended on us, dogging our every move, taking particular interest in our faces. When the sun was at its highest point in the sky, sorties of horseflies and deer flies bombarded us from every direction—wave upon wave, determined to tear small chunks of flesh from our exposed arms and necks. There was no relief unless you were willing to apply 100 per cent DEET to your exposed skin, and even then, it was only effective if you didn't sweat it off. I sweat my DEET off within minutes. People fashioned hijabs and other forms of headgear out of towels and shirts, soaking them in bug dope in an attempt to escape the torment.[2] When an angry yell or scream was heard from across the block—and these were frequent occurrences—it was almost always bug related. Worst of all, no matter how vigilant you were in swatting insects away from your face, it was only a matter of time before a blackfly bit you on that special spot near your eye that caused your eyelid to swell shut, usually for the better part of a week, giving you the appearance of having just wandered off the set of a zombie flick.

People began to drop weight, often dramatically so. Even though I tried to make up for lost calories at dinner, I was shedding pounds faster than I could tack them back on. I began wearing a belt for the first time in years as my pants were falling off my hips.

By mid-contract, we had exhausted all of the ground within walking distance of camp. Sadly, my early morning escapades came to an end, but I kept working in the evenings. Barrett would leave a trike for me on the block—a trike that I had no trouble operating—allowing me to put an extra run in after everyone else called

---

2. "Bug dope" refers to bug spray or DEET insect repellent.

it a day. When I arrived back in camp later in the evening, I could always count on Debbie to greet me at the edge of camp, eager to get me caught up on all of the gossip she'd overheard at dinner. She'd sit with me in the Quonset hut while I devoured my dinner, picking away at her dessert and watching with incredulity as I inhaled one course after another.

One evening after I arrived back at camp a little later than usual, Debbie was nowhere to be found. Brushing aside vague feelings of abandonment, I used the opportunity to take a shower before dinner (the shower tent was nearly always empty in the evenings as people preferred to get clean immediately after work). Just as I was getting lathered up, I heard someone walk past outside and run a hand across the tarpaulin wall. Then the door opened and closed. I had company.

These showers were slightly more private than the setup in the previous camp. Rather than one large open space, there were three medium-sized compartments with two shower heads in each. A six-foot-high tarpaulin separated each compartment. Paying no attention to the person undressing in the next stall over, I gave myself a final rinse and reached for my towel. Then, suddenly, through the layers of mist and steam, a soft, sultry voice inquired, "How was your day, Non-Stop?" I remember wrestling with a temporary stammer as the honeyed tones of Debbie's query pinged and echoed across every cell in my body. "Ah, ahhhh... good... great!" I finally managed.

Here was the one woman I adored more than any other on the entire planet, naked, showering a few feet away with only a thin sheet of plastic separating us. She asked if I wanted to try some of her shampoo, an intense mint-oil concoction that was popular among tree-planters back then. I accepted and stepped back under the generous spray. As she struggled to pass the heavy jug over our tarpaulin divider, I spotted beautiful chestnut brown freckles randomly and wonderfully distributed across her bicep and forearm. As I considered this exquisite little facet of her anatomy, I realized how much of a mystery she still was to me.

That may have been the longest shower of my young life, with Debbie occupying one side of the tarpaulin divide, me the other, each savouring the moist steamy environment, getting caught up on each other's day. Of course, my mind raced, wondering if there was greater significance to the encounter—something more meaningful than merely washing away the day's sweat and grime. One thing was for certain: if her intent was to drive me crazy, she had succeeded admirably. I hoped that this shower routine would become our "new thing."

After our showers, as we were making our way to the Quonset hut, Debbie warned me that there was a scandal brewing in camp. Some of the treeplanters' wives back on Cortes Island had been alerted that their men were sharing tents with some of the young ladies in camp (a number of people on the crew called Cortes home, including Barrett and my sister Lina). Apparently, one of the foremen who had been busted—a twitchy character named Ted—was livid, determined to find out who the whistleblower was. Rumour was, I was at the very top of his suspect list.

Halfway through my dinner that night, Ted marched in to the Quonset hut and interrupted my supper with a blunt and accusatory, "We need to talk." I didn't like Ted. I hadn't liked him from the very beginning, especially after he labelled our rookie crew "The Lunch Bunch" after spotting us taking a break together on the side of the road on our first day of the season. He was, for lack of a better term, a major-league douchebag. He was a condescending prick who liked to peacock around camp as if he owned the place. With his chest pounding and the veins in his neck appallingly distended, he leaned across the table and with a hoarse whisper said, "Your sister informed my wife that I was sleeping with Jennifer." I was in no mood for drama that evening and simply replied, "What the fuck do you want me to do about it, Ted?"

Before I could expand on that sentiment, Barrett, who had been listening in from the next table over, chimed in with, "Let the kid eat his dinner, Ted—can't you see he's on a date?" Debbie howled out loud with laughter at the suggestion, and Ted shrivelled to half his size and stormed out of the Quonset hut, tripping and nearly falling flat on his face in the process.

As the contract stretched out into June, Debbie and I grew even closer. We continued to spend our evenings together. I showed her how to play a few chords on my guitar. She even stayed late with me on the block a few times to tack a few hundred extra trees onto her score. Regrettably, intimate evening showers did not become our "new thing," but I sensed that she was beginning to look at me in a different way. After everything I had experienced over the previous two months, I was also beginning to think differently about myself.

As we entered week five of the contract, and week nine of the season, I began to notice a change in the crew. Beaten down by the extreme heat, bugs, and general state of exhaustion, people began retiring to their tents earlier in the evening. There was less celebrating. There was less music. Even Curt, who was normally good for an hour or two of pickin' and grinnin', limited his sets to only twenty or thirty minutes per night. And there was something going on with the hardcore smokers on the crew. They were running out of tobacco. The ubiquitous pouches of loose tobacco that were generally left unattended on the dining tables in the Quonset hut were now being scooped up and pocketed when not in use. Tobacco had suddenly become a rare commodity, and a carefully guarded one at that.

In the trucks, on the way to work, we speculated on the desperate times that lay ahead for smokers unless Barrett was able to find a way to bring more in. We had a shipment of provisions barged in earlier that week, but tobacco wasn't on the list. The smokers joked about how they would soon be forced to raid the dirty stinking ashtrays in the trucks. I thought they were jesting. They were not! There came an evening when they collectively raided the ashtrays in all of the trucks, sifting through nine weeks' worth of discards, sorting and grading the used butts according to their level of raunchiness. Nothing was thrown out, though. Eventually, even the raunchiest of the lot were pulled apart, re-rolled and smoked. When the supply in the trucks was exhausted, the discarded butts that had been ground into the dirt outside the Quonset hut were next. Big Tobacco really had these poor folk by the short and curlies.

As our spring season entered its final shift, the black bears, which until then had kept a healthy distance from our camp, became bolder, attempting to break into the kitchen and Quonset hut late at night. One of the girls who was camped in proximity to the kitchen claimed that a black bear had actually poked its head in through the front door of her tent. That explained the blood-curdling screams I woke up to at 2:00 a.m. Curiously, these Williston Lake black bears all sported beautiful white patches on their chests, some larger than others, but always prominent. It gave them a cuddly-looking quality and we always stopped our trucks to admire them whenever they were spotted on the road. But beyond a few isolated incidents, they didn't pose much of a threat, and they remain a fond memory—one of the few fond memories I have involving bears while camping in remote locales.

We were coming down to the final few days of the contract, and as I would soon discover, these were often stressful times for the crew. People would grow anxious in the final push. We always knew the number of trees that remained to be planted, and in the final few days, simple arithmetic revealed the exact number of trees each planter would be required to plant in order to draw the contract to a close. Often that number overwhelmed people. Adding to the stress of this particular contract, we were forced to abide by an inflexible barge schedule. Three days' worth of trees would need to go into the ground in the space of two; otherwise we'd be forced to wait another five days for the next barge run.

A decision was made to start work an hour earlier the next morning, work a full day, drive back to camp for a one-hour supper break and then head back out to the block for an evening run. I was fine with the idea, but there was resistance among some of the more exhausted planters on the crew. When it came right down to it, we didn't have a choice. Geographically isolated contracts often end in this manner. It seemed to be the rule, rather than the exception, as I would discover over time.

The second to last day of the contract was brutal. We needed to pound in an extraordinary number of trees that day, and we didn't quite reach our goal. A decision was made to start even earlier the next day and work until the final tree went into the ground. We were encouraged to work together in small groups in order to play off one another's energy. This made sense to me. Debbie and I decided to pair up, and we carefully scanned the crew for a third partner. Kevin!

Kevin was a bred and buttered Cortes Island boy. He was one of the more straightlaced and likable guys on the crew. He was clean-cut, he didn't smoke, he didn't drink and he was always polite, almost to a fault. He was also a fastidious man. He actually washed out his tree-planting bags at the end of each shift—no one on the crew had ever seen anything like it. And he planted with a mattock, an old-school pick-like tool that required an entirely different skill set to master. Kevin was the only treeplanter I have ever met who planted with such an archaic tool. Debbie and I both respected him for that.

Everyone retired to their tents shortly after finishing supper. Knowing that our time together was coming to an end, Debbie and I embraced each other longer than usual that evening. When she retreated to her tent, I found myself all alone in the Quonset hut. It was a strange feeling, being the only soul awake in camp while the sun was still visible on the horizon. I used the opportunity to fire up the generator and pump for a nice long shower. I had a lot to think about.

After ten minutes of squatting under the intense heat and spray generated by the two shower heads I had angled to form a single power-ful stream, I barely noticed the sound of the shower door opening and closing. I expected Barrett, or one of the foremen, to barge in thinking someone had accidentally left the shower on, but the rap of the shower door was followed by silence. Then, softly, Debbie emerged from the layers of steam. She was wearing only a towel, which she allowed to drop to the ground the moment our eyes met. The image of her slowly advancing through the white vapor is one that is indelibly burned into my memory.

The final day of planting—the final day of my 1983 spring tree-planting season—was an emotionally charged experience. Barrett loaded Debbie, Kevin and me into his own personal truck and sped off ahead of the rest of the pack. A few minutes into the drive, Debbie leaned into my shoulder and fell fast asleep. We were both exhausted. We were too exhausted to show up for breakfast that morning. While attempting to choke down a few handfuls of granola for energy, I observed Barrett turning our truck onto a brand-new road system. We were to be "block-openers" on that final day of the season.

As we pulled into our new block, I nudged Debbie and directed her weary gaze toward the beautiful expanse of cream that was coming into view.[3] With a grin on his mug, Barrett instructed us to plant down the slope against the forest line to our right, hook up with a riparian zone boundary half a kilometre below and plant single lines of trees through the cream until we were instructed to do otherwise. From a treeplanter's perspective, it was a dream assignment. It was a massive area, encompassing at least one hundred acres. Normally it would take the three of us five or six days to plant an area that size. On that day, we would have company, eventually. Two or three other crews were expected to arrive by the end of the afternoon, promising to turn the area into an epic gang-plant.[4]

Debbie and I were operating on only three hours of sleep. It took an inordinate amount of effort just to put seedlings into our bags and strap them onto our hips. Looking down toward the bottom of our

3. "Cream" refers to an exceptional piece of land that has light slash and soft, yielding soil. Basically, it's fast ground and easy to plant.

4. "Gang-plant": a large group of planters who descend on an area, typically toward the end of a contract, forming a line, planting side by side until the area, or the trees, are exhausted.

private cream-show, we observed a thin layer of fog hanging over the lower third of the block, obscuring our bottom boundary.

There might have been a half-dozen words spoken between us during that first hour. The only sounds produced by our little trio were those of our shovel and mattock blades stabbing the ground and the occasional involuntary grunt as we worked our roots into the soil. As we planted farther toward the bottom of the block, we were treated to the vibrations of rushing water. The source lay hidden, buried deep in the lush foliage of the riparian zone below.

This was not a day for individual achievement. When someone bagged-out early, they grabbed trees from the bags of the person planting beside them, repeating the gesture over and over until the entire group was completely bagged-out.

At the end of the first run, back at the treecache, Debbie glanced at her watch, sighed heavily and declared, "One run down... seven more to go." This was going to be a long day, and emotionally, I was a wreck. The thought that I might not see Debbie again after this day was more than I could handle. I was gutted. But I managed to stay in character. Staying in motion helped conceal my anguish.

We worked at a steady pace all day long and by 3:00 p.m. there were ten additional planters in our area, turning our cream-show into a hub of activity. By 5:00 p.m. two more trucks loaded with planters had arrived and, as expected, the gang-plant was epic in scale. It's an extraordinary sight watching two dozen planters lined up, side by side, three metres apart, taking out giant swaths of land in a single pass.

By 7:00 p.m., operating on only a few hours of sleep, a half-dozen pieces of fruit and a few handfuls of granola, our little trio was plucked off the gang-plant and put on yet another special mission. Barrett transported us to the other side of the riparian zone that served as our bottom boundary. There, a new cutblock opened up. Our instructions were simple: plant along the bottom of the cutblock, along the treeline, and continue planting until our roadside cache was exhausted. Though we couldn't fully appreciate it at the time, this assignment was a gift.

The perimeters of most Interior cutblocks were lined with a fire road or trail back then—a beautiful, dirty and yielding swath of ground that made planting nearly effortless. This cutblock had such a feature, but it was twice as wide as normal.

Barrett left us with eighteen hundred trees in our cache. We bagged-up with three hundred each and began pounding away. The ground was so clean and fast that we bagged-out in less than forty-five minutes. When we arrived back at our cache, Barrett had left us an additional 150 trees. Expecting that this would be our final run of the season, we bagged-up with 350 trees each. The weight on our poor hips and shoulders was brutal, but the weight comes off fast when you're planting a tree every five or six seconds.

The sun was in full retreat when we bagged-out from our final run, and to our great relief, there were no more trees waiting for us at our cache. Our empty tree boxes had been broken down, flattened, and the tarp was folded—a clear indication that our day was done. The contract was over.

Tearing a page out of Karl Marx's playbook, we decided to pool our trees together and split them evenly three ways. Our net result: 3,100 trees each. Not bad for a day when I was ready to quit before it even began.

There was no party or celebration back at camp that evening. People were struggling, even falling to the ground, as they attempted to extricate themselves from the back seats of their trucks when they arrived at camp. Some people didn't even line up for supper—they simply staggered off in the direction of their tents. This crew was done.

I guess I wasn't surprised when Debbie pulled away from me at the end of the evening, insisting that we retreat to our separate tents. This was her way, her first step in drawing our relationship to a close. Though she didn't admit it, I got a sense that she was determined to rekindle her flame back home in Vancouver. I was too tired to think, and with a heavy heart I wandered back to my side of the woods and drifted off into a profound sleep.

The breakfast horn blew at 9:00 the next morning. By the time I arrived, half of the camp had already been torn down. The bright white and yellow canvas shell of the Quonset hut had already been stripped and folded, and only the metal frame was still erect, giving it the appearance of a giant prehistoric skeleton from a distance.

Barrett, his foreman and several veteran highballers were gathered around the only table still upright, some shaking their heads, some with incredulous expressions on their faces. When Barrett spotted me, his face lit up. Pointing in my direction, he called out, "There he is!" Motioning me to come join his circle of insiders, he declared that I was his top producer on the contract. I had planted more trees than even his most celebrated highballers. That felt pretty damn good, for a second or two; then I spotted Debbie toiling away in the kitchen trailer, helping Denny get things squared away. When she looked up and our eyes met, I detected no warmth, no longing, no affection. She wasn't approachable. I kept my distance.

When the water taxis arrived to take us back to Mackenzie, Debbie boarded the second boat, choosing not to ride along with me in the first one. It was a long ride back to town. I isolated myself, avoiding the chatter that centred on topics like, "What's the first thing you're going to do when you get to town?" and, "Who's the first person you're going to call?" The banter was too carefree, too untroubled for the state of mind I was in. The smokers on the crew, who had just endured four days without nicotine, sat with their eyes fixed straight ahead, rocking back and forth in their seats. We knew what their first move would be once we landed, and one would be best advised not to stand in their way when the boat docked.

Back onshore, after the trucks were unloaded from the barge and people began to claim their seats, preparing for the long journey back to Vancouver, Debbie pulled away from the crowd, walked over to me and said goodbye. Our eyes locked for only a brief moment before she cast her gaze downward. Her eyes were puffy and red from tears—somehow I found comfort in her sadness. Before I could ask whether I could reach out to her the next time I was in Vancouver, she gave me a hug and quickly retreated back to her truck.

I wondered if I would ever see her again. To this day, some thirty-six years and a good handful of meaningful relationships later, my love for Debbie endures. Whenever I detect the scent of mint oil, lavender or jasmine, a melancholy rolls over me, nearly reducing me to tears.

Crazy thing: when I arrived back in Calgary late the next afternoon, I half expected a victory parade. After everything I had gone through, I expected people to stand up, take notice and give me my due. Of course, after planting for the better part of three months at a pace that could only be described as reckless, I was entitled to such delusions.

Exhausted, heartbroken and desolate, I landed on my sister's doorstep and retreated to her guest bedroom. The next two weeks are a blur. They consisted of long periods of deep sleep and ruminations over lost love. I was inconsolable. I couldn't steer my thoughts away from Debbie. Barely a second went by when I wasn't thinking of her in some way.

As the summer matured and I began to heal, my thoughts eventually turned westward. I was waiting for the phone to ring. I was waiting for that important phone call from Barrett. It finally came late in the summer, just as the leaves around my sister's neighbourhood were beginning to change colour.

# THE GRIZZLY CORRIDOR

||||||||||||||||||||||||||||||||||||||||||||||||||||||||||||||||||||||||||||||||||||||||||||||||||||||||

It was the late summer of 1983. I was restless. Barrett's phone call couldn't have been better timed. The spring season that had such a positive and profound impact on my life was almost three months behind me. Barrett explained that he had just been awarded a treeplanting contract up Bute Inlet. I was invited.

We were to mobilize from Heriot Bay on Quadra Island in two weeks. After arriving at our destination, we'd establish a tent camp, though our meals would be provided by a nearby logging camp. It sounded good to me. I committed to the project without hesitation.

As soon as I hung up the phone, I searched for Bute Inlet on a map and was immediately struck by its geographic isolation. It stretched some eighty kilometres into the rugged coastal Interior from its mouth at Stuart Island to its head at the estuaries of the Homathko and Southgate rivers. There were no highways or roads leading in; access was by air or water only. The juices really began to flow when I learned from my sister that it was considered to be one of the most dramatic and picturesque waterways in the entire world. I was stoked.

Up until that time, my experiences in remote locales were limited to the Interior of central and northern BC. And as extraordinary as those regions were, veteran planters insisted that the coast, specifically the coastal inlets, was infinitely more wild and exciting. They regaled me with tales of glaciers, ice fields, giant cedars, boulders the size of condos and vast stretches of pristine wilderness. Bute Inlet, above all other coastal destinations, was given special standing for its exceptional beauty and mystique.

One day before I was to embark on the twenty-four-hour bus ride from Calgary to Campbell River, where I was to spend the night before crossing over to meet the crew on Quadra Island, I came down with a nasty flu virus, one that nearly knocked me out of the picture. My mom, being a registered nurse, didn't hesitate in hooking me up with medication she thought might help take the edge off of my long journey. Before I hopped onto the bus, she handed me a small bottle of pain-relief pills, some with codeine, some without. We didn't realize it at that time, but I had an allergy to codeine, one that produced hallucinations and extreme anxiety.

I was five hours into the first leg of my journey when the sun began to set over Rogers Pass. I found myself unable to settle my nerves, partly due to my feverish state, partly due to my excitement and anticipation over the prospect of a new adventure.

As night began to descend over the mountain pass, I thought about home. I thought about how much I was already missing my friends and family. I thought about my mom. I then remembered her care package and promptly put back two of the larger white pills, hoping a sense of calm and quiet would sweep over me.

From that point on, my memories are fragmented and vague. I remember an unfamiliar sensation sweeping over me. I remember becoming fixated on the jagged black shapes of the mountain ridges on the horizon. I traced their near vertical contours all the way down to where they transitioned into complete blackness below the edge of the highway. Everything had a somewhat surreal and interesting quality at first, but then things began to spiral out of control. Dark shapes and shadows began to emerge from the rock faces and conifer patches on the right side of the highway. Worse, the steep valley walls on the left began to crumble and collapse, threatening to crush and bury our bus under piles of rock and debris.

Until then I had never experienced what the hippies referred to as a "bad trip," but this certainly had to qualify. I remember the panic, the desperation as I attempted to calm myself down. I remember hyperventilating, closing my eyes and burying my face in my jacket, trying not to scream. I'm not sure if I was successful in thwarting those impulses as my next real memory was dragging my gear across the bus station parking lot in Vancouver, some twelve hours later. But that was only a fleeting impression. I have no recollection of boarding my connecting bus, crossing the Strait of Georgia by ferry or making the journey up Vancouver Island. Apparently, I had so thoroughly programmed the entire itinerary into my head that I didn't skip a beat. Waking up en route, hearing the bus driver call out, "Next stop Campbell River," was a monumental relief. My dreams up until that point were toxic, plagued with flashes of alien landscapes and baleful faces.

Nearly defeated by the residual effects of a fever and a bad codeine trip, I dragged my heavy gear from the bus depot in Campbell River to a hotel I had booked in advance. Spotting the Quadra Island ferry dock from my hotel window was comforting—it was the vessel I would need to board early the next morning in order to hook up with my crew.

The first leg of my journey was behind me. To celebrate, I turned the TV on to the movie channel, collapsed on the bed and drifted off into a shallow coma. Later that night, I awoke with a start to the sound of roaring engines. For a few crazy moments I had no recollection of where I was, or how I got there. Running to the window and peering out onto the street below, I could see only the vague outline of unfamiliar buildings draped in a thick layer of fog. I was lost. I had no sense of time or space. On the desk next to the TV was an assortment of pamphlets and menus that finally revealed my location, allowing me to crawl back into the here and now.

The engine sounds that triggered the panic attack sprung from a movie that was playing on TV—George Miller's *The Road Warrior*—an extremely disconcerting post-apocalyptic tale of a desolate world filled with fiendish, relentless antagonists. The intrusion from the television seemed fitting somehow, considering my current state of mind.

I shook off my dopey malaise early the next morning and managed to catch the first ferry over to Quadra Island. It was a short crossing. The warmhearted generosity of the local island folk made hitching a ride to the other side of the island an effortless task.

I arrived at Heriot Bay ahead of schedule. Barrett's trucks, which were in the process of being loaded onto a barge, were a comforting sight. Though I felt as if I had been dragged behind the bus for the entire journey from Calgary to the West Coast, my strength was beginning to return. I felt myself coming back into the light.

It was good to see Barrett. He elevated my spirit. He was his usual animated self, grinning ear to ear, looking for any opportunity to laugh out loud. The crew he had assembled was small. There were only a dozen of us. I was surprised to see six new faces, including two younger bucks named Ricky and Zach.

Ricky was a tall, lean and ruggedly handsome fellow. He immediately came off as loud and unrefined. He was the kind of guy who didn't give a shit about what others thought of him—an admirable quality, I thought. He too loved to laugh out loud and, despite his crass nature, I immediately spotted a friend in him.

Zach was the polar opposite of his buddy. He was a solemn man with piercing green eyes. He appeared restless, brooding. He had a simmering intensity that could be felt the moment you entered his space. Though I greeted him warmly, shaking his hand, I resolved to keep my distance for the time being.

Ricky had also brought along a friend, a gentle and attentive Doberman pinscher named Lady. She was smaller in stature than most Dobies I had met, but she was very well conditioned. She had strong lines. It was obvious that Ricky loved his dog and took exceptionally good care of her.

Also on the crew were three familiar faces from the spring: Kelly, my first foreman, Ron, the ex-high-school English teacher and Nick, a Stetson-wearing cowboy with a thick southern drawl. The one person I had hoped to greet more than any other was not in evidence. No one could tell me where she was or how she was doing. In a way, I was relieved Debbie wasn't there.

There was one detail concerning the Bute project that I must've missed when Barrett briefed me over the phone. We were to sail along with the trucks for the entire ten-hour barge ride to the head of the inlet. I was stoked. The prospect of slowly skirting some of the more isolated islands within the Discovery Island group, before entering the inlet itself, promised to heighten the level of adventure.

Our barge captain navigated our vessel with great finesse through the narrow, turbulent channels between the islands of Read, Maurelle, Raza, Sonora and Stuart. There were also numerous smaller islands, completely uninhabited, that created an obstacle course of sorts, requiring delicate navigation. Once we rounded Stuart, about four hours into the journey, Bute Inlet opened up before us. Though shrouded in layers of fog, it offered a glorious moment. We were now heading into mainland BC through an eighty-kilometre-long estuary; a classic fjord some four kilometres wide with steep mountains rising up to three thousand metres on both sides.

Shortly after we entered the inlet, the clouds opened up and light rain began to fall. As we made our unhurried advance through the calm, dark blue water, each kilometre revealed something singular, something extraordinary: spectacular waterfalls cascading from great heights, their genesis cloaked in thick layers of cumulus; granite cliffs rising many hundreds of metres above us—their extent was also obscured by the low ceiling; voluminous creeks emptying into the estuary with great drama. Every once in a while we'd spot a small abandoned cabin poking out of the forest, only metres above the high-tide line, on the verge of surrendering to the elements. I imagined grizzled old prospectors once having lived in them as they scoured the area for gold decades earlier.

The slow barge ride up the inlet was a lot to drink in. I used up more than half of the film I had brought along to document the adventure, unable to set my camera down for more than a few moments at a time.

Curiously, feelings of loneliness and isolation began to take hold the farther in we went. I suppose if we had flown, or travelled in a much faster craft, those feelings wouldn't have had the opportunity to develop. The barge, burdened with the weight of trucks, fuel, gear and personnel, plodded along slowly through the dark calm water. By hour eight or nine, not having seen any other vessel travelling in or out, those feelings of loneliness and isolation gave way to a general sense of unease. I know I wasn't the only one who felt it.

We arrived at the head of the inlet late in the afternoon. The plan was to drive the twenty-five kilometres to the Scar Creek logging camp, unload the trucks, and hike to a nearby creek where we'd pitch our tents. Once set up, we could sit down to a hot meal back in the camp dining hall. I had endured nearly forty-eight hours without any real food.

The road leading inland from the head of the inlet was built specifically for the purpose of harvesting trees and putting wood in the water.[1] It did not link up with any other road or highway network. It terminated where the harvesting ended. Beyond that were hundreds of kilometres of pristine, untouched wilderness unbranded by human footprints.

It was a good half-hour drive from the beachhead to the Scar Creek camp. Stepping out of the truck, I immediately sensed something

---

1. Putting "wood in the water" is the objective of most coastal logging operations. In this case, the trees are felled, yarded, loaded onto trucks, transported to the head of the inlet, dumped in the water and finally towed in large booms by tugboat to market.

off about the place. It didn't feel right. I quickly dismissed that first impression. I couldn't trust it. I was still suffering from the residual effects of a fever and a codeine hangover.

The camp was well organized. Aside from a large machine shop and mess hall, there were a half-dozen mobile-home-like structures sprawled out across two acres, erected to shelter the crews that worked to put wood in the water.

NO CAULKS BEYOND THIS POINT was the ubiquitous message in camp.[2] The sign was at every entrance to every building. It was especially prominent at the entrance to the kitchen and mess hall.

Across the compound was a recreation room where the loggers went to unwind after dinner. The door was ajar. I could spot several sets of eyes checking us out from within.

While we were unloading gear from our trucks, a group of loggers assembled on the mess hall porch. Judging by the sour expressions, this wasn't a welcoming committee. They didn't seem too thrilled about strangers rolling into their camp. I suppose they decided that we didn't pose much of a threat, though. They soon lost interest and went back to their meals.

Our late arrival left us with limited daylight. We needed to hike our gear to the creek and set up our camp before nightfall. Wafting across the compound from the kitchen was the wonderful aroma of dinner. Hot food would be waiting for us the moment we got ourselves squared away.

The trail that led to our camping area cut through a thick patch of conifers for the first two hundred metres, then dropped down to a sandy flat where it wound through another two hundred metres of thick salmonberry, terminating at a sandy ledge at the edge of a creek.

The creek was at its seasonal low, exposing a five-metre-wide swath of dry creek bed, checkerboarded by round alluvial stones

---

2. "Caulks" refer to workboots with metal spikes in the soles. They are worn to gain traction in heavily wooded areas.

rendered smooth and slick from fast-running water. The creek just beyond ran shallow but steady. On one side, a large boulder field interrupted its flow, creating deep shimmering pools beyond, and on the other, a sublime sight: the exposed creek bed transitioned into a long, soft carpet of grey, talc-like sand—a narrow swath at first, swelling out into a vast expanse some five hundred metres long and up to fifty metres wide.

Tall timber flanked the beach on the upper fringe, accentuated by cedar, balsam and hemlock. The creek defined the lower boundary, its flow occasionally disrupted by large protruding boulders, inducing sloshes and churns that reverberated throughout the corridor.

Beyond the boulder field on the other side of the creek, the terrain then sloped upward, gradually increasing in grade, the heavy brush giving way to towering cedars with smaller maples interspersed between them. It was an ominous backdrop. This was real wilderness. One had to wonder what lurked along those higher reaches.

The beach offered numerous possibilities for individual campsites, everything from compacted waterfront benches to private alcoves tucked in along the forest edge. Preferring privacy, I claimed a spot at the very far end of the corridor. It was a long walk to the trailhead that led back to the logging camp, but the spot was wonderfully secluded.

After an hour of dragging gear, levelling sand, and pounding tent pegs, we raised an impressive little tent village. One dozen nylon structures of every shape, colour and size extended some five hundred metres from one end of the corridor to the other. My contribution to the neighbourhood: a two-man pup tent with an orange shell and a bright blue tarp fashioned as a rainfly.

By then, the sun was in full retreat. Barrett calling us to dinner was music to my ears. With our tents pitched, our gear organized for the next morning and flashlights in hand, we made our way back up the trail to the dining hall.

The mess hall was set up like a cafeteria. At supper, the entire meal was laid out buffet style—all you could eat and then some. In the morning, there was an assortment of breakfast entrees, also laid out buffet style, but you could have your eggs made to order. We were responsible for bagging our own lunches, and there was a separate room where lunch items were laid out each morning.

A very generous dinner spread was set out for us that first night, and as we filled our faces, Barrett gave us a quick rundown of the house rules, which facilities were open to us and which were strictly off limits. Aside from the dining hall, we were granted access to a vacant unit at the far end of the camp. It had a bathroom, several shower stalls and a good-sized dry room in the event the sky opened up on us. The recreation hall—where the loggers gathered to blow off steam after dinner—was a big question mark. Access would be decided by the loggers and would be by invitation only. I was intrigued by that little detail.

I slept extremely well in my tiny pup tent on the beach that first night. Soothed by the sound of running water and an occasional breeze caressing the canopy of conifer limbs above, I was instantly lulled and transported into dreamland. Nothing could have shaken me out of my slumber that first night.

It was pre-dawn when I emerged from my tent the next morning. Feeling better than I had in days, excited at the prospect of hitting the slopes, I headed off in the direction of the logging camp, eager to get a jump on my day. Along the trail, I heard a dog barking in the distance. It wasn't a normal bark. It sounded anxious, strained. I remember wondering if it was Lady, and what it was that had her so agitated, so early in the morning.

I wasn't prepared for the reception I received when I stepped into the mess hall that first morning. Three dozen loggers, all in the final stages of polishing off their breakfasts, stopped in mid-chew and stared me down. Bulletproof faces. Row upon row of them. Not a smile or friendly gesture among them. This hostility was par for the course in many ways. These men were working in one of the most geographically isolated areas on the planet. They weren't used to outsiders coming in, violating their space, sitting at their tables, eating their food. Tread lightly, I thought. I made a beeline for the safety of the lunchroom around the corner.

The lunch spread that greeted me caused my jaw to slacken. It had every variety of cold cut you could imagine, along with supper leftovers, a dozen different types of cheeses, every conceivable type of condiment and sandwich topping, and of course, a respectable collection of bread and rolls. But what really floored me was the area devoted entirely to desserts. Those items occupied twice as much table space as all the other lunch items combined. There were apple, strawberry, rhubarb, cherry and blueberry pies. A variety of lavishly iced cakes occupied the shelf above. Cookies, tarts, turnovers, brownies, fruit squares, Nanaimo bars, eclairs, Danishes and doughnuts. It was total madness.

Back at the dining area I spotted Kelly, my foreman, setting a plate of bacon and eggs on one of the tables that were made available to us. Kelly was an intense fellow, but it was a palatable intensity. He had the biggest, roundest blue eyes I had ever seen. The rest of his facial features were obscured by a thick black beard that merged with his straight, bowl cut. Kelly always seemed to have a knowing grin on his face, as if he were able to read your deepest thoughts.

As I approached his table to bid him good morning, he looked up and asked, "You didn't think to bring a rifle along, did ya?" Before I could respond, the mess hall door flew open and Ricky and Zach barged in, deeply engaged in conversation, oblivious to the disapproving glares from the locals. It then occurred to me why Lady had been barking so anxiously earlier on, and why Kelly would ask such an odd question. From that point on, our mess hall conversations were dominated by the talk of bears. Grizzly bears.

The drive to our first cutblock was a short hop from the logging camp. Along the way, Ricky and Zach described spotting a bear on the other side of the creek at roughly 4:30 a.m. It emerged within fifty or sixty metres of their campsite (their tents were close to the trailhead). It was fairly dark at that early hour, but from what little they could see, they estimated it was a large animal. Lady was the first to detect it, picking up its scent from inside Ricky's tent. When Ricky turned her loose, she immediately bolted to edge of the creek to challenge it. When the bear was slow to retreat, Lady crossed over and gave chase. The confrontation lasted well over an hour. The barking I'd heard on my way to breakfast was apparently the tail end of that episode. This got me thinking about my preference for privacy at the far end of the corridor.

Our focus soon shifted to planting. Being the first out of the truck and the first to bag-up, I was the first carve off a piece of the mountain. This was my very first piece of coastal terrain. It was challenging. The slash was bigger and deeper than in the Interior. The stumps and root swells were often several metres in diameter, rather than just a foot or two. The brush was thicker and higher.

I couldn't get the thought of a grizzly encounter out of my mind. I was on edge all day, reacting to every little sound and vibration around me. The day progressed without incident, though, and as usual, it ended almost as soon as it began. Time flies when you're hard at work creating a new forest.

When we arrived back at camp at the end of the day, supper was already being served. Rather than using the camp facilities to wash up, I chose to hike back to my tent first. I wanted to change into clean clothes, but I also felt a need to face my fears. When I reached our line of tents at the edge of the beach, the setting was undisturbed in the cool early evening air. I quickly made my way to the far end of the corridor, changed clothes, washed up in the creek, and ran back to the dining hall.

It was steak night. Aside from the usual buffet and salad bar, which would have easily satisfied all of our appetites, we were asked how we wanted our T-bone cooked: well done, medium, medium rare or bloody.

Careful planning was required to transport one's entire meal from the buffet line back to the table in a single trip. The solution: concentration, good balance, a large tray and a few positive affirmations along the way. I used two plates, one for the massive slab of red meat, the other for the salad, baked potato and lasagna. I also juggled a bowl filled with onions rings, a handful of flesh-tearing cutlery and two tall glasses filled to the brim by the industrial-sized Tang dispensers at the end of the buffet line. Few of us possessed the skills required to transport our entire meal back to the table, intact, in one trip. Most people played it safe, taking two, even three runs at it.

I was the last one to leave the dining hall that evening. Eating was great stress relief, and the cook just happened to have an extra T-bone that he put aside for me. The head cook liked me. He said that I reminded him of his son. Not wanting to hurt his feelings, and not wanting to see good food go to waste, I took the last steak and filled a second plate with all of the extras. I was very much a numbers guy back then, and I figured I had consumed the better part of twelve thousand calories that evening—a personal record that stands to this day.

As I staggered out of the dining hall, I spotted Kelly yakking with one of the loggers on the stairs leading to the rec room. Moments later, I was introduced to his good friend Chuck, who just happened to be working out of the camp as a faller.[3] This was a very fortuitous development. This was also my first lesson in logging camp politics, and the pecking order that existed within. At the very top of the food chain were the fallers. Then came management, then the logging truck drivers, the machine operators and the chokers. Farther on down the list were the rats and vermin that scoured the grounds for garbage and scraps, and then there was us. Here's the thing though: the fallers ruled the roost—no exceptions. Chuck understood the dynamics and apparently had a chat with some of the boys ahead of time. If you were at the very bottom of the heap, as we were, but were somehow able to gain favour with one or more of the fallers in camp, as we apparently had, you rose sharply in the ranks. The rec room was ours.

---

3. "Faller": an individual who cuts down large trees with a chainsaw.

The rec room wasn't nearly as active as I had expected. There were a few people playing pool, a small group playing cards and a half-dozen others assuming comfortable positions on their favourite sofas. Everyone was paying attention to the TV when I walked in. It was a surreal experience: gazing at snow-capped peaks in the middle of some of the most pristine wilderness on the planet one second, then entering a room filled with the sounds and images of a Stevie Nicks video the next. The boys seemed to really like Stevie.

I had a good chat with one of the veteran loggers that night. He was incredulous that we were camping out on the corridor along the creek. Apparently, he and his buddies had discussed it over dinner and agreed that camping out in tents *anywhere* along Bute Inlet was certifiably insane. He described how this area supported a large concentration of silvertips (grizzly bears), many of which were in competition with one another for territory, especially along the sandy corridor we were calling home. He regaled me with one hair-raising tale after another. The common theme: Bute Inlet silvertips were freakishly large, extremely territorial and had no fear of man whatsoever. I regretted wandering into the rec room that night.

The sun was already dipping below the horizon as I set off down the trail back to the beach. Walking with trepidation, I held two long-handled planting shovels, one in each hand, ready to swing furiously if necessary.

My rec room buddy's bear tales rattled me to the core. One in particular really messed with my head. He explained that when the grizzlies around camp became especially bothersome—a frequent occurrence—some of the boys would raid the kitchen and make off with a couple of large roasting hens. After stuffing them full of dynamite and blasting caps, they'd drive out to the camp dump and lay them out on the ground. Backing their truck off to a safe distance, they'd wait and watch. To this day I wonder if he was pulling my leg.

When I made it back to the beach, Lady was pacing back and forth out in front of Ricky's tent, pausing to test the air every few seconds.

She ignored me and my friendly gestures, then crossed the creek and wandered into a thicket on the other side. Walking in the direction of my tent, I detected campfire smoke wafting in layers along the sand. James had made a very large fire out in front of his tent.

James was a character. He was a mountain man in the truest sense of the term. He loved to hunt, fish and harvest wild edibles. He was generally a pleasant guy but was all too often dismissive, moody, unpredictable. He was thirty years old, but his weathered face and deep-set eye sockets, dark from insomnia, lent the appearance of a much older man. He always seemed to sport a wiry seven-day beard that grew in sporadic clumps around his bony cheeks and chin. You could have scaled fish on that stubble. James was always the first to rise in the morning, beginning his day with four cups of thick black coffee, made thicker and richer with the addition of several heaping scoops of instant crystals. Between sips of sludge—that's what the crew affectionately called it—he'd hand-roll cigarettes from a pouch of loose tobacco and chain-smoke until the breakfast horn sounded. Incessant fits of hacking and coughing always followed.

Under normal circumstances, when James made a fire, it was an open invitation for anyone who happened along to stop for a visit. But judging by the diameter of his pit that evening, the reach of his flames and the massive amount of wood he had stockpiled, I knew this fire had another purpose. The atmosphere along our beautiful stretch of sand had changed. What was once warm and inviting had suddenly become cold and disquieting.

Shortly after I settled in with James around his fire, Barrett ambled along. Before I could repeat some of the story-telling highlights, courtesy of my new friend, the rec room raconteur, Lady began barking at something in the vicinity of the trailhead, some two hundred metres away. Her barks became progressively louder, as if she were pursuing something that was advancing in our general direction.

It was pitch-dark. We were a captive audience, the three of us. We stood probing the other side of the creek with our flashlights, looking for any signs of movement. Just then, emerging from the darkness behind us, wearing a hoodie and a rifle strapped over his shoulder: Zach.

"It looks like we're the only ones who came prepared," he complained to James, tugging on his rifle strap and looking past Barrett and me.

James walked back to the fire, where he produced a .303 rifle from under his blanket. "What's going on, Zach?" he asked.

"There's one helluva big bear out there," Zach responded, his hoodie concealing most of his face.

Ricky and Zach had heard it first—a series of thuds and cracks followed by a disconcerting silence as the bear descended from a ridge above their campsite. A few minutes later they saw it. It emerged without a sound, like a ghost, from a thicket on the opposite side of the creek. Though obscured in darkness, it was clearly an enormous animal. Even Lady seemed to waver, unsure of her resolve. Her hesitation was short-lived, though. She bolted across the creek in a fit of rage and gave chase, forcing the bear to retreat up-creek. Her barks could still be heard echoing across the corridor.

Satisfied that Lady had things under control, we sat ourselves down around the fire to ponder our predicament. Barrett then gave James the green light to tell a story he had been holding back—a story that lives with me to this day.

One year earlier, Barrett had been awarded a treeplanting contract in Bute Inlet, where he mobilized a crew to the same general area we were camped on. It wasn't long before two large silvertips—a five-hundred-pound female and an eight-hundred-pound male—had, through a series of hostile encounters, forced the crew to evacuate camp and retreat to a safe area while the situation was dealt with. The trees needed to go in the ground, so a decision was made to handle the crisis in-house. James, along with a First Nations man named Luke—a professional hunting guide who happened to be in the area at the time—were enlisted to hunt down and kill both bears. Apparently, this was the company's only play. Barrett's contract was time sensitive, a top priority. James took on the role of executioner out of a sense of duty. Luke was motivated by the prospect of two very valuable bearskins.

The crew vacated the beach early in the morning. James and Luke set up an offensive position behind a stack of fallen logs that acted as a blind, opposite several gaps in the forest both bears used to access the beach corridor. The female was the first to emerge. They shot it as it crossed the creek, both hitting it in squarely in the chest. It didn't drop. It charged the men and managed to close the gap between them by only a few of metres, taking five addition slugs to the chest before its legs finally buckled.

Both men decided to move upstream and positioned themselves on the wood supports of an old bridge that had once been used to access timber in the higher elevations above the creek. The bridge had since been dismantled, the road on the other side left to the elements, and the bears. This vantage point offered the same view as before, but it was elevated some six feet higher, providing an added measure of security. More than two hours went by, waiting and watching before they spotted movement along the treeline across creek. Then the male grizzly, enormous in stature, emerged from the woods, pausing only briefly to test the air before retreating back into the forest, perhaps sensing the two hunters who were positioned upwind. They had a clear line of sight on the bear, but it emerged farther down the creek than they had anticipated—it was slightly out of range. Manoeuvring them-selves into the prone shooting position, they knew it was only a matter of time before the monster made another appearance.

Twenty tension-filled minutes passed with no activity, only the wind and running water breaking the thick, tense silence. Finally there was a disturbance in the trees above an opening much closer to their position. This was followed by glimpses of the animal as it walked the length of a massive old-growth cedar log that acted as a buffer between them. James's voice began to crack as he described the events that followed.

The bear paused near the end of the log, leaned into it and pulled itself up into a standing position. It was suddenly exposed from the shoulders up, prompting both men to let fire with a single shot to the head. James described the bear's head convulsing violently upon impact, like a doorstop spring being pulled back and released. The bear dropped hard, falling completely out of sight behind the log. With rifles extended and safeties off, they cautiously made their way across the creek and approached the log. James carefully climbed it near the point of impact while Luke flanked it on the far side. To their horror, the bear was gone. The only remains: a large pool of blood containing chunks of bone, teeth and cartilage. And leading away, leading up into the forest, a thick trail of blood.

James and Luke tracked the bear for eight arduous hours up into the timber, some four thousand feet higher in elevation. The bear, knowing it was being pursued, somehow managed to stay one step ahead of the men. When it sensed them closing in, it would run farther ahead, temporarily widening the gap between them. This process of running ahead, resting and running ahead, went on all day. The areas along the trail where the bear rested were saturated with blood. A steady trail would then lead away, forcing the men to push higher, farther up into the timber.

In the end James and Luke failed to track down the mortally wounded bear and put it down for good. Defeated, both physically and mentally, they were forced to turn back as they were losing daylight.

Both hunters, stricken with grief, made their way back down the mountain toward camp. Adding to James's distress, Luke believed that a wounded bear's spirit, after dying alone and in great agony, would search for and inhabit the body of another bear, and would seek revenge on those responsible for its suffering. It was apparent to me that James didn't completely dismiss this folklore as nonsense. I could see the worry written across his weathered face.

That was the end of James's tale. After several moments of quiet reflection, Barrett broke the grim silence, blurting out, "You have room in your tent for one more, right, James?" That was good for one millisecond of comic relief. And it was on that slightly positive shift in sentiment that I managed to summon the courage to bid everyone a caustic "pleasant evening" and set about venturing back to the far end of the corridor where I had set up my tent.

James was a gifted storyteller. His grizzly tale made quite an impression on me. It really began to sink in as I wandered in the direction of my pup tent, probing the dark with my tiny flashlight. I wondered how I was going to survive the contract. I wondered how I was going to survive that very night. Being the youngest and least experienced buck on the crew, I felt I had a lot to prove. I didn't want to come off as a coward. I resolved to feign courage and ride it out, to stay put at the far end of the beach, hoping my fears were exaggerated. It was at about that stage in my thought process that I sensed I was being followed.

Barely a moment separated a state of sheer panic from buoyant relief as Lady emerged from the dark and entered my narrow beam of light. She was perhaps ten metres behind me, matching me step for step. When I called out to her, she ran up and greeted me, eager to reassure me that we were of the same pack. She continued along with me to the entrance of my tent before being called by a distant voice— Ricky was calling her home.

As I unzipped the flap to my tent, I tried to convince myself that Lady had my back, that she would look out for me. I had no way of knowing just how genuine Lady's commitment was.

That set the stage for my second night at Bute, camping in a tiny pup tent. Had I known in advance that the events James described had transpired only a year earlier, on the same stretch of sand, I might've reconsidered taking part in this project. I certainly would have arrived better prepared. I don't know why this tale didn't filter down into any of the late-night fireside chats we'd had earlier in the spring. I suppose there were reasons, many of which were personal, for keeping this ugly episode under wraps.

Inside my tent that night, while organizing my bedding, I reminded myself that the full extent of the threat was not known. There had only been two sightings, in the dark, and that was really all they were—sightings. That didn't allay my fears, though. I stretched out on top of my bedding that night, fully clothed, my down jacket zipped, my hiking boots laced up tight. With my right hand, I held a six-inch lock-blade knife, gripping it as if it were a lifeline. If a bear clawed its way in through the front of my tent, I'd cut an exit door out through the back. That was my plan—the only one I could think of.

I tried to find sleep that night. I lay motionless, stiff as a board. Sounds emanating from the creek and from the depths of the woods behind my tent were amplified. Every sense was fully engaged. I was locked into every vibration, every note, every rhythm of the wilderness around me. It was maddening. I felt as if were trapped in a vivid waking dream, one that threatened to escalate into a full-blown nightmare. Lady's barks could sometimes be heard at the far end of the corridor. It was somewhat comforting knowing that she was busy patrolling the area. But it was unsettling too, knowing that whatever it was, whatever was out there, had no intention of giving up its territory. It remained.

I soon realized the futility of drifting off into any kind of meaningful sleep that night. The fact that my shelter consisted of a flimsy nylon shell, a pair of flexible rods and a thin plastic tarp only served to heighten my anxiety, my feelings of vulnerability.

I watched every hour tick by from 9:00 p.m. onward. Every time I felt on the verge of drifting off, I'd hear a twig snap, a rustle in the forest behind me, or Lady barking in the distance. At 1:30 a.m., I was still wide awake. At that stage, other concerns began to press my thoughts. Planting trees on steep coastal terrain was more physically and mentally demanding than I had anticipated. Without proper sleep, I knew I'd be useless as a treeplanter the following morning. I then remembered the medication my mother had sent along with me. I was desperate. I reluctantly popped two of the smaller pills—the ones that were codeine free—hoping that they would at least take the edge off of my raw, jangled nerves.

I finally drifted off into a light sleep around 2:00 a.m., but it was short-lived. I was roused by the sounds of yelling, followed by Lady barking. These were not distant barks—these were clearer, closer and they were getting closer still. Then I heard what sounded like the hooves of a galloping horse on the compact sand out in front of my tent. Bewildered and weary beyond measure, I lifted myself up and pulled aside the nylon flap at the front entrance to my tent. What I witnessed through the mist-filtered light of a waning crescent moon was difficult to comprehend. A massive grizzly bear—the first grizzly I had ever laid eyes on—charged past the front of my tent only a few metres away. It was in a full gallop with Lady in a frenzied pursuit, nipping at its hindquarters. The chase continued well past my field of vision, into the blackness, and judging by the sounds of splashing water, across the creek and up into the timber on the other side.

I believe I entered into a mild state of shock at that moment, unable to grasp what I had just witnessed. The barking continued for another thirty minutes until Ricky's piercing whistles brought Lady home. I can't remember—one hour seemed to blur into the next—but I may have managed thirty or forty minutes of fragmented sleep from that point on.

Emerging from my tent at first light, I could see several groups of people huddled together in front of their campsites. I couldn't make out much dialogue, but there was a fair amount of animated body language accompanying their discussions.

Spotting Ricky and Zach at the far end of the corridor, I ran over to join them for a debriefing. It turned out that Zach had woken up to grunting sounds outside his tent. When he pulled back the flap to investigate, he found himself face to face with the grizzly. It was his hollers that triggered the bizarre chase past my tent.

There was a rage in the air. Everyone sensed it. A fair amount of soul-searching accompanied our breakfast that morning. This was

1983, in one of the most geographically isolated areas in North America. There was no easy exit. And there was no clear-cut resolution. James's horrific account of the manner in which they were forced to deal with two hostile grizzlies only one year earlier, along the same corridor, clearly exposed a lack of protocol in these situations. We didn't exactly have a fish and wildlife officer on speed dial. Our only mode of communication was a two-way radio phone, an operator-assisted party line strictly controlled by the logging camp manager. A satellite phone might have opened up more options for us, but that technology was years off. We were stuck in this place. We were on our own.

A quick brainstorming session after breakfast produced a sensible plan. Appreciating the fact that all wild animals have an innate fear of fire, we decided to construct two additional firepits at opposite ends of our tent village. This would augment the centrally located pit James had constructed the previous night. Further, we would collectively scour the forest floor and stockpile as much dry wood as possible. The idea was to create three large blazes that would be maintained throughout the night. Without hesitation, I assumed responsibility for feeding the flames at my end of the corridor.

Another grave concern: The Gauntlet—the trail that linked our tent village to the logging camp compound. Just over a metre wide, enclosed by thick brush on one side and dense forest on the other, it provided no way to circumvent a bear encounter by veering either left or right. The trail also meandered. It was impossible to see more than ten metres ahead at any point along the way. If you walked the path alone, especially in the evening, you were rolling the dice. To address this risk, we resolved to always walk in groups. Of course having Lady as a minder was the preferred scenario, and incredibly, she patrolled the trail diligently, acting as an escort whenever she encountered people. Between the three roaring blazes, our two high-velocity rifles, Lady and a heightened state of paranoia, we were optimistic that we might actually walk away from this contract unscathed. Physically anyway.

As if the situation back at camp wasn't enough to keep us all on edge, our drive to work presented an entirely different type of risk altogether. Our road access was carved out precariously along the steep, mountainous clearcut walls of the valley floor below.[4] Some of the terrain was so steep, the engineers who designed these access routes were forced to compromise road width. These "roads," marked by a succession of sharp switchbacks, were already beginning to erode only one year after they were last maintained to accommodate heavy machinery and logging trucks. Gaining access to the upper plateaus of these massive clearcuts required a slow, cautious, white-knuckled crawl, switchback after miserable switchback.

My job, sitting in the front passenger seat of the lead truck, was to communicate with the driver and alert him whenever we crept too close to the edge. Rock slides and general cutbank erosion often placed immovable obstacles in our path, forcing us to travel precariously close to the fringe in order to get around them. I hung my head out the window and watched as the distance between our front tire and the precipice edge diminished to a matter of inches as we attempted to navigate around large boulders. A drop of hundreds of feet would have been the consequence had the sloughing road margin collapsed under the weight of our truck.

This perilous access, which we were required to traverse twice a day, was so unrelenting, so nerve-racking, that James—the great grizzly hunter himself—refused to ride along with the rest of us, "trapped" inside the truck. He had an arrangement with Barrett and Kelly that prompted our little convoy to grind to a halt whenever we

---

4. In the 1970s and 1980s, sustainable logging practices weren't always followed and often took a back seat to economics. These valley walls often appeared as one continuous series of clearcuts, separated only by thin swaths of mature forest. Due to the steep grade, extreme rainfall and the slopes' inability to hold soil, it didn't take long for erosion to render these roads dangerous and impassable.

approached a particularly nasty section of road—James would hop out, climb on to the roof of the truck and ride unencumbered, free to leap to safety in the event we suddenly plummeted off the edge.

We lost a fair amount of enamel, every one of us, navigating these Bute Inlet logging roads.

The terrain we were planting also presented challenges. Aside from the steep grade, the brush was often well over our heads, making it difficult to size up our areas. It wasn't unusual to completely disappear after taking only a few steps off the road.

The slash that littered our ground was more than a metre deep in places, and it was unstable; it shifted as you attempted to walk over it. When you weren't tripping, falling or attempting to extricate yourself from yet another trap door, you were repeatedly probing the ground with your shovel blade, attempting to find soil that simply wasn't there.[5] In my sleep-deprived state, it was a miracle that I managed to plant nine-hour days without collapsing from exhaustion or becoming another silviculture accident statistic.

The end of a gruelling day on the slopes is normally received with sighs of relief, beaming faces and buoyant conversation. Here, the end of our day was met with hard swallows and strained silence. The descent back down the mountain was even more nerve-racking than the ascent earlier in the day. I put on a brave face, but in reality, I was scared shitless.

Within minutes of arriving home we immediately set about gathering stones and stockpiling wood for our newly constructed firepits. After igniting three large blazes, we made our way up the trail toward the logging camp, secure in having fortified our little village.

The greeting we received from the loggers as we entered the dining hall that evening ranged from derision to genuine looks of concern.

---

5. "Trap door": a hollow or crevasse that is concealed by a weak layer of slash or debris. It's not uncommon to break through the surface of such a trap, believing you are on solid ground.

CHAPTER FOUR

They all knew what we were encountering in the dark of night. Word travels fast in remote camps. One of the loggers I spoke with after dinner could only shake his head. Fishing in the creek we were camped beside was extraordinary, he said, but that no one in his right mind fished there—not without armed backup anyway. Once again, I wondered what I had gotten into.

After dinner that night, the atmosphere along our beach corridor felt less oppressive, less hostile. Lady could be heard barking off in the distance intermittently, but there were peaceful lulls that lasted for an hour or more at a time. It occurred to me that between our three raging fires and Lady's constant surveillance, we had persuaded the bear to keep its distance. My thoughts soon turned to bedding down and making up for lost sleep.

Before retiring to bed, I tossed several large logs onto the fire nearest my tent. The plan was to set my alarm for midnight, stoke the fire, sleep another three hours and then stoke it one more time before sunrise.

I suddenly felt secure inside my tiny pup tent. I continued to lie on top of my bedding, though, fully clothed, hiking boots laced tight, jacket zipped to the collar, lock-blade fully extended and ready to rip an escape route if necessary.

Before falling asleep, I witnessed a wonderful play of light, a beautiful glow generated by the flames, exaggerated by the translucent nylon fabric of my tent, which served as a stage of sorts. The flames danced and mingled across the walls of my tent, keeping me company as I drifted off into oblivion.

Fire-stoking duty, and the intervals of sleep in between, wove together seamlessly. It was actually a cathartic exercise, waking up in the middle of the night, coaxing a bed of coals back into a flame, piling on enough wood to create a blaze and then falling back to sleep amid a generous warm glow. For the first time since the whole ridiculous bear episode began, I felt a modicum of peace and control. Fire was my ally. It was a powerful ally. Or so it seemed.

I woke up the next morning just as the first rays of light were beginning to filter through the valley. I felt somewhat refreshed and rejuvenated, and that helped to clear my mind and restore my confidence. As I crawled out of my tent into the half-light and began a series of stretches to limber up for what promised to be a productive day on the slopes, I noticed a disturbance in the sand—a disturbance that wasn't there the night before.

My heart stopped when I examined the ground closer. Tracks. Bear tracks. They coiled around my tent within a metre of where I had lain. I looked over at the fire. It still had a thick bed of coals. It was still throwing off a fair volume of heat and smoke. Dread instantly replaced whatever sense of security I had enjoyed only moments earlier.

As I nervously surveyed the area around me, I discovered an alarming detail. The tracks were contained within a finite area around my tent before disappearing into the forest. This bear was following a different pattern. It managed to stealth its way in from the forest behind me, rather than from the timber on the opposite side of the creek.

At the breakfast table that morning, my report was received with wide eyes and heavy sighs. People were incredulous. No one else had discovered tracks in the vicinity of their tents, but no one could honestly claim that they had examined their own campsites thoroughly enough to eliminate the possibility.

It was a long day on the slopes, prefaced and concluded by the terrifying series of switchbacks that put everyone on edge, especially James. At the end of the day, the crew filed back to the beach, anxious to examine the area around their campsites for tracks. Afterward, several people came over to examine the tracks around the perimeter of my tent. The conversation was subdued. Ricky did suggest, however, that I refrain from stockpiling carrot cake and Nanaimo bars for the remainder of the contract. That was good for a muted chuckle or two.

When Ricky and Zach noted subtle differences between the tracks encircling my tent and those observed at the opposite end of the corridor, the discussion turned to the possibility that we now had two large bears on our hands.

What followed this sombre little gathering was impressive. Without a verbal edict, everyone spontaneously began to search for firewood, and within ten minutes, we had amassed an impressive pile of fuel that would carry me until the end of the shift.

That evening, while everyone was filing into the dining hall for supper, I went on a reconnaissance mission. Still rattled by the tracks I had discovered earlier that morning, I decided to explore the other half of the building that housed our showers and dry room. The second half of the unit was secured by a closed door with a crudely written sign that read, ABSALUTLY NO ENTRY. Needing to explore this off-limits area, I figured I could use the spelling error on the sign as a defence in the event I was caught trespassing by one of the camp staff.

The door opened up into a long narrow hallway with four doors on each side. Presumably, these doors opened up into vacant rooms— perhaps even rooms with beds. I checked every door. They were all locked. I had no real burglary skills to boast, and I had no intention of forcing my way in, but I had no qualms about sizing things up from the outside windows.

Locating a large sturdy plastic pail in the corner of the dry room, I walked around the perimeter of the building and used it to boost myself up to get a look in through the window of each room. To my dismay, nearly all of the rooms had been stripped of furniture and were being used for storage. One room at the far end of the building, though cluttered with boxes and what appeared to be broken-down kitchen appliances, had a half-dozen mattresses stacked in one corner. This was the option I was looking for. I coaxed the window open with ease, and after an inelegant display of gymnastics, I was in.

The room reeked of urine, mildew and deep-fryer fat. The mattresses that lay stacked in a heap in the corner were just plain nasty, and upon closer inspection, appeared to be rodent infested—holes had been burrowed into them from every angle. These were desperate times, though. I decided to use this room as a sanctuary in the event things began to spiral out of control back at the beach. Turning an old dishwasher on its side and arranging a number of wooden crates around it, I was able to fashion an elevated box spring of sorts. There was one mattress standing up lengthwise in the opposite corner of the room that appeared to be intact and relatively rodent free. If needed, I'd simply toss it on top of my makeshift box spring, and voila: instant bed.

Back at the beach, staring at the grizzly tracks that were still clearly visible, I assumed responsibility for feeding the fire at my end of the corridor for a second night in a row. This was met with little opposition. It wasn't a selfless act. I needed to be in control of the flames that night. For added security, I constructed an additional firepit on the other side of my tent. And just as the final rays of light were being consumed by darkness, I lit two infernos, the flames of which I'm sure were visible for many kilometres. I wasn't messing around.

From inside my tent you wouldn't have guessed it was pitch-dark outside. The flames from both fires lit up the area around my campsite like a baseball stadium at night. Between the light show and the sounds of the fires—the crackling from the wood fibres being pulled apart and breaking; the hissing and sizzling from the pockets of moisture trapped inside the wood, boiling and bursting free—sleep seemed to come easy.

An hour before my alarm was set to go off, prompting me to throw more fuel on my fires, a shot rang out from the middle of the corridor. Angry shouts and urgent barking followed. Squinting, I recognized the vague outline of James patrolling the area in front of his tent, anxiously pacing back and forth, fixated on the forest across the creek. I could also see that his fire had burned itself out, the coals barely visible from where I stood. He had his rifle extended, ready for war. He flinched when I called out his name, but then immediately marched toward me, mumbling something while pointing in the vicinity of where Lady was busy scouring the ground for scent.

To see James this unnerved was disconcerting. He explained that he had woken up to the sounds of loud grunts behind his tent. When he probed the darkness through his mesh window with his flashlight, he startled a bear that he said was bigger than any he had ever seen. He would later describe it as "special effects big." James was so rattled by what he saw, he fired off a warning shot through the roof of his tent while still inside, yelling at the top of his lungs, causing the bear to bolt across the creek. Lady arrived on the scene within seconds. We watched in silence as she scoured the area, barking incessantly, except when she paused to test the air for fresh scent. I asked if this was the same bear that had been tormenting us since we arrived. "No fucking way!" James insisted. "This is a fucking monster!"

I immediately set about throwing wood on James's fire while he stood guard. All the while, Ricky could be heard calling Lady home. She resisted his calls at first, intent on standing her ground—the scent was too strong.

Before long, Ricky, Zach, James and I were all huddled together, secure in one another's company. While James performed a dramatic re-enactment of the event, Ricky passed around a freshly opened pack of cigarettes. I eagerly accepted (I didn't smoke). We pondered the prospect of two large bears, possibly more, competing with us for control of our narrow stretch of sand. We concluded that events were escalating and that we could lose control of the situation very quickly. One thing was becoming clear: this was a major wildlife corridor, one that had likely been held by Bute Inlet silvertips for many thousands of years, and here we were camped right in the middle of it.

The boys escorted me back to my campsite and helped stoke my fires before retreating back to their own tents. After they left I piled more wood on both fires, and by the time I was through I had two blazes that defied logic. The flames licked the air some ten metres high, throwing off so much heat that the sand around my tent began to steam.

We woke up to rain early the next morning. Until then we had enjoyed good weather: overcast skies in the morning; sunny breaks in the afternoons; cool, still air in the evenings; cold, starry moonlit nights. The rain and low-lying cloud added an element of despondency, claustrophobia even, to an atmosphere that was already severely strained.

We walked to the mess hall as a group that morning. James provided the others with a recap of the events from the night before. His story was met with weary nods, expressions of resignation. I looked into people's eyes, and it was apparent that everyone was struggling. Most people had been unable to find any meaningful measure of sleep. At this rate, it was only a matter of time before people began collapsing from exhaustion or injuring themselves on the slopes. Something had to give, but until then we all just tried to maintain our balance, putting one foot in front of the other.

Predictably, the situation on the slopes began to deteriorate. Now that it was raining, the added layer of rubberized rain gear restricted our ability to move freely. Adding to the challenge, the terrain was becoming increasingly steep. This severely limited the number of trees one could plant in a day.

There was also a mental component: when planting steep terrain, one needs to increase the vertical distance between seedlings. Failure to accurately compensate for the angle results in a density of trees that is higher than what is prescribed in the contract. This can lead to "excess" fines—cash penalties—that can involve many thousands of dollars if the error is repeated across multiple areas.

Our crew planted a fair number of excess trees that day.[6] The forestry technicians that visited my land later that morning found nine

---

6. Excess trees occur when a treeplanter strays from the prescribed guidelines and decreases the distance between each tree planted. If the contractor doesn't detect the error early enough, it can result in an area that is overstocked with seedlings. If the problem is pervasive and shows up in the logging company's detailed inspections (plots), it can lead to an excess fine. Generally speaking, a contractor is given a 7 per cent margin of error for excess trees. If that percentage is exceeded, excess fines can add up very quickly.

trees in a sample plot, rather than the anticipated six. Fortunately, they cut me some slack, ignoring my 50 per cent excess infraction in light of my "good roots" (I managed to insert my seedling roots into the exact material they wanted to see them in—100 per cent mineral dirt).

The rain began to ease off by the end of the day. When we arrived back at camp, a group of us hiked back to our tents to get warm, dry clothes before hauling our soggy rain gear over to the dry room.

As I surveyed our long line of tents at the entrance to the corridor, I couldn't spot my bright blue tarp at the far end. Normally, it stood out like a beacon. A sense of dread swept over me, discouraging any further thought of approaching the area on my own.

Cautiously flanking the corridor, I paused at James's campsite where I could clearly see our line of tents. "Hey...my fucking tent is down!" I called out to James, who was now just a few dozen metres behind me. Without saying a word, James dropped his gear, rotated his rifle forward from behind his back and took the lead as we slowly pressed forward.

We were only a few metres into our cautious approach when Lady zoomed right past us, scaring the life out of me, but allowing us to close the gap with much greater confidence. Lady then slithered across the entire width of the beach, nose to the ground as if it were a powerful vacuum. The scent eventually led her into the woods behind my campsite. Soon after she disappeared into the forest, urgent barks could be heard deep within.

My tent lay flat, sprawled out on the sand; puddles of rain had collected in the hollows of its lumpy topography. Immediately obvious were several small tears along one side. The tarp, which I used in place of a rainfly, was pulled a good ten metres across the sand where it lay in a clump. There were large tracks and scrape marks everywhere. Between the two cold firepits, positioned as if it were a symbol of conquest—or defiance—was *the* largest pile of bear scat either of us had ever seen. Everything in my tent could be accounted for except for my foam pillow. James would later discover a piece of it washed up onshore farther downstream.

When Barrett failed to show up on time for supper that evening, we speculated that he was busy on the camp's two-way radio, working on an early exit plan. Though we didn't like the uncertainty, we didn't want to press Barrett on the subject. Pulling out of a project before the contracted number of trees is in the ground often lays the foundation for heaps of grief—legal and otherwise. It would take a lot of finesse to successfully pull us out early. The only thing I was certain of at the time: my nights of camping out at the far end of the corridor had come to an end.

While I walked back to the beach from supper that evening with Ricky and Zach, Lady suddenly bolted ahead of us. Ricky had become quite adept at interpreting her barks. A rapid series of barks, followed by a pause of a second or two, could be interpreted as an alarm, but not necessarily for imminent danger. A slow, drawn-out series of low-pitched growls and barks suggested that she was dealing with an imminent threat. A rapid series of high-pitched barks usually meant she was giving chase. At that moment, she was obviously in pursuit of something—her barks were growing increasingly distant.

Generally, Ricky wasn't too concerned with Lady's safety. He considered her far too cunning and agile for a bear to gain the upper hand. The recent rain did worry him, though. The round, moss-covered rocks on the exposed creek bed were now slick and greasy. He had seen Lady slip and lose her balance earlier that morning. We didn't want to speculate on the consequences were that to occur during an encounter with an angry bear.

I used the distraction created by Lady as an opportunity to head back to my tent, roll up my bedding and make my way back to the logging camp. When Lady was in hot pursuit along the timber on the other side of the creek, one could reasonably expect that the threat of a bear encounter was somewhat diminished.

It was nearly nightfall when I boosted myself through the window of the rat-infested room I had discovered the night before. Seconds later it began to pour rain. My timing couldn't have been better. A quick once-over with my flashlight caused a half-dozen large rats to scurry and bolt for cover. Most of them dove into the rotting heap of mattresses in the corner of the room. I used my flashlight sparingly so as not to attract unwanted attention. I quickly manoeuvred the one good mattress onto the box spring I had fashioned during my last visit and, within seconds, my light was out and I was lying comfortably on top of my crudely constructed bed.

The pounding of the rain against the metal sheeting on the roof of my shelter caused my mind to wander. I wondered how people were coping. I wondered if they would be able to maintain their fires throughout the night. I wondered if grizzly bears were less active in the pouring rain. I wondered if the scuttling sounds I was hearing were the scurrying of tiny feet across the linoleum-tiled floor, or merely the patter of errant raindrops against my window. I wondered when this whole miserable ordeal would end.

I woke up from a deep sleep several hours later sensing movement on my lower extremities. When I lifted my head, I made out the silhouettes of two large rodents, frozen in motion, staring right at me; one on my hip, the other on my knee. Horrified, I freaked out in a full-body convulsion, causing the rats to leap off and break for cover. As I checked my exposed arms and neck for bite marks, it occurred to me that these critters appeared to be well fed. Perhaps they were merely curious. My anxiety soon dissipated and I was fast asleep again. Before I knew it, there was activity outside, presumably the loggers occupying the building next door. It was 5:45 a.m. I had managed to sleep nearly the entire night away.

When I entered the dining hall that morning for breakfast, I realized no one was even aware of my late night caper. The looks on people's faces told the tale—it had been another long sleepless night on the grizzly corridor.

After breakfast I decided to brave the trail back to the beach, alone, to see if I could find Barrett. It had been several days since I'd had a real talk with him. Barrett always had a way of putting things in perspective. I needed to know what he was thinking.

I made the hike back to the beach cautiously but deliberately. At the end of the trail, at the ledge overlooking the creek, I spotted Zach crouching down at the water's edge washing his hands and face. The air was still, untroubled. Before I could call out a greeting, the calm was broken by a loud cracking sound emanating from higher up in the timber. It was the distinct sound of large wood yielding to extreme pressure. Zach heard it too and we both paused, anxiously examining the opposite treeline.

"What the fuck was that?" I called out, but before he could respond, there was another loud crack, then a series of small crashes followed by a clamour in the heavy brush on the other side of the creek. Then, almost as if on cue, a monstrous grizzly broke into the open and charged halfway across the dry creek bed before grinding to a halt. The monster locked eyes with Zach.

Zach was unarmed. His rifle was leaning up against a log with the rest of his gear on higher ground a good twenty metres away. With its head down, the bear slowly began to advance, closing the gap between them.

It was a grotesque creature. Its coat was dripping and there were long clumps of matted fur hanging off its shoulders and neck. Its eyes—narrow, cold, black as pitch—seethed with rage. Its lower jaw quivered as it began a series of short advances, sweeping its freakishly large head back and forth, snarling and snorting. Then, as abruptly as when it first emerged, it exploded into a full-bore charge, stopping hard at the water's edge within fifteen metres of Zach. This second charge caused poor Zach to stumble backward, as if hit by a powerful blast of wind.

The bear continued to advance, entering the creek, emitting guttural grunts and growls as it thrashed its head from side to side. At one point it paused and began slapping the surface with its enormous forepaw, sending gushes of water in all directions. The bear was less than ten metres from Zach. We were both paralyzed with fear.

Though the bear was almost entirely fixated on Zach, it was keenly aware of my presence only ten metres further up the bank. We both had to contain the impulse to turn and run for fear of triggering a decisive predatory response and having all of this bear's rage unleashed on us.

With its ears back, its teeth clenched, its eyes fixed on Zach, I knew a final charge was imminent, one that would lead to a vicious mauling. All I could think to do was slowly reach into my pocket and pull out my small lock-blade knife. Hands shaking, attempting to extract the blade without attracting the bear's attention, I suddenly heard a clamour on the trail directly behind me. Before I could make sense of the commotion, I was sideswiped by a black streak. It knocked me off balance. It was Lady. She leaped off of the edge of the bank and bolted toward the bear headlong. She entered the creek and engaged the grizzly from the side, forcing it to pivot away from Zach.

Lady was in full-on attack mode, weaving to the left, then right, running tight half-circles around the bear in one direction, then reversing back. The bear thrashed its head wildly from side to side, snapping its jaws, emitting horrible moans and snorts as it tried to gain control of the engagement. Lady was simply a blur of fury.

In the space of only a second or two, the bear went from seething rage to abject bewilderment as it attempted to square off against its new foe. It was no match. While it was attempting to back out of the creek and onto dry land, seeking a more advantageous footing against the humiliating assault, Zach managed to stagger away from the creek edge, tripping and falling as he made his way over the slippery rocks toward his rifle. I continued to watch, slack-jawed, speechless.

Lady continued her assault, even as the bear attempted to turn itself around and retreat. She would not back off. If anything, her attacks became more intense, biting viciously at the bear's hindquarters every time it attempted to break for cover. During the chaos, I caught a glimpse of Zach wrestling with his rifle. It had apparently jammed as he was attempting to chamber a round. He didn't have a clear shot anyway—the two adversaries were too tightly entwined.

Eventually Lady became winded and suspended her assault for a second or two. The exhausted bear seized the opportunity to turn and run. This immediately triggered another rush by Lady. The bear managed to push past a thick layer of willow, tripping and stumbling over the uneven terrain as Lady mercilessly pursued from behind, biting and gnawing the bear's hind legs. I watched clumps of fur fly.

They soon disappeared into the dense brush and up into the timber. Occasionally, a crash could be heard, followed by a rapid series of high-pitched barks—I imagined the bear stumbling in its attempt to gain elevation and Lady capitalizing on the mishap.

While Zach sat down at the edge of the creek bed and tended to his rifle, I maintained my position, surveying the timber above, waiting for Lady to return. I was also trying to process what I had just witnessed.

A good ten minutes after the two combatants disappeared, Lady's barks were still audible, but were competing with the sounds of the rushing water from the creek. Twenty minutes later her barks were coming from much higher up on the mountain. By that time, Ricky had arrived, wondering where his dog had wandered off to. Zach and I took turns recounting the incredible sequence of events that had unfolded before our eyes only minutes earlier. And we made it clear that Lady was a hero, that had she not arrived when she did we both would have been torn to shreds.

Finally Lady emerged from the forest on the other side of the creek. The bounce was missing in her step, she was drenched with sweat, her breathing was laboured and her tongue was practically dragging along the ground. But she was okay. With the exception of several broken nails on her front paws, there wasn't a single wound or mark on her body. Our reunion was an emotional one.

That day proved to be the final day of the contract. While the crew was busy tying up loose ends on the cutblock, Barrett was busy tying up loose ends on the business side of things. Though I wasn't privy to the exact arrangements Barrett was able to negotiate with the logging company, I got the impression that it was an amicable one.

The following day Barrett arranged for a barge to pick us up at the head of the inlet late in the evening. We had the entire day to break down our camps, raid the pastry counters in the mess hall and watch movies in the rec room.

It was pitch-dark and raining hard by the time we had everything loaded onto the barge. The journey back up the inlet was surreal. I sat in the front seat of a truck that was positioned facing forward, at the very front of the barge. Occasionally our momentum caused water to lap up over the bow and onto the windshield. The seas were dead calm for the most part, but the heavy, low-lying cloud and the blackness of night obscured everything around us. The steep valley walls, the snow-capped peaks, the cascading waterfalls, all were mere shadows and dark shapes off in the distance. I stayed awake and alert for the entire eight-hour journey to Cortes Island. I managed to stay locked in the moment the entire time. I felt more alive during that dark journey through the inlet than I had at any other time in my life. It felt as though the blinds on my little world had been pulled wide open and I was suddenly looking at the world through a different lens. I marvelled at the expanded view.

# GONE STRANGE

||||||||||||||||||||||||||||||||||||||||||||||||||||||||||||||||||||||||

LIKE SERIOUS ATHLETES, HIGHBALLERS ARE DRIVEN BY COMPETITIVE-
ness, driven by ego, driven by a need to prove something to themselves
and others. They've established and reinforced a series of chemical
pathways in their brains that are hardwired to every muscle, joint,
ligament and tendon in their bodies. These powerful mind-body connections cut through every form of lactic acidosis, pain and fatigue.
Highballers don't just reach for a second wind, they reach for a third,
and fourth, if necessary. They obsess on their watches, forcing their
bodies to pick up the tempo if a production goal is not met by a certain
time of day. The final hour of the day to a highballer is what the final
few metres of track are to an Olympic sprinter. (Fact: a highballer will
expend significantly more calories in a single day than a runner will
during a full marathon, except a highballer will run this race every day
of the season.)

The highballer designation opens doors. Contractors return
your phone calls. Often, highballers don't have to go looking for work,
the work comes looking for them. These men and women are in the
top four percentile in the industry, and they are in extremely high
demand. For me, this skill set opened up numerous opportunities to

travel and explore some of the most remote stretches of wilderness on the continent.[1]

In 1983 I entered the treeplanting arena and discovered an industry and culture that satiated my competitive nature and adventurous spirit. I was told by a number of veterans that what I managed to accomplish during my rookie season normally took three or four years to pull off. I was a *highballer*. And in this tiny corner of the world, I had standing. This status meant absolutely nothing in the real world—zip, zero, nada—but in the silviculture arena, I had the freedom to move around, from crew to crew, company to company. Along with this elevated status came an inflated sense of self-worth, an arrogance. In hindsight, I should have kept this ridiculous pomposity in check. But I was young, stupid and aggressive. I wanted to push boundaries to see what I could shake loose.

BUTE INLET COMPLETELY CHANGED THE WAY I THOUGHT ABOUT remote wilderness settings, and in particular, the apex predators that lurked along the edges. When I returned home, I bought a Remington 870 pump-action shotgun—a big gun that fired chunky three-inch shells. I learned how to handle it, and I experimented with many different combinations of ammunition. I was looking for the most destructive sequence of ammo that would stop a charging grizzly in its tracks. I discovered that loading the gun with two three-inch slugs at the back of the magazine, followed by several three-inch rounds of oo buckshot, would be my best defence under such circumstances. I came to this conclusion after obliterating countless concrete

---

1. Remote, hard to reach treeplanting projects—those that are accessible only by water or air—are generally high-overhead scenarios. Expenses can run many thousands of dollars per day. A contractor, wanting to maximize the number of trees put into the ground daily, in order to minimize expenses, will seek to fill as many spots on his crew as possible with high-production treeplanters, a.k.a. highballers.)

cinder blocks. The trick, and this involved a lot of practice—not to mention a horrible pattern of bruises along my inner shoulder and chest—was attempting to fire off all of my rounds without first being blown back flat on my ass. This was no easy task. The recoil from each single round was tremendous. But I speculated that if I were ever to encounter another hostile eight-hundred-pound grizzly bear, I would need to completely empty my weapon in order to survive the attack.

Bute Inlet was in my rear-view mirror. Next time I would be prepared.

The spring of 1984 ushered in my second year of planting trees with Barrett's company, and the amount of work he had lined up was impressive. The season would begin with a small logging camp-based contract along the Bowron River, followed by a significantly larger tent-camp project along the Mesilinka River, on the remote west side of Williston Lake. There was also a rumour that my sister Lina might make an appearance during the Mesilinka contract, a prospect that promised to add a wonderful dynamic to the adventure.

Though I barely knew my older sister—she managed to skip several grades in school and was on her way out the door while I still in training wheels—she was a source of inspiration to me. She became a world traveller, living a life most people could only dream of. As a kid, I'd receive postcards from faraway places, detailing her latest adventures. And once, perhaps twice a year, without warning, the back door would fly open and Lina would burst in. Her entrances never lacked drama. These surprise visits meant a lot to me. I ranked them on the same level as birthdays and Christmas. They rarely lasted more than a few days at a time, but they were always emotionally charged events, filled with epic storytelling, high spirits and excitement. And there was always something Lina held back from me during each visit, a surprise gift that she'd carefully tuck under my pillow, or inside the sleeve of my jacket before she mysteriously disappeared into the night. She never said goodbye to me. I don't think she believed in goodbyes. Lina was my hero.

In mid-April of 1984, my first treeplanting destination was a camp dubbed "Too-Much," situated at the back end of what was considered to be the largest clearcut on the planet at the time: the Bowron Cut. This clearcut, located along the Bowron River Valley approximately 120 kilometres east of Prince George, BC, was some three hundred square kilometres in size. The harvesting began in the early 1980s in reaction to a spruce bark beetle epidemic that ravaged the area through the 1970s. When the cut was fresh, the scale of the clearcut area was so vast, it was clearly visible from space.

On my way in to Too-Much, I stopped at Purden Lake to grab a last bite to eat before hitting the gravel. While finishing off my last few bites of pie, my waitress asked if I was a treeplanter heading to Too-Much. When I asked why, she pointed out the window toward a hunched-over figure perched on a rock bluff overlooking the highway and said, "That poor sap's been there for days. He's been waiting for you to pick him up." Baffled, I crossed the highway and called up to him, asking if he was one of Barrett's new guys. Excited, nodding enthusiastically, he gathered his gear and climbed down from his roost.

His name was Rob, and I had never met anyone quite like him. He was one of the most garrulous characters you could imagine. I couldn't keep up with him. He was exhausting. He kept finishing my damn sentences. To account for his predicament, he explained that he had mixed up his dates, that he had been dropped off at Purden Lake three days ahead of schedule. When he realized his mistake, he pitched his tent at the top of that rock bluff. He figured that it was only a matter of time before someone heading in to Too-Much discovered him. When I suggested that a simple phone call might have secured a more reliable outcome, he shrugged off the advice, insisting that it wasn't worth the expense of a long-distance phone call. This guy was too much—he was headed to the right place.

We must have passed more than a hundred loaded logging trucks hauling wood out of the valley on the way in to Too-Much. Not having a radio, we had several close calls on some of the tighter corners on the road. I wouldn't have been able to hear the truckers call out their positions on the radio anyway—Rob refused to stop talking.[2] The heightened level of activity was typical for this area. This was perhaps the most actively logged region on the entire planet at the time.

When we arrived at Too-Much, it was a beehive of activity. Trees were being harvested, yarded and hauled away at a dizzying pace. In the camp itself there were barely enough beds available to accommodate our crew. We were forced to double and triple up in rooms that were built to house a single person. It was a good thing we were a tight group.

It was good to see familiar faces from the previous year. Ricky, Zach and James were there, and so were Brandi, Kelly, Kevin, Nick and Dr. Josh. Sadly my soulmate wasn't on the crew list. I would later learn that Debbie was engaged to be married that summer—engaged to a man who didn't deserve her. It deflated me on the spot.

The Too-Much contract was a brutal project. The seedlings we were required to plant were roughly four times larger, and heavier, than anything we had ever dealt with. Normally I could carry up to five hundred seedlings in my treeplanting bags. With these new super-trees, the maximum number I was able to jam into my bags at one time was ninety, one hundred tops.

Adding to our misery, the checkers who were employed to oversee the project turned out to be miserable, power-tripping tyrants.[3] Never

---

2. "Radio" refers to a two-way radio, one that allows access to a specific frequency in order to communicate with other drivers along an active logging road network. By stating your exact location—usually via numbered markers posted on the side of the road—and receiving the locations of other vehicles relative to your own, accidents can be avoided. A radio is often a mandatory piece of equipment on such road systems, being the only way to prevent potentially deadly head-on collisions.

3. Checkers are forestry technicians employed by logging companies to oversee a contractor's work. By checking the quality and density of the trees planted, via a series of detailed inspections or "plots," they ascertain the overall quality of a plantation to

could I have imagined such a hostile group of individuals being put in charge of such a conscientious crew. If they discovered minor faults in small, confined areas within the context of a large cutblock that was otherwise planted perfectly, the shit would hit the fan, as if those minor flaws were indicative of the entire plantation. They seemed to throw fines at us just for sport. They even had the audacity to unholster calculators in the field to demonstrate what our individual errors might ultimately cost our company. It was an oppressive atmosphere. There wasn't a single individual on the crew who didn't feel like crawling under a rock at the end of each day.

The Too-Much contract lasted twenty-one miserable days, and I managed to work every single one of them, including a half day at the very end. Knowing that the next contract along the Mesilinka River was going to be the main event, I volunteered to drive one of the company trucks up to the Mesilinka camp the moment the final Too-Much tree was put into the ground. Barrett had already set up camp along the Mesilinka River and was operating with two small crews. By skipping a richly deserved day off in town and driving up that very afternoon, I'd be in a position to hook up with the existing Mesilinka crew and go to work the very next morning. Workday number twenty-two was in my sights.

I had an important errand to run before travelling up to the Mesilinka River camp. I was instructed to pick up my six-year-old nephew, Lina's son Jaydin, from the bus depot in Prince George and bring him up to the camp with me. Jaydin was taking some time off school to broaden his horizons. I was thrilled beyond measure at the prospect of having my young nephew join our crew.

The Mesilinka crew was expected to grow to more than sixty souls. And the rumours were true: my sister Lina had assumed the role as

---

determine whether or not fines should be assessed against the contractor. Ideally their role is to provide useful feedback to the contractor (and crew) before such problems get out of hand. Their powers are broad. If they determine that a crew's work is sufficiently substandard, up to 100 per cent of the funds due to the contractor can be withheld.

head cook. I couldn't have been happier. I had seen Lina and Jaydin only twice over the previous decade. I couldn't imagine a more perfect setting to reconnect with them. There was one major concern though: Brandi. Barrett's girlfriend from the previous season had been planting with us at Too-Much. There was a possibility that she would be joining us for the Mesilinka show. Lina was well aware of Barrett's fling one year earlier, and I knew that if Brandi dared show her face in camp, all hell would break loose.

Truth be known, I liked Brandi. I got to know her. I even teamed up with her, planting side by side on several occasions—and if I'm to be 100 per cent honest, we were rather smitten with one another. I could have easily seen our mutual attraction evolving into something much more meaningful.

I tried to delicately broach the subject with Brandi regarding her plans after Too-Much, the Mesilinka contract, Lina's (possible) presence there and the potential for World War III. I hoped she would keep her distance.

After picking up Jaydin at the bus depot and stocking up on road snacks, we hit the highway. Jaydin immediately struck me as a cool kid. He was born on the Indonesian island of Bali and had seen more of the world in his six years than most people experience in an entire lifetime. He was a handsome boy—tall, lean and agile. He was the spitting image of his dad, a man who had a profound impact on my life when I visited Lina on Cortes Island ten years earlier. The long road ahead provided the perfect opportunity to get caught up with my young co-pilot. And we had had a fair amount of catching up to do.

The road leading into the Mesilinka River camp, along the west side of Williston Lake on the BCFP (British Columbia Forest Products) mainline, had to be experienced to be fully appreciated. This road network was so vast, it reached so far into the backcountry and had so many confusing junctions, it wasn't uncommon for treeplanters to lose their way, run out of gas and not be discovered for days.

I had a good map and was able to navigate the road network reasonably well, but it required hours of hard driving; hard in the sense that the road was extremely challenging. There were sections that were washed out from recent flooding, sections that had potholes the size of swimming pools and junctions that didn't make any sense whatsoever—not according to the map I was given anyway. This was likely due to the construction of new roads that branched off the mainline—new road systems that were under constant development. This was a prime example of humans reaching deeper and deeper into the wilderness in order to satiate our appetite for virgin stands of timber.

After travelling hundreds of kilometres over rough gravel, with the hour approaching midnight, we finally spotted a few flickers of light clustered at the edge of a small cutblock alongside a river. This was our camp on the Mesilinka, a waterway burdened with an enormous volume of spring runoff. Its roar competed with the music on our truck radio as we drew closer. It was difficult to make out, but on the other side of the river, sprawled out across a vertical rock face were the words JESUS SAVES slathered in thick white paint.

Pulling into camp, we were greeted by Barrett and Lina. They had been patiently waiting up for us, soaking away in the hot tub. The hot tub was a new feature in Barrett's camp. Made entirely from metal and permanently affixed to a trailer, it simply required a parking spot, river water and a wood fire. Barrett and Lina were hot tub aficionados. If I had to guess, I'd say they soaked away a minimum of 10 per cent of their adult lives. They had a hot tub back home on Cortes Island. All of their friends owned one too. When they went out socially, they rarely left the house without towels. I was never able to get used to the idea of stripping down to my birthday suit and jumping into the same tub with as my bare-naked sister. For Lina, it was as natural as filling her lungs with air.

After Lina finished lavishing Jaydin with hugs, she greeted me warmly, but I was left wanting. Our embrace lacked the intensity I had imagined. I always seemed to be left wanting more where Lina was concerned. Barrett pumped my hand with the kind of gusto that only the best of friends bestow upon one another. As always, it was impossible not to be moved by his larger-than-life presence and charisma. It was on occasions like these that I couldn't help but feel the most helpless crush on the man.

After a few minutes of catching up, I bid the trio goodnight and watched as they walked away hand in hand to a tent they had pitched on the bank overlooking the river. It was good to see the three of them together as a family.

I was without a home. I scoped out the setting and determined that it would be futile attempting to set up my camp in the dark. It would have to wait until morning. After raiding Lina's meticulously clean kitchen for a few choice morsels, I retreated back to the truck and settled in for the night, using my sleeping bag as insulation from the cold night air.

It was around 2:00 a.m. when I thought I felt the truck move. Checking the emergency brake and wiping away the condensation from the windows, I couldn't detect anything out of the ordinary. Several minutes later, after settling back down, I heard a loud crash, the distinct sound of metal on metal. A half-dozen flashlights flared up and began probing the darkness, trying to zero in on the source of the commotion. That was followed by a cacophony of shouts as the blur of a large bear streaked past the front of my truck. I hardly reacted. I couldn't have cared less. After twenty-one straight days of planting, a long torturous drive and workday number twenty-two only hours away, exploring the insides of my eyelids took on much greater urgency.

Lina firing up the camp generator at 5:00 a.m. was my wake-up call. Four and a half hours of sleep was better than none, I reminded myself as I kicked open the truck door and stumbled out.

Before unloading my gear and scoping out the terrain for potential campsites, I couldn't help but notice how absolutely gorgeous the setting was. The Quonset hut was set up on a landing beside the river, elevated several metres above the raging torrent below. A steep trail, only a few metres from the entrance to the Quonset hut, led down to a flat ledge at the water's edge. The landing itself was large enough to accommodate all of the other camp structures, including a small community of personal tents. Occupying the perimeter of the landing was Barrett's entire fleet of trucks, as well as a number of personal vehicles. Expanding out beyond the landing in the shape of a giant teardrop was a ten-hectare cutblock. It was flat, and the ground was clean and silty, offering numerous opportunities to set up one's personal campsite. A thick stand of mature spruce and black cedar lined the edge of the cutblock, lending our small community a sheltered feel. A more idyllic setting for a treeplanting camp, I could not imagine.

When I bid Lina a cursory good morning as I strolled past her kitchen trailer that morning, she suggested that we try to find time to chat before I set off to work. She had a way with words, my big sis: "Can't talk now, pussycat. Fifty greasy little piglets just took on the glow," she said, referring to the breakfast sausages that just went under the broiler.

I followed a game trail along the upper bank of the river until the obnoxious sound of the camp generator was completely drowned out by the rushing water below. I settled on a flat mossy bench, at a junction where the game trail met the forest, at the very edge of the cutblock. The river itself was a mere stone's throw away. My proximity to a well-established game trail was cause for concern, but I planned to cuddle with my shotgun at night.

A treeplanter would be hard pressed to find a more perfect campsite. I had the river directly below me to lull me to sleep at night, the shelter of the forest behind me to block the wind and rain, a thick bed of moss to bed down on, and a good trail leading back to the main camp in the event that I was without a flashlight at night. This was to be my home for the next two months.

I had purchased a much larger tent, one I could actually stand up in, and I brought along an extra-large hammock net that I slung between two cedar trees. I made note of where to establish my firepit, but that would have to wait until the end of the day. The workday loomed.

There were two small crews working the Mesilinka project at the time, and they had only just started the contract a few days prior to my arrival. The bulk of the crew—the group that had just been sprung loose from the Too-Much project—were in transit and were expected to begin trickling in later that day. In the meantime, I would be "guest planting" with Ron's crew.

As far as characters went, Ron was a contender for the most sophisticated, the most refined and certainly the most interesting. He was a wonderfully articulate man; a former high school English teacher with a master's degree in English literature. There was a casual elegance about him. He possessed a quality, a gentleness that immediately set you at ease. Ron seemed to sense the good in everyone. I can't recall a single occasion when he spoke disparagingly behind someone's back. He was also a handsome man, sporting a well-groomed chevron moustache, which complemented his prominent cheekbones and angular jawline. Best of all, he liked to puff on a half bent Dublin pipe, which he'd meticulously clean, load and tamp down with the sweetest smelling pipe tobacco whenever he kicked back. Ron was a fascinating study for a kid my age.

Ron was a class act all the way, but his crew, as I would soon discover, had the lowest energy of any group I had ever encountered. When we arrived on the cutblock, I was the first one out of the truck and the first one to hit the slopes. When I arrived back at the main tree cache a little over an hour later, there were still people loitering around the truck who had yet to lace up their boots, let alone begin planting trees. This was an absurd waste of time. The ground we were planting was absolute cream—clean, fast and lucrative. Even in my sleep-deprived state I managed to pound in four hundred trees in just over an hour. This went on all day—I'd come back from a run and encounter several people sitting in the truck, reading magazines, taking naps, running down time.

At day's end we all gathered in front of the truck, and Ron, wanting to pound home a point, asked people to holler out their tree scores while he recorded them into his book. "Eight hundred," called out one. "Six hundred," said another. Occasionally someone called out, "One thousand." One guy on the crew, an eccentric French Canadian character named Marc, proudly called out, "Fifteen hundred for me, Ron." This was met by a chorus of "oohs" and "aahs."

Ron saved me for last, inquiring, "What'd you pound in today, Non-Stop?"

I felt a tad self-conscious being put on the spot, but replied firmly with, "Twenty-three hundred, Ron."

Heads cranked hard over in my direction. Half of the crew thought I was joking, thinking I was some sort of a smartass. The other half didn't know what to think.

"Nice score, and you managed that on what—two hours' sleep?" Ron had made his point, and I have to admit, I felt like a bit of a superhero all of a sudden.

Rather than several four-by-four crew cabs, Ron drove a big yellow "crummy"—a one-ton truck with a large bus-like compartment on the back, which comfortably transported the entire crew of eighteen planters. It made for some diverse and spirited discussions, especially on the drive back home at the end of a hard day on the slopes.

On the ride back to camp after that first day, I got to know Marc a little better. He was a tall wiry man with a lean chiselled face. He had short jet-black hair and proudly sported a thick handlebar moustache. Marc was one of those French Canadians who picked up English as a second language halfway through his life, but his command of the language was remarkable. He had a way of articulating his thoughts, a way of trotting out adjectives that would light up any discussion or debate.

"Do you have any idea what your sister is doing?" he asked.

I had an idea of what he was getting at, but I played dumb, shrugging my shoulders.

Sweeping his outstretched hand across the crew huddled in behind us, he declared, "No one who's tasted Lina's food can stand the suspense—it's driving us mad." He was referring to what Lina might have on the supper menu that night. Shaking his head, he went on, exclaiming, "I can't concentrate on my work after 2:00 p.m. I'm totally fucking useless after three!" He continued, celebrating Lina's culinary skills—skills that he said transcended anything he had ever experienced.

Lina acquired her gift to layer, combine and heighten flavours from Southeast Asia, where she spent much of her adult life. She was often radical in her use of herbs and spices. It was nearly impossible, except by the most finely tuned palate, to unravel the underlying flavour profiles of any one of her hundreds of culinary masterpieces.

Despite Lina's strict adherence to vegetarianism, her treatment of animal protein was masterful. Example: if she were preparing whole sockeye salmon, she'd first make a series of deep slits along the entire length of the fish in order to embed sea salt, lime juice and citrus zest. After grilling it to charred perfection, she'd present it on a long ornate ceramic platter adorned with at least a half-dozen small ceramic bowls containing various concoctions and sauces, each incorporating varying degrees of sour, sweet, salt and heat—some with creamy bases, some with tangy acid bases, most with a generous layer of fresh herbs embellishing the surface. With Lina in the camp kitchen, dining was a spiritual experience.

And Lina loved making entrances. The introduction of dinner that night was met with a crescendo of excited murmurs. Having a flair for the dramatic, she unveiled one entree at a time. It was fun watching people become weak in the knees as she and her assistant entered the dining area, balancing large platters of steaming hot food over their shoulders, the aromas permeating every corner of the Quonset hut.

Treeplanting contracts didn't get any better than this. The money was fat, the setting was extraordinary and my superstar sister and nephew were in a tent next door. I felt like a very lucky man. After dinner that night Jaydin showed me the fish he'd caught in the river earlier that day. Even though Jaydin was barely a second grader, he was an expert angler and had hooked four beautiful rainbow trout, each weighing three or four pounds. These were to be added to whatever he could catch the next day and would serve as a blank canvas for Lina's artistry.

I was exhausted. This was workday number twenty-two for me, and after several unsuccessful attempts at cornering Lina's attention for more than a few moments at a time, I ambled off to bed. As the evening turned into night, I could hear the sounds of vehicles homing in on our camp. Members of the Too-Much crew were making their way in gradually, arriving in dribs and drabs, right up until the wee hours of the morning. At one point, I woke up to what I thought were angry voices in the general direction of the main camp. I quickly dismissed them.

Arriving at the Quonset hut shortly after the breakfast horn blew, I felt something was amiss. I couldn't find Lina anywhere. She wasn't toiling away in the kitchen. She wasn't in the Quonset hut or anywhere else you might expect to find the head cook. Then I spotted her down at the river's edge, squatting on a flat rock next to the raging torrent, looking out over the surrounding landscape. When I called out to her, there was no response. She appeared to be meditating. I was dressed in full gear, head to toe, with boots, long pants and a heavy down jacket. Even with all of my layers, I was still shivering in the icy morning air. Lina was at the water's edge, where it had to have been several degrees colder, wearing nothing but a sheer dress and flip-flops. The biting early morning air held no sway over her. It was unbelievable to me how she could control her body temperature, even in the most extreme conditions.

As I entered the Quonset hut and surveyed the crew, I was able to zero in on the source of the strange tension that permeated our camp that morning and, likely, the anger that had violated the stillness of the night only hours earlier: Brandi.

While the crew was finishing up breakfast and making final preparations for their day on the slopes, an eruption of angry shouts broke out in the middle of the landing, in full view of the entire crew. Lina and Brandi were squaring off face to face, and it was ugly. Lina wanted Brandi gone. Immediately. Brandi pleaded with Lina, attempting to convince her that she was only there to work and that she desperately needed the money. When Brandi refused to back down, Lina threatened, "Well, it's either you or me, lover girl."

As far as the crew was concerned, no one, and I mean *no one*, wanted to see Lina leave, for obvious reasons. But the crew also felt a certain loyalty toward Brandi. Even I was torn. Eventually the two combatants separated. Brandi jumped into one of the waiting trucks and we all departed for the slopes. The mood in the back of our crummy was subdued. I looked over at Marc, and it was clear that he was horrified at the prospect of losing Lina. It was simply more than he could bear. I too was concerned, but poor Marc was becoming unglued.

It was a stressful morning. I used the heightened tension to help me arrive at a difficult decision. Ron needed a highballer to help motivate his crew, and Kelly—my foreman from day one—already had a solid contingent of pounders. I decided to defect to Ron's crew for the duration of the season.

Curiously, when we arrived at the block that morning, everyone emerged from the yellow bus, laced up their caulks, bagged-up with trees and hauled ass. Ron had played his hand masterfully the previous day, highlighting my simple, commonsense work ethic, shaming his crew into following my lead. Working off percentages, he saw his commissions ratchet significantly higher from that day forward.

When we arrived back at camp at the end of the day, I noticed that Barrett's brown Subaru was missing. I knew, even before I was told: Lina was true to her word. She had hung up her apron, jumped in the Sube with Jaydin, and made tracks. What a disaster. My dream contract had, in the course of only a few hours, devolved into a seamy chapter out of a really bad soap opera. Brandi took things hard. She knew she was the catalyst for all of the unwelcome drama. I spotted her stomping off in the direction of her tent, tears welling up in her eyes.

My initial reaction was to pick up were Lina left off, to confront Brandi and demand that she remedy the situation. But as treeplanters, we're conditioned to accept dramatic and unexpected turns of fortune; we're conditioned to accept phases of adversity as the norm, rather than the exception.

Murphy's Law seems to kick in as a matter of routine, sometimes with craziest of frequency. Anything that can, will happen in these isolated wilderness settings. And then there are the personalities; the industry seems to attract more than its fair share of passionate people, from every walk of life—forces of nature in many cases. This dynamic alone lays a foundation for the unexpected. We all sucked it up. We all moved on. Except for poor Marc—it took him longer than most to pick up the pieces.

Lina's sudden departure left a major hole in the operation. Her kitchen helper, Pauline, was forced to rise to the occasion that night and attempt to table a meal for fifty ravenous treeplanters. She pulled it off though, with the help of Carrie, a treeplanter who volunteered to assist.

But the Universe wasn't quite finished with us that day. Late that very night, a huge black bear broke into the storage tent and devoured a large quantity of food. It also destroyed a half-dozen large containers of beans, rice and other dry goods. The usual litany of yells and screams followed, waking up half of the camp. A second incident occurred a few hours later when Carrie ventured into the woods near her tent for a restroom break and nearly bumped chests with the same bear. Her screams could be heard right across the entire valley, and that was the incident that put the entire camp on edge. There was work to be done securing and protecting the perimeter of our camp if we were to continue for another eight weeks.

The next evening, James and I nominated ourselves to provide an armed presence around camp after dinner. Truth be told, I was just looking for an opportunity to show off my big gun and look cool in front of the ladies.

We checked the sights on our weapons and fired off a few rounds for good measure, attracting a good amount of attention in the process—people weren't used to hearing firearms discharged in camp, and they did not like it! Our plan was to position ourselves and stand guard on the roof of Ron's big yellow bus, the highest vantage point available. We positioned the bus facing the wide-open cutblock. It gave us a clear view of the entire treeline. We suspected that the bears were using the treeline as cover to stealth their way closer to our food supply.

As we made ourselves comfortable that first evening, perched on top of the big yellow crummy in lawn chairs, it wasn't long before we spotted a black shadow, prowling along the far treeline, weaving in and out of the woods before disappearing into the cedars behind my tent. Minutes later, a large black bear emerged. We allowed the omnivore to advance within one hundred metres of the supply tent before letting go with two blasts from each of our weapons, into the air, over its head. The manner in which the poor bear panicked and retreated back into the woods suggested that this was the right tack. This first encounter, which was witnessed by a number of people, suddenly lent validity to our roles as armed sentries

By the third day of the shift, the entire crew had arrived and we were some sixty planters strong. This was one heterogeneous cast of characters. There were a total of three nuclear physicists on the crew (including Barrett), at least seven medical students, a half-dozen or so English majors, two marine biologists, several law students, a plethora of artists and musicians of every kind, a cowboy from Texas, two Afrikaners direct from South Africa, a Vietnam vet who had seen active combat, a model from Singapore, a recently landed immigrant from El Salvador and, as we later discovered, a psychologist disguising herself as a fine arts student, who was there to study the impact of extreme labour on individuals living in close quarters to one another in remote wilderness settings. Apparently this study would later form the foundation of an article that was published in an academic journal.

My favourite people on the crew were the salt-of-the-earth types, which included Ricky and Zach. These two had set up their own independent camp farther down the road alongside a tributary to the Mesilinka River. Their setup was impressive. It included a large army tent, electric lights and a generator. Their female companions, who were not treeplanters, had come along for the adventure. When it was dinnertime, Ricky and Zach would roar into camp on their dirt bikes, *Easy Rider*-style, with the ladies on the back hanging on for dear life.

After dinner, we'd hang out for a few minutes in the Quonset hut where I'd watch as they meticulously extracted seeds from their big buds of "killer weed." After twisting up an assortment of "fatties," they'd conclude the ritual with ostentatious sweeps of the hand, sending dozens of noxious seeds flying in every direction, landing on the dirt floor. This became a nightly ritual for Ricky and a number of other devoted Rasta types on the crew. After a few weeks, the enormous volume of cannabis seeds that hit our floor could be felt crunching beneath our feet as we walked along the aisles of the Quonset hut. I didn't partake, myself. Sentry duty required a clear head and a steady hand.

I continued my relentless pace of working every single day, including our days off. On those days, I'd allow myself the luxury of sleeping in for a few hours in the morning before absconding with one of Barrett's trucks and heading off to the cutblock. I figured that as long as I could sleep in every now and again, I could maintain the pace indefinitely. I was wrong. At around day fifty, I began to malfunction. Mornings were becoming increasingly difficult to navigate. I woke up later and later each day, barely allowing myself enough time to storm into the Quonset hut, scavenge whatever breakfast scraps I could find and then make a mad dash for the truck that was already in gear. It became a daily joke among the crew, whether or not I'd make it to the truck by the 7:00 a.m. departure time. I always did, but rarely with more than a few seconds to spare.

Knowing that it was only a matter of time before my body shut down completely, Barrett and Ron looked for ways to take the edge off my day, setting me up in areas that they thought would inspire me. On one occasion, they found a beautiful manicured cutblock that sloped down a hill, ending at a small spring-fed lake at the very bottom, and set it aside for me.[4] It was late May and we were at that stage in the season where the midday sun was beginning to take its toll, forcing us to consume unnatural amounts of water in order to stay hydrated. Having a spring-fed lake at the bottom of my area was a gift, the kind of gift a treeplanter rarely experiences. As I planted my way down the hill, I planned each run so that I bagged-out within metres of the shoreline. Then, it was a simple matter of dropping my gear and plunging into the clear cold water. It was an exhilarating experience. Eight runs per day meant eight rejuvenating swims at the end of each run. After a few days of this activity, my mind and body were in harmony again.

James and I kept up our vigil on the roof of the big yellow bus every evening without fail. By that stage of the contract, Ron's crummy had become quite the hangout. People would join us after dinner, climbing up with their lawn chairs, often with a beer in hand, settling in for the evening, eager to help us spot movement against the distant treeline. Bears were spotted every single night as they homed in on the scents and smells that wafted from our kitchen and supply tent, and the foul smells from the trash that had been piling up over the weeks. And it was always the same scenario: a bear would tentatively emerge from the forest, test the air, advance along the treeline, and the moment it broke from cover and ventured too close, we'd let fire with a few well-placed shots over its head, causing it to turn tail and bolt back into the woods.

There was one perfect evening while on bear duty that sticks in my mind above all others, one that held our senses captive. A thunderhead

---

4. Prior to the advent of the Forest Practices Code in the 1990s, logging companies were not required to maintain treed buffer zones around bodies of water. Small lakes and streams were sometimes logged to the very edge.

rolled in twenty minutes before sunset, treating us to a dramatic light show, releasing just enough precipitation to nourish the parched ground around our camp. After the storm passed, as the moisture on the grass and foliage began to evaporate, a thin layer of fog formed, blanketing the entire landscape. The land and air had become so completely still and hushed, you could hear a moth's wings flutter as it drifted by. As we were drinking in the dewy sweet air around us, we spotted a dark shape at the farthest point along the treeline, approximately four hundred metres away.

There was a surreal, almost dreamlike quality to what happened next. A massive black bear, the largest either of us had ever seen, broke out into the open and began advancing toward camp. It was like a ghost. Layers of mist and fog partially concealed its lower extremities. It appeared to float across the landscape. It didn't follow the usual routine of clinging to the treeline like the other bears. It approached as if unmoved by our presence.

Alarmed by the animal's sheer size and apparent lack of fear, James and I watched anxiously as it continued its steely advance. Having the only weapon capable of firing high-velocity rounds, James took control of the situation. The roof of the bus offered just enough room to stretch out, and that was exactly what he did, sprawling out into the prone shooting position, taking careful aim with his rifle. When the bear was within two hundred metres of our bus, James let fire with a single round. James's precision with his .303 was surgical. He managed to graze the hairs on the top of the bear's head, causing it to react violently. Terror stricken, the poor creature tore up swaths of earth, sending moss flying in all directions as it abruptly reversed course and bolted back toward the forest. James looked up after the drama ended. "I've killed enough bears for one lifetime," he said. We never saw that animal again.

We did have one repeat offender. A medium-sized black bear, perhaps two hundred pounds, always seemed to evade our careful monitoring of the terrain around camp. On several occasions it managed to gain access to our supply tent and make off with food before we were alerted. People also encountered it on their way to the privy at night, and this was becoming a concern. I always managed to frighten it off with a couple blasts from the shotgun, but it always returned one or two nights later. The crew, most of whom were sensitive to the rights of all living things, reluctantly came down on the side of safety versus conservation. They wanted it dead.

Then one evening, someone called out, "Bear in the river!" Scrambling down off the bus and running to the edge of the riverbank, we spied it: our problem bear, swimming hard against the current, steadily advancing to our side. By the time it made land, it was a good two hundred metres downstream from our camp. It was using the shoreline along the river's edge to gain a back entry to our supply tent. This was one clever bear. I cut it off with a well-placed shotgun blast over its head.

I didn't want to kill the bear. I know James *really* didn't want to kill the young bear. So I brainstormed a plan. During the bear's previous raid, it had tripped over a pail of dried mung beans (we had every type of dry bean you could imagine in storage) and these tiny rock-hard beans looked to be about the right size. I grabbed a handful and went to work. Taking two of my three-inch Magnum oo buckshot shotgun shells, I untwisted the tight seal at the top of the plastic casing, emptied out the steel pellets and crammed dried mung beans tightly into the empty shell. Then I carefully closed the top of the shell casing and sealed the seam with a thin layer of melted plastic.

Two nights later our problem bear was spotted swimming across the river. I loaded my shotgun with one mung-bean round in the chamber and one at the front of the magazine, followed by several three-inch slugs, just in case. Positioning myself halfway between the supply tent and the forest edge, it was only a matter of minutes before the bear ambled along. When it was within ten metres, I popped up from my crouched position behind a stump, spooking the bear, causing it to turn and run. That was when I fired off a round, followed immediately by a second round, hitting it squarely in the butt. Feeling the sting of the beans on its rump, its hindquarters nearly ran ahead of its front legs as it made its frantic getaway. Firing another round into the air sealed the deal. It dove back into the river and disappeared. That was another bear we never saw again.

BY THE MIDDLE OF JUNE WE HAD BEEN AT IT FOR NEARLY SEVEN weeks. We had been battling intense heat, insane bugs and terrain that was becoming increasingly difficult to plant. Gone were the creamy cutblocks that allowed us to plant in excess of two thousand trees per day. It was now a challenge to crack eighteen hundred. To compensate us for the added difficulty, Barrett increased our tree price by 20 per cent, allowing us to maintain our earnings average. Barrett was under no obligation to do that—it was an act of generosity that set his company apart from most others.

The blackflies that had been present since the very beginning of the contract were now at their peak, and they gorged themselves on us whenever we dared show some skin. At one point, there were a half-dozen planters in camp with eyes that had swelled shut from blackfly bites. I was one of them.

At this stage of the contract, I was having trouble negotiating simple things, like getting organized in the morning, keeping track of my gear, stringing enough words together to form a complete sentence. I was pushing seventy straight days of work at that point, and mentally speaking, one day simply blurred into the next. I actually lost the ability to speak coherently during the final days of the contract. Unable to summon the energy to hand-wash my filthy work clothes, I simply packed my dirty laundry into my hammock net, tied it off with a length of rope and tossed the bundle out into the river with a rock.

On the positive side of the ledger, the money was piling up. I was also in the best physical condition of my life, despite my obscene behaviour at the dinner table (I was always the first guy to start eating and the last to finish). I was determined to continue pushing myself non-stop until the end. Our contract was in the final inning and a long, glorious summer lay dead ahead.

It was the middle of the last four-day shift of the season. There was a buzz in the air. We hadn't seen our families, a real bed, a TV set or a pizza delivery guy in over two months. I had a young nephew in Calgary whom I was especially fond of, and I desperately wanted to see him. The idea of finishing the contract, breaking down camp and making a beeline to the big city was an intoxicating prospect. But we had two difficult days ahead to muscle through.

Our last series of cutblocks had required a helicopter as a landslide had wiped out our road. Normally I would have been excited by the prospect of a helicopter, but I was too exhausted to give a flying fuck.

On the morning of the second to last day of the season, the Bell 206 JetRanger had put us up on the mountain without a hitch, but the question was whether it would be able to pull us off at the end of the day. There was a massive storm front moving in. We'd watched it building in strength to the east of our location all day long. If conditions continued to deteriorate, the 206 would be forced to ground itself. There were three large crews that needed to be airlifted back to the staging area at day's end, and our crew was scheduled to fly out last.

I managed to survive that second to last day, planting my usual quota of trees, but rarely had I ever looked so forward to the end of a workday.

Minutes before the helicopter began pulling our crews off the mountain, it started to rain. We were worried. We watched as it began to shuttle people from the first crew, three at a time, back to the staging area at the bottom of the valley. Timing the cycles and running the math, it appeared that it wouldn't get around to us for at least another forty-five minutes.

After thirty minutes went by, the storm system that had been taunting us all day long parked itself directly on top of us. Intense rain was accompanied by vertical lightning strikes. We all huddled together under a large tarp in an attempt to stay dry, watching as the helicopter tentatively continued to pull crews off the slopes. Then, with great incredulity, we watched as it suddenly veered off in the opposite direction, becoming smaller and smaller until it completely disappeared from sight.

We had been abandoned. This was 1984—if there was portable radio technology available to communicate with helicopter pilots back then, we certainly weren't in possession of it. Our predicament was grim. Our forsaken crew was stranded on a mountain with ten kilometres and a landslide separating us from our truck. If that wasn't enough, it was pouring rain and the air was filled with electricity.

Weighing our options, of which there were only two, we decided to attempt the hike out, hoping that the landslide—the barrier that was responsible for our predicament in the first place—was traversable.

Decked out in full rain gear, we began our descent. The wind and rain were against us, adding resistance to each step we took. As we walked, we were preoccupied with the obstruction that lay ahead of us. Then we saw it. Off in the distance, a massive landslide that had wiped out over four hundred metres of road, along with about twenty hectares of terrain below it. As we closed in on the fringe, we could see numerous sections of unstable rock interspersed among larger areas of exposed bedrock and hard-packed clay. Water was coursing all through it, and it was perilously steep in spots.

We began to traverse the rubble in a single line. Our progress was slow, and the unstable slope was made even more precarious by the rain, which had thoroughly saturated the soil. Every third or fourth step, the ground under our feet would shift slightly. Every few minutes I would lose two or three metres of elevation, sliding downhill as layers of rubble would suddenly shift under the pressure of my weight.

Adding to our stress, lightning was striking the landscape around us, creating mini tremors under our feet. We carried long-handled shovels with steel blades on the end, and some of us were wearing metal soles or caulks on our feet. We were far too exposed for a lightning storm of that magnitude. At times, small rocks appeared to cling to my boots from all of the electricity in the air. It was total insanity.

I led the procession through the slide, and I struggled to choose the most stable route. My goal was to meet the road on the other side, but layers of fog and steam obscured my view. Toward the final third of our crossing, we had a large section of loose gravel, broken rock and boulders to contend with. It was impossible to continue traversing the slope without periodically sliding downhill and triggering small rock slides (it was for this reason that we walked in a single line with several metres between us). I expected to witness at least a couple of twisted ankles along this final stretch, perhaps even a fracture as some of the shifting rock was large and jagged.

Reconnecting with the road on the other side of the slide was a great victory. Huge sighs of relief echoed across the entire crew as we climbed back onto stable ground. It was a miracle that no one was severely hurt. It was a miracle that no one was struck by lightning. The entire crew managed to cross over unscathed, aside from a few nasty scrapes, gashes and bruises.

The rest of the trudge back to the staging area was arduous and exhausting, but when our big yellow crummy finally came into view, all of our misery was released. We erupted into a fist-pumping mass of cheering idiots that would've rivalled any rabid mob of European soccer fans.

When we arrived back at camp, Barrett and the helicopter pilot were waiting to greet us, offering apologies and sympathetic pats on the back as we filed out of the bus. I was having none of it. Barging right past them, I went straight for the buffet line. Within seconds we were all jockeying for position at the supper counter. This was not a time for courtesy or manners. This was a time for food—and as much as I could pile on my plate without straining myself.

After inhaling two heaping platefuls in record time, I took my third course outside as the rain appeared to have tapered off. Looking out over our village, I spotted James sitting on top of the crummy in his lawn chair, clutching his rifle. It had been over a week since we, or anyone else, had spotted a bear anywhere near our camp. When I called up to him and asked him for permission to come aboard, he glanced down at me with a look of melancholy in his eyes. I knew exactly how he was feeling. Though our armed vigil over camp was often viewed as a chore, a responsibility, we revelled in our roles as camp protectors. It made us feel important. It was fun. And we were damn good at it! James wanted to experience that glory one last time. I decided to join him. Pushing my appetite aside, I climbed up, rolled a cigarette from his pouch of loose tobacco, and smoked it down as we both sat in silence, scanning the landscape for apex predators. It wasn't long before the sky opened up again, forcing us to abandon our post and seek refuge inside the Quonset hut.

When the breakfast horn sounded the next morning, ushering in our last day at the Mesilinka contract, I considered the idea of simply boycotting the whole morning ritual and taking the final day off. After all, I had just worked seventy-six days straight. Also, it was raining. Lying in my tent, unable to face the dim morning light with my puffy eyes, physically diminished and mentally spent, I pondered my options. Then I imagined the conversations in the trucks on the way to work that morning: *Who the fuck does he think he is?* and *What gives him the right?* With that motivational bit of self-talk, I pulled myself out of my horizontal state and put myself through the motions.

Barrett and Ron had a special mission for me on that final morning, one that snapped me out of my funk somewhat. I was assigned the role of block-opener. I was to be dropped off on a clearcut just a short distance from camp while the rest of the crew finished off the heli-blocks from the previous day. My instructions were simple: plant single lines of trees along the treeline until the rest of the crew joined me later in the day. Eventually everyone would descend on my block, creating one colossal gang-plant to finish off the remaining trees on the contract.

The rain and wind continued unabated after I was dropped off and left on my own. After I donned full rain gear, my strategy was to simply stay in motion. Each tree I managed to put into the ground would literally bring me one step closer to finishing the 1984 spring season.

Not long after I began planting, as I was approaching the treeline at the back of the block, I came across something odd. A large clump of black cedar jutted out from the forest edge into the open ground. Logging companies rarely left these types of tree clusters standing.

As I planted a line of seedlings around the perimeter of this curious formation, I discovered a hollow in the ground, encircled by upturned cedar stumps, their root swells interconnected, creating a lattice effect about one and a half metres high. The air around this unusual formation was completely still, even though a storm was raging only metres away. It appeared to be some sort of weather vacuum. Looking up at the top of the treeline, I saw that all hell was breaking loose. The entire canopy was thrashing wildly, but below, I was completely sheltered from the assault. At the bottom of the hollow was room for precisely three well-spaced seedlings. But rather than planting the trees, I did something else instead: I unbuckled my treeplanting bags—which were still half full—let them drop to the ground with a thud, climbed down into the bottom of the hollow, and laid myself out flat on my back. It was a different world down there. I was utterly in the moment. I had a glimpse of a world that was foreign to me. I watched rain droplets swirl along the top of the treeline, as if they were caught in a vortex, some crazy tug of war between the elements. Then, as if defying the laws of gravity, the individual droplets would pause, hang in mid-air, and suddenly freefall, plummeting with tremendous velocity onto my outstretched body. I could never have imagined rain falling so straight. I considered the physics involved in these behaviours among the elements. I began to consider other things too, and before long, I began to drift.

When I last checked my watch, shortly after beginning my run along the treeline that morning, it was 8:20 a.m. When I came to, hearing laughter and people calling out my name from the edge of the hollow, it was 2:30 p.m.! I somehow managed to lose six hours of my day, and I had no concept of the time lost. It was identical to the sensation I had coming out from under anesthesia after surgery. When I rose to my feet, seven planters from my crew surrounded me. Fifty metres behind them more planters were lining in. On the road above, two trucks had just arrived, emptying their human cargo. All I could do was shake my head, chuckle along with everyone else, and join in on the gang-plant.

Our final evening at the Jesus Saves Mesilinka River camp was a delicious affair. As the swollen layers of cloud that loomed overhead finally began to break up and dissipate, the idea of monumental bonfire materialized. We built it in the centre of the landing, between the Quonset hut and the trucks. Situated nearby was a table draped in linen. On it were arranged some of the most beautiful cuts of aged, marbled beef I had ever seen: T-bones, porterhouse, rib-eyes. Absolutely beautiful. Even the vegetarians in camp marvelled at the display, and I could sense, at least among one or two of the faithful, temporary carnivorous conversions were imminent.

As we waited for the fire to exhaust itself and reduce to a thick bed of coals, someone had the idea of a group photo, and before long, the idea gained momentum. It's not an easy task getting dozens of treeplanters assembled for anything after work hours, but we all felt it was important to memorialize this final moment. Ron's big yellow crummy would be the backdrop, and people found their places along its battered and beaten-up exterior. A dozen or so climbed onto the roof. Some climbed inside and hung their heads out the windows. But the majority of us stood or crouched down in front. Several of us had good cameras and used empty fuel drums as makeshift tripods, setting our automatic timers, allowing just enough time to run back and assume our positions. I have a great shot where I'm squatting on the ground with Barrett hovering over me, leaning out the passenger-side window of the front cab with a big pie-eating grin; and Gilles, the model from Singapore, winding up as if he's about to kick a field goal, my head being the intended projectile. Someone had grabbed the chalkboard from the kitchen, scrawled "GONE STRANGE '84" and put it in the foreground. This became a rather famous image around our little resource-based sector—one that I like to revisit from time to time.

Our charbroiled steaks that night were accompanied by all of the usual sides, including four dozen bottles of Pinot Noir and a smaller offering of Pinot Grigio. After we were done searing flesh over the coals, the fire was stoked back up and to such magnitude, twenty chairs were needed to close its circumference. A second outer circle of chairs gradually formed as the sun began to set. The empty wine bottles littered the ground around us, and as far as we knew, the camp had been rendered dry. No sooner had that lament surfaced when Barrett hollered out, "Anyone care for a cold one?" Most of us thought he was pulling our legs, but then a procession of planters emerged from the supply tent carrying flats of beer. Aranged in several stacks on a table, there appeared to be enough ale to take us well into the early morning hours. There was no doubt about it—it was going to be a good night!

As evening transitioned into night, and the drinking and conversation became more animated, I found myself swapping gazes with Colette. I had come to know Colette from the Williston Lake contract one year earlier. She was involved with one of the highballers on the crew at the same time I was chasing Debbie. When she showed up at the beginning of the Mesilinka River contract, she was alone. There was rumour that she was single. I heard another rumour, from one of the women on Kelly's crew, that she liked me. One week earlier, we had bumped into each other in the shower and taken turns scrubbing one another's backs—it seemed like a practical division of labour at the time. I tried not to read too much into it.

I gradually manoeuvred myself closer to Colette until our chairs were nearly touching. She was a beautiful woman. She was lean, with brown shoulder-length hair, full lips, a perky nose and deep brown eyes. She was a complex woman: unapproachable, imposing and tough as nails one minute; kind, delicate and yielding the next. We talked about ourselves and our experiences on the slopes. After a series of deep, long gazes, a few playful nudges and a sensuous exploration of the palms of her hands, Colette drew my attention down to her back-pack, which was sitting on the ground beside her. Pulling aside the top flap, she revealed an unopened bottle of Pinot. I was putty in her hands as we made our way back to my tent.

I've never understood how people can simply turn passion on and off as if it were a bedside lamp, but that was how the vast majority of people I knew treated these treeplanting romances. They treated them like affairs. When the season was over, the affair was terminated and people went back to their lives. For many, there was no room to over-lap worlds. I always wanted and expected more. I wanted something that transcended the physical boundaries of our tent village. I wanted worlds to collide. Eventually, I came to the simple conclusion that these women were more emotionally evolved than I. They were looking only to assuage an immediate need. I decided that I had a lot more growing up to do. The next day, Colette explained that she was heading out east to visit her family for the summer, and that she didn't have time to play house.

After we had packed up camp, Barrett instructed me not to get too soft over the next month or so. He had the inside track on a sum-mer project that would land us right back at the Jesus Saves Mesilinka River campsite within a matter of weeks. And with that prospect in mind, he allowed me to take one of his trucks back to Calgary to use during the break.

On my way back home, travelling through the Rocky Mountains via the Jasper–Banff highway, I came to a wonderful realization: despite the hardships, the gruelling work schedule and the lost love, I was really enjoying living my life.

CHAPTER SIX

# THE GAZELLE

||||||||||||||||||||||||||||||||||||||||||||||||||||

ROUNDING THE FINAL CORNER AS I CLOSED IN ON THE JESUS SAVES campsite beside the Mesilinka River, I spooked a mother black bear and her three cubs. It was an eerie experience. This was a stretch of road that rarely saw vehicle traffic, and I imagined that this was a first for those baby bears; their very first encounter with man—man and his machines.

It was mid-August, a mere six weeks after having "Gone Strange" earlier in the spring. I made my way up the BCFP mainline a full three days ahead of the crew. I wanted to take in the atmosphere of the Jesus Saves Mesilinka River campsite before the crew descended on it, turning it into Grand Central Station. I wanted to be the first one to arrive and the last one to leave, for reasons that were intangible and perhaps in some measure, spiritual. It was a gorgeous setting and a magical place, one I hadn't stopped thinking about since driving away six weeks earlier.

Our summer project would be the first of its kind in BC. It was to be a "hectare-based" contract. An experiment. Normally, we would be paid a set price per tree—the more trees we managed to plant, the more money we earned. On this project, planting large numbers of trees wouldn't necessarily translate into fatter earnings. On this project, everything, including the psychology, was turned upside down. In some respects, planting as few trees as possible became the objective.

We would be focused on covering ground. The number of hectares we managed to plant each day would determine our ultimate pay rate. Barrett explained that a team of surveyors was being sent in one week ahead of us. Their function was to carve up our larger settings into smaller individual pieces. Each piece—which would be measured and defined by a series of brightly flagged boundaries—would be accurately measured to establish its exact size. The size of each area would determine its ultimate value. So, if I were given a piece of land three hectares in size and Barrett was paying a rate of $250 per hectare, the area would be worth $750 to me upon completion. This concept sounded interesting to me.

One of the challenges every treeplanter encountered during the course of a season was getting jammed up in an area that was already partially stocked—an area covered in "naturals."[1] In many cases we were required to treat these naturals as if they were planted trees, forcing us to space our own seedlings away from them at an appropriate distance (just over three metres). Under normal circumstances, discovering a large concentration of naturals in your area was a major financial setback. If there was no room to plant a seedling due to a natural already occupying the spot, you were forced to walk, and continue walking, until the ground opened up again; until it became free of naturals. Walking, not planting, meant losing money.

Under this new regime, large patches of naturals suddenly became a major financial windfall. Rather than cringing at the sight of a thick carpet of naturals opening up in front of you, there was reason to celebrate—the cash register would ring without you lifting a finger.

---

1. "Naturals" are young trees that already exist on a cutblock. They are the result of seeds having been released by the surrounding forest. These seeds, released by mature trees, are carried off by winds and eventually fall to the ground. If they happen to land on the fertile soil within a cutblock, they sprout and grow into natural seedlings.

If I was dealt a piece of land three hectares in size, and 50 per cent of the area was covered in healthy naturals, I'd bank $375 before planting a single tree. Booyah!

As I pulled into the landing alongside the river where our camp had stood only weeks earlier, I was immediately struck by the pungent smell of weed. I recalled several patches of skunk cabbage in the area from earlier in the spring and assumed they were the source. While unpacking my gear from the truck, though, I was hit by another wave of the skunky aroma, except this time it was much stronger. And then I saw it: near the edge of the river bank, in the exact spot our Quonset hut occupied earlier in the spring, a lush plantation of marijuana plants, basking in the warm direct sunlight, their broad feathered fronds yielding to a gentle breeze.

There were at least three dozen budding plants, all pushing a metre or more. Clearly this hemp garden was not produced by design. This was the harmless act of a clan of Rasta types whose nightly ritual was to use the dinner tables in the Quonset hut as deseeding stations for their giant buds of herb. Sweeping the forsaken seeds off the table and onto the dirt floor of the dining area was their way of cleaning up after themselves. With the volume of seedy weed that was consumed in camp during the spring, thousands of seeds must have hit the dirt over the course of the season and since germinated. I couldn't wait to see Barrett's reaction.

My three days of solitude at the Jesus Saves campsite were glorious. It was a thrill having it all to myself. I loved being able to cast a lure into one of the many deep shimmering pools, where rainbow trout liked to congregate, without tripping over the intake hose to the water pump. I luxuriated in my lounge chair, dozing off to the murmur of the river below, without the rumble of the kitchen generator competing for attention in the background. Several times, when I closed my eyes and began to drift, I could swear I heard voices from the spring, like residual spirits trapped by the surrounding forest and rock, forever destined to echo across the landscape.

To keep the bears at bay in the evenings, I made a huge bonfire and kept it stoked throughout the night. I spoiled myself. I roasted potatoes, mushrooms and asparagus over the fire. I filleted the rainbow trout I caught during the day and stretched their thick slabs of succulent red flesh across cedar planks, setting them to cook slowly against the glowing coals, occasionally basting them in a rich slathering of butter, lemon juice, rosemary and tarragon. I also brought along a bottle of single malt scotch, and a small but noble collection of cigars. I was determined to have a fine time before chaos descended.

By the third day, I had established an elaborate campsite, leaving no detail unattended. Aside from my main tent, I erected a second smaller tent for my work gear, a hammock for unwinding at the end of a hard day, and an extra-large tarp stretched out high overhead for protection from the elements. I also blazed a path to the riverbank, where I positioned two sprawling lounge chairs facing west. In front of this lounging area, I dug out a large firepit and lined it with smooth alluvial river stones. My hope was that a certain companion would share one or two evening sunsets with me, even though I hadn't talked to her since we parted company six weeks earlier.

By noon on that third day of my retreat, truck engines could be heard labouring off in the distance. Minutes later, thick columns of grey dust were visible above the trees, billowing up behind a long convoy of heavily burdened vehicles. This first group was hauling everything: the kitchen on wheels, the Quonset hut, the generators and pumps, the piles of two-by-fours and tarps, the plumbing, the mountains of food and of course, the CRC Ltd. slow cooker—Barrett's hot tub on wheels.

When we were done with the hugs and handshakes, I directed attention to the source of the skunky aroma everyone seemed to be puzzling over. Incredulity was immediately replaced by falling-down, clutch-your-ribs laughter.

And what to do with the pot plants? Leave them be? Pull them out by their roots and toss them? Harvest them and become the camp distributor? We eventually resolved to move the Quonset hut three metres over to allow the ganja to continue its ethereal ascent. Ultimately the crew would decide their fate. I suspected the herb's days were numbered.

Personal vehicles began limping in later that afternoon, and by 4:00 p.m., most of the fifty-person crew had arrived. I had been keeping an eye out for a certain someone, expecting she'd hop out of one of the many derelict cars and vans that somehow, miraculously, survived the punishing journey in. As the sun began to set, I feared that she might not show.

Just as I was about to retreat to my tent and take a nap, a beaten-up vw van rounded the final corner toward camp. I told myself that if she wasn't in that vehicle, she wouldn't be coming. Behind the wheel was my good friend Marc. There was no one in the passenger seat beside him. I began to feel very alone in the world all of a sudden.

As I waited in line to shake Marc's hand (he was a well-loved man) the side door to his van suddenly slid open and out stumbled one somnolent Colette. She was dressed in a cute set of denim coveralls, the pant legs cut down to short shorts. She had her hair cut short too, much shorter than mine, and she was glistening with coconut-scented tanning oil. My heart began to pound when her eyes met mine. She bypassed the welcoming committee, threw a big hug around me and wouldn't let go, transferring much of her residual coconut oil over to my exposed arms and chest (I rarely wore a shirt at camp). I was happy, and more than a little excited when she whispered, "I forgot my tent, Non-Stop. Any extra room in yours?"

When we were safely out of sight from the rest of the crew, having hauled her gear halfway up to my campsite, we spontaneously dropped everything and kissed so passionately, we thought for a moment that we had chipped our front teeth.

Laughing like two children without a worry in the world, we disappeared into my tent and whiled away the rest of the afternoon and a good part of the evening. I didn't feel guilty having stepped away from the crew—I had spent four hours earlier that afternoon helping set up the main Quonset hut and shower stalls. I had done my part. When we finally came up for air, there wasn't a soul in sight. We made our way toward the Quonset hut and kitchen, forced to tiptoe through a tight cluster of tents that had sprung up along the game trail leading back to camp.

As we pigged out on leftover pasta and salad in the Quonset hut—we had apparently missed the supper bell by several hours—Colette looked up and asked me what I was smiling about. I wasn't aware that I was smiling at all, but then it all of a sudden hit me.

"I'm just really enjoying life," I said. "Especially now." Her face lit up.

THE NEXT MORNING WE CAME TO OUR FIRST LARGE CUTBLOCK FOR A big pre-work meeting with several high-profile registered professional foresters (RPFs) and a contingent of company checkers. We were assembled to talk about this new concept of hectare-based planting.

This was the first project of its kind in the province; we were to be the very first treeplanting crew to implement it. Apparently only a handful of people had been informed ahead of time that our summer project was an experiment. There was ambivalence, confusion and a posse of shaking heads occupying the front row. Most of the crew had issues with the new approach. I was cautiously optimistic.

One of the reasons for the switch in tactics was to reduce what they called "waste." What they really meant was that they hoped this new strategy would reduce the number of trees that were being systematically "stashed" each year.[2] They believed that stashing occurred as a matter of routine with many treeplanting companies. The

---

2. "Stashing" is the act of burying, hiding or destroying trees for profit. It can be called a number of things: theft, destruction of property, fraud, etc. It was a contemptible act, one that often resulted in immediate termination. It was also possible to be charged with an offense under the Criminal Code of Canada if the contractor or logging company decided that firing was insufficient punishment. Of course, Barrett had a zero-tolerance policy on stashing.

hectare-based system removed the motive to stash trees, since one's earnings were not based on the number of trees planted, but on the amount of land covered.

There was nothing worse than being accused of stashing trees. Every highballer—me included—was often viewed with suspicion by certain people, especially if a tree total at the end of the day was significantly higher than the crew average. I decided that this contract would be my opportunity to demonstrate once and for all that I was the genuine article, that my reputation as a highballer was well deserved.

During the Williston Lake contract one year earlier, I was determined to end the project as the highest-producing planter in Barrett's arsenal. Somehow I managed to pull it off. My status as top-shelf highballer remained intact throughout the Too-Much and Mesilinka River contracts earlier in the spring as well. On this project, I was determined to bank more hectares than anyone else on the crew.[3] By the end of my first day operating under this new regime, I immediately recognized the potential.

Back at camp, James and I assumed our usual roles on bear duty. This made James very happy. When Colette joined us on the roof of the crummy that first evening, people began to talk. Suspected camp romances were fertile ground for gossip in treeplanting circles. But by the end of the first shift, we were all so exhausted from the relentless pace and midsummer heat, no one really seemed to care, or even notice, that I had a difficult time keeping my hands off of Colette.

I found myself wondering, as I had only a year earlier with Debbie, what would happen between Colette and me at the end of the season. I had a crazy notion that we would carve out a little nook for ourselves back in the city and become a real couple. I suspected that Colette had other plans though. I also suspected that I might never develop the emotional maturity to treat these treeplanting romances for what

---

3. The competitive behaviours exhibited by highballers were best characterized as "borderline psychotic."

they really were: escapes, distractions, meaningless affairs. But for the time being, we were really good together. I tried to focus on living in the moment.

Within a week or so we had caught up with our surveyors. We were chewing through the ground faster than they could carve it up for us. The experiment in hectare-based planting was working out extremely well for many of us. Rather than bag-up a backbreaking number of trees, I found myself carrying lighter loads, which allowed for greater agility and speed. I was planting nearly 1.7 hectares (4.2 acres) per day, and when my area offered large concentrations of naturals, significantly more.

Barrett was paying $250 for every hectare planted. The contract was turning into a major financial windfall. And any suspicions among certain crew members that highballers, like me, were ever guilty of stashing trees—those suspicions were cast aside when they witnessed the vast expanses of terrain I consumed each day.

Midway through the contract, the surveyors had fallen so far behind that when we arrived at a new setting, the perimeter was the only known dimension—no individual areas had been established. This afforded the opportunity to section off our own pieces. This is where it got interesting. The surveyors were to come in, after the fact, and run measurements on the areas we defined ourselves. On one such block, I was the first to arrive and was instructed to carve off enough ground to last three or four days. Though the new ground appeared to be one massive clearcut, it was actually a link in a long chain of cutblocks that extended five hundred metres up the side of a mountain, and at least four kilometres farther down the valley. Feeling ambitious and wanting to test myself, I made a bold move: I laid claim to nearly 50 per cent of the first cutblock. I had a good feeling that the surrounding forest had thrown off a generous dusting of seeds over the previous summer and that the winds placed most of them directly on my piece, generating carpets of lush, healthy naturals throughout.

The scope of my new area was daunting. It encompassed three deep ravines—hundreds of metres apart—running vertically from the timberline above to the main access road below. Unsure if I could even put a dent in the area over the course of a four-day shift, I bagged-up with five hundred trees and set off on a reconnaissance plant to see what I could see.

Before I was able to plant my way to the top of my new area, I noticed two trucks had pulled in on the road below. It appeared that I was already generating controversy with the size of my piece of land. Within a few minutes Ron and Kelly came into view, huffing and puffing, having made the climb to give me a piece of their mind; to inform me that I was "out of my fucking mind."

Kelly was pissed off. He went into a bit of a rant, informing me that if the surveyors arrived at some point during the shift, their first order of business would be to subdivide my area several times over. Ignoring Kelly, I turned my attention toward Ron and demanded that he have a little faith in me. I needed Ron to give me at least two days to see how far I could get before sending in reinforcements. Ron agreed, saying, "I'll guard-dog it for now, Non-Stop, but if you can't take out a goodly chunk by the end of tomorrow, expect company, pal." That was exactly what I needed to hear. That was what made Barrett's company great: managers like Ron who had your back when you needed them most.

I watched Kelly and Ron argue as they descended back down the mountain toward their trucks. Looking out over the vastness of my piece, I knew I really needed to up my game if I was to plant the entire area in only four days. I also needed a healthy population of naturals, distributed over large areas, and from where I stood, I wasn't seeing them. But the land was clean, the slash was light and the soil was yielding. It was an extremely fast piece of ground.

It took me the better part of two hours and five hundred trees to complete my reconnaissance run.[4] I estimated that my area was at least ten hectares (twenty-five acres). Running the math, dividing ten

---

4. A "reconnaissance plant" is an exploratory run where a treeplanter plants a single line of trees along the entire perimeter of his or her area, with the exception of the very

hectares by four days, I realized that I would need to plant the equivalent of five football fields per day. I had already blown through a quarter of my day and had barely scratched the surface.

At the end of day one, after having planted 2,400 trees, I looked down from the top of my piece. There were people packing up their gear on the road below. I couldn't make out who they were. I couldn't even discern whether they were male or female. I knew I had made a serious error in judgement. The distance from the top of my piece to the bottom road was still the better part of a half a kilometre. I had bitten off far more than I could chew. Admitting this to Ron and Kelly would be a humbling experience.

While Colette and I were cuddling in bed later that night, she informed me that word had gotten out that I had lost my mind; that I had carved off more land than the entire company could plant in a week. She also heard a story that I had threatened to brain Kelly with my shovel if he ever set foot on my land again. Stories tend to get exaggerated in treeplanting circles.

Colette was on Kelly's crew. They were headed to the same valley early the next morning to occupy ground farther down the road from me. Being the focal point of controversy, I knew that a lot of eyes would be monitoring my progress. And I would be on full display for everyone to see, having occupied an area that was elevated higher than everyone else in the valley. The pressure was most definitely on.

I woke up earlier than usual the next morning, stretching out my major muscle groups for a good twenty minutes before Colette emerged from our tent, all bed-head and beautiful. The only thing that occupied my thoughts more than the formidable task that lay ahead was Colette, and unfortunately I was already beginning to feel my heart break.

When we sat down to breakfast that morning, people on Kelly's crew offered heaps of free advice. "You'd best power down an extra bowl

---

front. This is performed in order to evaluate the terrain; to ascertain its various changes, challenges, and advantages.

of Wheaties there, Non-Stop," and, "If you get lost on your piece, don't panic—we'll form a search party at the end of the day."

The second Ron's crummy came to rest at the bottom of my piece, I flew out the door, stuffed five hundred seedlings into my bags and stormed up the treeline on the far right side of my area. When I was about halfway to the top, I came across three beautiful healthy naturals in a row. Pausing to scan the terrain around me, I observed a wide swath of fir naturals to my left, their light-green leaders covered in dew, glistening in the early morning sun.[5] They stood out like beacons, like Christmas ornaments, and like a child on Christmas morning, I greeted the discovery with joyous abandon.

By midday I had planted a dozen lines across the top of my area, and at that point, I began to merge into a seam of naturals that carpeted the upper right half of my piece. All of a sudden, I was walking more than I was planting. There were sections where I encountered a dozen or more well-spaced naturals in a row, negating the need to plant a single seedling. As my enthusiasm swelled, my pace began to quicken. In the areas that were devoid of naturals and required straight planting, I developed a method of leaping between spots. Rather than two measured strides between trees, a single leap produced by pushing off from a crouched position covered the same distance while eliminating a full step. This allowed me to accelerate my pace.

This little innovation in technique, though physically demanding, sprang from genuine childlike excitement. I embraced it. And little did I know, I was being watched closely by a group of planters who were sitting on the bottom road taking a lunch break.

A group of women on the crew—after watching me bound from spot to spot—came up with a new name for me: The Gazelle. I was flattered when the name caught on. Treeplanting nicknames don't always

---

5. The light harlequin-green colour on the delicate top leader of a fir natural represents brand-new growth from that very spring and summer.

After a long day of travel by barge, water taxi and truck, we settled in and set up camp along the remote eastern shore of Williston Lake.

On my second night camping along the grizzly corridor at Bute Inlet, I sat down by the campfire for a moment of reflection.

The break between contracts was barely sufficient for crew to stock up on supplies, develop film and catch up on some desperately needed sleep.

We glimpsed the steep Bute Inlet clearcut from the other side of the valley.

A treeplanter in the centre of the frame is concealed by the wild overgrowth at Bute Inlet.

In my second season of treeplanting, we encountered mean trees with giant bare roots that were larger and heavier than the typical seedling.

We toured along the end of the valley at Bute Inlet before setting sail in the direction of home.

A chain gang of at least twenty-five planters loaded multiple trucks full of seedlings from a tree cache located deep in the forest.

During the Mesilinka contract, road access was wiped out by a landslide. Helicopters were brought in to put us on top of the mountain.

Abandoned at the top of the mountain by our helicopter pilot, we pondered the idea of making the long trek back down the mountain and across a landslide to reach our trucks. I'm sitting with my arms crossed.

"Gone Strange '84," a long spring contract along the Mesilinka River in northern BC, drew to a close with one last group photo. I am pictured squatting to the immediate right of the chalkboard, surrounded by friends.

We arrived by float plane at Rivers Inlet with the snowline threatening to shut us down on all sides.

We finished planting a Rivers Inlet clearcut, but our work wasn't over just yet.

Our final day at Rivers Inlet took us to the other side of the inlet to plant out our remaining trees. Without caulks on our feet, we risked falling into a cold April ocean.

highlight the most favourable attributes of the individual. I got lucky with that one, and my fellow crew members made sure the name stuck.

At the end of day two, it was difficult to say for sure, but I felt I had covered nearly 40 per cent of my area. Wanting to continue riding the positive wave of momentum I had enjoyed all day, wanting to go into the evening, I tracked down Colette and asked her if she wouldn't mind driving back out at sunset to pick me up.

"If you work late, are you going to be of any use to me tonight?" she replied.

I promised her that I'd make it worth her while, and after a few nibbles to her neck and ear, I strapped on the bags and marched back up the slope.

As I watched the last set of taillights disappear below the road, I experienced the same familiar conflicting emotions again; feelings of loneliness and isolation, together with the excitement of being left alone on the side of a mountain. The roar of the truck engines could still be heard, for a minute or two, but they were soon drowned out by the hums and murmurs from the surrounding landscape. It was the end of August, and it was one of those late summer evenings when a transition could be felt all around. A chill hung in the evening air where no such chill could be detected only days earlier. The sun was slightly lower on the horizon, giving way to slightly shorter days, longer nights. And life along the forest floor appeared more hurried, more anxious, as marmots and other critters scrambled to prepare for the inevitable grip of colder days.

As always, a wonderfully complex host of sounds and vibrations began to emanate from the cutblock and surrounding forest as the sun's rays softened, yielding to the slow but steady approach of night. The mind becomes vigilant. The senses sharpen. I might not have paid attention to the sound of water coursing across the slope earlier that afternoon—I certainly took notice now. The long drawn-out creaks generated by mature trees at the edge of the forest, straining under the pressure of their own weight, were suddenly front and centre in my mind, where they barely registered only hours earlier. Perhaps most unsettling were the birds of prey that cruised overhead for unsuspecting rodents in the dimming early evening light—the sudden gushing sounds generated by air wrapping around their wings as they homed in on their targets. Every sound was amplified. Every vibration was significant. Of course, this was all part of the allure of staying late, being the only human on the mountain.

I had managed to knock off another decent swath of land by the time I heard the rumbling engine of a truck turning the corner at a junction five kilometres down the valley. Walking through my open ground on my way back down the mountain, I observed a sparser population of fir naturals than I had hoped for. I still had my work cut out for me if I was going to meet the four-day deadline imposed by Ron and Kelly, who I knew would be waiting for a progress report once I arrived back at camp.

Stepping off the block that evening into the warm embrace of my beautiful friend was a soothing way to end my day. On the way back to camp, Colette revealed how people were divided over whether or not I could finish my area by the end of the shift. Wagers were being placed. Apparently my decision to stay late that night fuelled the speculation. Many viewed it as an act of desperation. There was a split between genders too—the women believed I could pull it off, while most of the men thought I was completely out of my mind. Kelly still insisted that it couldn't be done. He had apparently walked over the lower half of my piece earlier that day and determined that it was simply too vast for *any* single planter to cover in the time remaining.

Kelly had reason to be worried. A crew of checkers was due to arrive on the last day of the shift to run quality and density checks over the entire block. Just about everyone who had areas next to me were in the process of wrapping them up and moving on to the next cutblock down the valley. An efficiently run operation does not permit loose ends. If I were the only person left planting on the block, while everyone else had moved farther on down the valley, it would look sloppy. It would stand out as a glaring loose end.

Pulling into camp, before I could even begin to extricate myself from the front seat of the truck, I was mobbed by Kelly, Ron and a small group of planters who presumably had just laid down significant wagers on my pending success or demise. Not wanting to partake in a big brouhaha, I guaranteed the boys that I would finish the area by the end of the shift. I believe Ron had faith, as he always seemed to. Kelly couldn't be swayed.

That night, even though I'd made certain promises to Colette earlier in the day, she insisted on taking care of me instead. Stretching out on the queen-sized foam mattress in our tent, I was treated to the most thorough and healing body massage I had ever experienced. She started with my neck and shoulders, slowly working her way down my torso. She wasn't always merciful. She worked on every major muscle group, often probing the deeper tissues, inducing involuntarily yelps and squeals along the way. I lost track of time. I began to drift when she started over with a less vigorous manipulation of the muscles, one that consisted of a series of exquisite circular strokes and caresses. That may have been the first time since I was an infant that I fell asleep on my stomach.

I woke up at 2:00 a.m. and found Colette seemingly fast asleep next to me, facing away. Before I could reach over and caress her back, she rolled over and with her eyes still closed, whispered, "Sleep, baby."

I woke up the next morning at 6:40, twenty minutes before the trucks were set to roll. Colette was nowhere in sight. When I started down the trail toward camp, she greeted me halfway—she was just coming to get me. Inside the Quonset hut, she had a plate of food, a bagged lunch and a steaming mug of coffee waiting for me on a table next to the wood stove. She had even filled all five of my water jugs, which she placed next to my gear in front of the crummy. I couldn't remember ever being pampered to this degree, not in my entire life.

As we made our way to the trucks, she took me by the shoulders and said, "You're going to find out soon enough, but I put $25 down on you!" This caused Ron, who was just within earshot, to burst out laughing, slapping his hand down on the hood of his truck. I had a good chuckle too. Before I could ask her if the massage was her idea of influencing the outcome, she insisted that she would have given me the five-star treatment regardless. I believed her. I was flattered and humbled that she had that much faith in me, making that kind of wager. That was a lot of money back then.

I attacked my area that morning with urgency and determination. *Panic* might be a better word for it. The carpets of naturals I'd enjoyed earlier in the shift began to thin out as I made my way toward the centre of my piece. I had to rely on speed and athleticism to plant out my remaining area. In my haste, at the end of each run, rather than walk down the mountain to my tree cache on the road below, I developed an exhilarating means of barrelling down the slope in order to save time. Every ten metres or so, in a full run, I'd launch myself off of a rock or stump, which would allow me to soar through the air due to the angle of the slope. I would land running, on the balls of my feet, with tiny rapid steps, gradually expanding into longer strides before picking my next target to leap from. It was invigorating. It was also reckless. But I honestly felt the sensations of flight—the same sort of feeling one experiences catching air while skiing. On more than one occasion, I built up so much momentum that I'd overshoot my tree cache and end up in the cutblock below the road. That little bit of fun reinforced my new tag, The Gazelle, in a major way.

By midday, discouraged by the lower third of my area, I planted to the top of the last vertical section, a section I had basically left alone. It was a swath of ground that had been cut off by a ravine that ran from the top of the mountain down to the very bottom road. This was my wildcard. The area was a complete mystery to me. As I began to plant it from the top down, I observed something extraordinary: a carpet of big beautiful fir naturals appeared to occupy the entire slope. Heart pounding and adrenaline pumping, I chewed through the ground and advanced down the mountain so fast, I caught myself giggling. Aside from the near certainty that I had this monstrous piece of land whipped, the economics of single-handedly finishing the area began to flash in my mind. If this was a ten-hectare piece of land as I suspected, and I was able to complete it in only four days, I would be averaging 2.5 hectares (six acres) per day at a pay rate of $250 per hectare. That translated into earnings of $625 per day ($1,360 in today's dollars).

Later that night, comforted by my success on the block earlier that day, Colette and I retreated to our campsite early. I built a nice fire on the bank overlooking the river and arranged our two lounge chairs around it in order to take full advantage of the warm glow. It was a beautiful evening. The sun was beginning to dissolve under the horizon, the air was still, and my fire was throwing off a generous volume of healing warmth. It was a perfect end to the evening, but my friend was in pain.

Colette had a difficult day on the slopes, having suffered several hard falls, sustaining large bruises on her hips and thighs. It was my turn to render first aid. I fetched some ice from the kitchen freezer, broke it up in a plastic bag and wrapped it in a soft towel. I alternated it around her upper and outer thighs, wherever the bruising was most prevalent, all the while rubbing her shoulders, stroking her hair, and occasionally nibbling her neck. When the fire died down, we retreated back to the tent where I caressed the smooth skin on her shoulders and back until she fell asleep. I felt her heart glow that night. I also sensed that she was concerned over how close we were becoming. I caught her wiping away a tear only moments before she drifted off.

At the end of day four, a half-dozen checkers arrived on the block and invaded my piece, running a series of pay-plots.[6] After running at

---

6. Pay-plots are a final series of quality and density checks that determine how well an area has been planted. They determine the ultimate rate of payment owed to the contractor. Generally, any quality score over 92.5 per cent results in 100 per cent payment to the contractor. Any score below 92.5 per cent normally results in "quality fines" (deducted from the total value). The lower the percentage score, the lower the payment due to the contractor. Scores approaching 70 per cent can have disastrous

least two dozen pay-plots across my area, I watched anxiously as Ron conferred with the head checker near my far boundary. I was reasonably confident that my work had passed inspection. But one can never be 100 per cent certain—every checker seems to have a different set of criteria for what they consider to be a properly planted tree. Ron, charging back down the slope in my direction, was cause for concern. It's rarely a positive sign when someone makes a beeline in your direction after being given pay-plot results. If everything had passed final inspection, Ron would have simply tossed me a wave and continued about his business. I was prepared to hear the words, "We have problems." This is every highballer's nightmare.

Speaking in slow deliberate terms, he reported: "The guy in charge wished every area he checked was as well planted as yours. Congrats, Mr. Gazelle." He said nothing else, not a damn thing, then turned and walked away. As he drove off, he gave me two quick celebratory bursts from his horn before disappearing below the road.

After finishing my area and receiving a passing grade, I was still missing one critical piece of information: the exact size of my area. I was convinced that it was at least ten hectares, but I wouldn't have that figure until the surveyors ran the measurements and crunched the numbers. I'd need to wait until the very end of the contract for that minor detail.

Back at camp, with the pressure off, and the prospect of sleeping in the next morning with my winsome friend, I started drinking a little earlier, and a little more enthusiastically, than was my usual style.

As the sun began to set, the boys lit a match to what turned into yet another towering Mesilinka River bonfire. Booze materialized mysteriously out of nowhere—Barrett's doing. There were stories. There

---

financial consequences and can result in the withholding of 100 per cent of payment. In addition to quality issues, if too many trees are planted in a sample area, "excess" fines come into play.

were laughs. There were dramatic re-enactments of people being chased by wasps. There were lovers sharing a single chair, committed to preserving the moment, and there was the occasional woebegone mien from those who appeared to be all alone in the world.

A little after midnight, after a final load of wood was tossed onto the fire, the weight of which kicked up a remarkable volume of sparks, directing our attention skyward, we suddenly realized how detailed the cosmos was and how much activity was occurring directly above our heads. There was some sort of meteor shower in progress. Shooting stars were streaking across the midnight sky with awe-inspiring frequency. Colette tugged at my arm, pulling me in the direction of the trail leading back to our tent. "We're sleeping under the stars tonight, lover," she whispered.

We dragged our bedding out onto the lush, dewy moss in front of our tent, stripped off our clothes, climbed in under our down quilt and lay, bodies entwined, gazing up at the tapestry of light and space. Colette, always the planner, had a thermos of cold lemonade, a bottle of white wine, two long-stemmed glasses that she poached from her mom's kitchen cupboard back home and a fatty she secretly sponged off Ricky. Our passions aroused, heightened by the streaks of incandescent light across the midnight sky, we gazed up at the heavens, sipped wine and made love until light suffused the distant horizon.

The next day, waking up close to noon, we were shocked to discover that nearly a dozen planters had packed up and moved on. We were into the first week of September. Certain people apparently needed to be sitting at attention in a classroom the very next day. The contract was winding down, with only a half-dozen days remaining. I knew I had to explore the immediate future with Colette. I was becoming rather accustomed to waking up next to her in the morning.

After raiding the kitchen for acceptable brunch fare, Colette and I went for a stroll along the river. There I learned that she and a girlfriend were heading to Europe together in a month. It was a trip they had been planning for over a year. After that, they planned to cross over to Australia, buy touring bikes and explore as much of that continent as possible.

Colette and I made the most of our final days together as a couple. We entertained the idea of getting an apartment together once she was back in Vancouver. Of course, I knew that was a long shot. Still, I considered it a remote possibility, and to that my hopes clung.

We ended the Mesilinka River contract on September 12. After a heart-tugging farewell, watching Colette drive away in the same vehicle she arrived in, I lingered long enough to watch everyone else depart. I was the last remaining soul at the Jesus Saves Mesilinka River campsite. I wanted to pay one last visit to the setting at the edge of the woods where I had fashioned our little campsite, our little nest. I wanted to see if I could still sense her presence. A gentle breeze caressed my face and hair as I approached the spot, reassuring me that I could.

As I took one last look around from the bank of the river where the Quonset hut stood, I noticed that the marijuana plants, which had been standing at least four feet high only hours earlier, had been clipped down to tiny nubs. That put a smile back on my face.

The final measurement, according to the surveyors, of the monstrous piece of ground that helped earn me the appellation The Gazelle: 11.42 hectares.

CHAPTER SEVEN

# THE TROPICANA

||||||||||||||||||||||||||||||||||||||||||||||||||||||||||||||||||||||||

I SPENT THE FALL AND WINTER OF 1984–85 ON CORTES ISLAND, A
Salish Sea paradise during the summer months, a lonely rain-swept
rock during the winter. Lina owned a waterfront house on seven
and a half acres at the south end of the isle near the tiny village of
Whaletown. I was house-sitting for her while she and Jaydin were in
Bali. She abhorred the rainy West Coast winters.

In hindsight Cortes Island wasn't an ideal destination for a
twenty-one-year-old man who had just experienced more adventure
and romance in the previous eighteen months than he had in all of
the rest of his years combined. It was a good place to lie low for a while,
though. I used the opportunity to maintain an extremely healthy lifestyle: running, hiking, digging clams, jigging for cod from a kayak,
collecting oysters, reading and playing a lot of guitar.

A musician friend of mine in Calgary, worried that I was giving
up on my dream of becoming a professional guitar player, pushed into
one of those crazy all-night lineups and purchased a beautiful Marshall
amplifier at a 75-per-cent-off sale, sending it to me the same day by bus.
Taking advantage of the area's ubiquitous fog, and not having visible
neighbours on either side of me, I would sometimes haul my gear onto
the deck facing the bay, crank the volume on my new Marshall up to

eleven and run a freshly rosined violin bow across the strings of my Les Paul Custom guitar. The feedback and echoes rolled out over the bay and could be heard for a good many kilometres inland. James, who lived on the other side of the bay approximately three kilometres away, informed me that the locals were beginning to suspect that a large pack of wolves had recently swum over from the mainland and had settled on the south end of the island. It was their only explanation for the crazy howling sounds that permeated the fog, invading their peaceful community from time to time. I delighted in fuelling imaginations. I was a bit of brat back then.

Since Barrett didn't have an early coastal season lined up in 1985, Ricky and Zach hooked me up with a contractor who had two months of planting near Port Eliza, on the remote west coast of Vancouver Island, beginning in early February. The contractor, Ryan, operated a company called FC Ltd. One brief telephone conversation with Ryan in mid-January put me on his crew list. There was no need for a formal resumé or reference check—Ricky and Zach were my guarantors.

I hooked up with Ryan's crew in Campbell River a few weeks later. It was a great-looking group of people. Ryan himself was a force of nature—all six foot eight of him. He had wavy red hair that crept down his cheeks, ultimately breaking out around his chin in a wild flourish. He wore a red plaid jacket, a tight-fitting T-shirt stretched out over a happy belly, suspenders, loose-fitting jeans- and black leather work boots. Basically, he was your quintessential lumberjack. He had a self-confidence and intensity that immediately put me on edge, though. I gave the man a wide berth. When he looked at you with his piercing brown eyes, it was like being zeroed in on by a traffic cop, one who just clocked you doing twice the speed limit in a school zone. But as I would soon discover, rounding out all of these rugged external features was a self-deprecating man, a gifted storyteller, a masterful piccolo player and a wildly creative humorist. I never laughed so hard as when I was around Ryan.

Ryan's crew looked strong, but it leaned more toward men—a dynamic that would take some getting used to. Still, there were several women on the crew that nourished the imagination, and to this end, perhaps my sisters were right: I do tend to fall in love with every girl I meet.

We were instructed to drive across to the other side of the island, spend the night and then load our gear, work trucks and crew onto a freight and passenger ship that serviced the more remote communities along the west coast of Vancouver Island.[1] Seeing that I didn't have a ride, Ryan asked if I wouldn't mind driving one of his trucks to the designated loading dock. The plan was to hook up with the rest of the crew early the next morning. I accepted.

When I arrived at the dock later that evening, I thought about touring the town to get a feel for the community. It was my first time on the west side of the island. I tucked Ryan's truck into a parking lot close to where it was to be loaded early the next morning and set out on foot to explore the area. But before I was able to take more than a few steps, an angry voice called out, "You're not allowed to park there, asshole." When I pointed to a sign that specified PUBLIC PARKING, the voice, coming from behind a cluster of trees at the edge of the parking lot insisted, "That sign don't mean shit." Obviously, I wasn't about to venture too far away, fearing that the man behind the voice might attempt to vandalize Ryan's truck. Rather than get a room at a nearby motel that night, which I was very much looking forward to, I stuck with the truck. This wouldn't be the first night I'd be forced into the role of guard dog due to threats uttered by disgruntled locals.

Sure enough, the next morning, several of Ryan's vehicles that had been parked overnight in a lot nearby were vandalized. It was an outrage. The real worry was reserved for the personal vehicles that

---

1. I'm leaving out the names of specific towns and proprietors in this chapter due to the hostility we encountered with certain locals—a seasonal disorder no doubt, one brought on by the ongoing labour disputes. Also, treeplanters always seemed to occupy a spot at the very bottom of the resource-industry food chain, a designation that persists to this day.

would be parked in the same zone of hostility for the better part of two months. With the exception of Ryan's two work trucks, this was the end of the road for our vehicles. There were no roads leading in to where we were going.

Later that morning, as the ship's crew were nearly finished loading our gear, including our two four-by-four crew cabs that were finessed on board with the use of a large crane, Ricky and Zach were nowhere to be found. I was getting concerned, but as usual, their entrance needed to be memorable. Not only were they nail-bitingly late, they drove right up onto the pier as if they owned the damn thing, pulling right up alongside the ship. Before Ryan could say anything, the boys began offloading everything from long sheets of plywood, to heavy bundles of canvas, to what looked like a generator, stereo equipment and living-room furniture. Ryan was gobsmacked. He obviously hadn't counted on this extra freight, nor had the captain of the ship—but in the end, they made it all fit.

Ricky and Zach also brought along two close friends: Lady, the fearless Dobie who my saved life at Bute Inlet, and a puppy from one of her litters—a one-year-old pup called Rio. It was a nice little reunion once the dust settled and everything was tucked away.

We were fogged in for the better part of the journey up the island, but when the low-lying cloud softened, parting for only a minute or two, we were treated to glimpses of a coastline that was as lush and beautiful as it was rugged and foreboding.

When we finally reached Port Eliza, after our trucks and gear were offloaded, we gained access to a road system that had been constructed specifically for the purpose of logging the rich seams of old-growth timber in the region. At that time, old-growth conifers were still abundant on the west coast of Vancouver Island. Trees that were hundreds of years old, over ten storeys in height and three metres in diameter were not uncommon. Each tree had character—a unique personality—and in clusters they formed canopies that supported and concealed worlds both mysterious and forbidden. Ecosystems completely independent from the ground below appeared to leap out from them. I spent many hours lying on my back at the base of old-growth cedars, gazing up into the tapestry of twisted, braided and intertwined limbs. It was a wonderful way to separate oneself from the woes of the modern world.

After a thirty-minute drive along the Port Eliza mainline, we arrived at a wall of old-growth cedar trees that formed a long, protective barrier along the coastline. Beyond the wall of cedar was a large bay. The beach that lined the bay was as exquisite as anything I had experienced in the Hawaiian Islands. It stretched out in both directions for at least a hundred metres before surrendering to the rugged, craggy coastline. What set this beach apart from all others was a formidable wall of beached logs that had been pushed right up to the edge of the forest floor, some fifteen metres above the high-tide line. Clearly, this was the aftermath of a series of powerful Pacific storms. I was told that this area, like many areas along the west coast of Vancouver Island, had its own distinct weather patterns. Hurricane-type storm systems could whip up at any time. This beautiful, lush and volatile stretch of coastline would be our home for the next four weeks.

The mossy open areas in between the giant cedars made perfect foundations for individual campsites. Scoping out the area thoroughly, I settled on a spot that was well beyond the perimeter of the main camp, directly below the largest old-growth cedar I had ever seen. I had been warned that I could expect a winter storm of such ferocity that typical tent layouts would buckle under the pressure of the extreme winds. With that in mind, I designed a configuration that incorporated mountain-climbing ropes and a number of rubber bungee cords to help secure my tarpaulin rainfly—a system that I hoped would flex and stretch, rather than pull, tear and blow away. When I was done pounding tent pegs and cinching ropes, I backed away to admire the engineering and construction from a distance. It appeared solid, yet flexible. Then I made the mistake of taking a closer look at the cedar canopy that hovered some nine storeys directly above my tent.

Each twisted and malformed limb appeared to weigh several hundred pounds. I decided that it was best not to obsess on minor details.

After only two days of planting trees, in what turned out to be exceptional, uncharacteristically mild weather, I came to discover that not all crews are created equal. Some operate under markedly different philosophies. Aside from Ricky, Zach and a handful of like-minded souls, the balance of Ryan's crew were deliberate underachievers. It appeared to be some sort of code of conduct. I was even scolded one evening by one of Ryan's regulars, an eccentric French Canadian fellow named Benoit, who attempted to convince me that there was no need to produce large numbers of trees on this contract. He insisted that I drop the competitive attitude and slow down. Curiously, hushed tones accompanied his reprimand. Clearly, he didn't want to be overheard at the dinner table. Wanting to test his resolve, to put an end to the claptrap, I interrupted him rudely, loudly, asking, "Really, Benoit? I need to slow down and plant fewer trees?" Ryan, listening from the next table over, was not impressed. Not one bit.

This crew certainly had its share of quirky components. Two couples on Ryan's crew immediately came into conflict. It seemed that the women were acting in an overly flirtatious manner. I actually discovered one poor dejected soul sobbing in the woods behind my tent one evening. Apparently, certain lines had been crossed.

There was one veteran planter on the crew who was there without his spouse. He was a devoted husband—while he was back home in Alberta anyway. He had a young lady on the crew in his romantic crosshairs, an English lit student named Sherry.

There was also a mysterious loner on the crew who was rumoured to have been engaged with a weapons think tank, until he woke up one day and decided that he needed to "improve his karma" by heading north. Apparently, he hit the road without having been formally debriefed by the weapons manufacturer that employed him. I was told that he lived in a log cabin on a remote Gulf Island in the off-season, with his two lovers.

Brett, our cook, was one of those gifted chefs who caused you to wonder, *How the hell did he get mixed up with a treeplanting company?* Not only was he a masterful saucier, he was remarkably skilled at resolving domestic issues—therapy that could have been dispensed full-time for the first few weeks at Port Eliza.

And then there were Ricky and Zach! The mountain of wood, hardware, furniture and electronic equipment they packed onto the boat morphed into a fully functional clubhouse. While the rest of us were living in tiny pup tents, with only a thin layer of foam separating our stiff, sore and battle-weary bodies from the cold, hard earth, they erected a twenty-person army tent with a three-metre-high ceiling. It had wood floors, a porch for storing gear and an airtight stove in the centre of the tent that converted the cold winter air into T-shirt weather within a matter of seconds. They had a Honda generator in the back that ran electricity through a number of hanging chandeliers, a stereo complete with turntable and speaker cabinets, and a string of twinkling Christmas lights adorning the front entrance. After I picked my jaw up off the floor, I noticed that they had three oversized cots set up, each lined with six inches of luxurious compressed foam. There were only two of them—I had to ask, "Who's the third cot for?" Ricky, who was busy attempting to drain a full bottle of beer in a single gulp, simply pointed at me, as if to say, "Duh...it's for you, numbnuts."

I resisted Ricky's generous offer for nearly a week. That was when the first storm hit. It was midway through the second shift at Port Eliza. The wind began picking up with an alarming intensity, and within twenty minutes we were being pummelled by gale-force winds. It was nearly impossible to stand upright, let alone walk a straight line in full planting gear. The forest around us sustained the worst of the assault. Limbs and huge chunks of wood, ripped from the exposed trees that lined the edge of our cutblock, crashed to the ground with loud cracks and thuds. By that time everyone had instinctively moved downslope, away from the havoc. There are few things more frightening than staring up at a giant stand of conifers as they bend, heave and contort under the pressure of a powerful squall.

Ryan was initially reluctant to call it quits that day. Hampered by a listless crew, he needed every ounce of production he could squeeze out of us. But it wasn't long before he was hanging onto the side-view mirror of his truck, barely able to hold his ground, blasting his horn through the open window as a signal to evacuate. That was the first time I had ever witnessed winds strong enough to part a man's beard right down the centre of his chin.

Driving off the cutblock required great care as objects large and small were being hurled at us. I saw full boxes of seedlings, weighing forty to fifty pounds, cartwheeling across the road in front of us as we made our escape.

Ryan was freaking out as we cautiously made our way down the valley back to camp. The Quonset hut was his main concern. Though it was secured by long steel spikes sunk deep into the ground, there was a risk that if the canvas flaps at the entrance weren't zipped up in time, the entire structure could launch skyward with the first violent squall and disappear out to sea.

When we arrived, the Quonset hut was still holding its ground, but there was damage to the other structures around camp. Along with several personal tents, the shower unit was flat on the ground, in pieces, and personal items of every description were strewn about, some making for open water out in the bay. The tarp covering my tent had taken a medium-sized tree limb to one corner, ripping it free from the bungee and rope supports. By the time I arrived, the tarp had basically turned into a giant kite, whipping and thrashing in the residual wind. Had the tree limb hit the tent dead centre, it would have destroyed it completely. Ricky and Zach's clubhouse survived unscathed. I checked in that very night.

Living at the Tropicana, as the crew called it, was decadent. It had nearly every luxury a treeplanter could want in the remote wilderness. Here I also enjoyed the company of two great dogs that were every bit as entertaining as my hosts. In the evenings, after dinner, we'd sit ourselves down around the airtight stove, dial into any one of the dozens of radio stations on the other side of the Pacific via Ricky's shortwave radio, and wait for the inevitable influx of tourists to arrive. The Tropicana was the crew's destination of choice in the evenings. There was always something going on: music, poker, storytelling, laughs, stupid pet tricks. When the guitars came out, it was standing room only.

At the end of the third shift, a number of Ryan's regulars were organizing a hike to the top of a mountain, the site of a First Nations burial ground according to local legend. Overhearing our discussion in the truck on the way back from work, Harrison, the guy who'd run away from a lucrative career figuring out better ways to blow shit up, spoke out for the first time since the contract began. "If you go up there, *no one* touches *nothing*," he warned. "Especially the skulls at the entrance!" If I was on the sidelines prior to Harrison's exhortation, I was at the front of the line by the end of it.

The next day after breakfast, there were enough people interested in the graveyard tour to fill a crew cab and then some. Brett, our chef and marriage counsellor, decided to tag along as well, forcing Ryan to cough up a second truck. The plan was to hike up to the burial site, which would take the better part of two hours, round trip, then continue to a beach farther up the coast. Once there, we'd play a bit of Frisbee football, have a little picnic, and soak up some west coast rays. The air was cool. The sky was clear. It promised to be a good day.

The burial ground trailhead could easily have been missed. There wasn't so much as a sign or marker indicating its origin—only a narrow opening through the thick brush at the end of an overgrown spur road. The trail itself was broken and sinuous but otherwise easily traversed. Though we were forced to walk single file, boisterous conversation and laughter accompanied our group nearly all the way to the top of the mountain.

As the trail levelled off on a plateau, one that supported an unusually sparse forest of stunted conifers, a voice from the front of our procession called out, "We're getting close, boys 'n' girls!" Suddenly, a palpable sense of gloom seemed to envelop our little group. Our laughter and carefree banter trailed off. Silence shrouded the remainder of our ascent. Even our two canine companions, Lady and Rio, appeared subdued.

Then, there it was: a dark hollow in the side of the mountain. At the entrance to the cave sat a large boulder that partially blocked the entrance. On the top of the boulder sat a single human skull, placed there, perhaps, as a sentinel to ward off unwelcome visitors. The cave entrance itself was almost three metres high and consisted of heavily stratified black rock that created naturally protruding ledges on which a number of human skulls had been positioned, facing outward, guarding the entrance.

Half of the crew refused to explore the cave beyond the disembodied gatekeeper on the boulder out front. The other half of us cautiously inched our way in, exploring the interior that gradually tapered down in height and width. Being a tall guy, I was forced to crouch down to reach the very back, some fifteen metres farther in. No one had remembered to bring along a flashlight. Though our light was poor, the cave walls appeared to be lined with a good number of human skulls, bones and other objects—perhaps the personal effects of the deceased. A hole at the very back of the cave dropped straight down into another chamber, one I was lucky to discover without accidentally falling in. We didn't bother probing the depths of the lower chamber. It was too narrow and dark. Our ghoulish curiosity was soon satiated. I for one had never seen a human skull before, let alone a community of them watching over me from every angle.

Our buoyant spirits were restored once we made our way past the oddly stunted conifer forest that defined the plateau leading away from the cave. It was like a veil had been lifted, allowing us to be ourselves again.

For the next leg of our adventure we drove up the coast to a beach, a secluded spot that I was told had to be seen to be believed.

Brett needed to prep our dinner for later on that evening so he drove back to camp in one of the trucks. This left us with only one vehicle in which to cram nine bodies—six inside the cab, three in the rumble seat in the back box. I amiably volunteered to rumble. Had I known in advance that the drive would require the better part of an hour, and a fair amount of elevation gain over a rough road, I would have fought for a seat inside the cab.

A tight series of switchbacks forced us to reduce our speed to a crawl as we zigzagged down the side of a mountain, gradually reaching the flats below. We came to rest against a pile of boulders at the edge of a small landing. From there a short hike through a cutblock brought us to the edge of the sand.

I could immediately appreciate what all of the fuss was about. It was a gorgeous setting. The beach, more picturesque than I could have imagined, extended at least five hundred metres in each direction. Adding to our excitement, waves more than a metre high were breaking and lapping at the gently sloping shoreline. As they receded in an effervescent backwash, they pulled tiny rounded pebbles back down along the bubbling, percolating fringe, creating a wonderful shimmering sound as they were consumed by the sea. The sand had a slightly coarse texture, but after baking in the mid-morning sun, it felt like a gentle massage under our bare, boot-weary toes. Scattered along the entire length of the beach, poking up randomly from the sand, were long smooth slabs of rock, polished to a glassy sheen by the elements. Often, these slabs lay just below the surface, except for their jagged corners and edges. We needed to be mindful of these hazards as we set off to play.

Our game of Frisbee football began innocently enough. As competition mounted, there were a number of highlight-reel catches. I made a few myself, hoping to impress one particular member of our crew—Sherry, the English lit student from Vancouver. Scotty, one of Ryan's highly competent foremen, not wanting to be outshone in front of his beautiful wife, attempted a diving reception and landed directly on top of one of the semi-submerged jagged rock slabs. When he finally managed to pick himself up, he was butchered all along his right hip, rib cage and shoulder. The wounds were mostly superficial, but he had lost a fair amount of skin and was bleeding profusely. Our afternoon beach follies came to an abrupt end.

After dressing Scotty's wounds with tape and gauze from the first-aid kit back at the truck, we got organized to head back to camp. That is, until the key turning in the ignition was met only by a weak clicking sound. The battery in our truck was dead. There was no explaining it. The headlights had been turned off, nothing requiring electricity had been left on and the truck had been parked for less than thirty minutes. It didn't make sense. The truck had been running flawlessly all contract long. A few feeble attempts at push-starting it generated only frustration and laughter—the landing was too tight and the road was on an incline, making it extremely difficult to generate sufficient momentum. The reality of our predicament hit home with a wallop: it wasn't even noon, and no one back at camp would likely begin to worry about us for another seven hours, after we failed to arrive home for dinner.

No one could recall seeing any other vehicles on the road in the two weeks that we were operating along the Port Eliza mainline. If there were other crews working in the area, we rarely crossed paths. For the most part, it was wonderful having the roads to ourselves, but for the purposes of hitching a desperately needed ride back home, we were shit out of luck that day.

Before we started our long trek, we wondered: Should Scotty stay behind and wait with the truck, or join the rest of us in our fifty-kilometre trail of despair back to camp? Insisting that he wasn't crippled, he joined our unhappy group of hapless hikers.

Concern for Scotty aside, I was disappointed. I had plans for the rest of my afternoon. I'd been looking forward to a long snooze on our beach between a pair of logs I had scoped out on the sand a day earlier. I was going to crash in a sleeping bag, curl up in the fetal position and heal.

We set out on a steep forty-five-minute climb to the top of a ridge overlooking the beach. We needed to make this climb in order to hook up with the mainline, which led back to camp. Fifty kilometres divided by a walking rate of maybe six kilometres per hour—I decided it was best to leave that bit of arithmetic alone. Then Gunther, an extremely fit regular on Ryan's crew, stepped up to the plate and announced that he was going to run the entire distance back to camp, assuring us that he had completed a number of full marathons in his day. Not that we wanted to discourage Gunther, but we had our doubts. The road leading back had a lot of ups and downs, it was midday, the sun was beating down and—this was a big *and*—Gunther wasn't 100 per cent certain that he knew the way back. Off he went anyway. We cheered him on with enough fanfare to put a good bounce in his stride, a bounce we suspected he lost the moment he dropped out of sight.

By hour four of our little walking tour, we had broken off into four separate groups, all advancing at varying speeds with approximately one kilometre separating the first group from the stragglers picking up the rear. Ricky and Zach, very perceptively and graciously, dropped back behind me and Sherry, allowing us some time alone.

Sherry was an impressive woman. Her intellect dwarfed mine, but not in a way that intimidated me. In fact, it had the opposite effect. I found her knowledge of all things literary incredibly alluring. She had a really earthy quality too, to the point that if you simply sized her up from a distance—with her blond hair that always looked like she'd just braved a windstorm—you might not have given her a second thought. But when she spoke—oh, how I loved to hear her speak! The tone of her voice was so pleasing, the flow of her words so silky, so rhythmic, I often found myself lulled into a semi-hypnotized state. I had an obvious challenge though: I sensed that she was interested in one of the married men in camp—a man who regarded the sanctity of marriage as a somewhat antiquated notion. Fortunately, this individual wasn't with us that day. I decided to let her choose.

It was now dark. We spotted two bright beams of light bounce off a timber-lined ridge at the far end of the valley. Without a doubt, it was our ride home! We were the only crew operating in the area, the only humans around for perhaps a hundred kilometres in every direction. It was Ryan behind the wheel, and in the front seat with him, one tapped-out marathon runner—Gunther. The poor guy managed to run nearly the entire distance back to camp before being intercepted by Ryan five hundred metres outside of camp. He didn't even get a chance to ring the alarm bell. We all decided to treat him as a hero anyway.

Ryan and Brett drove back to the beach to retrieve the abandoned truck. It started up on the first turn of the key!

AS WE APPROACHED THE END OF THE THIRD WEEK IN PORT ELIZA, Ricky, Zach, Sherry and I were called in for a private meeting with Ryan and Scotty. They offered us the opportunity to separate from the main crew and take on a special mission. This would entail sailing back down the coast and hooking up with two trucks. Once mobile, we'd travel up to the north end of the island and embark on a series of planting scenarios that required, as Ryan so generously put it, "a crew with a certain flair."

We were all sufficiently flattered by the offer and agreed to the arrangement without hesitation. What we weren't made aware of at the time was that the project was bid "site unseen"—the individual sites were not visited and examined prior to a bid being submitted. They were assessed and bid using aerial photographs, topographic maps and verbal descriptions. This is normally a recipe for disaster as maps and aerial photos do not reveal the actual physical characteristics of a setting. We embarked expecting adventure and fat dividends. I would soon be reminded that lofty expectations in this industry are best kept in check.

After making our way back down the coast on the same freight ship we had travelled up on, we ventured off in two trucks that were waiting for us at the loading dock. We were a six-pack: Scotty, his wife and planting partner, Elsie, Ricky, Zach, Sherry and me. It was a tight crew and we really enjoyed one another's company—a very important consideration with small treeplanting crews. Actually, Lady and Rio made us eight.

Our first project required travelling up the northwest side of the island, but since it was too dark to properly navigate the complex network of logging roads at night, we decided not to push it. We would travel as far a small town that was in the vicinity of one of our "missions," sleep in the trucks overnight and worry about setting up camp early the next day.

During our long drive up-island, feeling a sense of liberation at being cut loose from the main pack, I decided to do something I hadn't done since the Mesilinka River contract six months earlier: I agreed to join everyone in smoking a big fatty—a "gagger," as Scotty liked to call them. When we were within a stone's throw of our destination, we looked for a place to stop and blaze up. We found an ideal spot at the edge of a lake, one that had a large open area between the shoreline and the road.

It was nearly 9:00 p.m. and now pitch-dark. When we cut the engines, there was an ineffable calm in the air. The steep rock faces and forests around us fell into hushed silence as if eager to eavesdrop on what we had to say as we emerged from our vehicles. As the weed was passed around our tight little circle, I warned everyone that I might need a space helmet.

As we finished our gagger, Scotty rushed back to his truck, fished around behind his back seat, and called out, "I have something for ya, Mr. Gazelle." Grinning, he produced a Frisbee from behind his back, and with the flick of a switch tucked under the rim, he activated a series of blinking red lights around the disk's perimeter. There was a collective gasp.

What started out as gentle tosses around a tight circle morphed into an incredibly vigorous and acrobatic game. Eventually we were testing how far apart we could stand and still make contact with our intended receiver. The patterns of light we produced as the disk streaked across the pitch-dark sky were overwhelming at first, but they soon became awe inspiring. It wasn't long before we were making receptions and tosses that would have rivalled even the most hardcore Frisbee athlete. We played with the light and darkness for well over an hour, laughing, cheering, oohing and aahing. We would have played longer had it not started to rain. And within a few minutes of us all taking shelter in the trucks, it began to pour.

There wasn't much to see as we rolled into town, not in the dark anyway. A grand old hotel stood in the middle of things. It served as a watering hole and meeting place for the tiny, resource-dependent community. These were tough times in the resource sector. It seemed that the main labour union was always duking it out over wages and benefits with the big timber companies on the island. This often resulted in strikes and work shutdowns. This also created tension between the out-of-work loggers and those of us who rolled into town gainfully employed.

I was the first of our little troupe to enter the hotel bar that evening. When I walked through the door a group of older men in their mid- to late fifties all looked up from their warm glasses of beer at the same time, with the same wretched scowls on their faces. "You're not a fucking treeplanter, are ya?" the one closest to me demanded.

I was joined by Ricky and Zach moments later. We managed to find a safe zone at the back of the bar. The three of us together, under saner circumstances, likely would have appeared too formidable for anyone looking to pick a fight, but anything can happen where unemployment, anger and alcohol are involved. When I inquired about the rest of our crew, Zach said that Scotty and Elsie were guarding the trucks. Both had worked the area in the past, and experience had taught them that vehicles left unattended at night ran the risk of being broken into, vandalized or worse. Sherry was too afraid to venture inside.

After a mug of draft, I cautiously ventured over to the other side of the bar to use the washroom, careful not to accidently jostle anyone or anything. When I opened the door to the washroom, I noticed a figure hunched over, peering out through one of the stalls. He appeared to be hiding, cowering. When I asked him if everything was all right, he answered back in a thick Eastern European accent, "No, it's not very all right."" I think he sensed that I was a good guy, and before I had a chance to take care of some pressing personal business, he offered me a fifty-dollar bill if I would escort him safely to his truck. He was a geoduck fisherman who'd had a bit of an altercation with some of the locals prior to our arrival. He was hiding in the men's room to avoid a beat-down. Incredulous, I summoned Ricky and Zach, and after a brief huddle and a few choice words of reassurance, we escorted him out of the hotel bar, directing our most menacing glares at anyone who dared disapprove of the attention we were giving our new friend. There was no resistance, inside the hotel or out, and I'm proud to report that no protection money changed hands. Before we could wish our new friend good luck, he slipped away into the cold wet night. What a crazy fucking town!

To avoid starting a brawl back inside the hotel, we returned to the trucks and called it a night. Ricky and Zach cuddled up with Lady and Rio in their truck; Scotty, Elsie, Sherry and I cuddled up together in ours.

Early the next morning, we made our way to one of the small cut-blocks on our list—one that was centrally located. It turned out to be a good spot to set up camp, being somewhat sheltered from the elements. We settled on an area at the back end of the block, on a flat bench elevated six metres above a fast-running creek. The place had atmosphere, character. After setting up camp, we went over our maps to produce a plan for the remainder of our day. Our special mission included five cutblocks, encompassing 120 hectares spread out over a vast area. Aside from their isolation from one another, each area presented a unique challenge. We decided to attack the block farthest away from our camp first. It appeared, according to the description in the notes, to have the least amount of slash. We hoped it would be an easy block to start off on. What we overlooked were the tightly spaced contour lines on our maps.

When we arrived at the bottom of the block, we were shocked to discover that it wasn't a typical coastal setting. It was a series of steep clearcut areas interspersed between sheer rock faces and vertical cliffs. It was a nasty-looking piece of ground. It was also a fill-plant—a crew had attempted to plant the area in the past but was unsuccessful in establishing a healthy plantation. It had gaps. It didn't comply with the strict standards of the Ministry of Forests (MOF), a.k.a. the Forest Service. It required the planting of additional seedlings—our seedlings.

This project was actually being supervised by the MOF, and we were to expect regular visits by a Forest Service officer who would be inspecting our planting, organizing our tree deliveries, and ensuring that we kept to the schedule. My experience with the Forest Service was limited, but in the past, when we spotted their spruce-green trucks turn onto our cutblocks, it was like the cops showing up at a late-night party. Some of us referred to them as the Nervous Service.

My first day of planting on this special mission taught me an important lesson, one that governed my actions from that day forward. As we divided up the block, I volunteered to take on a particularly horrendous-looking section on the extreme right of the mountain. It was a clean-looking piece of ground, but treacherously steep. As I began planting, the heavy, swollen grey clouds that had been taunting us all morning suddenly unleashed a torrential downpour, and with the powerful wind that was already present, we were suddenly contending with horizontal sheets of rain. As I reached the top of my area and proceeded to worked my way across the slope toward my opposite boundary, the storm began to intensify. I was forced to turn away and work facing the slope with my head down. The sideways rain, propelled by violent gusts of wind, stung my exposed face. The rain was also creating channels of runoff—the soil had become completely saturated.

At the far corner of my piece I detected what appeared to be a crevasse or fissure cut into the side of the slope, but I had no way of determining its dimensions. Since this was an MOF contract, I knew that the checking would be strict. Suspecting that no stone would be left unturned in the search for planting infractions, I was determined to plant my way right up to the very edge of the crevasse. That was a mistake.

As I pushed myself sideways across the slope, struggling to maintain my footing, unable to read the ground anywhere around me due to the intensity of the wind and rain, I reached a point where I couldn't take another step. I needed to backtrack. To size up the ground below me, I cranked my head around and peered through the sharp, stinging sheets of rain. It didn't take long to realize I was in trouble. I was at the edge of a precipice. I had inadvertently worked my way along a thin ledge and was perched at the very end of it. The slope directly below me dropped off at least twenty metres at an eighty-degree angle. I couldn't move forward, and I didn't have the traction to work my way back. I was basically clinging to the slope for dear life. I began to panic. My legs began to tremble. Desperately, I jammed my shovel into the ground directly in front of me in order to stabilize my position. The extreme grade of the slope caused my shovel blade to enter the soil at roughly chest level. Continuing to panic, with no one in sight, I managed to transfer my shovel to my left hand while gripping the edge of the fresh gash I had cut into the slope with my right. Then, through a series of clumsy left-handed shovel stabs next to my left foot, I managed to chisel out a small foothold, allowing me to transfer my weight slightly to the left. This began the slow process of reversing back the way I came. I carved out a succession footholds with my shovel in this manner, slowly shifting my body back along the thin ledge, hugging the slope for dear life the entire time. Eventually, I reached a point where the grade eased off, allowing me to turn myself completely around.

Somehow, I managed to survive that ordeal. Had I not brainstormed the idea of carving out footholds with my shovel, exhaustion, runoff and gravity would have precipitated a decisive fall—one that would have ended in death. The significance of that event was not lost on me.

The storm continued to build in intensity. No one could maintain a firm footing. Our direct exposure to the elements made planting this steep terrain too precarious. We decided to pack up our gear and attempt to salvage what was left of our day back at the block we had set up camp on. I was too embarrassed to tell the crew about my debacle on the slopes. They could sense I was rattled though.

Today, a treeplanter would never find himself in that situation. The perimeter of any such danger zone would be surveyed and roped off with bright fluorescent flagging tape ahead of time. It would be treated with the same delicacy and deliberation as a crime scene. There would also be a pre-work meeting, on-site, where specific attention would be paid to such hazards before anyone was allowed to venture within one hundred metres of it. Back then we were completely on our own. The call was entirely ours to make.

When we arrived back at camp later that morning, the storm was throwing everything it had at us. The creek below our camp, running with only moderate volume earlier in the day, had become a raging river. Though we were somewhat sheltered by the brunt of the storm, the unusual topography of the valley funnelled the wind in an unpredictable manner. This was yet another epic weather event, and I was suddenly feeling inspired again.

With my confidence and sense of adventure restored, I bagged-up with a full load of trees and began planting along the perimeter of the creek.

This cutblock was unusual. It was a wonderful setting at the bottom of a valley. The soil was composed of fine silt and could not have been more yielding. Close up, the block appeared to be well on its way to becoming a mature forest, but when I peered through the lush greenery, I saw large open areas between the tall conifers—areas that required the company of our seedlings.

As I planted along the perimeter of the block along the top of a cutbank at the edge of the creek, I could clearly sense the water level rising by the minute. The surrounding mountainsides were trembling under the volume of runoff coursing down their steep slopes. The tall conifers seemed to bear the brunt of the severe winds, but the occasional gust was able to punch through, threatening to knock me flat on my ass.

At around noon, the storm shifted into a higher gear. Overhead, the tops of the taller fir trees began bending and contorting, exposed to the full fury of the storm. Sharp snaps and cracks were followed by giant thuds as the tops of the weaker, more exposed conifers began to break off and crash to the ground. It was exhilarating. Nearly falling to my death is one thing, but this was some wild stuff.

As I continued to plant along the creek, Scotty managed to track me down to make sure I was okay. No one else was willing to brave the elements and he felt it would be better if I joined the rest of the crew, huddled in the security of the trucks. "No fucking way," was my curt reply. Scotty was a good foreman. I respected him. But this was an event that I needed to experience up close. I was also pounding in a good number of trees.

I was having a blast until a powerful gust of wind blew me backward, off the steep bank, five metres down into the raging torrent below. I hit the water ass first and was immediately submerged. I distinctly remember the sensation of hitting the bottom of the creek bed with my butt before being swept downstream. Coughing and choking up water, before I could even think, let alone react, I was driven by the current up against a large log that was protruding from shore. The log was jammed into the creek bed at such an angle that the motion of the water actually pushed me back toward land. It all happened so fast, I still can't piece together the exact sequence of events. Crawling back onshore, coughing up gobs of brown silty sludge, I lay in a heap until I was able to thoroughly flush the creek from my lungs. It then took me a good half-hour to regain my bearings and find my way back up the steep bank, back to solid ground.

I had two close calls within the space of only a few hours that day. Not wanting to temp fate any further, I decided to call it quits and join the others.

The special mission that had generated so much hope and excitement at the outset turned into a complete gong show as the season progressed. Aside from the one good block that served as the foundation of our camp, the four remaining cutblocks were absolutely brutal. They were also priced far too low to make any sort of meaningful money. The near vertical hell-block that nearly claimed my life was left until the very end. The bulk of Ryan's main crew merged with us in mid-April, and it was decided that the entire crew—all eighteen of us—would blitz the block en masse and be done with it once and for all.

When we arrived at the hell-block on the final day of Ryan's coastal season, we discovered a locked gate at the entrance to the road leading in. It was another five hundred metres beyond the gate to the base of the block. Walking in, with trees, appeared to be our only play. Ryan stood back and examined the block from a distance. Calling me over to consult the map with him, he exclaimed, "Please tell me I'm looking at the wrong block." I assured him that his eyes weren't deceiving him.

"That's not a block," he bellowed. "That's a fucking cliff!"

What happened next I have experienced only twice in my twenty-seven years in the silviculture industry: Ryan instructed the crew to get back in the trucks. He told us that we were going to walk on this particular cutblock. "Walking" is the equivalent of breaking a contract. Here, he refused to put the lives of his crew at risk on terrain he deemed too dangerous to set foot on. Just as we started to drive off, the MOF officer in charge of the project arrived to unlock the gate. Ryan stopped his truck just long enough to roll down his window and ask, "Do you really expect me to put my people up on that cliff?" Without allowing the poor flustered guy to answer back, Ryan abruptly ended the discussion, saying, "Doesn't matter. We're fucking off." He peeled off, sending gravel flying in all directions.

When a contractor fails to complete a contract, the timber company can legally withhold funds for the entire project, causing great financial harm to the contractor and crew. One month later, I received a cheque in the mail for the full amount of what was owed. Ryan obviously worked out a compromise with the MOF. We all suspected that he would.

When I arrived back home in Calgary, there were numerous messages waiting for me on my answering machine. Barrett was anxious to get in touch with me to discuss his spring season. It was set to begin in only a few days. There was no time to rest between contracts. Less than forty-eight hours later, I was hightailing it to the BC Interior.

CHAPTER EIGHT

# THE ESCAPE

||||||||||||||||||||||||||||||||||||||||||||||||

Spring 1985 with barrett's company was a season of intense hard work, extreme heat, relentless blood-sucking insects and the occasional animal encounter—bears and humans alike. It was a satisfying season from a financial point of view but with none of the shake-your-head-in-amazement type of craziness I had come to expect planting trees in remote locations. At one point we were prepared to pull up stakes and evacuate when a forest fire threatened us from the north, but nothing came of it as the winds changed direction and the blaze eventually burned itself out.

Later that spring, my next adventure was with a company working in the Swan Hills region of Alberta, home of the infamous Swan Hills grizzly bear—some will swallow hard at the mere mention of the place. Setting foot in my first Alberta treeplanting camp was like entering the Dark Ages. The Quonset hut, which was standard equipment for most BC companies, was instead a small, single-compartment army tent, one that was in such poor condition, the scent of mould and mildew permeated the air inside and out. Its drooping canvas roof and walls would flap violently, even in the slightest breeze. The kitchen, which is normally offset from the dining area, shared the back half of the tent, allowing only two small tables and a dozen chairs in the space that remained. More than half of the crew of twenty-five were forced to eat their supper while standing. Veteran planters told me that this arrangement was par for an Alberta bush camp.

There were no showers. There was a creek but nobody, and I mean *nobody*, braved the frigid current, judging by the obvious lack of personal hygiene in camp. People wore their dirt and grime like a second (and third) layer of skin. It wasn't unusual to see a person return to camp at the end of the day with mud smeared across his face and neck, and one week later, spot the same individual wearing the same crud. When I arrived at this camp, I was sporting a leather jacket, black boot-cut jeans, highlights in my hair and a diamond stud in my left ear. People must have thought I was from another planet.

There were no established outhouses. People simply wandered farther and farther away from camp as the contract progressed. You had to be extremely careful where you stepped when strolling through the woods, especially at night. Instead of generators, electric lights and refrigeration, there were kerosene lanterns and meat pits.

Meat pits! In the absence of electricity, perishable items were stored below ground. The theory was simple: if the majority of your meat was brought in frozen, and if you were able to dig a pit deep enough into the mud, the temperature at the bottom of the pit would be cool enough to safely store your meat for up to two weeks. The shortcomings of this logic were obvious. Two weeks during the dog days of summer was pushing it. After day seven, they were laying out the welcome mat for every conceivable strain of pathogen and bacteria on the planet. In an act of self-preservation, I vowed to convert to a strict vegetarian diet after day five.

There were no real roads to speak of. The outlying cutblocks were accessible by ATV only, and due to the lack of ATVs on-site, we were expected to walk between four and eight kilometres to work each day, without any form of recompense. If you were female and friendly enough with one of the tree delivery guys, you could sometimes hitch a ride on the back of their ATV part way. For the rest of us, hoofing it was the only option. Enduring a punishing one-hour hike through muskeg and mud before strapping on the planting bags and hitting the slopes took some getting used to.

I did meet some truly amazing people in this camp, though. Even though it was an Alberta company, the crew was almost entirely Québécois, and these particular guys knew how to make the best of even the most miserable conditions.

One gloomy, wet morning, after a grueling eight-kilometre hike through hell, I detected the sweet aroma of coffee wafting through the trees from a cutblock next door. Peering through the forest, through the cold fog and rain, I spotted a small group of men gathered around a tiny Bunsen-burner stove with what appeared to be an espresso maker perched on top. The gurgling and hissing sounds drew me in like a moth to a flame. They spotted me snooping, called me over and put me at the front of the line, passing over a mug and a can of milk, one they had looted from the camp kitchen earlier that morning. My eyes lit up as they poured out a steamy espresso, scalding the milk at the bottom of my eagerly extended cup. How could I fail to be anything but completely enamoured by such a generous display of camaraderie and affection? These guys, despite their filthy and grubby appearance, were every bit as refined and sophisticated as my citified chums back home. Perhaps more so.

After two weeks of living in primeval conditions, I was looking for an exit. I required only one additional excuse to justify pulling up stakes and hitting the road. It wasn't a long wait. Two incidents, only twenty-four hours apart, would send me on my way: 1) Late one night a black bear was shot attempting to gain access to the meat pit. It took two bullets to the chest, then fell backward into the pit where it bled out and died on top of our food supply. 2) After returning to camp the following evening and discovering that the cook hadn't prepared enough food for supper, and couldn't be bothered to produce more for those of us who arrived home late and hungry, I was ready to brain someone with my shovel. I hit the road instead.

*

THE 1986 SPRING PLANTING SEASON WITH BARRETT'S COMPANY
began with a series of groans and collective sighs. The hectare-based
planting system was still being applied to Barrett's ground. Although it
had been an extremely lucrative proposition in the past, it had lost its
allure. It had lost its jackpot potential. Presumably, logging companies
had caught up in their backlog of planting older cutblocks. The older the
cutblock, the greater the number of naturals occupying one's land. The
glory days were over. We were now planting fresh cutblocks—blocks
that weren't given sufficient time to generate healthy populations of
naturals. Naturals were our key to success and they had become few
and far between.

The spring season was interesting in other respects, though. I was
joined by an older cousin, Darren, who followed me into the industry
after being regaled with tales of big money, high-country adventure,
cream and sports bras. Darren was a tall, lanky character with curly
black hair, dark piercing eyes and a thick brow that he loved to fur-
row whenever I spoke to him. This idiosyncrasy always put me on
edge. It made me think that my diction was off. It created a strange
tension between us. Darren was a character, though. He had a wonderfully twisted sense of humour. He was also a huge pro-wrestling
fan, obsessed with the subculture. Shortly after arriving in camp, he
insisted that he be referred to as the "Bone Crusher." After a few days,
the entire crew appeared to be on board with the crazy appellation,
shortening it to simply "Crusher."

We were engaged in one long contract that spring. It began in mid-
April and was scheduled to take us right into mid-June, with Barrett
following up on numerous leads in an attempt to extend our season
even further.

Our tent camp was located along the remote western shore of the
catastrophe that was Williston Lake. At that point in time, the water
level had receded to the extent that a one-kilometre halo of dry lakebed
surrounded the reservoir on all sides. We were actually able to drive

our trucks out onto the exposed lake bottom and set up the bulk of our camp there. It was an unusual setting. The entire lakebed, for as far as the eye could see, was completely devoid of any living thing. It was completely barren. There wasn't so much as a single tuft of grass poking up out of the soil. But dotting the sterile landscape, like the skeletal remains of a massive herd of roaming animals that were suddenly struck down by some cataclysmic event, their ghostly remains frozen in time, were the stumps of trees that were once a great northern forest. Years of wind and water had eroded the soil from around these stumps, their exposed lateral roots reaching outward, as if having writhed in pain in their final few moments of life. To some this backdrop was extremely unsettling. To others, the stumps and outstretched root masses were practical, useful features, providing shelter for their tents from the wind as well as a nifty framework from which to secure ropes, tarps and clotheslines.

Due to the fact that the setting was so completely wide open, I was forced to pitch my tent well over a kilometre from the main campsite—it was the only way to escape the grumble of the kitchen generator. I found a great spot, surrounded by a number of upturned stumps and criss-crossed logs, the likely result of a series of violent storms when the lake was at a much higher level. Learning my lesson from previous seasons, and wanting to create a campsite that was more than just a basic shelter, I unfurled and suspended the mother of all tarps, creating a spacious canopy that overlapped my tent on all sides. Out of the countless nooks and crannies within the root systems that surrounded my tent, I fashioned a vanity of sorts, setting up stations for washing and shaving, complete with strategically placed hand mirrors, metal basins, water bottles and toiletries. Twenty metres away from my little fortress I constructed a firepit. I lined it with beach rocks and encircled it with several large logs to act as backrests—I was hoping to have company at some point over the course of this long contract.

This project was being run by Ron, and was one of two large contracts Barrett had secured for CRC Ltd.'s 1986 spring season. Kelly was holding onto the other set of reins. His contract was also up the west side of Williston Lake but, strangely enough, our crews never crossed paths—not even once. This gives you an idea of the vastness of the area.

Where I was earning an average of $400 per day only seven months earlier, now I had to work overtime in order to crack three bills. Exacerbating the difficult conditions was a lack of any meaningful measure of rain. Aside from providing relief from the intense heat, rain softens the ground, making it easier to penetrate with your shovel blade. Uninterrupted stretches of hot weather can bake the surface of a south-facing cutblock—especially those with a high component of clay in the soil—into a hard shell that requires twice as much energy to plant.

As the contract wore on, there were times when I would pause in the middle of my day and lean on the end of my shovel, chest heaving and sweat gushing from every pore, and feel completely overwhelmed as I surveyed my land. My resolve to press on would waver. That was a new sensation for me. It felt as though I was pushing myself twice as hard as normal in order to make significantly less. It was a sobering and demoralizing reality. The fact that I was getting bogged down meant that everyone else was too, particularly those who lacked the experience and physical endurance to push themselves all day long. The atmosphere around our camp suffered greatly as a consequence. When the weather is good, the ground is fast, and people are making money, the air in the Quonset hut at dinnertime is energized, filled with laughter and animated conversation. There's nothing quite like it. When the crew struggles with seemingly non-stop hardship and adversity, with no financial recompense to ease the pain, the air inside the Quonset hut resembles that of a morgue.

Not everyone in camp was feeling beleaguered. We had an amazing new crew member named Margo. She was a dance student from Vancouver, a pretty young woman who always had a smile on her face and something positive to contribute to every conversation. And she always had something to contribute. Margo was *the* most garrulous individual I had ever met. If you engaged Margo in conversation, you had her absolute undivided attention, and in some cases, that was more than people could bear. Don't get me wrong, I loved Margo. Aside from having a smoking hot body, she was a fascinating study. I marvelled at her positive energy. Her ability to pull back the curtain of gloom that seemed to envelop every one of us, her assurance that brighter days lay dead ahead, was an enviable quality.

One historic day, during a vehicle breakdown, everyone piled out of their trucks and formed a giant circle to shoot the shit while repairs were being rendered. Margo, needing to pee like Sea Biscuit but not wanting to stray too far from the conversation, backed away just far enough from the circle, pulled down her pants and undies in a single motion, squatted, and let 'er rip. Unfortunately, she was slightly uphill from the rest of us, and within a few seconds, a powerful stream of urine breached our circle and began forming a series of pools around our feet. Stunned silence was immediately replaced by fits of laughter when someone blurted out, "Wow, Margo, that's quite the gusher." The name stuck, and from that point on, everyone in the company, and eventually everyone from companies all around the province, referred to Margo as "Gusher." Darren, the "Bone Crusher," found the whole peeing episode rather amusing, and before long, they were an item. Naturally, they became known as "Crusher and Gusher."

Crusher and Gusher occupied a tent in the heart of a small, tightly packed community near the edge of camp. While they were enjoying the honeymoon phase of their relationship, they apparently made a lot of noise, sometimes well into the wee hours of the morning. Their neighbours were mortified. People began arriving for breakfast later than usual showing obvious signs of sleep deprivation. They even approached me, asking if I could somehow intervene. I tried. I attempted to convince Crusher to move his tent to a more secluded location. When he refused, I begged him to consider turning the volume down on their late-night mating rituals. It was pointless. My consultations only seemed to strengthen Crusher and Gusher's resolve to explore the depths of their passion in the loudest manner possible. People had had enough. The small community pulled up stakes, seeking refuge among less dissolute neighbours.

A number of Crusher and Gusher's refugees found sanctuary in the suburbs, closer to my neighbourhood, a good kilometre away from the madness. Before long, my campsite became a popular meeting place in the evenings. My fires were easily spotted from the far end of camp. People began showing up on foot and on mountain bikes. On several occasions, they arrived by the truckload. It turned into a really nice social scene. People even showered and dressed for the occasion, the women arriving with their hair all done up, donning their favourite tunics, tight-fitting jeans and tees. The crew really needed this. It was a gruelling contract and we finally had a means to escape—a way to bond together as a group in order to keep our spirits up. And without Crusher and Gusher's frenzied courtship, our little social club would never have come together like this.

The evenings of our days off were high-spirited affairs, with upwards of twenty people making the journey from across the sand, bringing along liquid refreshments of all kinds, musical instruments, treats poached from the kitchen supply tent and, of course, copious amounts of weed. Due to our extreme physical exhaustion, these gatherings usually wound down around midnight, with only a few hardcore types hanging on past 1:00 a.m. It was during one of these late-night transition periods, when the crowd began to thin out and the atmosphere around the fire softened, that we experienced a violent rush of air directly above our heads, followed by a series of swirls and gushes as a large winged vertebrate retreated back into the dark. The nearest treeline was over three kilometres away. We puzzled over why a bird—likely a large bird of prey—would travel such a great distance to buzz our little gathering. Then a short while later it happened again, except this time it felt closer and more threatening. This second aerial assault caused us to lean way back into our seats and search the night sky, hoping to catch a glimpse of the winged intruder. Instead, our attention was drawn to the full-blown meteor event developing above us. This brought to mind the last time I took in a meteor shower. It was while camping at the Mesilinka River, nearly two years earlier, with my good friend Colette. The torrents of memory came rushing back, flooding my senses like a winter tide. I was feeling alone in the world all of a sudden. Wanting to heighten the intensity of the moment, I interrupted the normal path the weed took as it circulated around the fire, taking several puffs before sending it back on its normal track. The people who knew me were shocked at my sudden indulgence.

Though the possibility of a face full of talons kept us on edge, it was difficult not to be completely entranced by the balls of molten rock that crashed through the atmosphere, streaking across the sky in a series of flashes and sparks. The last log went on the fire at 3:00 a.m. I was soon fast asleep next to the coals under a thick quilt my mother had stitched for me. That was a good night. I woke up the next morning feeling more alive than I had in weeks.

AS THE CONTRACT STRETCHED OUT INTO THE LAST WEEK OF MAY, with little to no improvement in the ground conditions or earnings potential, we began to take out our frustrations on poor Ron. Based on the rate we were planting, we still had a minimum of two weeks remaining on the contract, and the days were getting longer and hotter. We hadn't seen a town in over two months. We wanted out. Ron, knowing a thing or two about keeping disgruntled crews in check, promised we would be compensated for our suffering, one way or another. Of course, it was no fault of Ron's that the ground conditions had deteriorated, or that we were wilting under the relentless late-spring heat, but we had collectively hit a wall. We were on the verge of breaking down physically and mentally. I lost over twenty pounds, which was excessive considering I had arrived at the beginning of the season already fit and lean.

It was during the second week of June that Ron received word that Barrett had pay dirt. It was the mother of all late-season scores. Barrett had been awarded a large contract and it was 100 per cent scarified ground.[1] Scarified ground is fast ground. Cream. Adding to the prize, the price per tree was to be an astounding 17¢, and the duration of the contract would be three whole weeks. The project was ours and ours alone—no other crew was invited. I knew that if I were firing on all cylinders, I would be planting a minimum of 2,500 trees per day. At 17¢ per tree, that meant that my daily earnings would skyrocket from $280 to $425 (the equivalent of $860 in 2019 terms). I'd be happier than a pig in shit, surrounded by an entire litter of similarly happy swine. This lit a fire under us. We managed to finish off the Williston Lake contract in nine days, rather than the projected fourteen.

The plan was to take a day off in town, rest, stock up on provisions and then meet the following day at a diner on the side of the highway outside of McLeod Lake. There, we would hook up with Ron and Barrett, have a quick meeting and then convoy out to the next contract, our sights set on cream and fat tree prices. I couldn't remember ever being so excited at the prospect of starting a new project.

When I arrived the following day for our scheduled rendezvous, I was shocked to see a large number of familiar-looking vehicles lined up in the parking lot next to the café. They belonged to Kelly's crew. When I opened the door to the restaurant, it was standing room only. Aside from Ron and the rest of my crew, Kelly was there with thirty of his guys. Barrett was running late and had yet to arrive. When I asked Kelly what was happening, the answer was not what I wanted to hear. As it turned out, this was not going to be the three-week-long cream-show we were hoping for. In my mind, it was about to become one giant clusterfuck, and I didn't want any part of it. It's simple arithmetic: when you double the size of a crew, you reduce the number of

---

1. Ground is considered "scarified" when a large earth-moving machine prepares it, pushing the debris into piles or rows, exposing the soil on the surface in the process. While it churns the decomposing litter layer on the surface into the soil below, it also creates an extremely fast planting medium for the treeplanter.

workdays by half. Our three weeks on the literal promised land was about to be sheared down to a mere ten days. I was livid!

I disappeared from the restaurant for twenty minutes, making use of my calling card at a pay phone on the side of the highway. When I re-entered the restaurant, I approached Ron. "I'm outta here."

In my whirlwind of phone calls, I discovered that Ryan had a large contract near Elko, close to the Roosville Canada-US border crossing in the East Kootenays. He was desperately looking for good planters. Though my experience with Ryan at Port Eliza fifteen months earlier was mixed, I really liked the guy, and by the sounds of things, he really needed my help.

I was careful not to make a scene. There was already a commotion brewing inside the tiny restaurant. I confided in only a tiny circle of friends about my plans. I didn't want my abrupt departure to trigger a mass exodus. Sometimes, that's all it takes to open up the flood gates— one key player walking away.

As I attempted to quietly slip away, Kyle, one of my closer friends on the crew, informed me that he and two others were planning to follow behind me. Just what I was afraid of. I rushed out of the café before anyone else could corner me, making my escape from the parking lot just as Barrett turned in off the highway.

The logging road leading up to Ryan's camp—a sharp turn off Highway 3 just south of the town of Elko—immediately began to climb in elevation. This steep trajectory continued for the better part of an hour, the road clinging to steep valley walls on one side and dropping down into an abyss on the other. Adding a degree of anxiety to the journey was the evidence of large-scale erosion. The entire area was unstable. Freshly dislodged rock littered the narrow road. A path just wide enough for a single vehicle to pass had been cleared. Just when I thought the road was about to level off, a new series of switchbacks would begin creating a relentless, seemingly endless ascent up the mountain. Finally the road plateaued and the steep valley walls dropped away to my left. It was there that the first few multicoloured nylon pup tents came into view.

As I drove slowly through the centre of camp, I was struck by how tightly people were packed together. Though space was at a premium— the valley walls continued to rise steeply above the road and drop off sharply below—there was more than enough room to spread out. I was puzzled. There's normally a very good reason when people choose to camp in such proximity to one another.

The atmosphere around camp was strained, subdued. I felt it the moment I stepped out of my vehicle. As I began my search for Ryan, I noticed that most of the tents around camp had bodies inside them. According to my intel, this was a workday, the contract only having begun one week earlier. It was the middle of the day and the majority of Ryan's crew appeared to be lounging in their tents. Something was amiss.

Poking around the various structures in camp, I saw a tall figure hunched over at the back of a trailer, busily stacking boxes. Ryan was startled when I called out his name. It was immediately apparent that he hadn't been in contact with his office. He had no idea that I was coming. There were no effusive hugs, handshakes or pleasantries, just a simple acknowledgement and an urgent wide-eyed query: "How many people did you bring?!"

He gave me a detailed account of what had unfolded prior to my arrival, events that were forcing him to seriously consider dropping the contract and walk away. Having abruptly walked on Barrett's contract and then travelling clear across the province to get here, I did not want to hear this at all.

The entire crew had contracted giardiasis, otherwise known as "beaver fever," caused by an intestinal parasite, *Giardia lamblia*, that colonizes and reproduces in the small intestine. Nearly everyone on his crew was down for the count.

The majority of Ryan's planters were experiencing symptoms that ran the gamut from general fatigue to vomiting. Their primary source of drinking water, a creek that ran through the centre of camp, was the culprit. After the crew began exhibiting symptoms, Ryan discovered a fresh deer kill upstream. It had been subjected to a feeding frenzy by a number of predators, their abundant feces obviously ground zero for the contamination. Fortunately, there were other sources of fast-running glacial runoff nearby.

Ryan was at his wit's end. I hated to see him like this. He was contemplating shutting the contract down, packing up and driving away. Not only did he have a camp full of sick kids to worry about, he had the logging company giving him the gears. They warned that if he couldn't ramp up his production to at least twenty thousand trees per day, immediately, they were going to pull his contract. He was currently producing only six thousand trees per day with his ailing crew of twenty planters. For a contractor, there are few scenarios worse than this. Though there were extenuating circumstances at play, getting shut down by a logging company is a humiliating experience, and word travels fast in treeplanting circles. Potential future clients and treeplanters alike tend to shy away from companies that suffer this humiliating fate. I know I steered clear of them.

I told Ryan that another two or three highballers were on their way. I also suggested that others could arrive by nightfall. Truthfully, I had no idea who would show up.

Shortly after I settled in, Kyle arrived. Shortly after Kyle arrived, Crusher arrived (without Gusher). And just before sunset, four more planters arrived from Barrett's crew. After sizing up the new arrivals, I told Ryan to expect a minimum of ten thousand trees out of our crew alone. He thought I was overly optimistic, especially since we weren't acclimated to the higher elevation (our camp was at an elevation of over twenty-five hundred metres—a number of our cutblocks were much higher). I insisted that if he motivated his sickly crew to produce ten thousand trees, we'd make up the balance. He needed twenty thousand trees to go into the ground the very next day—minimum.

That next day, despite the extreme elevation and challenging ground conditions—Ryan's cutblocks were overgrown with rhododendrons and were difficult to manoeuvre on—the seven of us managed to pound in an astonishing twelve thousand trees. As word spread around camp that the new arrivals had asserted themselves in such spectacular fashion, Ryan fielded nearly his entire crew the following morning. By the end of the shift, he was producing thirty thousand trees per day. Sometimes all it takes is a bunch of new kids showing up on the block to kickstart a crew. We discovered that the effects of beaver fever, though debilitating to a degree, were apparently not severe enough to shut these folks down completely. Some people could still function. It was possible to rise to the occasion and make a meaningful contribution.

I soon discovered the reason Ryan's crew had huddled their tents together so tightly. Two medium-sized grizzly bears—youngsters who had recently been given the boot by their mom—were making trouble in camp and on some of the nearby blocks. These bears, forced to survive on their own for the very first time in their lives, were looking for easy pickings. A treeplanting camp, with its abundance of aromas, was a tempting target for the hungry pair. The two had attempted several kitchen raids during the first few nights of the contract. Several treeplanters also reported encounters with the bears on the block, claiming that they exhibited stalking behaviours. There's nothing more disconcerting than a bear that won't turn tail and run when you confront it. Being stalked by twin grizzly bears...that's a different kettle of fish altogether.

There was a third unsettling element that infused the atmosphere around Ryan's camp with fear and anxiety. All around us, the unstable terrain was in a constant state of flux. While we lay in bed at night, it wasn't unusual to hear a rock slide somewhere off in the distance. Late one evening, a massive rock slide, emanating from an elevation much higher than our camp, came down with such force, it nearly shook us out of our sleeping bags. The accompanying boom and roar was every bit as deafening as a rolling prairie thunderhead. Its origin and path seemed so immediate that for several moments, I was convinced we were about to be crushed under millions of tons of rock. People emerged from their tents into the black of night in a state of panic and confusion, milling about aimlessly in their PJS and nightgowns, uncertain of their fate. The scene resembled an asylum break in a really bad B movie.

It took several minutes for the canyon to purge the fractured, weakened layers of rock along its steep walls. The roar eventually gave way to a muffled rumble, trailing off into a series of reverberations felt hundreds of metres below our camp. After everyone calmed down and retreated to the illusory safety of their nylon cocoons, gravity continued to play havoc with the residual rock on the freshly scarred landscape. Slides, albeit minor ones, continued throughout the night, the echoes of the cascading rock ricocheting up and down the canyon, making meaningful sleep nearly impossible.

I looked for evidence of the slide the next morning but couldn't locate its origin. The valley walls around us were so steep that gravity sucked the entire load of rock straight down into the abyss. Discussion at the breakfast table that morning was dominated by the tragedy that befell the town of Frank. In 1903, Canada's deadliest rock slide wiped out much of the small town, killing ninety people. Frank was a mere sixty kilometres away from us as the crow flies. Our collective anxiety ratcheted higher.

By the end of June, the contract was beginning to wind down, and despite the parasitic infestation, Ryan's company was firing on all cylinders. The mood around camp was as buoyant as could be expected. I had made the right move leaving Barrett's company when I did. Not only had I secured a satisfying amount of lucrative work, I helped Ryan pull one out of the fire. I owed him that. Earlier that spring, I had committed to working on one of his projects and then backed out at the very last minute. That was a shitty thing to do.

ON THE NIGHT BEFORE OUR FINAL SCHEDULED DAY OFF, AS I WAS relaxing outside the Quonset hut and sipping beer, a fellow named Nigel came over and tapped me on the shoulder. Nigel worked part-time with Search and Rescue. He brought his two work dogs to camp, a German shepherd named Char, and a black lab named Kora. They followed him everywhere, but at this moment they were nowhere in sight. I immediately sensed something was wrong, and when he asked me to follow him, I wasn't even remotely prepared for what he needed me to see. Both dogs, secured in the box of his truck, were riddled with porcupine quills around the mouth, throat and snout. Many of the quills were buried in their gums, noses and the roof of their mouths. Some appeared to be broken off below the surface of the surrounding tissue. Nigel asked if I knew what to do. We were at least three hours from the nearest vet, assuming one could be located at that late hour, and both dogs were in absolute agony.

I was puzzled by why Nigel had chosen to come to me in particular. But as luck would have it, I *did* have a few insights: I had once skimmed over a magazine article that was applicable. As a kid, I had a subscription to *Field & Stream* magazine. One memorable issue included a centrefold instructional guide explaining what to do in the event your pooch ever tangles with a porcupine. I had taken the time to scan the centrefold instructions, briefly, as any curious nine-year-old kid would. I caught the gist of what to do and somehow managed to retain that info. I recalled that the dog in the magazine had only a few quills protruding from its snout, though. Nigel's poor dogs had apparently tried to ravage the creature.

The first thing we needed was sedation. I ran back to my tent and grabbed the bottle of Valium my mother had sent along with me at the beginning of the season, for nights when sleep was elusive. My flurry of activity attracted attention, and by the time I arrived back at Nigel's truck, a half-dozen people were gathered around offering their help. While Nigel and I forced the dogs to swallow the tiny blue pills, not having a clue if Valium was even safe for dogs in the first place, I instructed everyone else to scour the camp for burlap sacks, rope, bungee cords and as many pairs of needle-nose pliers as they could find.

After twenty minutes, the sedative seemed to kick in. Both Char and Kora appeared somewhat calmer, less agitated. We carefully inserted each dog butt first into the burlap sacks, which were tripled up for strength. We pulled the material up to their napes, leaving only their heads and necks exposed. We then carefully tucked both their front and rear legs into their chests and began tightly binding their bodies with rope and bungee cords. The process was difficult and required the effort of a half-dozen people as the dogs struggled desperately to free themselves. The result, however, was two completely immobilized bundles with only the dogs' heads exposed. Onto the next step.

We worked on each dog for no more than ten minutes at a time, allowing them to rest and settle back down between extraction sessions. While several people balanced and secured the dogs on the tailgate of the truck, Nigel and I worked on pulling quills with hastily sterilized pliers, starting with the easiest extractions first, gradually working our way along the teeth, gums and snouts.

There are hundreds of tiny barbs located along the first four millimetres of a porcupine quill, so each one took a surprising amount of force to extract. The deeper they were buried, the more brute strength was required. The quills that were broken off and embedded below the surface of the skin or gum line were left until last. All the while, the poor dogs cried out in agony, eventually exhausting themselves, whimpering as they exhaled.

We managed to extract every last quill. The entire procedure took two hours from beginning to end. When we finally declared victory, people erupted in spontaneous applause. Hugs were exchanged, tears were shed, people were high-fiving and cans of beer were swapped. For my efforts, Nigel pressed a fat doobie into my palm, along with a beautiful Cuban cigar he had been saving for a special occasion. I gratefully accepted the gesture. I was looking forward to cutting loose after such a traumatic ordeal.

Later that evening, someone yelled out a warning that our two neighbourhood grizzly bears were lurking on the road just outside of camp. My tent was in the immediate vicinity of the sighting, but I was too amped up from dealing with Nigel's dogs to really care.

After chugging a couple of well-deserved beers and smoking my cigar halfway down, I asked my good buddy Kyle if he'd be interested in joining me back at my tent for a few puffs from the doobie Nigel laid on me. Kyle simply nodded, wide eyes, gaping smile.

What I wasn't aware of—something I wished I had known in advance—was that the weed circulating around Ryan's camp was from a rogue grow-op hidden somewhere in the deep recesses of the West Kootenays, near the town of Nelson, a region that would eventually become world-renowned for its high-potency bud. The spliff that I held in my hand had a THC component that was far more potent than anything available on the market at the time—that is how it was explained to me the next morning when I was seeking an explanation for the hallucinations.

As Kyle and I sat in my tent, with the door flaps tied wide open in order to fully appreciate the sun that was just beginning to set behind a snow-capped ridge, we sparked up the spliff and inhaled its toxic fumes. Still vibrating with excitement and a profound sense of accomplishment, I took one careless pull after another. And then something very strange began to occur: rather than the usual rush of excitement, elevated heart rate and fits of laughter, both Kyle and I stopped talking. Our expressions froze and we began furtively surveying our immediate surroundings. It didn't take long to realize we were in big trouble.

The last rays of the setting sun highlighted the anxiety written all over our faces. These last rays, which were fractured and splintered by a thin stand of conifers out in front of my tent, began to appear denser, more liquid-like. Before long they appeared to act as a conduit, transporting colours and shapes down from the sky, spilling them out onto a lush carpet of moss that encircled the entrance to my tent. Then, incredulously, I watched as the colours and shapes began to take form. They began to morph into cartoon characters that proceeded to march into my tent, right past Kyle, over my lap, and out through the meshed screened window behind my bed. It wasn't just one or two animated characters sauntering on through; it was an ensemble, a long procession of critters, saluting me as they filed past one by one. When I looked over at Kyle, I could see that he was fixated on something else entirely, something that was higher up in the trees but equally mesmerizing. It took a while before I was able to regain control of the speech centre in my brain, and when I finally did, blurting out something completely nonsensical, Kyle startled as if he had been zapped by an electric current. That was when the laughter kicked in as we both realized just how far outside of our comfort zone we had been transported. The laughter slowly helped us dial things back. We gradually latched back onto reality

After approximately one hour, the effects of the THC had largely worn off. We were in control of our faculties once again, able to examine our experience from a slightly less "animated" level. It was at this time, in the blackness of night, that we both heard a rustling sound coming from an area behind my tent—an area I couldn't see due to the scarcity of windows in my tent. When we heard a similar disturbance several minutes later, we both agreed that it had to be something large, perhaps an elk or a deer. I then remembered the grizzly sightings, the warnings that echoed across our camp only a few hours earlier. I was suddenly forced to shake off the haze, sharpen my senses and focus. As I pondered the potential aftermath of one or more hunger-crazed grizzlies shredding the walls of my tent and gaining entry, I reached for my 870 Wingmaster, a weapon I had slept with ever since my ordeal at Bute Inlet three years earlier. Pulling my shotgun out from under my foamy, I instructed Kyle to position himself up against the back wall of my tent with me, facing the ruckus emanating from the gloom outside. Incredibly, the threat began to escalate. A series of low-pitched growls was followed by the outline of a claw that began to scratch the side of my tent in one long downward motion, stretching the fabric to the point of tearing. Without hesitation, in a cold display of self-preservation, I savagely pumped my shotgun, clicked off my safety and was on the verge of unleashing a hail of unimaginable violence when I heard a voice suddenly cry out, "No, no, no—it's me—*it's only me!*"

With a lantern in hand, we ran outside and discovered my cousin, the Bone Crusher, lying on his back, staring blankly up into the night sky. He was hyperventilating.

It turned out that this was Crusher's idea of a practical joke. Apparently, he forgot that I slept with a cannon. Realistically, I was one exhalation away from blowing him in two. The damage my three-inch 00 buckshot would have inflicted upon his body, at close range, would have been catastrophic, unsurvivable.

I'm not sure how the local constabulary would have treated the crime scene. Any number of charges could have been laid against me. The one positive to come out of that whole ridiculous episode: Crusher appeared to have himself a little accident when he heard the pump on my shotgun.

ONE WEEK BEFORE THE CONTRACT ENDED, WHILE THE CREW WAS toiling away on the slopes, Ryan invited a group of government health officials up to visit our camp. Their inspection of Ryan's camp, which was a top-shelf facility by any measure at the time, formed the basis for a report and a subsequent list of recommendations that became mandatory protocol across the industry. A short while later, all treeplanting contractors were required to adhere to a strict set of guidelines regarding kitchen cleanliness, refrigeration, food handling, and safe drinking water for their employees.

Ryan's contract ended ahead of schedule. Everyone was happy, including the logging company. As we lined up for a payroll advance, Ryan furnished each one of us with a stool-sample kit. We were instructed to visit our family doctors immediately after arriving home and furnish them with a sample of our shit. If the samples revealed the presence of parasitic protozoa, we were to go on a regimen of medication that waged war on our gastrointestinal tract. I'll withhold the details on how that one played out for yours truly, but suffice to say, I endured only one dose of the medication before being rushed to the emergency room.

I had just a few weeks of vacation before my summer planting season began, and I spent it flat on my back, recuperating from that single dose of beaver fever medication.

SUMMER 1986 WAS EVENTFUL. WITHIN THE SPACE OF SEVEN WEEKS, I planted for seven different companies. It all began back where it first started for me, with what many considered to be *the* best treeplanting outfit in the entire universe: CRC Ltd. I was worried that I wouldn't be invited back after my abrupt departure earlier in the spring; I even heard a rumour that Barrett was forced to drop a large amount of work due to an exodus that he believed I had orchestrated. That was only a rumour, though, and Barrett welcomed me back with open arms.

Barrett had two projects lined up for that summer, one large, one small. I was offered a position on the smaller satellite project. It was too good to be true. We pitched our tents beside a fishing lodge along the shore of a picturesque lake. The lodge kitchen provided our meals. It was an intimate crew—a six-pack—equally divided between genders. We gelled together as a unit from the get-go. We were tight. We ate our meals together in the evening. We took group strolls along the lakeshore after dinner. We watched movies together in the lodge rec room at night. We genuinely enjoyed one another's company. There was also a fair amount of sexual tension among us. We were all single, all looking for experiences beyond the cutblock—all wanting to probe the depths of our new friendships. But somehow we managed to keep things platonic. It was almost as if no one was willing to risk damaging the wonderfully rare dynamic we had established as a planting unit. And this was one powerful crew. Though there were only six of us, we easily out-produced crews twice our number. When we hit a cutblock, we mowed it down with impressive speed and power. The forestry checkers, unable to keep pace with us, begged us to slow down on several occasions.

It was at this stage of my treeplanting career that I first began experimenting with a Sony Walkman. The Walkman destroyed my hearing, but my eclectic collection of mixtapes helped tack an additional 10 to 15 per cent onto my daily tree total. The only drawback: I was oblivious to every other sound around me. During the hot summer months, throughout the BC Interior, yellow jackets liked to make their ground nests in our fresh cutblocks. They excited easily, and if you ventured too close, their frenzied buzzing offered ample warning, allowing you to take evasive action before they swarmed you. With the volume on my Walkman cranked to the limit, unable to hear their agitation building, I was swarmed repeatedly. I lost count of the number of stings I received that summer. Not only did I get tagged planting too close to a ground nest, on several occasions I managed to step directly on top of one, completely oblivious to the rage percolating under my feet. My reaction, suddenly realizing that I had a dozen or more angry stinging insects crawling up the inside of my pant legs, generated tremendous entertainment value for those planting nearby.

Due to the speed and power of our little crew, our satellite project finished ahead of schedule. After a brainstorming session on the last day of the contract, we decided to try something none of us had ever attempted, or even entertained. Rather than work the phone and look for employment the traditional way, we planned to head down the highway, visit MOF offices, find the approximate locations of tree-planting companies who were active in the area, and simply show up unannounced. It was a bold plan.

After some research, we targeted a stretch of terrain off Highway 5 between the towns of Valemont and Clearwater, BC. The first tree-planting camp that we descended on was run by a company called MT Ltd. The man behind the company was a very cool fellow named Rock. Rock had a large crew already in place, but their planting average was quite poor at only seven hundred trees per day.[2] He blamed the weak production on a number of factors, including the oppressively hot

---

2. Crew average or planting average: this number is calculated by taking the total number of trees planted in a day and dividing it by the total number of planters on the

weather and ground conditions that were less than ideal. Rock was happy to have us.

Rock's crew appeared to have mixed emotions over our unannounced arrival, but I suspected there were some who welcomed the additional help, hoping we would bring an early end to their miserable summer season.

Our little crew hit Rock's ground hard that first day, causing our roadside caches to run out of seedlings on several occasions. By the end of the day our six-pack pounded in a total of fifteen thousand trees, compared to the seventeen thousand trees the balance of Rock's crew put into the ground—they were a crew of twenty-five! When word of our crazy numbers got out, there was a lot of talk behind our turned backs. Many among Rock's regular crew were convinced that we were stashers who had buried thousands of trees that day. They were convinced that planting in excess of two thousand trees per day, on that type of rough terrain, was a physical impossibility. I think even Rock had his suspicions, but he gave us the benefit of the doubt. The accusations were insulting, but we took them in stride.

The next day, I had a number of visitors in my area. We all did. There were several foremen, including Rock himself, who monitored our work closely. They stood off in the distance, often concealing themselves behind a stump or log, clocking our progress at regular intervals throughout the day. They used a standard test for determining the veracity of a highballer. They would count the number of trees planted within sixty seconds, and repeat that exercise several times over. If I was claiming a score at the end of an eight-hour day of 2,500 trees, I would need to be planting at least five trees every sixty seconds. But when you factor in time lost due to hiking back to the cache, bagging-up additional seedlings, and the occasional break, ideally they would want to see a minimum of six planted trees per minute. They clocked my

---

crew. Example: if a crew of twenty treeplanters plants twenty thousand trees in a day, their crew average is one thousand trees on that particular day.

progress at least a dozen times throughout that day to determine if the oppressive midday heat adversely impacted my pace. That day, our elite team of boys and girls managed to beat our previous day's number by one thousand trees, planting nearly sixteen thousand trees in total. Rock's entire crew was gobsmacked when he informed them, in no uncertain terms, that our six-pack was on the level, that we were the real deal. That event elevated our little crew to rock-star status. No one had ever seen anything quite like it. Even I was amazed at the energy I was able to generate that late in the season.

We hoped to get at least a week's worth of work out of that camp, but only managed to eke out five days. After Rock's contract ended, we heard rumour of a company working a large contract with a fair amount of fast ground operating near the town of Blue River.

By the time we left Rock's camp on the final day of his contract, it was too late to begin scouring unfamiliar logging roads for treeplanting camps—they can be elusive at the best of times. Deciding to make camp somewhere along Highway 5, we made our way toward Blue River in the dark of night. A few dozen kilometres ahead of us, a strange glow could be seen midway up a mountain, extending across its entire width. As we drew closer, the unmistakable smell of smoke began to permeate the air. The forest fire appeared to be completely out of control as it reached up for fresh fuel along the steep mountain wall. We decided to backtrack until the air became more breathable. We ended up pitching our tents on an open patch of sand next to the North Thompson River with the blaze on the mountain still within view.

One of the conversations around our campfire that night, initiated by the women, dwelled on how remarkable it was that no one on our tiny crew had hooked up yet, not even for a single night. That sounded like a dare if I had ever heard one.

I was especially fond of Joan, but I had no way of knowing if those feelings were mutual. She was a reserved, self-effacing Prairie girl who was quick to blush. While watching movies back at the fishing lodge weeks earlier, she'd leave her chair, flushed and self-conscious, whenever sex spilled over into a scene. She had an earthy quality that I found extremely attractive. She was also an incredible athlete on the slopes, possessing great agility and awe-inspiring speed. Joan was all business, unwilling to communicate—not even a cursory greeting with friends planting nearby. I really liked Joan, but I didn't know how to approach her. I suspected there was warmth and passion there, somewhere beneath her inscrutable exterior, but I didn't know how to tap into it. Our elite unit of (chaste) superheroes chose to remain celibate that night.

The next day, after searching a network of logging roads off Highway 5 for the better part of six hours, we finally homed in on our next target, halfway up a mountain tucked into the heart of a lush riparian zone. It was 7:30 p.m., well past the supper hour, and when we pulled into the staging area near the entrance to their main Quonset hut, a number of people emerged to check us out. Curious, wide-eyed glances quickly gave way, after a few hushed whispers, to a collection of cold, inhospitable stares. These people most certainly did not appreciate our presence. We needed to talk to their boss—a man named Kelvin. We had heard stories about this guy. He was supposed to be a character.

Unable to flank the bulletproof faces at the front of the dining tent, we decided to draw straws to determine who would push past the blockade and venture inside. I drew short straw, and after a few hard swallows, I jumped out of the truck and approached the mob with a loud and boisterous, "Howdy, boys!" It was easier than I thought to push past them and gain entry, but Kelvin was nowhere to be found. He appeared to really have his shit together, though—the inside of the Quonset hut was impressive, orderly. The shelves were stacked with the kinds of nosh you'd only find in the better camps. Even his dining room furniture was of the highest quality. At a table at the far end of the room sat a guy wearing headphones. He appeared to be doing paperwork. Tapping him on the shoulder and gauging his reaction, I instantly knew this wasn't our guy. His name was Marv, and he was an agriculture student that Kelvin had hired to help run the show. An agriculture student supervising a treeplanting crew. That was a first.

Climbing back into the truck, I could only report that my new farm friend Marv was under strict orders not to disturb Kelvin while he was taking his after-dinner nap. Marv did promise, however, that he'd talk to the head honcho the minute he emerged and let him know that we were seeking an audience. This is not what the crew wanted to hear. We were losing daylight and we needed to know if the welcome mat was out or if we should hit the road.

We decided to wait for Kelvin at the far end of the camp next to a creek. Stretching out on a bed of moss, we made light of our predicament. We broke out some food, a bottle of wine and had ourselves a little picnic. An entire hour went by and there was still no sign of Kelvin. Then, finally, Marv made an appearance and relayed a message that Kelvin would not be granting us an audience after all; that it would have to wait until the morning. Once again, this was not what we wanted to hear, but at least he didn't tell us to piss off.

Our little group of dynamos, humbled by the cold shoulder, set up camp on a grassy bank next to the creek. I decided to sleep in the front seat of the truck. Pitching a tent seemed like too much work, and besides, I wasn't even sure if we'd be invited to stay.

As I was getting myself prepared for bed, I was struck by the image in my side-view mirror of two lovely women wearing red tunics. As they drew closer, they appeared to be curious, perhaps wondering who the new people in town were. Walking past the front of my truck, they paused, glanced in and smiled warmly. My heart skipped a beat. I was in love—again. I was also intrigued when they joined hands shortly after our eyes met. As they disappeared into the forest along the creek, I had to rub my eyes. I wondered if they were even real.

It was nearly dark when my friends blew the candles out in their tents. It had been a long day. The season was getting long in the tooth. Getting comfortable, reclining and closing my eyes, I began to drift. Then, suddenly, there was a tap on the passenger-side window of my truck. Squinting, I discerned the outline of a man looking in. It was our guy. It was Kelvin. As he climbed into the passenger seat of my truck, I pretended I wasn't shocked by his late-evening attire. He was dressed in a white and black kimono, purple socks and a pair of fuzzy white slippers. He thought he saw a light on in my truck, he said, and decided to pay us a visit after all. What followed was not the type of conversation I had imagined us having. He didn't seem too impressed with my crew's resumé. He was far more intent on impressing me with how brilliant he was as a silviculture contractor. For two excruciating hours this went on; tale after tale proving how shrewd he was in the business, how adept he was at negotiating outrageously fat tree prices. I had never met anyone so intent on talking themselves up.

It was nearly midnight when Kelvin finally grew weary and announced he was off to bed. It was almost as an afterthought when he said, "Oh yeah—tell your crew breakfast is at six. The trucks leave for the slopes at seven sharp." This guy was too much.

Kelvin ran a tight show. He immediately recognized the strength in our crew and cut us loose, allowing us to carve off enormous chunks of land. Among the six of us, we laid claim to over twenty-five hectares of cream.

At about noon on that first day, I recognized two women who were working an area below me as the ladies in red who strolled by my truck the previous evening. They planted trees for a few minutes, and when they realized they had my attention, they removed their tie-dye tees and proceeded to plant topless. This wasn't a big deal. Many of the women I worked with enjoyed planting topless. It was a common sight back then. These two appeared to be doing it strictly for my benefit, though. Once again, I was intrigued.

In talking with one of Kelvin's regulars later that day, I discovered that these two women, Katera and Shyra, were members of the Rajneesh movement, a religious group led by a spiritual guru from India. Some, including my mother, would've immediately slapped the "cult" label on the Rajneesh. I didn't have any opinions at the time, but Katera and Shyra were making a bit of an impression on me.

After dinner that night, I set up my tent in a secluded area near a bend in the creek, a good one hundred and fifty metres away from my closest neighbour. Even though our anticipated stay was a short one, perhaps three or four days, I decided to build a firepit. I wanted a nice warm glow to relax by in the evening. Everyone else on my crew decided to retire early that night. We were all at that stage in the season where sleep took priority over everything else. Nearly everything else.

As I was throwing a final load of wood on the fire, I caught a glimpse of the two Rajneesh women walking along the road. When they paused at my truck and peered through the trees, spotting me and my picturesque little campsite, I pretended not to notice them. I wasn't sure if I'd be comfortable with their company. I was a little wary of their whole freedom thing; that and the alternative values that they likely embraced. But before I could slip away into the security of my tent, they strolled into my campsite and introduced themselves.

Katera broke the ice. She was of medium height with a lean frame. She had extremely short brown hair as if she had shaved her head only a month earlier, and it was just beginning to grow back in. Even with her brush cut, she was an extraordinarily beautiful woman. She had a number of piercings, including one in her nose, and a good many bracelets that she proudly displayed around her wrists and ankles. She carried herself with a certain authority, which I must confess, I found slightly intimidating (I was raised by powerful women). She also had an unadorned, matter-of-fact manner of talking, as if she had all the answers, or that she'd heard it all before. Though I felt somewhat uneasy around her, I was also curious—I sensed a slight air of vulnerability whenever our eyes met.

Shyra was tall with wide hips and a slightly plump frame. Her long dark-brown hair, still damp from having showered earlier, was swept over to one side. She had a pretty face. I was especially fond of her profile, which for some mysterious reason completely altered my first impression of her. Shyra wasn't nearly as poised as her friend. She spoke in soft tones. I had to chuckle when she whispered into her friend's ear, expecting Katera to articulate her thoughts.

I began to feel a strange calm sweep over me, something I don't often experience in the company of strangers. Riding the unexpected wave of cool composure, I offered to fetch them a blanket to sit down on next to the fire. Gazing at one another and smiling, they both nodded.

As a slight chill developed in the air, and as the girls began to cuddle, I naively asked if they'd like me to fetch them another blanket. Chuckling at my suggestion, Shyra whispered something into her friend's ear, causing Katera to look down at the ground, as if she needed time to think. Then, slowly raising her head to engage me, she said, almost impassively, "Shyra thinks you're beautiful."

Both women studied my reaction intently as I searched for a response—any response. But before I could speak, they rose and walked over to my side of the fire, Katera settling in close behind me while Shyra kneeled down in front. Katera asked me to close my eyes as she began rubbing my shoulders and neck. I felt compelled to play along. With my eyes closed, Shyra took both of my hands into hers and laced our fingers together. She then began massaging my palms and the back of each hand, taking care to work each individual finger. The scent of lavender and patchouli permeated the air around us. Then, unexpectedly, shockingly, I felt Katera's lips on the back of my neck. She paused briefly to whisper into my ear, "Your hands, use them to explore Shyra's face." I complied once again, inwardly marvelling at how wonderful and natural the entire exercise felt. I imagined myself blind as I reached up and began exploring the soft contours of Shyra's forehead, cheekbones and chin. I then used the tips of my fingers to delicately trace the outline of her eyes, nose and lips. As I ran my fingers down the side of her temples and behind her ears, I detected a faint gasp. Next, I could sense Shyra's sweet breath as she slowly began to lean forward. She then began kissing the front of my shoulders, working her way up along my neck and chin, eventually settling on my lips. The sensations were exquisite. I then sensed both women in motion around me and a different set of lips on mine. They continued to switch positions, rotating around me, taking turns kissing my lips, then the back of my neck, ears and shoulders. As I began to lose track of who I was kissing, both girls suddenly stood up, each taking me by the hand, pulling me forward. When they finally allowed me to open my eyes, both women had managed to completely disrobe, their discarded tunics lying in clumps on the blanket next to the fire. I was being led to the entrance of my tent by two of the strangest, most beautiful and alluring women I had ever laid eyes on.

I was brought up in a fairly strict and conservative household. I was taught from a very early age not to engage in any activity, sexual or otherwise, that was not becoming of a true gentleman. Further, I was taught never to entertain or even fantasize about engaging in any such activity. I was *not* the kind of guy who spent the night with two women at the same time. But these two had a way of disarming every inhibition that, until then, had kept my reasonably strict value system in check. This was one of the most erotic experiences of my entire life. It was also one of the most profound and liberating experiences of my entire life, but I knew then, deep down, that this sort of encounter would never happen again. Ever.

The next evening it happened again. On the third night a similar scenario played out, but it ended with me waking up at the other side of camp the following morning, in Shyra and Katera's tent.

My treeplanting production took a hit over the remainder of the contract as I wasn't getting nearly the amount of sleep required to maintain an aggressive planting pace. The crew I had been travelling with were disappointed that I had suddenly abandoned them in the evenings, but they knew what was going on. The entire camp had to know what was going on, judging by the cold shoulders and disdainful looks I encountered. My status as a highballer was at risk, but the trade-off was acceptable—I had made two very good friends.

On the evening before the final planting day of the contract, Shyra informed me that Katera had an upset stomach from something she had eaten at supper, had thrown up several times, and was resting in bed back at their tent. She told me that if Katera was feeling better later on that evening, they'd both come over and sit with me around my fire. Before I could express my genuine concern, Shyra kissed me on the chin and quickly retreated back in the direction of her tent. That was the last time I saw either one of them.

The next morning, there was a small red silk scarf, carefully knotted at the top with teal-coloured ribbon, dangling from a branch out in front of my tent. Inside the scarf were two small pieces of quartz the girls had found at the top of their area a few days earlier, quartz crystals that they excitedly revealed to everyone in the truck on the way home from work that day. When I walked to the other end of our camp, their tent and vw van were gone. No one talked to them before they left. No one saw them leave. They exited my world as mysteriously as they had entered it. I still wonder if they were even real.

Our group of highballers broke up at the end of Kelvin's contract. We all went our separate ways. It had been a long season. Some of us had been planting since early February and the last day of summer was fast approaching.

At the tail end of my season of guest planting and contract hopping, I hooked up with several other companies in the southern part of the province, a few days of planting here, a few there. My final adventure that year was with an Alberta company, along the remote banks of the Wandering River in Athabasca County. Once again, it was like entering the Dark Ages. Shortly after arriving, I decided to leave when I discovered that our only source of drinking water was the Wandering River itself—untreated, warm and slightly milky. I had learned my lesson from drinking untreated water. I walked without planting a single tree. My season was done.

By the fall of 1986, with four full seasons in my rear view mirror, I came to the realization that this career path I had chosen, this lifestyle I had embraced, offered far more than mere financial reward. It opened the door to a world that very few people, especially those who work behind a desk, ever get the chance to experience. Shit tends to happen, with the craziest of frequency when you place yourself in the path of a tribe of roaming treeplanters. The adventure never plays out the same way twice. You come together in the middle of some of the most remote and pristine wilderness on the planet, and once there, you live, work and experience things that will entertain your thoughts and haunt your memories for the rest of your days.

# CHAPTER NINE

# THE PROMOTION

||||||||||||||||||||||||||||||||||||||||||||||||||||||||||||||||||||||

THE LIFE. A TREEPLANTER'S LIFE. I ONCE OVERHEARD MY SISTER describe it to a friend as a "dog's life"—dirty, punishing, unrelenting. I suppose there's an element of truth to that, especially today, in a culture where the vast majority our needs can met without ever having to leave the security of one's living room. But for me, The Life opened the door to a world that is concealed to most; a boundless universe of beauty, complexity, mystery, subtlety. I loved the sensations I experienced standing alone on the side of a mountain, in the evening, with no one around for miles in all directions. I struggle for the words to describe the stillness and quiet I encountered in these moments—a calm, interrupted only by my own careful and measured movements across the slope, or by the vibrations of nature itself.

The life I had come to know as a simple treeplanter changed dramatically over the course of my fifth season in the treeplanting arena. Those moments of stillness and quiet reflection, those opportunities for spiritual and cognitive growth, were unceremoniously brushed aside in order to make room for more pressing matters. I suddenly found myself engaged in a challenge that was full-on, all hurried, all urgent, all stress, all the time. Management.

In 1986 there was a big shakeup in the silviculture arena. The federal government discovered a massive backlog of unplanted cutblocks across the province of BC. They, along with their provincial counterparts, threw unprecedented sums of money at dealing with the backlog. It meant that a lot more trees were about to go into the ground. In 1987 it also became mandatory for logging companies to replant 100 per cent of the forests they cut down, rather than the 20 per cent they held themselves accountable to previously. If that wasn't enough to goose the industry, that period also witnessed a sharp acceleration in logging. All of these combined factors forced a dramatic and rapid expansion within the silviculture industry.

The fall of 1986 presented an extraordinary opportunity for BC treeplanting contractors. Companies grew exponentially overnight. Companies that, until then, had operated with barely a six-pack or two expanded to a half-dozen crews. Companies that had operated with only thirty planters expanded their workforce to a hundred or more. Companies that were already large to begin with became monsters. And curiously, employees who were mere treeplanters only one year earlier—kids, basically—were suddenly thrown into high-stress management positions. That was where I came in.

When I arrived back home in Calgary in the late summer of 1986, after a rather remarkable series of adventures on and off the cutblock, I had a stack of messages waiting for me. They were all from Barrett. He was expanding CRC Ltd. big-time. He wanted me involved. He wanted me to run a large training crew of university students the very next spring. Preparations had to be made. There were a number of needs: land needed to be viewed, bids needed to be submitted, university students needed to be interviewed and Barrett needed to know if I was willing to rise to the occasion. How could I say no?

Within forty-eight hours, I was on my way to Vancouver to meet with Barrett and his inner circle of foremen and advisors. Our strategy was simple: throw bids at everything we could lay our eyes on in the

Prince George–Mackenzie region. With that basic strategy in mind, we hopped in our trucks and made a beeline for the Interior and boarding the Prince George viewing train.

After several months and thousands of kilometres of logging roads—not to mention countless greasy spoons, seedy motels and bid forms—Barrett's company managed to secure a formidable amount of work for the 1987 spring season. Dozens of additional experienced treeplanters were hired, and dozens more rookies were recruited off campuses. This was repeated across the entire sector for what promised to be the greatest silviculture clusterfuck in BC history. If things played out according to plan, certain contractors were destined to become very, very rich. Of course expanding one's company exponentially overnight can result in many unintended consequences. Murphy's Law can be a bitch.

I didn't have much control over the actual hiring of my rookie crew. I merely visited a number of campuses in BC and Alberta, conducted interviews, took notes and then passed along recommendations to Barrett and his office staff. When I travelled to Prince George in April of 1987, all I knew was that thirty-four students would be awaiting my arrival at the Nechako Inn. From there I was to escort them to a logging camp near McLeod Lake and begin moulding them into a competent planting unit. I was given three weeks to accomplish this daunting task. Barrett assured me that the training ground would be very accommodating for a rookie crew: flat, clean, lots of soil, easy to plant.

Teaching rookies how to plant trees was only one of the challenges I faced that spring. The McLeod Lake contract was like any other contract. My plantations would be rigorously inspected and audited by company checkers. There would be no leniency for my rookie crew. No kid gloves. I was expected to whip these kids into shape and nix any bad habits before they could develop into quality or excess fines. The pressure I felt rolling into the Nechako Inn parking lot that day was enormous. I did have help though: Wes, a competent planter and foreman, would be helping me out for the first half of the project.

When I arrived at the Nechako Inn to greet my rookies, I discovered that only a handful of the students I interviewed earlier in the year had made the final cut. They were strangers to me for the most part, but my first impression was very positive. Everyone appeared to be in high spirits, and they all appeared to be in good physical condition. Barrett had also hired a decent number of women. Aside from my thirty rookies, Barrett sent along two experienced highballers to serve as role models: Shiori and Cindy. I had worked with these women in the past and they were both gifted planters.

Being a young single guy, at the height of my various appetites, I fell in love three or four times over within the first few minutes of meeting the crew. But my assignment was more important than any other consideration. In the weeks prior to embarking on this adventure, I'd spent many sleepless nights lying in bed, staring up at the ceiling, wondering if I had the capacity to lead people. I was determined to stay 100 per cent focused, or at least somewhere in the mid -80 per cent range.

After transporting the crew to the logging camp and getting them settled, it was time to attend my first meeting with the logging company officials who awarded us the contract. This can be an intimidating experience, especially for a rookie foreman. I was immediately put at ease, though—these were very sensible, down-to-earth people. Also, the checker in charge of overseeing the project pointed out one of the women on my crew as his cousin. I wasn't sure if this had been a strategic hire by Barrett, but I suspected so. And what a brilliant hire it was.

Running a training crew came naturally to me. I found myself able to break down and articulate every aspect of the treeplanting process, including strategies to stay motivated. By day two, all thirty rookies seemed to be well on their way. By the end of day four, with nearly everyone showing natural ability and steady progress, we were ready for a day off.

There was girl on the crew who was the object of intense scrutiny and speculation during that first shift. Her name was Joanne. Hers was the tiniest frame I had ever witnessed donning a set of treeplanting bags. She had an air of calm about her—some mistook it for diffidence. At the end of the second day, I was horrified when she revealed severe blisters over both of her feet and ankles, a consequence of breaking in new hiking boots on broken terrain. I was shocked that she was still able to walk, let alone hit the slopes the next day. She pressed on. She ignored what must have been unimaginable pain and continued to keep pace with the rest of the crew. Some people were convinced that it was just a matter of time before she dropped out. She did no such thing. At the beginning of the second shift of the contract, I spotted her walking off her area, standing on the road next to her tree cache, hand on hip, feigning impatience. She proudly presented the land behind her with a sweep of the hand, declaring, "I'm done this bitch—what's next?" I had given her an area that should have kept her busy all day—she finished it in only a few hours. Never underestimate the ability of people to prove you wrong. Joanne was on track to plant one thousand trees by the end of the second shift. She was outpacing everyone, including two triathletes on the crew, by a very healthy margin. She became my top rookie planter. She was determined to achieve highballer status by the end of the season.

At the end of the second shift, the trucks were idling, pointed in the direction of town. The crew craved city lights, and they wanted to head in directly after supper. I was more than willing to oblige. When we landed at the Nechako Inn in Prince George later that evening, we discovered that the motel was overrun with treeplanters and that they were light on rooms. The crew was forced to triple up. Melanie, a lifeguard and university student I had become good friends with over the previous two shifts, proposed that she and I share a small room. Melanie was a tall, lean woman with short brown hair and beautiful blue eyes. She was an athlete, a beach volleyball champ who would have made it to the big time had the IOC recognized it as an official Olympic sport back then. She had a lot of attitude, a lot of moxie. She was a large presence on the crew, but she could also be very gentle and attentive.

I watched her take time out of her day to console another planter who had taken a hard fall and suffered a bruised hip. It struck me what an amazing mom she would make someday.

Trying not to read too much into Melanie's proposition, I checked in and tossed her a room key. She wanted to go blow off some steam with the rest of the crew that night. The only thing I could envision for the rest of my evening was falling into bed and not surfacing until checkout time the next day.

The crew was off to the Midnight Express, a polished dance club in downtown Prince George, but Joanne and few of her friends were the holdouts. They weren't into the dance club scene, not that evening anyway. Instead, they convinced me to hang out with them at a local pizzeria, where I regaled them with tales from a grizzly corridor. We were back at the Nechako Inn by 8:00 p.m. I was tucked in and sawing logs by 8:05.

I didn't hear the door open later that night. I didn't even feel her climb into my bed, but at 2:00 a.m., I woke up with a naked female body next to mine. Melanie, laying her head on the pillow next to mine, only an inch from my face, whispered, "Hi-ya boss."

Prior to the start of the season, I vowed not to get involved with anyone on the rookie crew. Aside from the poor optics, I didn't think I could handle the distraction. Of course, being a typical, weak-willed male, I'm somewhat pathetic when it comes to women. I'm pretty much at their mercy 100 per cent of the time. I think Melanie sensed those qualities in me and decided to take advantage. I was grateful she did.

TOWARD THE END OF THE MCLEOD LAKE CONTRACT, WANTING Melanie to experience the atmosphere of the cutblock in the evening when no one else was around, I asked her to join me during one of my nightly tree-runs.[1] After I'd distributed my truckload of trees among

1. A nightly "tree-run" is an exercise where a foreman loads a truck with boxes of seedlings, delivers them to the cutblock and distributes them to the various roadside

the individual caches along the road, I cut the engine and asked her to go for a walk to the end of the block with me. Melanie immediately understood the significance of the ritual. The cutblock, bustling with activity only hours earlier, took on an indefinable, eerie quality that evening. She almost didn't recognize the area she had been toiling away in earlier that day through the filtered evening light. She began to notice things for the first time, like the strange features along the tree-line that defined the limits of her area. There were several snags along the forest edge—at the very top of her piece—that towered over every-thing else for hundreds of metres around. And perched on a branch at the top of the tallest snag: a beautiful broad-winged hawk, scanning the surface of the ground below, looking for movement among the for-est of seedlings Melanie had planted only hours earlier. She squeezed my hand several times as we silently took it all in.

As the McLeod Lake contract drew to a close, some three and a half weeks into the season, every single rookie who had shown up at the beginning was still hanging on. I had never heard of a training crew holding together like this, not without coughing up at least one victim. The norm would have been a 15-20 per cent attrition rate. This was a testament to Barrett's ability to spot latent talent. Not only had we churned out a very decent crop of new planters, we scored 100 per cent payment across the entire McLeod Lake contract—a feat that no one expected, especially Barrett. I was feeling rather pleased with myself. It went straight to my head.

The next project for the rookie crew was halfway up the isolated western shore of Williston Lake. My co-manager on the rookie project, Wes, went ahead one week earlier to get things started with another crew. To gear up for this contract, we first travelled to Prince George and swapped out our trucks for two small buses. Each bus was capable of carrying twenty people and gear. It being a transition period for all of us, I was desperate to blow off a bit of steam as I had been working

---

caches from which they'll be drawn the next day.

non-stop for the better part of a month, attempting to keep pace with a large crew that was growing stronger by the day. Aside from the relentless pace during the day, my evenings, beginning from the time we returned to camp, were an endless series of Q and A sessions. Everyone seemed to have issues, concerns or complaints. Sometimes it was advice or guidance people were seeking. Sometimes they just wanted attention, they just wanted to yak with the foreman. It was impossible to sit down at dinner without being mobbed by a pack of wide-eyed kids, all looking to get something off their chest. I wasn't used to this kind of attention. I was exhausted.

I was looking for an opportunity to cut loose—to become one of the guys again—even if for just a few hours. I found that opportunity in the six-hour drive up to Williston Lake. That morning, we were joined by Terry, another rookie foreman who would help me run things on the next contract. I knew Terry. I trusted him. Taking pity, after enduring a litany of moans and groans about my lack of R and R, he offered to take complete responsibility for leading both buses to the next project. He insisted that I kick back and relax for the entire six-hour journey. I accepted the offer. I think I even welcomed it with a big fat hug.

My only concern at the time was the possibility of getting lost. The complex road network along the west shore of the lake could be extremely confusing at the best of times. Taking a wrong turn, getting lost and running out of gas in the middle of nowhere with thirty rookies in tow—that would be an unqualified disaster. Terry assured me that he knew the road leading in like the back of his hand. I put my faith in him. I was thrilled at the prospect of cutting loose for a few hours, and on that cue, I bought myself a big bottle of tequila for the numerous pit stops we planned to make along the way.

The first leg of our journey was wonderful. It was a beautiful spring day and industrial traffic on the mainline was non-existent. Terry was driving the first bus, leading the way in, with my friend Les at the wheel of the second bus following up behind. Les was a gentle giant, proudly standing six foot seven. He was what I called a "balancer," someone who managed to get along with everyone. There was a quiet confidence about him. A non-smoker and non-drinker, he was a man with a rigid moral compass. He was also a man who craved any added responsibility I could throw at him. He happily assumed control of the second bus that day. I was one of his many giddy passengers. We had our stereo volume cranked to the maximum during the journey, and whenever a particularly danceable tune came on, Les would lay on the horn, bringing both vehicles to an abrupt halt in the middle of the BCFP mainline. Within seconds, everyone on board both buses would spill out into the middle of the road and dance. It was the damnedest thing I'd ever seen! And of course, the beer, tequila and other hard stuff would flow. We repeated this exercise more times than I can recall. The only rule I insisted on, one that Les and Terry enforced with a watchful eye, was that there was to be no drinking on the bus while we were in motion. This, of course, necessitated an inordinate number of stops along the way.

Approximately four hours into our journey, my memory becomes a bit hazy. I remember both buses coming to rest at the edge of a small lake. I remember Melanie sitting on my lap. I recall jumping out of the bus and dancing to "She Sells Sanctuary" by The Cult, a popular band at the time. I remember chatting with our mutual friend Stacy, who was consuming alcohol at a much faster rate than I. Stacy was a law student from Vancouver. She was outgoing, beautiful and impossibly voluptuous. We all knew that she was destined to become a great litigator some day. Her intellect and authority caused many of us to sit up straight, at full attention, whenever she opined on a subject. I was attracted to Stacy. I was in awe of her. She reminded me of a great love I once had, a love lost during my first season of planting trees with Barrett's company.

I have a vague recollection of sharing my bottle of tequila with Stacy. Beyond that, I'm at a complete loss. Melanie reluctantly helped fill in the blanks the next day. Apparently, after shooting back a crazy amount of blue agave, fingers entwined, Stacy and I snuck to the back of the bus and began making out with such intensity, people were considering throwing cold water on us.

When I woke up early the next morning, stretched out across the back seat of the bus, I discovered that twelve full hours were missing from my memory. It was twilight. The sun was just beginning to rise. When I looked around, the bus was completely empty. I was the only passenger on board. As I staggered toward the front of the bus, squinting, attempting to make sense of the situation, I slowly began to piece things together.

On the side of the road, spread out along a grassy bank on the opposite side of the ditch: two dozen treeplanters sprawled out in sleeping bags. They were arranged side by side. They were fast asleep. It was a surreal and disturbing image. It resembled a scene from the Jonestown massacre. As I stumbled out onto the hard gravel, rattled, head pounding and thirsty unlike anything I had ever experienced in my entire life, I spotted the second bus parked farther up the road. Another dozen or so people were passed out along the ditch next to it. Terry had lost his way and driven the buses until they completely ran out of gas. My worst nightmare had become reality.

It was an extraordinary scene: the sun rising amid a cloudless sky in the middle of a great northern forest, two buses broken down on the side of an isolated logging road, three dozen weary treeplanters wrapped like mummies in sleeping bags highlighting every synthetic colour ever conceived (from salsa-red to gemini-green) strewn out across a lush, grassy embankment, and a wild-eyed rookie foreman, stumbling and staggering along the edge of the road, unable to comprehend the carnage laid out before him. It is not a fond memory. It is, however, an indelible one.

Melanie was the first to wake up. She acknowledged my presence but refused to talk to me. Terry woke up next, shaking his head repeatedly in disbelief. This was a major fuck-up. It was a complete and utter disaster. Barrett was expecting us to arrive the previous night. We were scheduled to begin work that very morning. Three dozen plant-ers sidelined along with their two hapless foremen meant Barrett was losing a significant number of production hours. I knew he would be furious. I certainly would've been. I immediately understood that I had no choice but to take full responsibility. I had visions of Barrett pointing me in the direction of the highway. Again. This was not my finest hour.

We were discovered later that morning by Barrett himself, who must have used some sort of psychic ability to track us down. He didn't appear to be overly upset by my screw-up. He actually made light of the entire situation as we began refuelling both buses with jerry cans he had loaded in the back of his truck. I could sense his disappointment, though.

Things went downhill dramatically from that point on. One of our buses had apparently bottomed out on a rough patch of road while it was being driven aimlessly into the night. It had developed a slow leak in the oil pan. The very next day, driving back from work, the engine seized and the bus ground to a screeching halt. It was a complete write-off and the tow bill alone cost Barrett $1,500. That was a fence that couldn't be mended.

My relationship with Melanie was not an easy mend either.

Melanie was forced to leave halfway through the Williston Lake contract. She was competing in a nationwide lifeguard competition, an event that she and her crew were favoured to win. I drove her into Prince George on a day off, three days before her crew was scheduled to compete. It was difficult watching the taillights of her bus disappear below the highway.

Things went from bad to worse during the final project of the 1987 spring season. This last one was run out of a tiny resource-based com-munity in northern BC. It was a contract that I'd viewed myself, but when I travelled there the previous fall, recent flooding had washed out a number of the roads in the area. Access into many of the indi-vidual cutblocks was destroyed. I hadn't been able to view 90 per cent of the project. I had no way of determining how good or bad—how fast or slow—the terrain was. I recommended an outrageously high bid price in order to compensate for the elevated uncertainty and risk, but the forester in charge of the project managed to convince Barrett it wasn't nearly as challenging as my notes suggested. It was. In fact, it was worse. Much worse. This is something a contractor sometimes faces in this sector—unscrupulous foresters who will say anything to elicit the cheapest bid possible. Financially, I suspect Barrett had his head handed to him on that one.

I was forced to share the responsibility of running the final project with another supervisor, one who resented my presence there. We fought constantly for control. The conflict led to broken lines of communication and a poorly run campaign. I was embarrassed by my behaviour, but in my defence, I was forced to work with a real tool.

Adding to the negative atmosphere around camp, we heard rumours that a pair of escaped convicts were hiding out in the area. Worse than that—much worse—we were forced to deal with an extremely edgy black bear population. Severe dry conditions throughout the spring had placed enormous stress on wild edibles, making it difficult for bears to find sufficient nutrition. Most of the black bears I encountered had protruding rib cages. They were hungry, disoriented and altogether unpredictable. On one occasion, while I was delivering trees to a cutblock on my quad, I crested a steep hill and spotted a large, malnourished black bear standing in the washout at the bottom of the road. Normally the sight and sound of a large quad would be enough to scare the wits out of any bear, causing it to turn tail and run. Not this guy. As I descended the slope toward him he actually turned and confronted me. Unable to stop, let alone jam the machine into reverse due to my heavy load and momentum, I was forced to swerve dangerously around the bear to avoid hitting it, nearly flipping my quad in the process. I barely managed to maintain my balance. It was a good thing I did. The bear chased after me, forcing me to push a box of seedlings off of the back of my quad in an effort to distract it. It worked. I was able make my escape unscathed.

When I returned an hour later the bear was gone, but it had completely ravaged the box of trees I had put in its way. As I was cleaning up the mess, two company checkers arrived on foot, and despite my explanation for the hundreds of seedlings that lay half eaten and scattered about, they fined me $250. The official explanation: "poor stock handling"!

That final contract of the 1987 spring season sucked the spirit out of me, and as it wound down, I was forced to make a difficult decision. That proved to be my final chapter with Barrett's company. I cut myself loose and never returned.

# STARTING OVER

||||||||||||||||||||||||||||||||||||||||||||||||||||||||||||||||||||||||

THE PHONE CALL USUALLY COMES JUST AFTER CHRISTMAS, OR EARLY in the new year. It's a heads-up, a wake-up call for the season that is fast approaching—a season that could begin as early as February. By the end of the phone call, with an actual start date to work with, that feeling begins to sink in: the realization that your days of freedom are drawing to a close.

Start dates are often meaningless this early in the season, though. You could be delayed at least a week or two by a cold front meeting precipitation over the coast, causing the snowline to drop, sometimes significantly. It's impossible to plant trees when there's snow covering the ground. These delays are often met with sighs of relief by those who aren't quite ready to face the harsh reality of the BC coast in early February (the coastal region of British Columbia is the only place in Canada you'll find treeplanters working in the winter months). The prospect of rainy, windswept slopes can be extremely daunting for those of us who prefer warm jammies to sweat-soaked rain gear. For some, an early season delay feels like a stay of execution. When that inevitable confirmation call finally does come, the one that declares "It's go time," you normally have two or three days to get your sorry ass in gear.

During the off-season, I hooked up with a company based in the Slocan Valley in the West Kootenay region of BC. EG Ltd. had a good reputation, and they promised me as much work as I could handle.

It was the first week of February in 1988 when I received that confirmation call. Two days later I hopped a bus bound for Port McNeill on the north end of Vancouver Island. It promised to be a long and taxing journey westward. I started feeling homesick the moment my gear was tucked in under the bus's belly. As we pushed past the Calgary city limits toward a wall of mountains that appeared to want to block my advance farther west, I pondered the prospect of five months away from home—five long months working with a crew I had never met, in a region I was completely unfamiliar with. I felt lonely, isolated, adrift. I had left Barrett's company only months earlier, and it felt like I was starting from scratch, forced to demonstrate my mettle and prove myself to a group of complete strangers. As always, this bounty of negative emotions one entertains at the beginning of every treeplanting season coalesces with positive memories from seasons past, forming one big twisted ball of schizophrenia, a condition that always manages to unravel after the first day of planting is in the rear-view mirror.

The twenty-eight-hour bus ride up to the north end of Vancouver Island gave me plenty of time to reflect upon my experiences from the previous season. Shortly after the debacle with Barrett's company, I had taken a gamble on yet another Alberta company, this time in the Red Earth Creek area in the northern part of the province. Somehow I endured three whole weeks of their unique version of "The Life" before walking away. Having witnessed yet another reckless attempt to store meat and perishable goods in a pit dug into the midsummer mud, I limited my carnivorous appetites to seven days, after which I once again became a strict vegetarian. Three days after I made the conversion, half the crew came down with severe food poisoning, the aftermath of which I only wished I could have un-seen. It began with a suspicious assortment of meat chunks laid out on the breakfast counter early one morning. It ended with a dozen people who were barely able to crawl out of their sleeping bags, emptying the contents of their stomachs and bowels onto the ground just a few feet from the entrance to their tents later that night. As I was forced to make wider and wider detours around the worst-hit areas of camp, "Never again," I decided. Never again would I indulge another Alberta-based company.

The ferry crossing over the Strait of Georgia from Horseshoe Bay to Nanaimo probably should have been cancelled that day. Massive storm swells made the journey unbearable. Everyone on board planted themselves firmly in their seats on the passenger deck to ride out the storm. Normally a storm of that magnitude would perk up my ears and get the juices flowing. Not that day. I knew that in less than forty-eight hours I'd be donning full rain gear, getting pummelled by the elements while attempting to traverse steep coastal terrain. I tried not to think about the weight of the seedlings on my shoulders and hips, the weight I'd be forced to bear as horizontal sheets of rain slapped me in the face. Every time the ferry hit a large swell and landed with a hollow thud, I swallowed hard.

The final leg up-island by bus was equally hellish. The farther north we travelled, the more intense the storm grew. When I finally reached Port McNeill, it was dark and the rain was coming down with such intensity, I was nearly soaked to the bone making the short walk from the bus stop to my motel. I wasn't due to hook up with my crew for another fifteen hours. I still had time to change my mind.

Sitting in my tiny motel room, listening to the storm lash at my window, I contemplated coming up with some lame excuse and jumping on the next bus headed back east. Aside from the hostile elements and the likelihood that I wouldn't see the sun for the next three or four weeks, I had to prepare for the possibility that this new crew could turn out to be a bunch of mouth-breathers. I couldn't bear the thought of being forced to live in extremely tight quarters with a bunch of imbeciles. I also realized that everything I considered indispensable in the world—friends, family, pillow-top mattresses, Indian curry—would be completely beyond my reach for the next five months. It was a good thing that the motel had several movie channels and a pizza oven. Without those distractions, I likely would have talked myself right back onto the next eastbound bus.

Fourteen hours later I was huddled in a boat with seventeen strangers, getting jostled around on high seas. Our destination was Gilford Island, a large island wedged between Vancouver Island and the mainland. It was an inaccessible rock with no regularly scheduled ferry. It had seen its fair share of logging activity, though, hence our visit.

Our foreman, Gary, an affable, easygoing character, informed us that we would be sharing our accommodations with a crew of loggers, and that with our arrival, it would be a full camp. I hated logging camps that were filled to capacity—there's little worse than sharing a roof with people who can't stand the sight of you. Gary also informed us that the logging company, which had operations spread out across Vancouver Island, was using this particular camp as a juvenile detention centre of sorts to house the social misfits it was keeping away from the rest of their employees. Obviously these crappy details weren't disclosed to us until we were beyond the point of no return. Had I known about this arrangement in advance, I likely would have expanded my search for a new company, especially considering that this first contract was projected to run at least four weeks. Typical, I thought. One more crazy episode.

When we arrived at the Gilford Island camp, it was close to the supper hour. At first glance, the camp appeared to be in very good condition. There was a series of long, newer-looking trailers arranged in neat rows, one large double-wide trailer that housed the kitchen and dining area, and several smaller trailers that appeared to function as dry rooms. Walking past the dining trailer, I noticed a series of holes—the type of holes a shotgun loaded with oo buckshot might inflict—scattered all across the front entrance. This was only speculation on my part, of course. And if that wasn't enough of a welcome mat, a half-dozen punks who had apparently been waiting patiently for our arrival sprayed us with imaginary machine-gun fire the second we opened the door to our trailer. More puzzled than alarmed, we wondered what these little reprobates would dish up next. As we were settling into our rooms, the same group of pinheads formed a line and took turns violently hammering on our walls and doors as they filed past. When they reached the end of the hallway, they turned around and attempted a second pass, that is, until several of us stepped out from our doorways and blocked their path. I don't know what these degenerates were expecting. Obviously, they hadn't considered the possibility that they'd encounter men nearly twice their size, men not easily rattled. That little standoff put an end to what was likely a whole laundry list of pranks. This group of miscreants, who occupied several rooms at the front of our trailer, were outnumbered and were going to have to learn some manners. That was my thinking anyway. Of course, we were vastly outnumbered across the entire camp, but as it turned out, these little asshats didn't have much in the way of backup.

As I lay in bed that first night, I could feel our trailer shudder and shake. Horizontal sheets of rain lashed at my window with such force, I was afraid the glass would shatter. I thought about my imminent debut on Gilford Island terrain. My hope was that Gary would have mercy on us and start us off on something gentle, something sheltered from the gale-force winds—a flat piece of terrain perhaps, one easy on both mind and body. Admittedly, this was a tall order for the coast.

During an intense storm, when you're completely exposed to the elements, planting steep terrain often requires twice as much time and energy as normal—you literally need to fight your way from one spot to the next. There are also many dangers present when planting trees during severe high winds, the more obvious being the possibility of a large conifer along the treeline cracking under the pressure and coming down on top of you. Even if you're nowhere near the impact zone, it's possible for large chunks of wood to break off and barrel downslope, propelled by grade and gravity. These are the types of close calls we encountered back in the day. Today, crews are not allowed to work during such conditions. Period. Today even rainfall is carefully monitored, and if it exceeds a certain amount within a specific time frame, the entire division is shut down to all activity, including road traffic. But these were the days when no such guidelines or protocol existed. If they did within other areas of the resource sector, they simply did not apply to treeplanting companies—not to the companies I worked with anyway. We hit the slopes no matter what nature threw at us. This obviously exposed us to great risk, but it also exposed us to a level of adventure that was several orders of magnitude higher than one would encounter in today's strictly controlled work environment.

The first two weeks of Gilford were brutal. Though the intense wind eventually died down, the rain stayed constant. Worst of all, the temperature often dipped down low enough to thicken the rain, turning it into sleet. It wasn't quite cold enough to collect on the ground, but cold enough to make our lives absolutely miserable.

I had a glove system for dealing with the wind and rain. I wore a thick rubber inner glove that was snug, but not tight, and a nylon outer glove with rubber mesh webbing. It worked great under most conditions, but not when the air temperature was near freezing. On such days, the cold penetrated right down to the marrow of my fingers, rendering them stiff and numb, making it nearly impossible to finesse a seedling's roots into the ground. It was on one such day, when the rain had turned chunky, that I noticed the fellow sharing my tree cache doing something unconventional. His name was Ted, a.k.a. Ted-Head. He had a large tub of petroleum jelly on the road next to his gear. He was dipping into it between each run, smearing the gunk all over his bare hands and fingers before pulling his rubber gloves over top. I soon discovered that I had missed a step the first few times I happened to witness this disgusting display: he was also sprinkling a few pinches of orange powder into the finger slots of each glove before slipping it back on. After I let up poking fun at him for this nasty ritual, he revealed to me that the orange powder was cayenne pepper. He encouraged me to try it. I was at my wit's end trying to maintain the circulation in my fingers that day. Reluctantly,

I sprinkled some of his cayenne pepper into my rubber gloves, dipped into the industrial-sized jug of ice-cold petroleum jelly he left out for me and swished the glop all over my hands and fingers before guiding them back into the amply seasoned finger holes. In less than a minute my fingers were wonderfully warm and tingly. Ted-Head was a veteran treeplanter. He had a lot of tricks like this up his sleeve. I still had a few things to learn.

The rest of Gary's crew were competent and experienced, and they presented me with a good deal of competition for the top highballer spot. Though his crew didn't include quite as many women as I would have liked—presumably because of the delinquents who inhabited the logging camp—Gary promised a better gender balance the moment we hit the Interior later on in the season. Like Gary, the majority of his crew hailed from the Kootenay region of the BC Interior.

One of his regulars, a charismatic highballer named Brock, would eventually become my planting partner. I rarely took on planting partners due to the politics involved, as well the different planting styles that often create conflict, but Brock and I had a lot in common. I also really admired the guy.

Planting with a partner or with a team takes practice, and it takes consideration for the person working next to you. It involves the proper use of natural boundaries, that is, not forcing the person following you to climb over large obstacles in order to meet your line of trees. When you find another planter you respect and admire, with the same planting style, speed and etiquette, it's a rare thing.

Back at camp the extreme weather was causing tempers to flare among some of the camp's more crotchety inhabitants. It wasn't uncommon for a shouting match to erupt between two or more people, often from opposite ends of the dining hall. These uproars would always get broken up by a supervisor who would interject twice as loudly, turning the dinnertime ambiance into a total brouhaha. These outbursts had great entertainment value. Many of them ended with one or more hooligans being sent back to their rooms without dessert. Priceless stuff!

The extreme weather on Gilford Island also played havoc with the soil conditions. The ground on some of our steeper cutblocks, saturated over weeks of relentless rainfall, became slick and difficult to traverse. We were constantly slipping and sliding downslope, and when this occurred you'd grab onto whatever you could to prevent yourself from sliding farther. It seemed that of all the vine-like vegetation one could latch onto in such a crisis, nine times out of ten you'd end up grabbing devil's club: a sprawling shrub with long cane-like stems covered in sharp, stiff thorns—the type that easily penetrated your work gloves, sinking deep into your flesh. It was a rare day when you weren't temporarily sidelined, picking devil's club from your hands. Every year, around November or December, the devil's club thorns that were buried deep into my thighs and calves—the ones I neglected to extract—would start migrating to the surface by the dozens. This annual migration, cued by the emergence of tiny pus-filled bumps with black dots in the middle, was always an event.

The saturated soil also made slash and large debris unstable. On one very memorable occasion I came across a large slab of wood occupying a steep section of ground near the centre of one of my areas. It was a three- by one-and-a-half-metre chunk that had been split lengthwise, the aftermath of a mature tree falling against a sheet of bedrock and exploding upon impact. Pointing downslope like a giant toboggan, it was a bizarre obstacle, one you don't often encounter on steep terrain. I remember briefly sizing it up. It was too high and wide to hop over, and the manner in which it was positioned on the slope made it tricky to manoeuvre around. Cognizant of the risk, I straddled the giant slab, intending to roll off on the opposite side in one fluid motion. But the moment I transferred my weight onto its centre, it dislodged from the greasy slope and began careening down the mountain, me riding it like some hapless cartoon character. The brief spurt of momentum I experienced hurtling down the centre of my area was absolutely terrifying. It could have ended badly. As luck would have it, approximately twenty metres downslope the front of the slab slammed into a large stump, causing it to grind to an abrupt halt. This sudden cessation in momentum catapulted me at least six metres through the air. I landed hard, back-first on top of a slash pile, then continued to roll and slide another fifteen or twenty metres before crashing into another stump. I was hurt, but I was able to get back on my feet and walk within ten minutes. The damage, which I wasn't able to properly assess until I showered later on that evening, included several bruised ribs, a severely bruised back and thigh, as well as a sprained elbow and knee. My treeplanting bags, which were half full of seedlings prior to the wild ride, were nearly emptied, the seedlings having been randomly distributed all over the mountain.

The Gilford contract marked the first time I had been put to work in an area that was subject to heavy deer browsing. In such areas, the deer populations were out of control, posing a threat to the plantations we were attempting to establish (deer love tender young seedlings, especially cedar). In order to protect our young forests from the ravenous herds, we would insert a metre-high mesh plastic tube over the top of each freshly planted tree, securing it to the ground with a long metal stake. These rigid protective tubes were called vexars. Normal protocol involved planting the trees one day and then immediately vexaring the trees the following morning, before the deer had a chance do any real damage. But on one of our designated vexar days, we discovered that 80 per cent of our cedar seedlings were missing. They had been chewed right down to a nub. Forced to change our strategy in order to stay one step ahead of the greedy grazers, it was decided that we would plant trees for the first half of the day, and then spend the second half applying the protective vexars.

The very day that we were to switch to this new strategy, a miracle occurred: the rain began to lighten and the clouds began to part. The ubiquitous layers of fog that had enveloped us magically began to lift. For the first time in weeks disembodied voices that penetrated the fog, echoing across the slopes, could be traced to their source. Most surprising of all, when the fog dissipated, it unveiled a small herd of deer that had been following thirty metres behind me, step for step, taking turns devouring my cedar trees within minutes of my tucking their roots in the ground. Several other planters in the area had similar escorts tagging along behind them as well. A person could only laugh.

Twenty-four hours after we left Gilford Island, the entire coast got hit with a March snowstorm. A subsequent cold snap caused the snow to stick, shutting the coast down for four long weeks. This put our next coastal contract on hold. While the Kootenay crew travelled back home, I chose to hang out in Vancouver, keeping a daily vigil on the coastal mountains, waiting for the snowline to creep back up. It was a long wait, much longer than anyone could have predicted.

It was early April when I reunited with my crew. We met in Port Hardy, a small town near the very northern tip of Vancouver Island. There we boarded a float plane destined for the remote Rivers Inlet, a deep fjord located on the central coast five hundred kilometres north of Vancouver. Back then, there was only one logging camp at the mouth of the inlet. It was a good camp with a very decent class of logger inhabiting the facilities.

The Rivers Inlet contract turned into a tough coastal grind. The ground was incredibly steep in places, and good soil was often difficult to find. Making the situation even more challenging, the company checker in charge of the project was an ex-treeplanter. He was a difficult man to please (checkers who are ex-treeplanters know all of our tricks—that can be a problem). A good number of our cut-blocks received hefty quality fines, mostly due to seedlings planted in unsuitable material.[1]

---

1. Planting criteria can vary from contract to contract. In this case, tight restrictions were placed on the types of soils in which we were allowed, and not allowed, to plant our seedlings. The preferred soils were not easy to find at times, while the poorer soils— those we were instructed to avoid—were often found in great abundance. Planting trees in "unsuitable material" often results in quality faults. If these faults are repeated across large areas, quality fines come into play.

Clearly visible from a number of our cutblocks was an enormous shelf of ice hanging over a sheer rock face on a mountain ridge some thirty kilometres away. We could only assume that there was a large volume of snow and ice—a glacier or icefield—creating pressure directly behind it. This shelf of ice was massive. It was more than a kilometre across. Brock and I were planting partners at the time, and whenever we stopped for a short break, we would sit facing the ice shelf with our backs up against a log, marvelling at its sheer scale, mesmerized by the brilliant shades of blue that permeated its mass from one end to the other. During one such break, on a day when the sun's penetrating warmth allowed us to strip down to our T-shirts, I managed to look up from my tuna salad just as the entire shelf of ice let go. It broke off from the edge of the ridge, dropping hundreds of metres, disappearing well below my line of sight. The image of it letting go was surreal, and it was accompanied by absolute silence. Three seconds later, all hell broke loose. As the ground around us shook, there was a sharp clap followed by a deafening roar, like a thunderhead had just opened up directly over our heads. As Brock was spinning around, struggling to comprehend the auditory and seismic activity, I sat frozen, slack jawed, wide eyed. I was so completely blown away, I could only point up at the bare, exposed ridge, prompting Brock to exclaim, "What happened to our glacier?!" I don't know how long that shelf of ice had been hanging there: years, decades, longer? I was the only soul on the crew to witness the event.

On the final day at Rivers, Brock and I took a water taxi to the other side of the inlet, where we were put to work on a flat piece of land that was bounded by a meandering, fast-running creek. Only minutes after taking the lead, while planting a line of trees along the edge of the bank, Brock excitedly called out, "Hey, check this out!" When I looked up, he was waving what appeared to be a metal wok above his head. As we continued planting, stabbing the thick moss with our shovel blades in search of soil, we began breaking glass with every other poke. Excited and mystified, we dropped to our hands and knees and began peeling back the layers, exposing a number of broken plates, metal objects and pieces of glass. As we continued to excavate the area, we also discovered a good number of hand-blown bottles and several pieces of ceramic pottery. Before long, we managed to expose a large number of curious items. It was obvious that we were standing on top of what was once a thriving community from East Asia. We speculated that it might have been a timber mill from back in the day. Whatever the case, it was decades old—perhaps a half century or more. We came away that day with a bag full of seamless hand-blown bottles, a beautiful clay pot and a number of antique glass pieces. Brock and I barely had time to scratch the surface of what ultimately lay buried beneath that thick layer of moss—we were under enormous pressure to plant out our remaining trees before day's end.

ONE OF THE WORST THINGS THAT CAN BEFALL A TREEPLANTER WHO IS just beginning to hit his stride midseason is a severe flu virus. That's exactly what happened to me as I made my way from the north end of Vancouver Island to Boundary Country in the West Kootenay region. It was the first week of May and I was on my way to hook up with several EG Ltd. crews who were ganging up on a large Interior project. By the time I reached Nelson, a picturesque little town nestled in the heart of the Selkirk Mountains, I had a temperature of 104°F. Every muscle and joint in my body was in full rebellion. Adding to my misery, a low-pressure system had just settled in over the region, promising at least a week of solid rain.

When I arrived at the remote Burl Creek tent camp, I was in rough shape. I had made a bit of a name for myself as a highballer with EG Ltd., having planted two difficult contracts on the coast with Gary's crew, but now I was on Ross and Rob's turf. I hadn't met these two yet. It was their show, they were in charge, and they were the two guys I needed to impress. Asserting oneself and demonstrating one's ability to plant good-quality trees, in large quantities, was often rewarded with perks. Management would often set aside large areas of creamy ground for a select group of highballers. These perks, which were always awarded surreptitiously, translated into better money, but you needed to prove yourself worthy first. At the time, I wasn't sure if I had the energy to pitch my tent, let alone hit the slopes as a highballing madman.

EG Ltd.'s camp was as elaborate as anything I had seen anywhere. At the nexus of a sprawled-out community of personal tents stood a nerve centre consisting of a massive dining tent, a full-length school bus that had been creatively converted into a kitchen and a very decent shower setup.

Having just arrived from the coast, we were joining a project that was already in progress. As I wandered among the crew who had just arrived home from work, I was shocked to discover that aside from Gary's crew, whom I had been working with since early February, I didn't recognize a single soul. I would have expected to greet at least a half-dozen familiar faces from having worked five years in the industry—five years working with nearly a dozen different companies. That was when I realized that these two regions, though both in the BC Interior, were quite distinct. Crews rarely crossed over between them. It was as if they were two distinctly separate cultures. There was one notable exception: Margo, a.k.a. Gusher, my cousin Crusher's girlfriend from two years earlier. She arrived in camp later that evening. And curiously, the entire crew also called her Gusher. Though there was a clear disconnect between regions and cultures, the legendary peeing incident from two years earlier, and nearly one thousand kilometres away, lived on in these parts. The crew was blown away when I admitted to having witnessed the fabled event.

It took every ounce of energy I had to construct my campsite after arriving that afternoon. My fever and chills were beginning to intensify. I was in absolute agony. I might have been a formidable highballer, but I was an insufferable wimp when it came to viruses. Adding to my misery, the skies opened up and drenched half of everything I owned before I was able to tuck my gear and bedding under cover. The moment I succeeded in squaring everything away and drawing the zipper down on my tent, I collapsed on top of my soggy bedding. I slept right through supper and into the wee hours of the morning. Waking up in the middle of the night, delirious from fever but famished from not having eaten in over fourteen hours, I crept stealthily into the kitchen and raided the goodies the cook had prepped for the next morning.

Raiding the fridge is always a risky manoeuvre in any camp situation. The trick is to cover your tracks and not get too greedy. Rather than digging into a bowl of something and removing scoops, it's better to carefully take an even layer off of the top, smoothing back the surface, before replacing the plastic and returning the item to the exact spot where you found it. One also needs to walk on tiptoes so as not to cause the floors to creak, potentially alerting the cook who is always camped in proximity to the kitchen. I have fond memories of my midnight kitchen raids. It was a rare morning when I didn't arrive for breakfast on a full stomach.

I learned something about my competitive nature during the first three days of the Burl Creek contract. Though I was as sick as a dog— lying in bed at night shaking with chills, waking up in the wee hours of the morning in pools of sweat—I was somehow able to maintain my competitive spirit. There were several highballers on the crew, including my planting partner Brock, who I managed to keep pace with.

At the end of day four, just before quitting time, the rain subsided, the fog lifted, and the sun made a brief appearance causing the ground around me to steam. This is a special time, those moments after the sun's warming rays hit rain-sodden wood and soil for the first time in days. The sight and smell of steam billowing from the drenched landscape imparts a healing effect on the light-deprived body and mind. It was right at that very moment, as steam began rising all around me, I felt my fever break. It was like a hardened shell, one applying constant pressure around my skull, suddenly splitting down the centre and falling away. All at once my head was clear and my muscles decompressed. The sensation was extraordinary. It was a reawakening of the senses unlike anything I had ever experienced.

CHAPTER TEN

The remainder of the Burl Creek contract was extremely lucrative. Brock and I solidified our planting partnership, pounding in huge numbers of trees on a daily basis. On one particularly productive day, we managed to crack the three-thousand-tree threshold—a feat very few planters ever accomplished back in those days of tough checkers and exacting standards.

The Burl Creek contract was more enjoyable for some than others. My friend Ted, the man who had liberated my freezing fingers from the driving sleet at Gilford with his "a little dab'll do ya" cayenne-and-petroleum-jelly recipe, decided to experiment with some of the local mushroom populations. He chowed down on a false morel, believing it would impart a nice buzz. I don't know if he got the buzz he was looking for, but what it did do was knock him on his ass for the majority of the contract. Along with severe intestinal distress, Ted endured every other symptom one might expect from a bad 'shroom. Poor Ted-Head sidelined himself for what turned out to be the most lucrative contract of the year, but he was lucky in one respect: false morels have been known to kill people. Ted survived the ordeal.

The day Ted finally got back on his feet—the morning of the final four-day shift of the Burl Creek contract—he made another terrible mistake: he accidentally left his bear banger unattended on the dashboard of the truck while he ran back to his tent to retrieve something.[2] Murphy's Law was at it again. In the sixty seconds that Ted was away, one of the women on his crew jumped into the truck, found the curious-looking device just lying there, began playing with it and accidentally set it off. The frightening sequence of events that followed began with a massive boom—an explosion that occurred inside the

---

2. A bear banger is a device reminiscent of a James Bond–style pen. An explosive cartridge is screwed onto the end, and when a triggering mechanism at the opposite end is pulled back and released, the cartridge shoots a fiery projectile about ten metres into the air where it then explodes with the intensity of a loud gunshot. They are extremely effective bear deterrents, but need to be handled with great care.

confined space of the truck's cab, compounding and amplifying the effect. As thick, choking smoke poured out of the truck's windows and doors, people panicked, tripping over one another as they spilled out of the vehicle. People had no idea what was happening. Worst of all, the explosive projectile ricocheted around the cab of the truck before exploding next to the poor woman who was playing with the device, rupturing her eardrum. After the smoke cleared and the tumult was reduced to a dull roar, Ted was assigned the responsibility for driving the injured woman to the ER in Grand Forks some three hours away.

THE FINAL CONTRACT OF THE 1988 SPRING SEASON HELD GREAT PROMise. Our destination was a remote logging camp on a large lake near Golden, BC. It was a camp that could only be accessed by float plane or boat. This was one of those rare occasions when the camp was empty, except for the staff who managed it.

Tracy and Rick, the camp managers, were a strict middle-aged couple with specific expectations as to how we should all behave. The crew was in full-on party mode. It had been a long season and everyone was looking to cut loose. This didn't sit too well with Tracy and Rick. The stodgy couple actually attempted to insert "quiet hours" into our evening schedule. Big mistake.

This contract wasn't nearly as lucrative as we were hoping. The soil conditions were challenging and the supervising checkers were unusually strict. They seemed to revel in finding fault with our plantations. This created a slightly oppressive atmosphere around camp, one that EG management helped mitigate by chartering a float plane, filling it up with booze and flying it in just in time for the eve of our scheduled day off. This was a classy move by EG management, one that was not lost on us. Tracy and Rick, on the other hand, were livid.

I want to come clean about something that occurred during the final days of the contract. My habit of raiding camp kitchens at night was not restricted to remote tent camps, where gaining access was never a problem. I would raid any kitchen, even some of the more secure industrial facilities, if I felt that my caloric intake required late-night augmentation. Three days before the end of the contract, a kitchen employee who was flying out the next day put aside a quarter piece of chicken for his long journey home. It looked delicious. He placed this beautiful piece of fowl on a plate, covered it with plastic, and just left it there, unguarded. Surely he must have known how irresistible such an item might appear to anyone accessing the "employees only" walk-in refrigerator.

Early the next morning, there was a commotion inside the mess hall. When I arrived for breakfast the two managers and kitchen staff were deep in conversation over what appeared to be a crisis of some sort. When our entire crew was present and accounted for, Tracy demanded everyone's undivided attention. The first thought that came to mind was that a forest fire was raging through the area and that our evacuation was imminent—we had been smelling smoke over the previous couple of days, after all. Instead, Tracy revealed that a "theft" had been perpetrated in the kitchen overnight. It was the theft of a quarter chicken (one that was smothered in a sweet, tangy barbecue sauce, I might add). She was dead serious. They treated this "theft" as a felony offense. Further, they treated the walk-in refrigerator as a crime scene.

Sensing that our crew wasn't appreciating the gravity of the offense, they tried forcing our hand by demanding that the thief come forward, threatening consequences, far-reaching consequences that would affect everyone. It wasn't long before the crew, unwilling to indulge in Tracy and Rick's vitriol, began to chuckle. Having failed to impress upon us the enormity of the offense, they sat back down in resignation and endured muffled fits of laughter from one end of the dining hall to the other. Then people began making sounds that an egg-laying hen might make: "Bawk, bawk, bawk, bawk, bawk, b-*gawwgawwk*..." Tracy and Rick rose abruptly from their breakfast plates, threw their chairs back against the wall and stormed out of the dining hall.

Tracy and Rick wanted their pound of flesh. They tried taking the matter up with the forestry officials who were overseeing our project, as well as the owners of the camp itself, but apparently no one was willing to call in the local constabulary. This incident was talked about for years in EG Ltd. treeplanting circles, even decades. The thief never came forward, not even after the crime's statute of limitations ran out. Well, the chicken thief was *me*, in case you hadn't guessed.

I finished my first season with EG Ltd. with an impressive number of workdays under my belt. They were true to their word, offering me as much work as I could handle. They also allowed me to move among their network of crews, of which they had at least a half-dozen working at any given time throughout the season. The managers, aside from being extremely competent, were all characters too. I had found a new home.

When I arrived back in Calgary, having banked 120 planting days, and having planted over 200,000 trees, I slipped into my usual two-week coma, sleeping eighteen to twenty hours per day until my mind and body were synchronized again. At the end of each season it usually required a good friend or family member—someone who wasn't a tree-planter—to point out the gashes, gouges and partially healed wounds that covered my body after an extensive season of planting trees on tough terrain. It's only then, after someone stares wide-eyed at your exposed arms and legs, that you become aware of just how much abuse your body takes during the course of a single season. When I look down at my arms and legs today, even after being retired from the industry for a number of years, the network of scar tissue resembles that of a street map of some major urban centre.

Later that summer and fall, there didn't appear to be much going on along the slopes of the BC Interior. I succeeded in lining up less than two weeks of work. I was looking for at least six. That prompted me to make inquiries with several Alberta-based companies, something I vowed I would never do again. Having abruptly walked on a number of contracts in the past, I wondered if they would even take my call. When I contacted SFS Ltd. and talked to a fellow named Reggie, he explained that all of his crews were full, but that he'd let me know if something came up. I wouldn't have hired me back either.

After hanging up the phone, satisfied that I had covered all of my bases, I decided to commit to the modest amount of work that was offered to me in the BC Interior. Then the phone rang. It was Reggie. I'll never forget how he phrased his offer: "I don't have a planting spot for you, but I have a contract in Nordegg. Uhhh, you wanna run it?"

I was stupefied. Reggie barely knew me. We had only met on two prior occasions. Briefly. On one of those occasions, I'd pointed out glaring weaknesses in his operation, something most bosses don't appreciate hearing from new employees. My insights were valid, though. I suppose Reggie thought so too. He obviously thought I had something to offer—something beyond high tree counts and a snarky attitude. The very next afternoon I found myself sitting across from him at his office in Leduc, Alberta. After a brief discussion, he slid over a stack of maps, the name of a forester, the keys to several of his trucks, the contact numbers for a small support staff who were waiting anxiously on the sidelines, and a stack of company credit cards. Less than two hours later I was towing a flatbed trailer full of quads and trikes to a place I had never been, to hook up with a crew I had never met.

How could I have known that accepting Reggie's offer would trigger a sequence of events that would have such profound and far-reaching consequences? Everything in my life was about to change.

# THE INSANITY

||||||||||||||||||||||||||||||||||||||||||||||||||||||||||

IN THE FALL OF 1988 I WAS TOSSED THE KEYS TO A COMPANY I HAD worked for only briefly, by a man I barely knew. I puzzle to this very day over Reggie's rationale. Why would he bestow such trust on an outsider? He managed to pick the right guy, though. His timing was impeccable too. Deep down, I wanted another whack at management.

I hooked up with a crew of eighteen complete strangers in Nordegg, a tiny hamlet in the foothills of the Canadian Rockies. Together we successfully planted a large technical project under budget and ahead of schedule. Reggie was tickled pink with the result and immediately set me up with a second, even larger project—an extremely remote tent-camp scenario north of Fort McMurray, Alberta. This project involved working with an entirely different crew, and it too ended with very favourable results. And damned if I didn't have fun doing it, even though it was a logistical nightmare.

I was able to find a third project for the company on my own. It was a reclamation contract; a cushy one-week gig working for Syncrude Canada, also in the Fort McMurray area. It turned out to be extremely lucrative for everyone involved, and that bit of resourcefulness seemed to seal my fate with SFS Ltd. But it was during this contract that tragedy struck Reggie's crew. One of his timber cruisers had been mauled to death by a grizzly bear in northern Alberta. This is the sort of news that grinds into the psyche of every treeplanter, especially when it's so close to home.

It was mid-October when I finally had the opportunity to sit down and chat with Reggie again. On my way back home, I dropped by his office for a quick debriefing and to return the keys to his trucks along with a stack of company plastic. Reggie seized the moment to press me on my plans for the following spring. I hadn't made any real commitments, but my heart was with EG Ltd. of the Slocan Valley, the company I had worked with earlier in the year.

Sensing my indecisiveness, Reggie made an offer I was forced to consider on the spot: $300 per day plus expenses to run his entire portfolio of Alberta-based projects. The work would begin early in the spring of 1989. The details were sketchy, the contracts had yet to be negotiated, but he promised that it would add up to a substantial amount of work beginning in mid-April and running until the end of June. He was impatient. He wanted an answer immediately. I hemmed and hawed.

To sweeten the deal, he offered me the use of one of his trucks over the winter as well as part-time work with one of his (non-planting) forestry crews during the winter months whenever I needed the income. As the incentives piled up, and after a warm gaze from his secretary caught my eye, I felt compelled to accept the offer. Three hundred dollars per day was a respectable amount of money back then. And it would be two and a half months where I wouldn't be required to plant a single tree unless I really wanted to.

All treeplanters reach a stage in their career when they come to the realization that they cannot continue planting trees forever. I wasn't at that stage yet, not even close, but I was able to envisage a day when I'd be forced to consider an exit.

As the 1989 spring season drew near, Reggie finally let me in on a few details. I was to start out with a large contract along the remote shores of Lesser Slave Lake in northern Alberta. My second project, nearly twice the size of the first, was even more remote, requiring a lengthy barge ride down the Athabasca River to an area north of Fort McMurray. The third and final contract was an unusual one. It was situated on a small island in the middle of the Athabasca River itself, which, I would soon discover, was over one kilometre wide in places. There was a hitch. Reggie was participating in a treeplanting boom in the province of Ontario, where his other two supervisors were focusing all of their time and energy. All of Reggie's experienced workers would be travelling to Ontario to meet the demands of the work he had secured there. This development stranded me without an experienced workforce. I had no other option but to train twenty-four rookies. This was not part of our original deal. I briefly considered walking out on Reg, but not wanting to show weakness, I went along with the plan.

The rookie crew, according to a list I was furnished with in advance, consisted mainly of students from the universities of Alberta and Calgary, and two hockey players from a college in Swift Current, Saskatchewan. They were mostly male, between the ages of nineteen and twenty-two, and, as usual, I wasn't given a chance to meet them in advance. I did have a chance to study their application forms, though. Noteworthy, under the heading that asked for their "outdoor experience," a number of applicants listed a single word: "Camping." *Camping!* "That's nice," I thought. The project wasn't due to begin for five days and I was already breaking out in a cold sweat.

The first project was a series of cutblocks spread out over a vast area of beaver dams, swamps and deep muskeg patches. Access consisted of a network of winter logging roads; running trucks and heavy machinery through these areas was only possible when the ground was frozen solid. Gaining access during the spring and summer months, for our crews and equipment, required resourcefulness, hard work and luck. Some of the roads weren't actually roads at all—they were cutlines: long, straight access trails carved through the forest by oil and gas companies in their search for underground fossil fuel deposits. No matter what the road design, access into these areas was dicey and required the use of ATVs. This was no surprise. I was aware of these objectionable details ahead of time.

I was given a small support crew for the duration of the season to assist me in maintaining supply lines and repairing access routes. This support consisted of a First Nations guide named Lance, who was a very competent woodsman I had come to know from a previous treeplanting campaign, and a guy named Danny. I was lucky to have Lance. I knew nothing of Danny.

The schedule was set. We had four days to travel to Lesser Slave Lake, drive in as far as we were able with our trucks, set up a staging area at the point where our road access turned to crap, and offload our camp and equipment, including our quads and trikes.[1] Then it was a matter of getting familiar with the vast network of winter logging roads and trails that criss-crossed the region. That was where our quads came into play.

We would immediately set out to locate our planting areas—cutblocks I wasn't given the luxury of viewing in advance. Once we had the entire project scoped out, we'd shift our focus to finding a suitable, centralized location to set up camp.

Our staging area at the junction marked the exact point where everything changed. It was like standing at the edge of a parallel universe. The only way to proceed beyond that point was either on foot or by ATV. Once we arrived, we only had a few hours' worth of daylight remaining on that first day. I thought that with a bit of luck, and if my maps were accurate, we might succeed in finding one of my larger cutblocks before sunset. These blocks were mere blips on a map, hidden somewhere in the dark recesses of what appeared to be an impenetrable wall of spruce, fir, pine and larch.

---

1. A staging area is often set up as a transition zone, marking the end of one mode of transportation's usefulness where another more suitable mode takes over. Ideally the location is a flat, wide-open area where equipment and fuel can be stored and accessed as needed.

While Lance and I mounted quads and set off to explore the area, Danny stayed behind at the staging area to begin offloading gear from our trucks and flatbed trailers. Lance and I travelled together that afternoon, consulting our maps every few kilometres, attempting to make sense of the complex network of roads and cutlines that appeared to shoot off in every direction.

Combing the area for three long hours, we were unable to find anything that even resembled a cutblock. Every road, every trail we followed seemed to come to an abrupt dead end without rhyme or reason. Discouraged but not disheartened, we made our way back to the staging area, jumped in the truck, and drove back to our tiny motel located on the side of the highway. I was baffled that our combined map-reading skills didn't allow us to home in on a single cutblock. I wondered whether we had the right maps at all.

Waking up at the crack of dawn the next morning, the priority was to find and scope out every single one of the two dozen cutblocks. I needed to scrutinize every minute detail—the terrain, the soil, the access leading in and out. Every damn thing. Failure was not an option. We each had a hand-held radio, a map of the area, a quad and several gallons of extra fuel in the event we were forced to travel farther than anticipated. I informed both Lance and Danny that we were not to return to the trucks—not for any reason—until we had met our objective.

We travelled together at the beginning of our day-two search. We knew that the majority of our blocks were distributed on the other side of a ridge, one that mocked us off in the distance some twenty kilometres beyond our first main junction. We had issues with that first junction, which was basically a Y in the road. It offered up far too many options. Whether we chose left or right, each fork immediately branched off into a succession of secondary junctions, none of which made any sense according to our maps. These secondary junctions would then splinter apart, creating a tangled web of random cutlines and trails. It was baffling. It didn't take us long to figure out that our maps were hopelessly outdated. At midday, after hours of searching without success, we were forced to split up and travel independently, resorting to a process of elimination. We'd travel up one access trail, and when that dead-ended, we'd try another, and then another, and so on. The barriers we encountered ran the gamut from simple dead ends where the road would inexplicably terminate at a wall of trees to beaver dams, small lakes, deep ravines or impassable bogs that were deep in muskeg—a watery, moss-covered slurry of decomposing vegetation that threatened to swallow us up, ATV and all.

By late afternoon, not only were we unable find a single block, we were getting hopelessly lost at times. It was, and remains, one of the greatest frustrations I've ever encountered. Day two ended with the same dreadful result as day one. We were exhausted, we were covered from head to toe with mud, our kidneys ached from being bounced around on our quads for hours on end, and we were pissed off. Adding to the pressure, Lance, who knew Reggie much better than I, recommended that I not contact him and ask for assistance. Apparently, we were completely on our own.

Day three began with a profound sense of urgency. I was scheduled to meet two van-loads of university kids in forty-eight hours, and at that point, I didn't even have a patch of green for them to pitch their tents on. I spent the majority of the day cursing at my maps. Nothing made sense. I experienced more dead ends. I was getting lost. I was getting stuck. There were times when I buried my quad so deep in the muskeg, I thought I had lost it for good. Toward the end of the day, without having made any forward progress, I felt a nervous breakdown coming on. Day three yielded the same inexplicable outcome as the previous two. We had explored, without success, every access road, every junction, every cutline, every seismic line and every goat trail in the region. In desperation we even followed road systems that shot off in the wrong direction, hoping they would eventually double back and hook up with other roads that would lead us in. Nothing worked. I was pushing a hard ten on the ol' tension meter.

It was day four. Late in the afternoon I was scheduled to meet a semi-truck back at the highway. It would deliver a massive, tank-like ATV on a flatbed trailer. This "Monster" ATV was to be my primary support vehicle. It would be deployed to haul large loads of trees, fuel and supplies between the staging area and camp.[2] The next day, at 10:00 a.m., I had another meeting back at the highway. This time it would be with Reggie. He was due to arrive with two large passenger vans full of rookie treeplanters.

In a complete daze, I ventured off on my quad. Lance and Danny followed up behind. Our plan was to explore a series of trails that, according to a new set of maps we obtained from an old gentleman who owned our motel, ran ten kilometres to the west before pushing north. This was our last and only hope of finding a way into our project area.

After several more hours of dead ends and immovable obstacles, I began to lose control, inwardly. The gravity of the situation was exacting a toll on my ability to think straight. The thought of taking responsibility for the well-being and safety of twenty-four rookies, without even a campsite to guide them to, was more than my diminished faculties could handle. I remember thinking, as I was searching aimlessly along a cutline, that if I were to crash my quad and break a leg, I'd get to go home. It's not an easy thing to admit, even decades after the fact, but I actually began to run accident scenarios through my mind, examining the ditch on both sides of the cutline, looking for good spots to stage an accident. I wasn't there yet. My level of desperation hadn't quite peaked. I was close. Then the most extraordinary thing occurred: the forest on both sides of the cutline completely dropped away, opening up into a massive cutblock of scarified ground. Eyes wider than

---

2. The "Monster" was an ATV that resembled a monster truck. It was an off-road vehicle with four massive tires under the front cab, and four additional tires under a second compartment that was used to haul cargo and/or crew. It was nearly solid metal, extremely heavy and could travel over almost any sort of terrain.

CHAPTER ELEVEN

saucers, I continued on and arrived at the edge of a ridge where I could see three additional blocks below me, several kilometres off in the distance. The polygonal shapes on my maps lined up perfectly with what I was seeing. I had found the contract! The timing of the discovery was nothing short of miraculous. I called in Lance and Danny, and we were immediately able to locate an idyllic campsite in the middle of all of the action—a beautiful riparian zone with a babbling brook running right through the centre. All of a sudden, inexplicably, everything fell into place.

Tight for time, I instructed Danny to begin hauling as much gear as he was able from the staging area to our campsite, which was a two-hour round trip by quad if you were hauling ass. Meanwhile, Lance and I raced back to the staging area, hopped in a truck and made our way back to the highway to meet the semi-truck that was due to deliver our Monster ATV.

As we were driving back to the highway, on what was a very good hard-packed dirt road, I remember marvelling at how upbeat I was suddenly beginning to feel, especially after contemplating the unimaginable only two hours earlier.

When we were within two kilometres of the highway junction, the clouds began to stack up and it started to rain lightly. Then it came down with a little more conviction, necessitating the use of my windshield wipers. The second my wipers began their sweeping action, both Lance and I looked at one another in worried silence. We could already sense the road beginning to deteriorate.[3] When we reached the highway junction, our semi-truck, along with its massive payload, had just arrived. I needed the driver to follow us back in, as far as he was able,

---

3. Dirt roads in northern Alberta deteriorate quickly in the rain. This is due to the high component of clay in the soil. When clay reacts with water it tends to gum up, making it too slick to travel on. Even the slightest amount of precipitation can render roads impassable to two-wheel-drive traffic. Within twenty minutes of continuous rainfall, these roads can be rendered impassable even for four-by-four trucks.

before offloading the Monster. My hope was that he could travel the entire distance back to the staging area, but as the rain continued to fall, both Lance and I registered our doubts.

There was no time for pleasantries. After a cursory handshake, I asked the driver and his partner if they had any intentions of "chaining up," that is, putting chains on their tires to maintain adequate traction on a road that was deteriorating by the minute. Chaining up was a big job for a rig that size. The driver, annoyed at my suggestion, insisted that it wasn't necessary. He was certain that the weight of the Monster alone would keep the rig anchored to the road. I was in no position to argue.

As I began to lead the way in, I was forced to put my truck in four-by-four for the first time since arriving at Lesser Slave Lake. It was difficult to drive in a straight line without fishtailing all over the road. Both Lance and I divided our attention equally between the road ahead and the side-view mirrors, keeping the semi-truck in our sights.

We maintained a safe distance between us, and everything appeared to be okay for the first three kilometres or so. Then we came to a wide sweeping curve in the road; a curve elevated some six metres above the forest floor. We managed to navigate the curve with only a few minor drifts and were relieved when the road straightened out immediately after. We then became fixated on the side and rear-view mirrors. The semi-truck had yet to come into view. Continuing to press forward, we were worried. We finally spotted the big rig as it entered the final stage of the curve. Then the unthinkable happened: it disappeared from sight. Without so much as a sound, the semi-truck sailed right off the edge of the road and into the forest below. For a moment I thought that my sleep-deprived state had caused me to hallucinate, but Lance pounding his fists on the dashboard triggered my reflexes. I stomped on the brakes, hard. As we doubled back, hearts in our throats, not knowing what horror awaited us, we were stunned to discover both the driver and his partner standing upright in the ditch, rubbing their swollen heads as they surveyed the accident scene.

The semi-truck was on its side, wedged against a tree. Its massive flatbed trailer was lying completely upside down, wheels still spinning. The truck's cargo—our Monster ATV—had somehow managed to land right side up and was perched on top of a cluster of spruce trees it had toppled and crushed as it rolled free from the rig. All of this havoc was strewn out over the deepest, lushest carpet of jade green moss I had ever seen. I was immediately struck by the juxtaposition of these deeply conflicting elements (the mind tends to wander when it hasn't rested in days).

After assessing the damage, we determined that the two men had suffered only minor injuries and that the damage to their rig was not catastrophic.

Using the Monster ATV's massive winch cable, Lance managed to right both the semi-truck and its flatbed trailer. He then winched them up the steep ditch and set them back onto the road where the two wobbly drivers promptly set about chaining up their tires. Lance and I watched in disbelief as they limped the injured rig back toward the highway. I knew from that moment on that Lance was going to be key to my survival that season.

There was one major problem with the Monster, though: it was a heavy machine. Lance had already done some damage to the road surface while winching the big rig back up the steep bank. And being ten kilometres away from our staging area, we had no other option but to drive it the rest of the way in. The sheer weight of the machine, along with its enormous tire treads, chewed up the dirt road, leaving a deeply rutted trail in its wake. Weeks later the oil and gas company discovered the damage to their road. They were not pleased. Reggie would later receive a $9,000 bill in the mail.

The three of us worked until 3:00 a.m., hauling equipment and fuel some thirty-five kilometres into the depths of the boreal forest where our idyllic campsite was tucked away. It was 5:00 a.m. when we finally arrived back at our motel room. I was due to meet the crew at 10:00 a.m., forty-five minutes farther down the highway. I tried not to think about how much sleep I was due, and how little I'd actually receive before being forced back in motion again.

Reggie arrived at 10:00 a.m. sharp with two shiny white passenger vans bursting at the seams with wide-eyed rookies and an impossible amount of personal gear. The first words to come out of Reggie's mouth: "Good golly, you look like you haven't slept in days."

Reggie was a tough nut to crack. I liked him, even though he preferred to keep me at a distance. He was a stocky fellow with a curious, round face. He had an effusive air about him. He wore a grin, particularly when there was nothing worth grinning about. Despite the daily uncertainty of operating in a hostile environment, Reggie maintained his cool. He kept things in perspective. In an industry that generated more than its share of nervous breakdowns, Reggie was unflappable. We seemed to share a lot of the same values, holding common ground on many issues, but we disagreed strongly on one key point: while I believed that a good job should always be rewarded with praise, Reggie believed that praise should be doled out sparingly, if at all. He felt praise would only lead to inefficiency and neglect in the end.

While the crew was busy loading their gear into the back of my trucks, Reggie took the opportunity to give me a little pep talk. He also gave me a brief history lesson concerning the project into which I was about to throw myself. He informed me that it was a direct award contract, one that he risked losing unless our pay-plots came in well above average.[4] He went on to explain how one year earlier he was nearly thrown out of the area. Lance was supervising the project. When the logging company checkers arrived to run their quality checks at the end of the campaign, they discovered that the seedlings were in poor health. Many of Lance's plantations failed to survive that summer.

---

4. A direct award contract is an arrangement that a logging company has with its preferred contractor. Awarding a contract directly bypasses the tendering process. A direct award is a show of confidence and the greatest compliment a logging company can bestow upon a contractor. Few treeplanting contractors ever achieve this standing.

"Poorly planted root systems" was the reason cited for the high mortality rate—a problem that could have been averted had it been detected early on. I reminded Reggie that he was saddling me with a rookie crew. Rookie crews will always have quality issues until they learn the ropes—a process that can take weeks. I also informed him that most twenty-four-person crews have at least two full-time quality-control foremen, in addition to the supervisor, to help enforce proper planting standards. I was entirely on my own for this project! Reggie dismissed my concerns, expecting me to perform a miracle. "We're counting on you," he insisted from the open window of his van before speeding off.

My first impression of the crew, as they busily unloaded their gear at the staging area and reloaded it into the back of the idling Monster, was positive. They all appeared to be in good physical condition. They also appeared to be a rather spirited bunch. Everyone, with a few notable exceptions, seemed genuinely excited to be there.

My first impression of my cook, Frank, was mixed. Frank was an older gentleman with a stolid demeanor. He was standoffish at first, but after a brief chat, I sensed a few soft spots. He appreciated his critical role on the crew. He understood the importance of producing palate-pleasing, nutrient-dense meals in sufficient volumes. I did sense, however, that he wasn't 100 per cent comfortable taking orders from a man less than half his age. I didn't mind that minor point of disconnect. It was the least of my worries.

With the crew loaded into the back of the Monster, I followed up behind on my quad, watching as Lance expertly negotiated the narrow passageways through the forest, tearing up great swaths of moss as he bullied his way through. The entire crew seemed to revel in every bump along the way. I had to laugh out loud as people hooted and hollered, like rodeo cowboys, with each rough patch in the road. This group was primed for adventure, and adventure was the one thing I was certain I could deliver.

Shortly after we reached camp, Lance pulled me aside. He had overheard Reggie talking about him, about the way he'd mismanaged his project one year earlier, and he resented the way he was character-ized. He said that there were extenuating circumstances that caused his project to run into trouble and that Reggie had left out some important details. I told Lance not to fret, that I wasn't judging him. I knew all too well how a contract in Alberta could turn south in a New York minute. Lance needed to hear that from me.

I liked and respected Lance. There was something wonderfully, pleasingly enigmatic about the guy. He was a tall, proud and handsome First Nations man with simmering dark brown eyes, shoulder-length jet-black hair, and a thick chevron mustache. He had a warmth and charisma that everyone found engaging. People felt safe around Lance. People wanted to get to know him. They wanted to be liked by him. Being a self-professed "pussy tease," it wasn't long before he was chat-ting up several of the women on the crew—women who somehow managed to sneak onto Reggie's (nearly) all-male crew.

Though Lance was dealing with both guilt over the previous years debacle, and anger over having been demoted to the role of support guy, he was nonetheless committed to helping me make this project work. "No matter what goes down, I got your back," he told me, and I believed him. I also instinctively knew that it had to work both ways. In the next sentence, he asked me to promise him something. He wanted me to agree to cut him loose midway through the season for at least twenty-four hours with no questions asked. I agreed. A person's word, as I would soon discover, was more important to Lance than anything else.

We couldn't have picked a better location for our camp. A thick cluster of conifer and deciduous trees cast a generous volume of shade around us. A cold spring-fed brook trickled past my tent with sufficient volume to impart a lulling effect—something that would help push away reality for a handful of hours each night. Our campsite was also flanked on all sides by a series of small cutblocks—terrain I planned to train my rookies on. The blocks were small enough that if our first attempt at creating a new forest failed, we might have the chance to make repairs before the company checkers descended on us, running their final inspection plots.

I had one meeting with the crew that afternoon. I told them, after they had gathered their gear and pitched their tents, to assist Lance, Danny and Frank in the construction of a fully functional camp and kitchen. Then and only then would Frank ring the dinner bell. I also instructed them to eat a good meal and to get lots of rest. The next day promised to be long and exhausting. I went back to my tent and was asleep within seconds of my head hitting the pillow. It was only two in the afternoon and I managed to sleep through the pounding of metal stakes, the ruckus of two-cycle engines, the excited shouts of overly enthusiastic kids at work, a dinner horn and the roar of the Monster as it cycled back and forth between the staging area and camp. I slept nearly fifteen hours straight, uninterrupted, until 4:30 the next morning.

The next morning after breakfast we all took a short stroll through the woods to our first clearcut setting. The aroma of bacon and eggs continued to waft through the air and settle in around us as I began to pontificate. Straight off, I needed everyone to understand how crucial it was to plant a healthy tree. To stress my point, I pulled back the Silvicool tarp from the tree cache, reached into one of the boxes filled with seedlings, extracted a bare-root tree from one of the bundles and held it up for everyone to see.[5] Clearly boring everyone with my little show-'n'-tell routine, I then declared, "This tree is dead!" In the twenty or thirty seconds that I exposed the seedling's roots to the warm spring air, the root hairs had shrivelled up, causing the seedling to expire. This got the crew's attention. The first step in planting a healthy tree is ensuring it survives the journey from the roadside tree cache to the soil. This little bit of drama also impressed Andre, a forestry checker

---

5. Bare-root seedlings are self-explanatory: instead of having roots encased in a cone of soil, they are almost entirely bare, with only a thin layer of soil protecting their delicate root hairs.

who had arrived early that morning insisting on being present every step of the way. There was a lot riding on the successful conclusion of this contract. With Andre present, the pressure was most definitely on.

I lectured the crew for two hours that morning. I covered every topic from tree quality to proper nutrition, to bear safety. (Andre was in the search party that had discovered the mauled body of Reggie's timber cruiser one year earlier. He was never seen without a defender shotgun slung over his shoulder.) I then had the crew watch as I slow-motion planted forty seedlings, pointing out every step in excruciating detail. Then, in order to tighten the learning curve, I had each rookie come forward, one by one, to plant ten trees at the correct spacing while the rest of us observed and critiqued. By day's end, I had twenty-four rookie treeplanters who clearly understood what I needed from them.

Midway through day two, I had everyone set up in their own areas and working independently. Wanting to insert an element of positive pressure, I informed everyone that their individual areas would be plotted on a permanent map and would bear their names for future reference. This wasn't entirely untrue—I was a stickler for detail. The crew's quality at the end of day two was good. It wasn't great, but I could spot improvement from one hour to the next.

By the end of the first shift, the crew was collectively planting thirteen thousand trees per day. That number exceeded my expectations by 50 per cent. In that time, I lost only one rookie, an army brat who went into shock at the back of his area. He was found listless and unable to communicate. At the end of the day, after he corralled his senses and regained control of his vocal cords, he confessed to not being able to keep pace with the rest of the crew. He was upset and he wanted to go home. Lance seized the opportunity to run to town, taking the poor kid out by quad on the morning of the day off, then driving him by truck to the bus station in Slave Lake.

As the contract progressed, the distance between camp and our planting areas increased considerably, necessitating the use of the Monster to transport the crew to and from camp. We needed to plan our trips to the outlying blocks carefully. The sheer size and weight of the Monster cut deep ruts into the cutlines and roads with each pass. On some of the wetter, softer road surfaces, a single pass with the Monster would create ruts that were almost a metre deep and a metre wide. After a second pass, the ruts were often waist deep. After three passes, some road sections were rendered impassable. As we began to destroy one important access route after another, we were forced to use the Monster in a most unconventional way. It was possible to detour around certain trouble spots by simply veering off into the forest, knocking down mature trees as if they were toothpicks. We'd flank these areas, mowing down vast stretches of forest, until it was safe to merge back onto the main road. We were forced to rely on this desperate manoeuvre more times than I'm comfortable admitting. I hate to reflect on the number of mature conifers we killed on this one contract alone.

It was becoming increasingly clear, as the contract matured and our access was getting used up, that the Monster was becoming more and more vulnerable to getting stuck. Lance managed to bury its wheels in deep muskeg more than once, bringing the beast to a worrying halt, but he always managed to winch it out using the surrounding forest as leverage. The real worry was getting it stuck in an area where there wasn't a strong enough conifer within reach of the winch cable. If that were to occur, the Monster could become a permanent fixture in the Lesser Slave Lake boreal forest. I really didn't want that kind of environmental nightmare on my resumé.

By the time the Lesser Slave Lake contract entered its final shift—after three very productive weeks—my crew of rookies had gelled into a tight unit. Andre's final report detailed a crew that more closely resembled a group of veteran planters than a bunch of university students who were planting trees for the very first time. Andre was not an easy checker to please. I was extremely proud of that result.

On the second-last day of the contract, we received a weather report via Andre's radio of a massive storm front approaching our area. With the road leading back to the staging area already severely compromised, any large volume of precipitation threatened to strand all of our heavy equipment, including our camp, out in the middle of nowhere. I made the decision to take a shot at planting one and a half days' worth of trees in a single day. The question was: could the rookie crew rise to the occasion?

The plan was simple. First, we'd head out after supper and plant for an additional hour in an attempt to put a dent in the tree count. Second, we'd start planting at first light the next morning and work until the final tree went into the ground. The crew, in spite of being thrown slightly off centre by the sudden pressure, collectively agreed to give it the old college try.

That next morning after breakfast, while giving the crew my best impersonation of Tony Robbins, reciting a veritable laundry list of negative consequences should we fail to plant out our remaining trees by sunset, Frank and Danny began dismantling camp. The minute Lance finished dropping everyone off at the block in the Monster, I instructed him to hightail it back to camp and begin hauling ass, transporting our camp and equipment back to the staging area. I was stressed. We needed to stay one step ahead of the storm. By midday, with an uninterrupted view of the northern horizon, we watched the storm building in intensity and advancing by the minute. Some people on the crew found the predicament exhilarating. Others were rattled by the race against time and nature.

Our final afternoon at Lesser Slave Lake was one for the books. I strapped on the treeplanting bags, and together with my crew managed to plant out the last of our seedlings by 7:00 p.m. We were completely surrounded by the storm at that point. Andre and I transported the crew back to camp on our quads and trailers, eight at a time. This was in order to allow Lance to continue hauling gear back to the staging area, uninterrupted, in the Monster.

To my horror, there was a mountain of gear still waiting to be hauled away when we arrived back at camp, and neither Frank nor

Danny had seen Lance in over five hours. Minutes later Lance emerged from the woods, on foot, like some wild bushman. Covered from head to toe in mud, limping and unable to control his seething rage, he exclaimed, "Yup! I buried that motherfucker but good!"

He described getting the Monster stuck in a patch of muskeg halfway between camp and the staging area. He tried to winch it out. He looped the winch cable around three separate trees but ended up tearing each one out by its roots. The Monster was buried right up to the top of its back wheels. It wasn't going anywhere. Lance figured we'd need at least fifteen metres of heavy-duty chain to extend the winch cable, giving it enough length to latch onto a group of trees that were currently out of reach. We possessed no such length of heavy-duty chain.

We were losing daylight fast. The rain was beginning to come down with conviction. Without so much as a coffee break, we threw ourselves back in motion. While Andre and I used the quads and trailers to begin ferrying personal gear back to the trucks at the staging area, everyone else followed up behind on foot. The idea was to unload the gear, whisk back and then begin ferrying people. If the crew continued to walk, closing the distance between themselves and the trucks, our cycle times would steadily decrease. On our first run back to the staging area, we spotted it. The Monster was buried right up to the cab, just as Lance described. Only the very tops of its tires were visible above the muskeg. It looked hopeless. We speculated that this could well be its final resting place—a miry muskeg grave that, over time, would consume its entire mass.

By the time we hooked back up with the crew on the main trail, they had managed to walk a good four kilometres, cutting our ferrying times down significantly. Now that we were hauling people, getting stuck wasn't an issue as they'd simply hop off during the rough spots and push us through, allowing our quads to maintain forward momentum. The hardcore nature of this group of boys and girls was impressive. They were actually having a blast in the bog and muck.

After dropping the first group of people off at the staging area, despite a spirited protest, I decided not to allow them to blast off to town ahead of the rest of the crew, even though there were enough bodies to fill a truck. I've always believed that travelling together as a unit is good protocol. It's safer that way.

It was 11:00 p.m. by the time we were all safely loaded into the trucks and in motion. Though it was the first real road we had seen in over three weeks, the rain had turned it into a slick, greasy mess. With the trucks in four-wheel drive and the crews hopping out every few minutes to help push us through the sloppier sections, we eventually made our way to pavement.

Within twenty minutes of acquiring keys to their motel rooms, the crew's lights were out. They were done. My plan was to have Reggie pick them up and take them back to Edmonton the next morning. Reggie always made himself available for this sort of thing. I called him at 6:00 a.m. the following day, and three hours later he had the entire crew packed into the same white vans they'd arrived in three weeks earlier. The crew had two days off in the big city. I remained behind with Lance and Danny. There was work to do.

I had two days to get the Monster unstuck, haul the rest of our gear and equipment back to the staging area and begin mobilizing our quads in the direction of Fort McMurray.

Believing that Lance and Danny could handle the task in one day, I gave Lance the company plastic and told him to make it happen. Having averaged only five hours of sleep per night over the duration of the Lesser Slave Lake contract, I had but one goal for the rest of my day in town—to survey the insides of my eyelids.

Later that afternoon, mud-encrusted fists were pounding at my motel room door. It was Lance and Danny. The Monster was still buried in the bog. They had purchased twenty metres of heavy-duty chain from the local hardware store, attached it to the cable on the Monster's winch and begun systematically ripping trees out of the ground by their root systems. Every single tree that was within reach of their extended winch line was torn out of the earth. Lance described one large tree holding firm as he punched the accelerator while simultaneously winding in the winch cable. The Monster was just beginning to climb out of its hole when the tree suddenly exploded, splintering into pieces, causing the beast to lurch back into its swampy hollow. Aside from its enormous weight, its gigantic wheels were completely buried in muskeg, creating significant suction that was difficult to break. They were on their way back to the hardware store to purchase an additional twenty metres of chain. He guaranteed that would do the trick. He said that with any luck, they'd be back at the motel by midnight. I promised them that cold beer and pizza would be waiting for them when they returned.

Midnight came and went. Finally there was a knock on my door at 1:30 a.m. Lance and Danny stormed into my room. They were inconsolable. They threatened to quit. The additional twenty metres of chain only helped precipitate further deforestation. Shaking off their rage, they settled into their beer and pizza, food that they had been fantasizing about throughout the entire ordeal. Afterward we racked our brains. The fruit of our brainstorming session: buy more chain. Buy every last metre of chain the hardware store had in stock, wrap it around the entire damn forest and winch that sucker out once and for all.

The next morning, the second the hardware store manager flipped over his OPEN sign, we stormed in and emerged minutes later with a dolly loaded with over sixty metres of heavy-duty chain. When we arrived back at the scene of the crime, the carnage was mind-boggling. There were over two dozen trees lying criss-crossed all over the forest floor, some snapped in two, some splintered into shreds, some with their root systems twisted and contorted beyond recognition from having been unceremoniously ripped from the earth.

We assigned Danny the unenviable task of digging a channel around the base of each wheel to help break the suction that was holding the brute down. While Danny was up to his armpits in muskeg, Lance and I laboriously dragged chain through what was left of the forest, weaving and linking nearly two dozen trees together, forming a snare of sorts. When Lance fired up the Monster and began winding in the slack on the winch cable, the trees captured in the snare—some twenty metres across—began to quiver and quake. The outer trees immediately began to snap and crack under the strain. As weaker trees were wrenched out of the ground, one by one, several large conifers that formed a tight cluster at the centre of the snare held firm. With great drama, the Monster began climbing out of its pit in a series of violent jolts and thrusts, and in one final wild lurch forward, it emerged from its watery grave and rested on higher ground. Mud and brown sludge oozed from every component. It was a sight.

It took us fourteen hours to haul the camp back to the staging area, load our ATVs onto the trucks, and park the Monster where it could be retrieved by the trucking crew. We made it back to our motel room at 3:00 a.m. We were scheduled to meet the crew in Fort McMurray at 10:00 a.m. that very morning, some four and a half hours away. This left us two and a half hours to sleep! We forced ourselves back into motion at 5:30 a.m. and began the long journey to Fort Mac, stopping only briefly to guzzle coffee.

The next project was every bit as ridiculous as the first in terms of "What could possibly happen next"? It took three modes of transportation to get the crew, quads and camp shipped to our next destination. The journey required one hour in a four-by-four truck, forty-five minutes in a Monster ATV (a different Monster), one and a half hours on a barge down the Athabasca River, followed by a short hike up a steep bank to a clearing in the forest. It was here that we would construct our camp.

Reggie had mobilized two support crews to the project seventy-five hours in advance of our arrival, each crew alternating in twelve-hour shifts to maintain a twenty-four-hour supply chain. Crews painstakingly hauled in trees, fuel and equipment by land and water. By the time I arrived with my crew, 75 per cent of Reggie's largest (newest) camp was waiting for us in large piles along the river's edge. My quads, trailers and Silvicool tarps from the previous expedition continued to flow in our direction over the next twenty-four hours. In total, four full days were required to haul everything downriver to where it was needed. It took an additional twelve hours to piece our camp together and get things organized. Incredible!

Reggie had a philosophy regarding these logistically challenging projects. He believed very few contractors possessed the expertise and coping skills (and nut sack) to pull them off. He felt that it was our responsibility to step up and take them on. It was good having Reggie on site with us that day, but I was operating on only two hours of sleep. I was way too exhausted to discuss philosophical concepts with him.

At my insistence, Reggie tacked four additional women onto the crew list, as well as three experienced male planters who I knew from previous planting campaigns. In total I had a crew of thirty, including my rookie crew that was fast becoming a well-oiled planting machine. Our tree quality was good and our production numbers were respectable, but once again, I was on my own to manage this crew. I had no support staff in the field helping me ensure that our plantations would survive their first year in the ground. Under normal circumstances, I'd have two or three foremen checking tree quality full-time. Exacerbating my concern over the potential for setbacks, our new checker—a famously unsympathetic fellow named Eric, was known across the industry for having co-invented the infamous "Ring of Death"—a metal ring with a precise diameter of twelve inches, used to assess quality faults and levy fines. The criteria on this particular contract required that all vegetation and debris be scraped away from the surface of the ground, down to exposed mineral dirt—a process known as "screefing"—to form a circumference with a minimum diameter of twelve inches. The seedling, according to the terms of the contract, was to be placed directly in the centre of this screef. The contract was very specific and strict, stating that failure to screef away debris and vegetation to the minimum required diameter would result in a planting fault. If enough planting faults of this type were identified across any single cutblock, fines would become an issue.

Eric carried around his Ring of Death whenever he ran quality checks. He'd simply slap the ring down over a planted seedling, and if so much as a single blade of grass dared to make an appearance inside of the metal circumference, he'd hit the planter with a quality fault. It was a brutal system of assessing planting quality, and its application became widespread across certain regions of the province. His Ring of Death was likely responsible for the assessment of tens, if not hundreds of thousands of dollars in quality fines over the years.

Eric planned to be with us for only a short time before being replaced by another checker, but I was nervous, and rightfully so. After I introduced him to the crew, Lance pointed at the collection of metal rings dangling from the handlebars of his quad and suggested, "You might want to lose those for this one." Lance's quip came off as a bit of a threat, and I sensed the tension immediately begin to build. It was not how I wanted to start things off.

Walking the ground of a nearby cutblock while the crew was busy piecing our camp together, Eric briefed me on what he would be looking for, and as expected, he introduced me to his Ring of Death. Eric, for the most part, seemed like a reasonable guy. When I argued that he might be unfairly relying on a non-biological gadget as a means to determine the health of a biological organism, he listened intently and I could immediately sense some give. The meeting ended without a resolution, but later on that evening, he surprised me when he offered to sideline his metal gadget for the duration of his stay. It was a solid victory. The reputation that preceded Eric turned out to be way overblown. He was a rich character and all-around great guy. We became good friends in the end.

Our Athabasca River campsite was perched at the edge of a plateau overlooking the mighty Athabasca, some forty metres below. Extending beyond the plateau, an overgrown road wound through a dense forest of spruce, pine and larch. The setting offered the crew numerous options for raising their own personal camps. There were dozens of lush, moss-lined meadows tucked in among the tall conifers, some shaded by the forest canopy, some exposed to sunlight, depending on the time of day. For a shower, one had to walk through the main camp and scale down a steep bank to the river, where several stalls were constructed out of two-by-fours and tarps. The shower itself was a simple affair, invented by Reggie. Water was pumped directly from the river and fed through a large copper coil that was fixed to a metal tripod. A second metal tripod held a large propane-fuelled Tiger Torch that blasted a powerful flame over the copper coil as cold river water circulated through it. With careful tweaking of the flame, the perfect water temperature could be attained. The water then flowed directly into the shower head.

My crew of thirty souls stands out as one of the more entertaining crews I've ever had the pleasure to work with. Frank, our cook, had a wonderfully twisted sense of humour and just seemed to be from another planet altogether. Lance, my tree-delivery guy, mechanic, road repairman, bridge builder, troubleshooter and miracle worker, developed the uncanny ability to anticipate my every move, my every need. He even became adept at finishing my sentences. He was like the older brother I never really had. My other support guy, Lance's cohort Danny, turned out to be a bit of a dud. I rarely dealt with him. As far as I was concerned, he was Lance's charge.

The crew was young and full of piss and vinegar. Of the thirty souls, two standouts were Curt and Wheezy. They were the two hockey players from Swift Current. Wheezy stood all of six foot eight inches. He had a genuinely cheerful disposition, as if he found life slightly more entertaining than the rest of us. When he talked, he liked to lean heavy on the consonants, and he was incredibly loud, showing no hint of self-consciousness whatsoever. His best friend Curt, who loved to play pranks on his giant unsuspecting companion—the type of pranks that often ended in Wheezy writhing on the ground in pain—was impulsive, unconstrained, obnoxious and, more often than not, wildly entertaining. Curt loved to challenge people by pointing out their flaws and weaknesses, preferring to take aim when their defences were down, usually early in the morning before they had their coffee. There were times when he liked to test my resolve by refusing to wake up in the morning. On such days, with only a handful of minutes remaining until our 7:00 a.m. departure, I'd be forced to fire off a round from my shotgun just outside of his tent—it seemed to be the only way to get his butt in gear. Each morning, in order to get the juices flowing, Curt would storm into the middle of his area, jump up on the tallest stump he could find, and belt out the Russian national anthem at the top of his lungs.

I had only one real career veteran on the crew—an older guy named Hank—who came on board at the start of the Athabasca River project. Hank somehow managed to impale his scrotum on a sharp shard of wood after only two days on the job, forcing me to airlift him out. The ER in Fort Mac sewed him up and he managed to make his way back, hooking up with one of my tree shipments four days later.

The women on my crew, including the rookies, were ruthless hardcore planters. They planted trees together, took breaks together, sat together at the dinner table and socialized together every evening in a circle. Their work ethic was exemplary. They were usually the first ones to bag-up in the morning, always the last ones to walk off the block at the end of the day. On my list of top-producing planters, the women routinely rounded out the top three spots.

We were well into the month of May. The weather along the river, approximately one hundred and twenty-five kilometres downstream from the town of Fort Mac, was ideal for planting trees. It was warm and breezy during the day, cool and still in the evenings. Everyone was in high spirits. Frank was even demonstrating a certain culinary flair in the kitchen, reinforcing the elevated atmosphere around camp. People were happy with the money they were making. And there were enough women on the crew to dilute the testosterone in camp. The increased female presence even encouraged a more frequent use of soap, shampoo and deodorant. Curt and Wheezy, enamoured by the new female arrivals, suddenly appeared cleaner, shinier and generally less malodorous than usual.

There was a harmless shower ritual that took place at the end of each workday. The women on the crew were always given the chance to use the showers ahead of the men (chivalry was alive and well in my camps). While they showered and squared themselves away in the privacy of the shower stalls and change room, the boys would all sit and wait their turn with their backs against a large log that lay parallel to the river on the beach. Though the log was at an appropriate distance and facing away from the showering activity, the boys were always on alert, hoping to catch a glimpse of a naked female body part.

On one such evening, I happened to be kicking back with the boys, waiting for the ladies to finish showering, when I noticed something unusual along the very top of the ridge on the other side of the river approximately two kilometres away. Everything suddenly appeared to be in motion, as if the towering conifers lining the horizon were being stroked by a giant invisible hand. Then the forest along the entire far slope began to gyrate wildly. I knew we were in trouble. I jumped up and demanded that everyone begin securing anything that wasn't nailed down. It was a futile command. Within ten seconds we were hit by a squall so powerful, those of us who weren't prepared were blown right off our feet. It was a violent, sustained blast of wind. Within seconds, everything was either levelled or airborne. Screams were heard from the plateau above, followed by two loud crashes. Insisting that everyone stay put on the beach, I scrambled up the steep bank toward camp. As I crested the hill, I saw that two massive trees had come down right next to the dining tent, one overlapping the other in an X formation. The entire forest canopy above was heaving, thrashing violently from side to side. Tree limbs were snapping off and raining down all around us. People were in a state of panic, tripping and falling over one another as they attempted to flee from the hail of debris. It was total mayhem.

Hollering at the top of our lungs, Lance and I managed to herd everyone down toward the river, the only safe zone where tree limbs weren't being hurled at us from every direction. People stumbled and slid down the steep bank—most were in bare feet or flip-flops. As I looked down at the riverbank from the edge of the plateau, half of the crew were lying flat on the sand and the other half were clinging to each other for support. Curt and Wheezy appeared to be fist pumping and cheering wildly. Drifting and bobbing a good distance down the river, barely within sight, were my three empty forty-five-gallon fuel drums, a number of bright red jerry cans, tarps, pieces of wood and every other object that wasn't nailed to the ground.

After fifteen or twenty minutes, the wind gusts abated. Rattled, we made our way back up the steep bank to survey the damage. As we walked over the compound, collecting tree limbs and clearing debris, we were hit by another sudden gust of wind. It was much less severe than the previous blasts, but it caused another tree to come down with a resounding crash, somewhere just beyond the perimeter of our camp.

Adrenaline still pumping, I hopped on my quad and surveyed the damage along our one and only road. I encountered a number of fallen trees within the first five hundred metres of our camp. I lost count after twenty. From the top of my nearest cutblock, I could see large swaths of forest—hundreds of mature trees—levelled. They had either been completely uprooted, or snapped in half like dry twigs. Elsewhere, off in the distance, there were entire sections of forest, acre upon acre, leaning at a forty-five-degree angle. I had never witnessed such widespread destruction in my entire life. I thought about calling Reggie on the two-way radio I had mounted on my quad, but what would I say? And what could I possibly expect him to do?

Damage to the camp was limited to three large tears along the top of the dining tent and a warped freezer lid that took a direct hit from a large tree limb, ruining the cold airlock. Most of our shower unit was sailing north along the Athabasca River. Just about everyone's personal tents were damaged. No one was severely hurt, though—only bruises, scrapes and one black eye from the airborne debris. We were incredibly lucky in that regard.

The windstorm that ravaged the area had weakened the root systems of some of the taller trees in the forest around our camp. Though

CHAPTER ELEVEN

these mature conifers didn't capitulate at the height of the storm, they were rendered unstable. Each night, whenever there was a gust of wind, or even the slightest of breezes, the trees around our camp would begin to rock and sway. Creaks and moans, barely audible at first, would crescendo as the condemned conifers oscillated. And at least two or three times a night these unsettling creaks and moans would usher in a horrendous crash, jolting everyone out of their sleep. Usually the doomed tree was a safe distance from our tents, but every now and again, the impact was right on our doorstep. I'll never forget those late-night tremors.

I had experienced the fear of lying awake in my tent in the middle of the night, wondering if the sounds emanating from the forest were a prelude to the unleashing of unimaginable violence, courtesy of a territorial grizzly bear—but this threat was different. It was real. It was pervasive. It was entirely random. And we had no means to defend ourselves against it.

After a good many sleepless nights and a quad accident on the block—one that bestowed superhero status upon Wheezy when his surging adrenaline gave him sufficient strength to lift the machine clean off my hopelessly pinned body—I decided to schedule some desperately needed R and R. While we were at work on the final day of that shift, I instructed Frank to thaw out the T-bone steaks Reggie packed in the bottom of our freezer for a special occasion. The plan was to build a large fire and grill our entire supper over the open flames. I also had two flats of beer; not enough for a party, but enough to take the edge off our collective anxiety.

As that final day of the shift wound down, Lance decided that it was time to call in a marker. There was barge due with supplies early that evening. He wanted to be on that barge as it made its way back upriver toward town. It wasn't great timing. There were a number of large trees down on the road leading into our next series of cutblocks. I needed him to get busy on the chainsaw, clearing access. When I responded with a resounding "No," he promptly reminded me of our pact, the one where I'd promised to cut him loose for twenty-four hours with no questions asked. As I hemmed and hawed over the prospect of losing my most valuable asset, he forced my hand by threatening to quit. "Go!" was my knee-jerk response. Watching him peacock back to his quad was worth the price of losing him. Before speeding off, he turned and hollered out for everyone to hear, "I owe you a big sloppy one, boss man." Lance!

That evening started off with a barbecue. With the pressures of work lifted and brushed aside for the next thirty-six hours, we revelled in the easy atmosphere around camp. After seasoning, grilling and devouring our meals, as the final rays of daylight were smothered by the cool curtain of night, we gathered around the fire, sipping beer and swapping stories. Then, just as Curt and Wheezy decided it was time to scold me over my thoughtlessness in not having provided enough alcohol for the occasion, we heard the distinct chugging sound of a two-stroke outboard motor. It could be heard somewhere in the darkness upriver, and it seemed to be drawing closer. It was unusual to hear a motorboat travelling the river at night. It was an eerie intrusion. I assumed that its destination was another bush camp farther downriver. Curt called out from the edge of the bluff, "Check it out! It's coming right at us!" We all rushed over and watched as a long river canoe—bright headlights fixed to its bow and stern—crawled up onshore alongside a small dock we had constructed out of logs and wooden pallets. The canoe appeared to be loaded down with something heavy.

Curt and Wheezy were the first to make their way down the bank to greet the captain, an older First Nations gentleman named George. When George pulled back the tarp, revealing his cargo, Curt and Wheezy began whooping and hollering. George explained to me that a man named Lance had offered him $100 to bring us ten flats of beer, thirty cheap cigars, three cartons of cigarettes and a bottle of single-malt scotch with the words BOSS MAN crudely scratched across the label with something sharp.

The atmosphere around our camp became decidedly animated from that moment on. Lance's surprise delivery inspired the largest cannonball chugging ring I had ever witnessed. There were at least twenty treeplanters, in one form of battle stance or another, boldly choking back beer after beer, flat after flat, until there were only a handful of participants left standing. Twenty treeplanters, next seen staggering around camp, slurring their words, telling anyone who would listen how much they meant to them.

Later in the evening, as people really began to cut loose and throw down their guard, we spotted three sets of headlights through the forest. We weren't accustomed to strangers riding into camp. It was an unsettling sight. While Curt and Wheezy attempted to convince everyone that it was the cops, I walked ahead to intercept the strangers. My concern turned to genuine delight when a familiar face came into view from behind the handlebars of a big red quad. It was my dear friend Robin, along with two of his forestry techs. They had arrived to replace Eric, who had barged back to town earlier that evening with Lance. I had come to know Robin from the Nordegg contract nine months earlier. Though he was our checker—the enemy—we had become fast friends. We felt an immediate kinship. We were the same age, we had similar interests and we admired the same girls on the crew.

Robin was one of the good ones. He didn't believe in using his position of authority to gain leverage over us. His motto was, "I'm here to work with you, and I'm here to learn." He and his two techs, having arrived only hours earlier, had set up camp twenty kilometres upriver from us. He said that he'd heard a rumour that a large volume of beer had found its way into our camp and he decided to investigate. How he knew this was beyond me. He refused to give up his source.

The next morning, I woke up to the aroma of steak and eggs. Several of the guys had set their alarms early enough to lay claim to one of the half-dozen T-bone steaks that were left over from the previous night. The majority of the crew were still lounging in their tents, happily enjoying the lull in activity.

Missing out on the last T-bone by a matter of minutes, I settled on the idea of a nice long shower instead. Making my way through camp, I noticed Curt had climbed up on the two criss-crossed conifers that came down during the windstorm, perching himself at the junction where one tree overlapped the other. He was relaxing in the morning sun, whittling a piece of wood. As I strolled past, he looked up, tossed me a wave and continued about his whittling. I remember thinking how unusually calm and contemplative he was—it was a side of Curt I didn't know existed.

Down at the river, while in the process of firing up the shower pump, I heard a long, drawn-out creak followed by a loud crash. I knew what had happened even before reaching the top of the bank. Halfway across the compound, surrounded by a half-dozen people, Curt was rubbing his head and favouring his left knee. Surveying the area, I saw the landscape had changed dramatically. There were now three large trees criss-crossing one another, instead of two. According to Curt, the third tree came down with little warning, landing hard at the base of the two trees he was roosting on. The impact created a teeter-totter effect that catapulted him some ten metres through the air. Curt, being Curt, was absolutely thrilled with the unexpected flying lesson. He couldn't stop laughing. When Wheezy and others showed up, Curt, despite his sore head and gimped leg, re-enacted the entire episode—over and over and over.

Shortly after the human-catapult show, Robin was back in camp with his two technicians offering me a preliminary report on how our planting quality was stacking up. Robin was happy. Our quality faults and excess trees were well within the allowable limits. For a supervisor responsible for tens of thousands of trees going into the ground each and every day, tension and anxiety are always in the air when a new group of checkers is out blitzing your work. There's nothing quite like a happy checker in the morning.

Receiving positive feedback from Robin went a long way toward numbing the effects of my hangover that morning. Emboldened by the positive report, I decided to ask Robin for an enormous favour, one that I was reluctant to lay on Eric. There was a growing pile of foul-smelling, slimy, decomposing trash stacked at the far side of the camp compound. I asked Robin for permission to burn it. It's always a touchy subject, burning garbage. More often than not the request is met with a swift unequivocal "No!" The alternative was hiking it down to the shore, barging it upriver and loading it into the Monster for a jarring forty-five-minute rodeo ride, followed by two hours in the back of a truck to the landfill. I laid out all of the putrid details for Robin to consider. I also threw in the very real concern that it would likely begin attracting bears if it continued to marinate in the hot sun. It wasn't an easy decision for Robin. Saying yes meant breaking the rules. But this was a special situation, being as isolated and transportationally challenged as we were. After weighing the pros and cons, with chin in hand and a few token scratches to the head, Robin finally relented. "Get the crew involved," he said. "We'll dig a deep pit and burn it." That made a lot of sense. We'd be able to bury whatever was left over.

In no time, I had six guys busy with shovels, led by one slightly gimped Curt and his cohort Wheezy. Within thirty minutes we had a pit that was over a metre wide, three metres long, and almost two metres deep. After lining the bottom of the pit with layers of cardboard and tossing nearly two dozen bags of rotting trash on top, I took a five-gallon container of mixed gas and began slowly pouring it onto the vile, nauseating mass. I must have been engaged in a riveting conversation with Robin at the time as neither he nor I—nor anyone else for that matter—were paying attention to the volume of gas I was pouring out. After nearly emptying the five-gallon jerry can into the pit, I created a long fuse by pouring the remaining gas out onto the ground as I backed away. Everyone appeared to be at a safe distance as I struck a match and tossed it onto the ground, igniting the fuse. We were not.

The explosion blew me backward two metres into a tree. The only image I recall was a blue vertical pillar, accompanied by an eardrum-bursting *whoomph*. Everyone who was standing nearby was blown backward and knocked flat onto the ground. The explosion launched the entire mass of stinking refuse into the air. Some of it was hung up in trees, but most lay in smoldering clumps, spread out over a large area of forest. Frank, who was watching through an open flap in the dining tent, blew his air horn non-stop until we had the entire crew assembled, darting through the forest, putting out dozens of small fires with their planting shovels. We barely managed to contain the small blazes before they grew out of control. Had it not been for Frank's horn and the crew's rapid response, we likely would have been forced into an evacuation scenario as the forest floor was tinder-dry and loaded with dead wood.

Everyone in the vicinity of the pit experienced impaired vision from the intensity of the blast. One of Robin's technicians was forced to take the rest of the day off, unable to drive his quad back to camp, requiring a full twenty-four hours before his vision was restored. I really outdid myself in the stupidity department on that one.

Lance arrived back in camp later that night and was immediately mobbed by the crew. Everyone knew that he was responsible for the boat full of spirits that arrived at our shore the previous night. Before I could thank him personally, Curt and Wheezy dragged him off to show him the tree that nearly launched Curt into orbit earlier in the day, and the garbage bomb that detonated soon after.

WE WERE INTO THE SECOND WEEK OF JUNE WHEN ROBIN NOTIFIED me that I was to receive a 30 per cent increase in the number of trees assigned to the contract. The news came as a shock. I was behind schedule as it was. My crew was strong, but there was no way we could handle the extra half-million trees—my project had a strict deadline and it was approaching fast. Then came the bombshell. My crew was about to double in size! Thirty new planters were due to arrive early the next morning and would be setting up camp twenty kilometres upriver in an area that was in proximity to the new cutblocks that had been added to my program. This new group was coming from another

Alberta company—one of Reggie's main competitors—and though they would be accompanied by two foremen, it would be my responsibility to set them up, direct their day-to-day operations and maintain their supply chains. Reggie had just added another ten hours onto what was already an eighteen-hour day for me. I was pissed off. The added workload didn't even come with an increase in pay. In hindsight, I should have negotiated some contingencies into my verbal contract with Reggie. In hindsight, I probably should have walked.

The new crew was well equipped, arriving with their own camp, setting it up at the edge of their largest cutblock. Unfortunately, it took me thirty minutes of hard quad riding to reach them from my end of the project. That was a one-hour round trip. I didn't have one hour to spare in my day. I didn't have one minute to spare and I needed to make this journey at least twice every single workday. The road access separating both operations was good, though, with several unbroken stretches that were high and dry, straight as an arrow. This afforded me the rare opportunity to open my quad up in fifth gear and accelerate as fast as the machine was designed to travel. And I needed the speed. Every minute that I left my crew unattended was a minute where something could go wrong—ours was fertile territory for Murphy's Law.

Fortunately, there was a lot of experience on this new crew, and they appeared to be fairly well disciplined. The foremen were two amazing young women named Janis and Charlie. They were a high-energy pair and they understood exactly what I needed from them. At a time when I couldn't afford to be distracted, not even for a moment, Charlie and I developed an instant attraction to one another. She took my breath away from the moment our eyes met. She was very petite, barely five feet tall, but she had a radiance and charisma that made her seem larger than life. She had short black hair, penetrating brown eyes, a tiny nose and ample pouty lips. She was a beautiful lass, through and through. I was in love. Again. Though we didn't spend a great deal of time together, we found our moments.

On one particularly manic day in mid-June, a day when I needed to be in both places at the same time, I decided to travel over to check on Charlie and her crew first. They were apparently having difficulty with some of the naturals they were encountering on their cutblock (they couldn't determine which naturals were good and which were bad—this was making Robin antsy).

The last four kilometres of the road leading into Charlie's camp were tricky. The road, which wound through a series of small cut-blocks, had several sharp curves as well as four deep washouts that were six metres across with sheer banks on both sides—the aftermath of severe flooding from earlier in the spring. All four of these ditches, spaced several hundred metres apart, required the utmost caution to negotiate. On approach, I would slow right down, and in low gear, carefully crawl down the steep bank on one side, around the boulders strewn along the bottom and then up the sharp bank on the opposite side. After visiting Charlie's side of the project, I always kept a heedful count of the obstacles as I raced back to my crew. Once I was past the fourth washout, I could punch the accelerator and race off at a dizzying rate of speed.

When I reached the other side of the project that morning, there was a conference going on in the middle of the road between Janis, Charlie and Robin. Their body language suggested no stress or tension whatsoever. I was informed that the problem had been resolved. It had been decided that all of the existing naturals on the block were unhealthy and were to be ignored altogether. Suddenly, there were no quality issues to speak of.

I was on cloud nine knowing that Robin was happy with the other crew's work. At the same time, I knew I had to get back to my own crew, and they were a good half-hour away. As I jumped back on my quad and put it in gear, my spirits were high. I was busting! A potential problem had been averted, Robin was in a good mood, Charlie winked at me as I passed her on the road, and the sun was shining brightly. It promised to be a glorious day.

As I cautiously crawled over what I thought was the final washout in the sequence of four, I punched the accelerator and hurtled off at a breathtaking speed. Then, suddenly, I came to a curve in the road that shouldn't have been there, causing me to drift wildly around the apex. On the other side of the curve, there it was: the fourth washout in the road that I thought was behind me. The washout that I'd lost track of in all of my excitement.

I had perhaps one full second to consider my options. Do I slam on the brakes and plow straight into the steep bank on the other side? Or do I attempt the impossible—accelerate and jump the damn thing? I opted for the latter. When I felt all four wheels leave the ground, I immediately sensed I was in trouble. I felt the heavy ass-end of my quad drop slightly in mid-air. I didn't have nearly enough speed, or height. Though my front wheels landed clean, my rear wheels caught the edge of the opposite bank, launching me over the handlebars and through the air like a rag doll. When I landed, I landed hard and rolled for a good distance. I glimpsed the blur of my quad cartwheeling past me, end over end within inches of my head. It continued cartwheeling down the road before disappearing somewhere into the cutblock below.

I could barely breathe. I tried to fill my lungs with air, but I could manage only short, stunted breaths. The pain in my chest and back was excruciating. After writhing around on the ground for what must have been thirty minutes, I finally managed to regain control of my limbs and stand upright. I was bleeding profusely from numerous scrapes and cuts along my arms, legs, abdomen and face. Blood blinded me in one eye. It felt as if I had just been fed through a meat grinder.

Limping along the road, following the deep gouges in the surface created by my acrobatic quad, I finally found it about thirty metres from the edge of the washout. It was lying on its side, wedged against a stump in the cutblock below. Thanks to elevated levels of adrenaline, I managed to right the quad, get it started and walk it back up onto the road. I spent another fifteen minutes hammering away on my crumpled foot pegs, gearshift and handlebars with a large round rock, desperately trying to make my ride operational again. My two-way radio—the only connection I had with the outside world—had been sheared off the frame during the accident and was nowhere to be found.

When I finally arrived back at the other side of the project, everything was fine. My entire crew was still in motion, still putting trees in the ground. I used the opportunity to clean off some of my wounds in a nearby creek. By that time the pain was beginning to radiate through my entire body. I had a twisted ankle, a severely sprained knee, a wrenched back, horribly butchered elbows and wrists, and it was clear that I had cracked ribs on both sides of my chest. Even after I cleaned up in the creek, people looked at me as if I were some sort of a monster. The gouges and open wounds on my face and arms were particularly off-putting.

Though I endured unimaginable pain over the next several days, I managed to maintain a degree of control over the project. Robin and Charlie helped pick up the slack on the far side of the project, insisting that I not attempt any long commutes on my quad until I began to heal. Lance also rose to the occasion, dragging the plot cord around, keeping track of the crew's quality on our end of things. Without them, the contract would have ground to an abrupt halt.

Charlie and her crew ended up breaking down camp and departing one week before the last tree went into the ground. Her company had picked up a contract of its own. I wanted to see her before she left, but I was still too busted up from my accident to travel the distance to say goodbye.

The Athabasca River contract was one of those projects that seemed to drag on forever. Everyone was exhausted from the summer heat, the blackflies and the relentless pace. When Robin informed me that he was taking a day off and heading into town, he asked me if there were any messages he should pass along to Reggie. I didn't know where to begin. I chose to forgo the gory details of my accident, and asked him to simply instruct Reggie to schedule a full day off in town for the crew. I needed one full day off in Fort McMurray, not including half days or travel days. No exceptions. I suspected that this might ruffle a few feathers.

On the final day of the contract, I pulled five planters out of circulation and instructed them to help Frank, Danny and Lance break down everything in camp with the exception of the kitchen appliances. I was worried about putting too much strain on Frank, who was beginning to show signs of a mental breakdown: talking to himself, flying off the handle for no reason, angry voices emanating from his tent in the middle of the night (note: he slept alone). The plan was to break down the entire camp, leaving the kitchen until last, allowing Frank to cook a full meal that we would eat picnic-style later that evening. Giving Frank control of a small crew he could boss around for a day seemed to placate him.

As it turned out, the timing and organization couldn't have worked out better. We pounded our last trees into the ground just as the final pieces of our camp were being stacked into neat piles along the river. As we sat down to eat, the river barge arrived to begin the lengthy process of hauling everything away.

The Athabasca River project was over. We had one contract remaining in our season. It was a short one, but I wanted everyone well rested for it. The prospect of hitting Fort Mac by noon the following day had everyone vibrating with excitement.

Waking up at first light the next morning, we broke down our tents and dragged our personal gear down to the barge. The barge crew and captain were fast asleep on the deck, cuddled up in their sleeping bags. They still had three solid days of work ahead of them, hauling our camp, ATVs and gear back to pavement. We were on our way out.

Not having given breakfast much thought—all we had were a few bunches of bananas and a dozen apples at the bottom of a box—I treated everyone to brunch at a greasy spoon near the edge of town. It was a nice way to ease back into the world.

I spent the remainder of that day quarrelling with Reggie over the phone in my motel room. He had ignored my instructions and scheduled our barge downriver for the very next day. I had made a promise. I'd assured the crew that they could sleep in the next morning and enjoy an entire day off in town. The next project was only a four-day scenario, but Reggie wanted to wrap things up as soon as possible. "The crew can have their day off on the barge," he kept insisting. "It'll be great fun." Neither one of us was willing to budge. After multiple, heated, exhausting exchanges over the telephone, he finally backed off, agreeing to reschedule the barge for the day after.

Back in those days, management viewed R and R as an unnecessary luxury, warranted in only the most extreme situations. This seemed to be a common mindset among Alberta-based companies, arising from the constant, urgent need to "make hay while the sun shines." Weather and deteriorating access conditions were a constant threat. Protocol often demanded that crews push themselves, and continue pushing until they collapsed from exhaustion.

The final project was a doozy. Somewhere out in the middle of the Athabasca River was an island that was 90 per cent clearcut. We were to barge in, find a spot to go ashore, set up a small, scaled-down version of our camp and plant the entire island from one end to the other.

After a slow three-hour barge ride downriver, we arrived at our isle. It didn't look like much from the water. It appeared to be one kilometre long, perhaps three hundred metres wide, and completely flat. While the crew unloaded the barge, Lance and I walked the ground to figure out a planting strategy. It was the damnedest thing: the logging company had left a few clumps of trees here and there, but aside from that, everything was clipped down to a nub, as if a giant lawnmower made several passes over it.

Before we cut the barge captain loose—after consulting with the crew members, who were unanimous in their desire to wrap the project up lickety-split—we instructed him to return early in the morning on day four. We were prepared to work from sun-up until sundown to finish the trees off in only three days. The pressure was on. Again.

Our Athabasca River Island camp was a shoestring affair. We had no generator, our fridge and freezer were replaced by large coolers packed with ice, our oven was replaced by three large Coleman stoves and our dining room was a small army tent. Even more limiting, the barge had no room for a quad. This meant that Lance and I would be forced to lug boxes filled with seedlings on our backs for the first day and a half, a scenario Lance found particularly distressing. Frank was our greatest concern, though. He was really beginning to lose it. He stopped talking to everyone—except himself. He also began to do strange things. At the end of our first day, we discovered that he had taken all of our bread—needed to make sandwiches for our lunches— and whipped up a giant vat of bread pudding. It was disgusting. No one dared touch it. Later that evening he made great drama out of dumping the entire vat of starchy mush into the river. Then he instigated an argument with himself inside the kitchen tent—an argument he apparently lost.

I had a short meeting with the crew early the next day and instructed them to throw heaps of praise Frank's way after supper that evening, even if his food offended the senses. We needed to prevent him from melting down completely. Strapping him to a log and setting him adrift down the mighty Athabasca was my Plan B.

Planting the island went without incident. We had the perfect number of trees and we managed to wrap up the project at the end of day three, allowing us to partially break down camp in preparation for the barge's return early the next morning. Frank grew sullen and listless. Some on the crew speculated that he had a condition and that he had run out of his meds weeks earlier and had been rendered chemically imbalanced. He appeared harmless though, and that allayed most of my concern.

The barge arrived early the next morning accompanied by a crew boat. The vessel had seats for eighteen bodies. We were a crew of twenty-eight. There was another boat on its way, but its ETA was unknown. The crew became fixated on the eighteen seats that were immediately available and rushed to claim them like it was some sort of life-or-death game of musical chairs. Not only did the prank leave ten people standing without a seat, the camp and equipment were still lying in piles onshore. A strange standoff ensued. Those who had secured a seat refused to relinquish it and help the rest of us load the barge. This spring planting season was obviously very long in the tooth.

Someone took a picture of me as I was pacing back and forth onshore, reading the riot act, attempting to convince people to give up their seats. I finally threatened to cancel both crew boats and force everyone to experience an all-day Athabasca River barge ride unless they complied. When I was shown that picture several weeks later, I didn't recognize myself: raging, mouth open in mid-holler, unhealed gashes on my chin and cheeks. It was an unsettling image.

After a convincing series of threats, the barge was finally loaded, and soon after, a second smaller crew boat pulled up onshore. Without hesitation, the crew—led by one ranting and raving camp cook—rushed to claim a seat on the larger of the two vessels. I happily jumped aboard the smaller craft with the remainder of the crew. As it turned out, the smaller boat travelled at twice the speed of the larger one. I attempted to convince our captain to slow down and travel alongside the larger vessel, but his schedule was tight—he needed to be much farther downriver later that morning. There were a number of incredulous faces on the larger boat. Curt and Wheezy nearly fell overboard while jumping up and down on their seats, shaking their fists in anger as we sped past.

It was a lucky break that I managed to get ahead of the rest of the crew. I had a big evening planned and I needed time to set things up. My intention was to reserve everyone a room, treat them to dinner and drinks and then follow up with a shindig back at the motel later that night.

We arrived at our trucks at the edge of town at 11:00 a.m. and were settled in our motel rooms shortly after. According to our captain, the rest of the crew was approximately one hour behind us. With the remainder of the crew in Lance's capable hands, I organized advance money with the bank, booked a number of tables at a restaurant and shopped for booze.

At 2:00 p.m. the remaining crew had yet to make it back to town. I was starting to get concerned. At 4:00 p.m., with still no word or sign, I began calling everyone I could think of to help figure out what had happened. I finally called Reggie—he began working the phone on his end. At 7:00 p.m., I still had eighteen missing crew members and no one could tell me a damn thing.

Tired of waiting impatiently in the motel room for the phone to ring, I decided to drive the short distance back to where the crew boat was due to land—there was no crew in sight, their trucks were still parked at the edge of the landing. It was just before midnight when I finally received word. A radio operator relayed a call from a trapper who lived in a cabin along the Athabasca River. The message was simply: "Crew is safe. Will be catching crew boat at first light. Will arrive home two hours hence."

I was at the landing at 6:00 a.m., and after I'd waited the better part of two hours, a large crew boat finally came into sight. As it pulled up onshore, my AWOL crew staggered off the boat, one by one, looking as if they had just returned from an all-night kegger.

This is the Coles Notes version of what transpired twenty-two hours earlier: Within minutes of our smaller crew boat overtaking their larger vessel, they had lost power and began drifting aimlessly. They were at the mercy of the current. The captain attempted to make emergency repairs to the motor but was unsuccessful. In desperation the crew grabbed their planting shovels and used them as paddles, managing to reach a small island, which they were able to latch onto. The captain, who forgot to charge the battery on his radio the night before, had no way of calling out for help. Their only hope was spotting and flagging down a passing vessel, but it was a slow day on the river. After several hours passed with no rescue in sight, Frank decided to take matters into his own hands. He began pouring gasoline out onto the water and igniting it, hoping an overhead plane would spot the flames. The crew was too stunned to intervene at first—I know I would have been. By the time they got between Frank and his matches, he had managed to ignite the dry brush along the edge of the island with one of his flaming puddles.

The fire quickly turned into a blaze. Horrified, the crew snapped into action and used their shovels to dig a firebreak in an attempt to prevent the entire island from being consumed by flames. It took them several hours to get the blaze under control, and by that time, an overhead plane had spotted the smoke. A helicopter was then dispatched to investigate. It arrived after the fire had been extinguished and spotted the stranded crew waving furiously at the edge of the island. The pilot managed to find an open area to land and was able to communicate with the likes of Curt and Wheezy face to face (I wish I had been there for that conversation). After unsuccessfully trying to arrange a crew boat—it was getting late in the day—the pilot radioed a trapper friend of his who lived in a cabin downriver. He happily agreed to shelter the crew overnight, and soon began transporting them, six at a time, in his small riverboat. He fed them macaroni and cheese—an important detail according to some—and then they all slept under the stars that night, laying out their sleeping bags on a large deck that overlooked the river. A crew boat was summoned at first light the next day and they were back under my wing an hour or so later.

The crew's conduct, having stormed the larger crew boat—pushing others out of their way in order to claim a seat on what ultimately turned out to be a stricken vessel—had an element of irony attached to it. I know it wasn't lost on them.

I reserved the motel for one additional night, letting the crew relax for the rest of the day. Later that evening, we were all seated at the restaurant along with eighteen pitchers of beer. In hindsight, I should have cut the beer consumption in half. We were kicked out of the restaurant before we even had a chance to dig in to our main courses. I've never seen so many doggy bags walk out of a restaurant at the same time.

When I arrived back home in Calgary several days later, the first person I went to see was my mom. Taking one look at my face, she broke down in tears, right on her front doorstep. In hindsight, I should have waited another week for the gashes on my mug to heal before surprising her at home. She then attempted, yet again, to convince me to quit the treeplanting business, to go back to school, to get a "proper job." She abhorred what I did for a living. She was convinced that if I continued on the same path, she'd end up outliving me—a nightmare every mother harbours deep down.

I wasn't quite ready to hang up my planting bags and shovel. Not yet anyway. Despite the challenges, the struggles, the hardship and the risk to mind and body, I was having a blast. I was living life and I was living it in the moment. And the icing on the cake: I had a brand-new batch of stories to trot out for anyone who was willing to listen. The only question being: would anyone believe even half of the crazy shit that I claimed went down that season?

# THE BREAKDOWN

||||||||||||||||||||||||||||||||||||||||||||||||||||||||||||||||||||||||||||

THE BRUISING, THE GASHES, THE SPRAINS AND THE CRACKED RIBS from my quad accident took another month to heal after I arrived back home during that summer of 1989. My spring season in Alberta, which turned into a veritable variety show of thrills, spills, mishaps and adventure, took a toll on me physically and mentally. Reggie's previous Alberta manager—the guy I replaced—had taken his own life, and though the details surrounding his tragic death were sketchy, I couldn't help suspect that the stress of the job played a part.

During my summer break, I chatted with a number of people who supervised treeplanting crews in BC. They all had an Alberta story. They all had ventured into the province at one point in their careers. For the majority of them, once was enough.

Earlier in the year, when I explained to EG Ltd (the company that treated me so well one year earlier) that I wouldn't be joining them for their 1989 spring season, that I had decided to take a shot at running crews in Alberta instead, they thought I was completely out of my mind. Having made a foray into the province themselves, *once*, they tried their best to dissuade me. Had I listened, I likely wouldn't have walked with a limp for the remainder of that year. I likely wouldn't have made my poor mom cry either.

I had plenty of time to think as I convalesced at my sister's house in Calgary that summer. By remaining committed to Reggie, I wondered if I wasn't setting myself up for more than I could handle. I loved the challenge, but I wasn't sure if I could stomach a repeat of the spring of 1989. From the moment I stepped out of my truck at the Lesser Slave Lake staging area, things had begun to unravel—the situation threatened to blow up in my face. Perhaps with a seasoned crew and a good supervisor backing me up, I might stand a fighting chance. But after polling my crew at the end of the season, no one expressed any real interest in returning for another round. I got the distinct impression that they had endured enough insanity for one lifetime. Those who did express interest in strapping the planting bags on again said that they'd likely seek opportunities farther west, in the province of BC.

Losing experienced treeplanters was part of the game back then for Alberta-based treeplanting companies. Many operators experienced ridiculously high turnover rates. Some unscrupulous contractors tried to coerce their employees into signing employment contracts that clawed back up to 30 per cent of their earnings should they leave a project prematurely. Other contractors deployed a so-called bonus system, one that added 20 to 30 per cent onto a treeplanter's earnings, if they managed to tough it out for the entire season. The "bonus" component of the arrangement wasn't a reward, though—it merely boosted one's earnings up to a level that might be considered adequate. These duplicitous measures violated every labour law, every sense of fair play, but very few individuals had the resolve to fight back when they were being shaken down. I was never forced to sign such a contract. No one had the guts to put one in front of me.

At the risk of breaking their contract with the company and losing a large percentage of their earnings in the process, people quit. They walked. Mass exoduses were not uncommon. When this occurred, the contractor was forced to scramble. If the company didn't have sufficient reserves on standby, ready to be immediately mobilized for the imperilled project, the site manager would often resort to stalking the streets of nearby towns, looking to recruit any derelict who happened along. I witnessed one of these acts of desperation once. I was determined never to be put in that position myself.

I needed to have a serious discussion with Reggie. I liked working for the man. I particularly enjoyed the freedom and autonomy he afforded me. I did not enjoy, however, the hour-to-hour uncertainty of operating in such hostile environments. At times, it felt as if we were camped at the edge of a whirling vortex, with certain catastrophe hovering nearby. I needed to convince Reggie to allow me to explore opportunities outside of the province—opportunities farther west.

After mulling things over for several weeks, I approached Reggie with a proposition. While I was willing to continue helping him manage his shitshows in Alberta, I asked him to consider bankrolling my campaign to carve out a niche in BC. There were a number of regions within the province that I considered prospective, areas where I had already worked as a treeplanter. Reggie was reluctant at first, but I kept working on him. I decided that if he didn't support me in the end, I would walk. It was as simple as that.

In the end, I got the green light to go ahead, to travel into BC, to kick open as many doors as I dared. Reggie and his office staff had already been working behind the scenes for over a week putting together a travel itinerary for me, one with a number of meetings scheduled with key foresters. Two days later, I was behind the wheel of Reggie's newest four-by-four truck, sights set on the nexus of the treeplanting universe: Prince George, BC.

I think every supervisor has a love-hate relationship with viewing. If you can afford to treat yourself well for the duration of a long viewing campaign, with good meals and a comfortable motel room to look forward to at the end of a day, it can be a tolerable experience. But the novelty of exploring logging roads from sun-up to sundown, with one hand on the steering wheel and the other on a sketchy map, can wear off pretty damn fast.

As usual, the regional maps I received from the various forestry offices—maps that we relied upon to explore every facet of the project—were hopelessly flawed. Unless you were already familiar with the road systems, you could expect to waste 50 per cent or more of your time driving in circles. All too often, the maps were a year or two old and didn't accurately reflect recent road construction—the roads that had been recently pushed into freshly harvested areas. I suspected certain foresters of harbouring sadistic tendencies, intentionally setting us up with spurious material in order to mess with our heads. Perhaps it was their way of testing our mettle, of testing our resourcefulness.

One had to take great care not to take unnecessary risks while viewing trees. Rolling the dice and driving through cross ditches or sections of washed-out roads could get you jammed up, stuck in the middle of nowhere with no one around for miles to bail you out. To help mitigate that risk, Reggie hooked me up with a two-way radio.

I viewed trees for eight long weeks that summer and fall. I lost count of the number of cutblocks I visited. All told I submitted bids on more than twenty-five million trees—trees that were destined to go into the ground the following spring. During the first week of October, bid results began trickling in. By the second week of October, I was alerted that I was the successful bidder on a large contract near the town of MacKenzie. This was the foot-in-the-door opportunity I'd been looking for. I was excited. I know Reggie was too.

On October 30, I decided that I had exhausted every opportunity to find work for our company in BC. But while I was packing up and preparing for the long journey back to Alberta, I discovered a manila envelope wedged between the seats of my truck. Inside were details of a two-million-tree contract, one I had neglected to slot into my viewing schedule. According to the viewing package, all two million trees were to be planted on 100 per cent mechanically groomed ground. It was all scarified. A total cream-show. There was no way I was leaving Prince George without throwing a bid at it.

Once again the regional map I was given to locate the project had me driving in circles. I explored the area for five or six hours without finding a single cutblock. I was about to give up. It was getting late in the day, the clouds were laden with precipitation, light snow was already beginning to fall and I needed at least one hour of daylight to help find my way back to pavement. Rolling the dice, I decided to turn up one last junction before throwing in the towel. Then the Fates interceded—at the very end of the road, rising up in front of me for as far as the eye could see, were hundreds of hectares of scarified ground.

I was thrilled, having found the object of my quest that day. I guess I was more than thrilled—I celebrated with a series of doughnuts out on the landing at the entrance to the first block. After letting the brat in me act out for a spell, I decided to take a cursory look at the area on foot before racing back to the highway. As I was parking my truck, applying the brake and shifting the gear, the stick suddenly snapped off in my hand. It snapped right off! Incredulous, I attempted to reattach it to the steering column. It wouldn't reattach. The truck was stuck in park.

I tried everything I could think of to put the truck back into drive. I slumped back in my seat after exhausting every pathetic attempt at remedying the situation, feeling waves of panic sweep over me as the reality of my predicament kicked in. I was stuck at the back end of the Bowron, about as far from pavement as a person could conceivably travel on that road system, and the weather was deteriorating. I did have the shelter of my truck, though. I was able to keep the engine running, which threw off as much heat as I needed, but that was of little comfort. Then the skies opened up. Snow began to fall, moderately at first, then in thick, unrelenting waves.

Within twenty minutes of having stranded myself, I was in whiteout conditions. The snow came down with such intensity, my visibility was reduced to almost nil. Every now and again it would lighten up ever so slightly, opening up a glimpse of the road leading in along the valley, but then everything began to blend, blanketed in at least a foot of white powder.

CHAPTER TWELVE

I worked my two-way radio, desperately attempting to secure a connection.[1] Each time I succeeded in reaching an operator in Prince George, she either had a difficult time hearing me or the signal would abruptly cut out. After forty-five minutes without success, I felt panic really begin to set in. The blizzard was showing no sign of letting up. I couldn't distinguish the road leading into the block from the rest of the terrain along the valley. Everything was buried under at least a half-metre of snow. My remote location, along with the severity of the storm, rendered my radio useless. I began to lose hope, but I had to keep trying. It was my only play.

After I connected with and then was abruptly cut off by over two dozen radio operators in the Prince George region, an operator from the Fort Nelson area mysteriously picked up my signal. I was shocked when she announced Fort Nelson as her location. It didn't seem possible that my radio could reach that far north, but the connection was clear, and she was able to understand every word I was saying. I explained to her that I was in trouble, that I needed her to find me a tow-truck driver in the Prince George area. Understanding the gravity of my situation, she immediately dialed a twenty-four-hour towing service, and after several long, torturous rings, I heard a woman's voice come over the phone.

When my radio operator explained that this was a two-way radio call emergency, neither of us were prepared for the woman's response.

---

1. The truck-mounted two-way radio is a curious device. Aside from allowing you to communicate with other travellers on the road, it can connect you with a radio operator, depending on the remoteness of your location. When you hold down the transmit button for three seconds and then release it, an operator's voice should come on. The operator will immediately announce his or her location and ask you what number you would like to call. They will then dial the number for you, acting as a go-between or middleman. Usually, the operator will make initial contact with the party you're attempting to contact before handing the conversation off to you. The operator will then remain on standby in the event you require further assistance.

The raspy voice at the other end of the line explained that her husband—the tow-truck driver—was unable to come to the phone. He was busy transferring fish from a small aquarium to a larger aquarium they had just purchased from the mall earlier that afternoon. When she began describing how beautiful the new aquarium looked in their living room, my radio operator cut her off, abruptly, reiterating that this was an emergency. Clearly annoyed, the woman explained that her husband was less than twenty feet away and that she'd relay everything that I had to say. I then took over the conversation, summarizing my situation as clearly and concisely as possible.

I was forced to listen as the couple squabbled across the room, as country music filled the background, expecting my radio signal to cut out at any moment. He kept asking his wife the same questions over and over, demanding greater detail regarding my exact location and situation. She was becoming increasingly vexed. While noisily supervising the transfer of their pet fish, she talked at me and barked back at him at the same time. Meanwhile, I was being buried by a blizzard several valleys away from them (the extreme weather apparently hadn't hit this couple's front yard yet). I wondered if I was even being taken seriously. I could only hope and pray that my radio signal would hold out long enough to secure a rescue.

When the tow-truck driver heard the word "blizzard" repeated enough times, he stopped playing around with his fish, wrestled the phone away from his truculent spouse and began talking to me directly. Finally I had this guy's undivided attention. He insisted that he knew exactly where I was, based on my descriptions, and even went so far as to describe some of the more prominent topographical features in the area.

He knew where I was! For the first time in well over an hour my triple-digit heart rate began to dial back, my breathing became less laboured, less asthmatic. He said that he'd have to travel across town to get a much larger rig, based on the conditions I was describing. I was told not to expect him for at least three hours. When he hung up the phone, my radio operator, who had been anxiously monitoring the conversation the whole time, came back on and asked how I was faring. But before I could extend my most profound gratitude to her for having saved my life, the signal mysteriously cut out.

As the hours passed and the veil of night descended, darkness highlighted the contours of the snow-covered landscape. My truck was positioned facing the open valley. It was an eerie setting. The snow continued to fall, sometimes driving at an angle, sometimes falling vertically. Every once in a while I went for a short walk in the thigh-deep snow, and each time I jumped out of the truck, the snow was several centimetres deeper. I had to have faith that the driver knew what he was doing, that he had the common sense to chain up before venturing into the Bowron River Valley. There was over a metre of snow on the ground and I couldn't imagine any vehicle pushing through unless it was a heavy one—a heavy machine with over-sized tires wrapped in thick chains.

After three hours turned into four, I became fixated on the vague outline of a steep hill three kilometres farther down the valley. As I watched for evidence of a foreign source of light, any shift or alteration in the texture of the distant snow-covered forest, ridges or rock faces—one that might suggest the encroachment of a vehicle's high beams—my imagination began to play tricks on me. There were several occasions, minutes apart, where I celebrated my rescue prematurely, only to be disappointed. As four hours turned into five, panic began to set in again. I began to imagine the worst. I imagined my rescuer getting stuck, driving off the road, or worse.

Finally, there was a perceptible and continuous play of lights along the white rolling contours at the far end of the valley, one that morphed into a powerful fixed beam of light as a large truck emerged from behind the hill. I watched in rapture as it closed the distance between us. It couldn't have been travelling more than twenty kilometres an hour, labouring to maintain forward momentum through snow that was now well over a metre deep.

Flashing my headlights to signal my position, I was shocked at the size of the rig he had brought in. It was large enough to haul a logging truck. The driver was exactly as I had imagined him: baseball cap, beard, cheesy mustache, and a huge grin knowing he'd be ringing the cash register at the end of the night. It was worth every penny, though. The drive back down the valley, even though he had cut himself a path coming in, was a slow and often perilous crawl. When we finally reached the highway, we celebrated with hoots, hollers and well-deserved pats on the shoulders. When we reached Prince George, he dropped me off at my motel, gave me a few leads on the best watering holes in town and offered to drop my truck off outside the dealership on his way home. My viewing campaign officially ended that night.

SEVERAL DAYS LATER, THERE WAS EXCITEMENT IN THE AIR AT Reggie's office. I had landed the company's very first BC project, and I was confident that if I could successfully execute on this first contract, many more would follow. I'd then have solid footing in an area where I was comfortable operating—an area that wouldn't chew me up and spit me out during the course of a season.

As fall turned into winter, Reggie informed me that the majority of his Alberta spring season had been pushed back into the summer. There would be only one large contract to run in Alberta before travelling to the BC Interior. The Promised Land: that's how I planned to characterize the journey with my crew.

Then the phone rang early one December morning.

Three years earlier, I had entrusted my entire life savings to some people who were very close to me. After their business venture went belly up, they refused to take responsibility for the debt. This forced me to take legal action. The phone call I received that December day was from my lawyer in Vancouver. Things were about to get very busy where my lawsuit was concerned. I had to be prepared to travel to Vancouver for depositions, a summary trial and a full-blown trial if all else failed. I needed to ensure that my schedule was flexible for the entire spring!

When you're running treeplanting contracts, your schedule is anything but flexible. It's full-on, often eighteen hours per day

CHAPTER TWELVE

(particularly in Alberta), without so much as a single day off. Breaking away from my role as a supervisor would be an impossibility. I had a choice to make: drop my lawsuit and remain committed to the 1990 spring season I was instrumental in piecing together with SFS Ltd., or pursue the lawsuit, forcing Reggie to find someone to cover for me. It wasn't an easy decision to make. I chose to go to court.

Breaking the news to Reggie was difficult. He was flabbergasted at first. But to his credit, he understood. He told me to go and do what I needed to do, and to hurry back when I was done. I couldn't shake the feeling that I had turned my back on him, that I was leaving him high and dry, especially since it was my idea to make the big push into BC. But the money I was seeking to recover in court was worth three times as much as I could make in any single season of planting trees or running crews. At the time, it felt like the right thing to do.

With one simple phone call, I was able to secure a temporary spot as a guest planter on one of EG Ltd.'s crews for the spring of 1990—a position that EG management promised would afford as much flexibility as I required to travel back and forth between the worksite and Vancouver. I thought that with any luck, I would see an early resolution to my litigation.

I began planting trees on the coast with EG Ltd. in February of 1990. Though I was focused on the work, I was in a state of limbo. At the time, it seemed that everything in my life was in a state of conflict, a state of flux. I was anxious over my imminent court case in Vancouver. I was anxious over the bind I had put Reggie in. I was anxious over a woman I had become quite enamoured with, one who was unsure of her feelings toward me.

Over the spring, after making several trips to Vancouver, I gradually regained control of things. I managed to score a minor victory in my lawsuit. I also managed to win the heart of the woman I had become rather fond of, though our time together was cut short when life got in the way. But my concern for Reggie, the crew and the BC project I had fought so hard for was difficult to shake.

Later on that season, at the end of May, we were planting in a remote valley east of the town of Revelstoke, BC. This area is unique in that its weather patterns are similar to those along the coast, receiving unusually large volumes of rainfall compared to other regions of the Interior (it has the giant red cedar trees to prove it). It had become one of my favourite areas in the province to work in, despite its rain-swept slopes.

It was the afternoon of Tuesday, May 29, 1990, on a dreary, foggy and melancholy mountainside. I remember every aspect of the setting, every nuance of light and sound. My buddy Lionel and I were on a solo mission, planting a steep cutblock wedged between two stands of giant cedars. The setting had a certain feel to it, an ineffable atmosphere. Shrouded in layers of mist, the river beneath us dropped off vertically from a series of benches into deep pools of churning white water, settling only briefly before dropping off again and again, eventually disappearing into the brume below. The maelstrom forced us to holler, even from short distances, in order be heard over the turbulence. It was one of those moist days when, rather than rain or drizzle, the low ceiling of cloud imparted a fine mist into the air around us. The volume of precipitation wasn't enough to justify donning rain gear, but after hours of exposure, we were soaked to the bone. Around mid-afternoon, feeling the chill from a sudden high-elevation breeze, Lionel retreated back to the truck for a blast of heat. He emerged a short while later, muttering something about a news report he'd heard on the radio, one that detailed a tragic accident involving a treeplanting crew from Alberta. Concerned, I asked him if he'd caught the name of the company involved. He wasn't sure, but it was a name he wasn't familiar with. "Did the name of the company resemble SFS Ltd.," I asked. "Yeah," he said. "I'm pretty sure that's it. Why?"

The following day a number of Alberta newspapers carried the story: "A van carrying twelve SFS Ltd. treeplanters from the Fox Creek area of Alberta to the Prince George region of BC flipped over and rolled multiple times, tossing out its passengers, killing seven people."

# CHAPTER THIRTEEN

# THE RECOVERY

||||||||||||||||||||||||||||||||||||||||||||||||||||||||||||||||

I CAN'T IMAGINE ANYONE STRAPPING ON A SET OF TREEPLANTING bags for the very first time, burdened with the weight of a hundred or so seedlings and the relentless pull of gravity as he attempts to traverse a steep coastal rock face on a blustery day in early February, enduring hours of crawling, slipping and falling and then trumpeting at the end of the day, "Where has this gig been all my life?" A person would have to be completely deranged to utter such inanity. But after a week or two, after the mind and body begin to adapt, after a slightly firmer footing is gained and a greater sense of balance is realized, moments begin to work their way into the experience. They slide over you unexpectedly, magically. Moments like when the rain pauses, the clouds part and the sun reveals itself for the first time in days. It's an event worthy of your scrutiny. And as you shed your sweat-soaked rain gear, which is liberating enough in itself, you turn to discover a tapestry of landscapes that have eluded your attention for days; landscapes that until then were made secret by fog and low-lying cloud; landscapes so stunning, so captivating, the visual impact steals your breath and pushes you back against the slope. These moments are strictly between you and the universe.

I was fortunate to experience several such moments very early in my treeplanting career. For me, these were galvanizing respites. They helped nudge me past the physical and mental adversity I was grappling with at the time. I developed an appetite for these moments, a yearning. I tuned my senses to always be on alert for them. No matter how engaged I was with the task at hand, I always paused to survey the landscape around me. I took mental snapshots of any feature that stood out as unique or unusual. And every once in a while I'd capture something truly extraordinary; like the dramatic collapse of a mature conifer during a windstorm, the onset of a rock slide high up on a mountain before its rumble drew the attention of others, the epic collapse of a massive shelf of ice along the edge of a glacier, the sight of a newborn fawn gazing up in silence through the tall grass as I planted a seedling nearby.

Many people come away from their first full season of planting trees feeling as if they'd cultivated something pivotal in their lives, something that sparked and inspired inner growth—something that would live with them for the rest of their days.

Many ex-treeplanters who I talk to today, even those whose experience was limited to a mere summer or two decades earlier, become animated when they reflect back on those times. I always detect a certain longing when they call to mind their triumphs over adversity both on and off the slopes, and the rich camp life that fostered so many bonds and friendships, many of which endured the passage of time.

I was a wide-eyed kid when I first entered the treeplanting arena. I had no idea what to expect when my mother dumped me off on Barrett's lap that day in April of 1983. I was "wide-eyed" because I was immediately exposed to things that I thought only occurred in adventure novels and movies.

I soon came to the realization that my situation back then was different, that it was the remoteness and geographic isolation of my surroundings that generated the heightened level of activity I was experiencing. Perhaps Nature has become increasing possessive and protective of her last remaining vestiges of unspoiled wilderness, resisting our attempts to intrude upon them. Unlike projects located in proximity to paved roads where her sovereignty has been muted and suppressed to a degree, many of the settings I found myself in were raw, unrestrained, untamed and heavy with atmosphere.

Some of the wilderness corridors we occupied harboured undercurrents so weighty, it felt as though we were camped at the edge of an alternate universe—on the fringe of an invisible moat of volatility, one that threatened to overflow its banks and yank us in the moment we let our guard down. That is how it felt to a wide-eyed teenager anyway, one whose greatest wilderness challenge prior to this was helping his mom deal with a flat tire on the side of the highway.

Despite the gruelling pace, the adversity, the setbacks, the injuries and the omnipresent risk, I adored the life. After years in the industry, after surpassing the one-million-trees-planted mark, I continued to approach each day with a bit of childlike wonder. Even after blowing through two million trees, the wonder was still there, but I also liked to imagine, as I matured into a veteran highballer, that I could handle any adversity life threw at me, any obstacle the Universe placed in my path. I liked to think that, in a way, I was becoming invulnerable.

On Tuesday, May 29th of 1990, after hearing news of that tragic logging-road accident, that childlike wonder was ripped from my soul. Any sense of invulnerability that I might have imagined was unceremoniously stripped away. That afternoon, I wandered off to the far side of the mountain and planted out the rest of my day alone. The surreal atmosphere on the block that day—the mist, the fog, the turbulence below—deflected and diminished reality somewhat, as if I were in another world, another time. But reality loomed.

As details of the tragic accident filtered in, I formed a mental picture of how events unfolded. SFS Ltd. had just wrapped up their contract in Alberta. They were on their way to their next project, the contract I'd succeeded in securing for them eight months earlier. The crew didn't set out together. They set off in a number of vehicles, travelling independently of one another. A van carrying twelve crew members went ahead of the rest of the pack. They were on their way to a nearby town to pick up additional treeplanters before continuing on to BC. For whatever reason, they pulled over at the edge of an extremely steep embankment. Something—whether it was a strong gust of wind or a driver error—caused the van to leave the road. It rolled down the embankment, flipping over multiple times, throwing nearly everyone out before coming to rest at the bottom. Five people died at the scene, one person died en route to the hospital, and another died in hospital later that night.

Had I been there to supervise the project, this tragedy would not have befallen this crew. To some, this reasoning may sound outrageous, but I assure you, it's immutable fact. Aside from the obvious shift in timelines that my presence alone would have shaped—a shift that would have altered and negated the entire sequence of events leading up to the tragedy—I never, *ever* would have allowed a single vehicle to travel out on its own between projects, let alone between provinces. I was, and always will be, a stickler for travelling together as a group. No exceptions. This punishing realization invaded my psyche and exacted a toll, dominating my thoughts by day, haunting my dreams by night.

I felt profoundly culpable for what occurred—guilty for not having been there to prevent the accident and responsible for having acquired the ill-fated project in the first place. I was tormented by the thought my own greed was to blame. Had I listened to my sister, taken her advice and dropped the lawsuit that forced me to abandon my post in Alberta, the local news outlets would have run a completely different set of headlines that day.

I planted out the remainder of my 1990 spring season solo, rejecting several offers to partner up with friends. That might not have been the wisest decision, being alone with my thoughts all day, replaying events, wondering how Reggie was coping, thinking about the unimaginable sadness families of the deceased crew members were going through. The truth is, I had a difficult time being around people.

CHAPTER THIRTEEN

I allowed weeks to slip past without contacting Reggie. I was putting off that conversation for as long as I dared. I was afraid of what he might say to me and I was ashamed for nurturing that fear. It wasn't until I was back home in Calgary, after weeks of rumination, that I forced myself to make that phone call.

I sat next to the phone for a good, long while before actually dialing Reggie's number. I wasn't sure how the conversation would play out. I anticipated, at best, indifference, and at worst, dead air followed by an abrupt disconnect. To my absolute relief, Reggie expressed no animosity toward me. He even sought to soothe any feelings of guilt he suspected I might be harbouring. He offered a brief summary of the events that led up to the tragedy (the actual cause of the van leaving the road is still shrouded in mystery), how he communicated with the grief-stricken families, and how he was present for the funerals. It was clear to me that he demonstrated real character during the crisis, reaching out the way he did. It couldn't have been easy. Further into the conversation, he attempted to shift focus to the future and speak in upbeat terms, but I sensed his uncertainty and profound sadness. It wasn't a lengthy conversation. There was no discussion concerning my return, which was also a relief—I didn't feel fit to take on any responsibility beyond my own personal well-being at the time.

I had no way of knowing that that would be the last conversation I would ever have with the man. I figured I would eventually return and pick up where I left off, but soon after our talk, Reggie ran into trouble with a large project in Alberta. It was one of those classic Alberta horror shows where company resources were insufficient to meet the challenges: too much energy was directed at overcoming the complex logistics, too little at ensuring their freshly planting seedlings would survive the summer. They did not. SFS Ltd.'s cutblocks failed final inspection. Aside from the wages owed to Reggie's employees, the day-to-day operations sucked up huge sums of capital. Reggie was ruined. The bank stripped him of everything he owned in the world, including his beautiful ranch.

Recently I discovered that Reggie eventually rose above his financial challenges, even managing to rebuild his empire, making a name for himself by becoming a pioneer in the application of new technologies in the forestry sector. Two weeks after he formally retired, he embarked on a road trip across the US with his wife, one they had been planning for a number of months. Four days into his newly acquired freedom, with the sun low on the horizon, he stopped on the side of a highway to take a photo of an old farmhouse. He didn't see the truck that hit him. Reggie was sixty-six years old when he passed away that day.

IN SEPTEMBER OF 1990, AS I CAME TO TERMS WITH THE TRAGEDY OF the van accident, I was ready for the world again. I decided to head back into action. I returned to where it all began for me, to Prince George, where I eventually hooked up with a company I had never worked for, or even heard of. The project was less than an hour's drive from a paved highway, and perhaps ninety minutes from the nearest fast-food drive-thru. I quit after only one four-day shift, realizing that what I had taken on wasn't real treeplanting. It was a scaled-down, under-bid, underpaid, sterilized version of what I was used to. I drove away feeling completely uninspired and underwhelmed, knowing that if I wanted the real thing, I would need to reunite with crews that specialized in geographically isolated projects. It was only in these remote locales that I believed I would find what I was looking for.

In the spring of 1991 I was invited to join a crew of highballers who specialized in technically challenging coastal projects. Planting trees along some of the more rugged and isolated settings in BC, and working with the best of the best—some of whom were legends in the industry—was exactly what I needed. This crew was at the top of its game and had little tolerance for weakness. I was forced to step up and rise to the occasion.

Over the next one and a half years we journeyed into some truly extraordinary faraway places: Phillips Arm, Ramsay Arm, Jervis Inlet, Toba Inlet, Kingcome Inlet, Bute Inlet, and others. I lost track of the number of islands we were dropped onto by helicopter along the Johnstone and Queen Charlotte straits. This was still a difficult period for me, though. I struggled with anger and depression. There were times when the slightest mishap would set me off. I know I was a real prick to work with at times. But I was back in motion, surrounded by vast expanses of untamed wilderness, thrown into one set of challenges after another. I felt alive again.

REALITY KICKS IN. ALL TREEPLANTERS REACH A STAGE IN THEIR careers where they're forced to come to grips with reality. Throughout my teenage years, I believed that my body was basically immune to permanent injury. I recklessly threw myself into every full-contact sport I could sign up for, believing every hit, every tackle, every fight would make me stronger in the end. It was a belief system that served me well in my youth. By the end of my fifth or sixth season of planting trees, after having sustained a number of serious injuries over the years, it was clear that I had a few chinks in the armour, that the impact of multiple injuries could potentially compound over time. It was a sobering realization. That's when I began to look for other opportunities within the industry, knowing that planting 200,000 trees per year—though still manageable at that point—was a pace that was increasingly difficult to sustain. So I took on many different roles with a number of different companies and crews. I worked as a simple foreman. I ran small satellite projects. I was sent on special missions. I also began taking on greater responsibility, supervising large projects across BC. Eventually I became a contractor, specializing in highly technical helicopter projects along the west coast of Vancouver Island and the mainland inlets. I managed to put together an impressive crew, and together we won an enviable number of direct award contracts. Though we kept an extremely low profile, we were a highly regarded outfit.

Throughout the years, the adventures continued to pile up. There is one standout from these untold tales, though, one event that stands apart from everything else: a crazy whirlwind treeplanting romance that led to the birth of a beautiful baby girl, my daughter Brigit.

It's been said that what makes a memory stick—the element that allows the experience to endure the passage of time—is when highly charged emotions accompany the event. I had plenty of those. Being a sensitive kid to begin with, enamoured with the enormity and complexity of nature, I was thrilled beyond measure to be plunked down in the middle of it. And with that emotional backdrop, being exposed to wilderness settings I had never before seen or imagined, I took it all in. I mentally recorded even the most minute details. Those memories are indelible. They are cached in my mind like movies on a shelf—all I need to do is select one and hit play.

It's mid-April. You're in a tent perched on the top of a hill overlooking camp. You're reluctant to leave the warmth of your sleeping bag, especially this early in the season when everything is coated in a thick layer of frost...

# ACKNOWLEDGEMENTS

SITTING ALONG THE EDGE OF A VANCOUVER ISLAND LAKE A COUPLE years back, swapping adventure stories with my new-found friends Gail and Brent Stoll, it suddenly occurred to me that my early years in the treeplanting arena might make for an entertaining read. Gail and Brent were my initial inspiration and for that, I can't thank them enough.

Other people who recognized the early potential of my manuscript include Jeff and Deb Hallworth, Eric Plummer and my good friend Peter Bell. Thanks, folks, for your generous support and feedback.

Writing can be an obsessive, lonely and solitary pursuit. My beautiful daughter, Brigit Nolan Meeker, didn't hold this against me. Thank you, Brigit, for your patience, your understanding and your unconditional love.

A hearty thank you goes out to Jade Hyde, Mali Hyde, Dave Nolan, Denise Saumer, Capucine Tseu and Rick MacCabe. All of these fine folks were tremendous sources of support.

A few names from back in the day I'd like to acknowledge: Robin Bellavance, Claudia Brown, Cindy Rose, Norm White, Meghan Anderson and my old treeplanting partners, Bruce Miller, Jesper Nielsen and Deano Rocco (rest in peace, buddy).

A special shout out goes to Tommy Humphreys for his generosity, his wise counsel and for helping me put a title on this book.

Lastly, I'd like to thank Carbon Based Lifeforms, the ambient music duo from Sweden, for repeatedly helping me get into the writing zone when I couldn't get there on my own.